"The technical precision of a Clancy novel and the emotion of a Henry James story. . . . One of the best books of the year—a can't-miss read!"

—Jason Shepherd, senior writer
Insight for Living

"A Machiavellian plot. . . . Cutrer and Glahn delve into the controversial world of cloning and genetics in relation to God's plan while offering a satisfying medical thriller."

—*Library Journal*

"Like much of modern medicine, the events in *Lethal Harvest* are almost unbelievable—but true! The strong presence of Christ throughout the novel highlights the sacredness of human life even in the coldest scientific experiments."

—Dr. David Stevens, president
Christian Medical & Dental Society

"A neuron-tingling, synapse-twisting thriller! *Lethal Harvest* brought me to the cutting edge of today's news and wrapped it in a challenging worldview. Give me more!"

—Bob Singleton, president
Singleton Productions, Inc.

"Readers will encounter the explosive potential for good or evil that awaits the human race as medicine, science and ethics attempt to dance with one another. For those who want to be prepared for what lies ahead, *Lethal Harvest* has an exciting and powerful message."

—Daniel L. Akin
Dean, School of Theology
Vice President, Academic Administration
The Southern Baptist Theological Seminary

"A swirl of mystery and romance, action and ethics, faith and science. A fast-paced read that addresses when life begins, the sanctity of marriage, and the change that faith makes in the heart of Christians. A good book for book clubs and discussion groups."

—Amy Nappa
bestselling author

LETHAL HARVEST

LETHAL HARVEST

WILLIAM CUTRER, M.D.
SANDRA GLAHN

kregel
PUBLICATIONS

Grand Rapids, MI 49501

Lethal Harvest

© 2000 by William Cutrer and Sandra Glahn

Published by Kregel Publications, a division of Kregel, Inc., P.O. Box 2607, Grand Rapids, MI 49501.

For more information about Kregel Publications, visit our web site: www.kregel.com

ISBN 0-8254-2371-6

Printed in the United States of America

1 2 3 4 5 / 04 03 02 01 00

To our parents

To Joan Cutrer and in memory of Ben Cutrer;
and to Willis and Ann Grafe—
with gratitude to God for their
constant love and support.

And to all the other thoughtful people of faith
who willingly struggle with the ethical/theological
issues of the day, seeking to live honorably
in a world growing ever more complex.

Acknowledgements

This, our third coauthored work, was made easier by the blessing of e-mail and the fifteen-year foundation of solid friendship that has taken us and our families to Russia, Mexico, and across the USA, adding to the richness of our lives and greatly aiding the process of cocreation.

We owe part of the inspiration for Marnie's character to the world's best nurse, Marnie Gaines, who helped make Bill's practice a place of both physical and emotional healing. We are both deeply indebted to her for multiplying joys and dividing griefs. We were also inspired by our friend Dr. Steve Harris—Bill's former partner and Sandi's physician—who teamed with Bill in practice for many years and has continued to provide compassionate, competent medical care.

We are grateful to Dennis Hillman and the staff at Kregel Publications, especially for their guidance early in the manuscript. And we wish to thank Reg Grant and the other professors who have molded our worldviews and helped us develop our writing voices.

We are also deeply grateful for the love, faithful encouragement, and competent input of Bill's wife, Jane; his children, Bill and Elisabeth Cutrer, Bob Cutrer, and Jennie and Casey Snow; Bill's brother, Ken; our friend Virginia Swint; and Sandi's husband, Gary.

Authors' Note

We have endeavored to write an engaging drama set in the context of real-life ethical dilemmas. The rapid advance of scientific knowledge in the areas of cloning and stem cell research limits the number of readers who can (and want to) read highly technical discussions of the subject. Given the social and spiritual implications of this research, however, it is a topic that demands not just the attention of the scientific specialist, but of us all.

While the plot and characters of *Lethal Harvest* are fictional, the techniques portrayed in this story are as real as today's headlines. We have taken the liberty of inventing a disease and a few technological procedures, but the research portrayed here (and its potential for good or ill) is both accurate and ongoing.

Chapter One

3:30 A.M. THE GLOVED FIGURE slid open the back door of the clinic and stepped inside. Removing a black box the size of a pocket calculator from his overcoat, he attached it to the master alarm touch pad. *Amazingly simple.* In less than fifteen seconds, he had bypassed the code and silenced the warning beeper.

Moving past the reception desk, he shone his flashlight along the floor and slipped down the hall to the door of the first doctor's office. With the light under his arm, he worked the lock, then entered and shut the door behind him. The beam from his flashlight circled the room until it stopped on a desk photo—a wedding shot of a smiling bride and groom, each of them dark-haired and slender. He moved the light to the photo next to it. In it, a little girl with brown hair was blowing bubbles. Another picture, this time a studio portrait of the same couple with the preschooler, confirmed he had the wrong office. He stepped back into the hallway, never noticing the most remarkable photo in the room—a signed photo of the doctor's family with the president of the United States.

Picking the lock on the next office door, he entered and quickly looked around. The computer monitor on the desk had been left on overnight and its screen-saver shed a ghostly light on the walls. He squinted at the photos decorating the office and, this time, when he saw seven or eight shots of a blond man, with a wife and three young children, he smiled grimly. He pulled out the desk chair and sat down. One at a time, he worked his way into each of the locked drawers. For the next thirty minutes, he meticulously examined files, charge bills, phone messages. Finally, he leaned back and was still. "Nothing here," he muttered.

Next, the computer. A password protected some of the files, but he could read their labels: Dell. Texaco. IBM. Westinghouse. General Motors. *Just financial stuff. Nothing interesting.* He opened and read some of the accessible files. Still nothing.

Back in the hallway, he easily located the long vertical files filled with medical records. And there, in the "P through S" section, he found the file he was looking for: Rivera, Leigh. He thumbed his way through the documents, stopping to photograph two "thank-you" notes, written about a year apart from each other. But these things were unimportant. *Nothing. Nothing at all!* He replaced the file, reset the alarm, and departed.

Three blocks away, he got into his Audi, lit a cigarette, and drove home.

Several restless hours later, he picked up the phone and pressed a long series of numbers. Far away in Culiacán, a city of several million near Mazatlan in

Sinaloa, Mexico, a phone began to ring. It was quickly picked up.

"Mayor Rivera's office," a voice answered. Carlos Rivera had installed a private phone line with instructions that it was always to be answered in English.

"I need to speak with the mayor."

"Yes. The mayor expects your call. One moment, please."

After a wait of about three minutes, Carlos, who spoke excellent English thanks to his education at the University of Texas, came on the line.

"What did you find?" he demanded.

"Nothing."

Carlos cursed. He then remained silent for so long that Victor felt compelled to fill the silence.

"I searched his computer files, read his e-mail, his phone messages. Her medical file. Only thing I found—two 'thank you' notes. Nothing beyond the usual gratitude, señor. Nothing suspicious."

"No doubt he is a smart man. He would be careful. When you find out more, you will handle things, no?"

"Yes. Of course."

The tall gentleman in the dark suit brushed the December rain off his overcoat, removed the garment, and draped it over his left arm. He checked the brass plate beside the door—"The Center for Fertility Enhancement"—glanced at the address in his hand and, opening the heavy wooden door, walked in. At the front desk he waited silently for the receptionist to look up from her paperwork.

"I need to see Dr. Lucas Morgan, please."

"Do you have an appointment, sir?" Lisa looked up. She had worked there for a few years, and she didn't recognize the man as a regular patient. Most men who entered the office for the first time had their wives with them.

"I need to see Dr. Morgan," the man repeated.

"Dr. Morgan is seeing patients, sir. Would you like me to give him a message for you?"

"I'm delivering legal papers, ma'am. I need to do it in person." He opened his suit coat just enough to indicate a letter in the inside pocket.

Lisa's eyes widened. "Just a moment." She started to push the button on the intercom, then decided to walk back and find Dr. Luc herself. "It could take a few minutes. The schedule is pretty tight on Monday mornings," she said.

And, actually, it was booked solid with new-patient interviews, ultrasound scans, and office visits. In fact, the doctor rarely took time for lunch. Hopeful patients with their lists of questions would be waiting quietly in the reception area, anxious to hear the doctor's interpretation of laboratory values or their in vitro fertilization—IVF—cycles.

Lisa found Dr. Luc in his office. He was on the phone and pacing. The thirty-nine-year-old physician was always on the go, never still for long. Lisa could tell from his side of the conversation that the voice at the other end was Tim Sullivan, the clinic's embryologist. She patiently waited for the two men to finish their rundown of the weekend caseload.

"Got some patients waiting. Glad you're on your way in. . . . Good. . . . Okay, bye." Luc finished his conversation and raised his eyebrows at Lisa, awaiting an explanation for her presence.

She bit her lip and, pointing with her thumb toward the lobby, said in a low voice, "There's a guy out there who wants to give you some legal papers. He says he needs to talk to you himself. Want me to have him wait?"

Luc stared at her momentarily, then smiled and ran his fingers through his hair. "All those traffic violations finally caught up with me, eh?" He had no idea what this was about, but he figured there'd be less talk in the office if Lisa considered the matter insignificant.

Lisa's mouth opened. "You don't pay up when you get a ticket? Gee, that seems sort of out of character. I thought you were a conservative, law-abiding doctor. I guess your speed-tempting Jaguar . . ." Realizing she was saying too much, Lisa stopped herself.

Luc just shrugged and maintained his no-worries look. "Send him on back."

"Dr. Lucas Morgan?" The man stepped through the doorway. Lisa considered lingering, but Luc's look told her she'd better not.

"Guilty. Or perhaps I shouldn't say that. How can I help you?"

"It's my job to present this to you, sir. It's an intent-to-sue document."

Luc felt his heart jump. "Who from?"

"Don't know, sir," said the man, shaking his head. "Delivering the envelope's my job. Knowing what's inside isn't."

"All right. Thank you," Luc muttered, not feeling thankful in the least.

"Appreciate your attitude," the dark-suited man said.

He started to walk out, then turned back to face the doctor. "You wouldn't believe some of the things people say when they get served."

Luc half smiled. The man offered a polite nod and disappeared into the hall. Sitting at his desk, the doctor put on his reading glasses and reached for his letter opener. He quickly scanned the document.

"Malpractice?" He felt a wave of nausea. Case number . . . plaintiff attorney. . . . His eyes fixed on the name Carlos Rivera, and his chin dropped. Carlos Rivera was the wealthy mayor of a large, modern city in western Mexico. His wife had undergone a successful IVF transfer in the past year. As far as Luc could remember, everything had gone perfectly.

He walked out to the rack in the hallway and pulled Leigh Rivera's chart. As he opened it, a photograph of beautiful twin girls fell out. *Somebody didn't close the clasp on this file correctly. We can't have stuff falling out of charts like this!* As he leafed through the documents, he exclaimed, "This is absurd! Incredible! A perfect outcome. I waived half their fee for the sake of 'international relations' and look what happens. What a rip!"

"What's a rip, Dr. Luc?" His office manager had been passing down the hall and overheard him. Luc muttered something unintelligible and walked back into his office. It was beyond understanding how the Riveras could name him in a lawsuit. He sat down behind his desk but, unable to remain still, he stood again and began to pace as he paged through the history and physical examination records of Leigh Rivera.

Leigh Rivera. I liked her. Delightful woman. A real California girl.

The mayor's wife was a tall blonde with crystal blue eyes, in contrast to her husband, who was comparatively short, with dark features. Mrs. Rivera's initial workup had proved normal, but Mr. Rivera had had a low sperm count. They'd come to the center because of its international reputation for excellence and the high success rates enjoyed by its three doctors, Luc Morgan, Tim Sullivan, and Benjamin McKay.

"That's right," Luc murmured. "Because of the distance, we decided Leigh and Carlos would be good candidates for IVF following gentle ovarian hyperstimulation." He read through the chart, remembering that Mrs. Rivera's response to hyperstimulation had pleased everyone. "Egg harvest under ultrasound guidance, easy retrieval," he quoted from the chart. He was remembering some of the facts now that the file had jogged his memory. *What could have gone wrong?*

He read a note in Tim's handwriting. The embryologist had indicated excellent egg quality. Normal sperm prep. It was a fairly straightforward case—take the eggs, expose them to the prepared sperm, watch for signs of fertilization. Allow the zygote to divide, reimplant three because the Rivera family wanted to avoid any risk of high-order multiples. Freeze the remaining embryos. *They didn't want to have to decide later about multifetal pregnancy reduction.* Luc nodded. *I totally agreed with the ethics.*

Luc's memory had always served him well. He'd graduated third in his class at medical school and since then had steadily risen to the top of his field, especially when he and Tim had discovered the Uterine Implantation Factor. After the *New England Journal* published their research, the phones at the center had not stopped ringing for a month.

An ideal scenario. They should have been thrilled. What in the world's going on?

Luc read that the initial embryo transfer had been unsuccessful, but Mrs. Rivera had returned alone during her next natural cycle. Three embryos survived the thaw from cryopreservation and had been transferred to her uterus. A twin pregnancy had resulted. *That's right! Second cycle. I came in over Christmas. Just about a year ago exactly.*

Looking closely at his notes, Luc felt his pulse quicken. His palms became so moist that the paper stuck to them. His own scratched handwriting confirmed that it was he, along with his nurse, who had performed the transfer.

Mrs. Rivera's "prime time" had fallen over the Christmas holidays. Tim and Marnie had taken a long-overdue vacation to Hawaii. Luc wished that he had scribbled down more details in the chart, but record-keeping wasted valuable time. Still, it was coming back to him. He had come in over the holiday, asking his nurse to join him— not too unusual since the peak moments for implantation are hard to control precisely. Mrs. Rivera was on a natural cycle and couldn't be controlled at all. Lab tests had shown the rise in her LH, signaling the hormonal environment would be perfect at just the wrong time as far as convenience went.

It would have been easier to do it with Tim present, because of his filing system, but Luc and his nurse had done the procedure without him many times. The way Tim stored and tracked the cryopreserved embryos was complicated, but he insisted on using his system. Color codes and numbers, as well as names. Computer records in addition to notebook copies. Checks and rechecks. No possibility for error—but inconvenient for anyone except Tim to decipher.

Tim and Marnie planned that vacation for months. Only time he's ever been away. With the file to jog his memory, more details came back. *I went to the lab. Didn't even try to open his computer files. Who knows what kind of security that self-proclaimed computer guru had. Searched through the notebook records for cryopreserved embryos.*

The clinic kept frozen sperm, frozen eggs, and the embryos all in separate areas of the refrigeration unit, each under lock and key. Only the three doctors had access. *I found Tim's books with the names and coding system. It took awhile to locate Mrs. Rivera's frozen embryos. Found them in the second refrigerated area. Code numbers matched with Mrs. Rivera's chart. Didn't see a color code on the dish, but everything else was perfect. Both the name and the code number on the specimens. It* had *to have been the correct embryos for transfer. Didn't have any other patient by the name of Rivera. The procedure went without a hitch. No problems. Mrs. Rivera was so grateful we'd agreed to come in over Christmas to do the transfer for her. She* liked *us. Now they're* suing *us?*

He pulled out the picture of two healthy infants, wondering if they'd died of SIDS or something. Then he stared at the harshly worded intent-to-sue papers.

The fact that he found nothing suspicious in the chart failed to soothe him. He reached for the intercom to ask Lisa to get Chris Winston, his personal attorney and tennis partner, on the phone. Then he thought better of it, called information, and dialed the number for himself. *No point in arousing her curiosity.*

Luc liked Lisa. She had a great sense of humor, and the patients always commented on how friendly she was. But the office staff talked too freely for his comfort.

Holding the phone to his ear, he kept leafing through Mrs. Rivera's chart, looking for some hint. *Why are they suing us?* The name of the attorney filing the document was unfamiliar to him. He swallowed hard when he thought of the bad publicity a high-profile lawsuit could bring to the clinic.

In a decade of practice, Luc had received two other letters suggesting a "cause of action." But in both cases, early in the discovery phase, no evidence of malpractice had been uncovered, and no one had ever formally pressed charges. There had never been a hint of impropriety. In an industry that suffered from bad publicity—sometimes deserved—Luc took pride in the clinic's perfect reputation.

"Attorney's office." The voice at the other end of the line sounded annoyingly cheerful.

"This is Dr. Lucas Morgan. May I speak to Chris Winston?"

Luc sat on hold for a few minutes, fearing he would have to leave a message. But finally Chris came on the line. "Hey, Luc. What's up?"

Luc felt a flood of relief when he heard his friend's voice. "I seem to have a problem here, Chris. I was just served some papers."

There was a momentary silence. "I don't suppose they were informing you that you'd just won the lottery?"

"I wish! No. I've been named the primary defendant

in a lawsuit. They're suing all of us, along with the clinic. Gee, Merry Christmas."

"Welcome to the club." Chris sounded unworried. "What do the papers say?"

Luc told him all he knew.

"Get me the case number and the name of the plaintiff's attorney," Chris said. "Better send me a copy of the medical file, too. Let me make a few calls, and I'll get right back to you."

"Thanks. Thanks a lot, Chris. I can't imagine there's any real problem here. It was the kind of case most patients dream about. A good outcome and a grateful family. I just don't know what their gripe could be."

"Sorry, friend." Chris's voice softened. "Just remember, it's not usually about good and bad, right or wrong. Justice isn't the issue. It's money. Money's the issue—and who gets the most."

Luc grunted his disapproval.

"Just hang in there. I'll get back with you as soon as I find anything out."

"Thanks, Chris."

Luc hung up the phone and leaned back in his chair. The reception area was now filled with patients, but he waited in his office with the door shut until he regained his focus. Abruptly, he stood up and shut the Rivera file, determined to leave his thoughts in the folder. But just as he laid his hand on the doorknob, he heard a knock.

Luc opened his door to find Tim Sullivan, his embryologist, holding a coffee cup. Tim was one of the skinniest rich guys Luc had ever known. He sure wasn't much to look at. Still, as the nephew of the U.S. president, the man possessed superior breeding and a bright intellect, even if he did dress like the old men Luc's dad played golf with. And he had managed to win the heart of Marnie Boralis, the stunning journalist who had covered their big breakthrough. "What's up? You had a visit from the law?"

"Word travels fast."

"Something about speeding tickets? Everyone's amused. Except that the reception area's backed up to Maryland." Tim remained oblivious to Luc's tension.

"I'm afraid it's a lot worse than that, Tim."

Luc briefly told his colleague the bad news and then, leaving him to mull it over, headed into one of the exam rooms to meet with a waiting patient. The embryologist stood reading through the file. Suddenly he sank into a chair and threw the chart down on the desk.

Lisa took the call just as she was about to leave for lunch. "Chris Winston here," said the speaker. "Is Dr. Morgan still in?"

"I'm sorry, Dr. Morgan is with a patient right now," Lisa told him. He surprised her by saying he'd hold. The moment the doctor emerged, she told him that Chris was on the line. He nodded, handed her a file he was carrying, walked quickly into his office, and shut the door.

He picked up the phone and pressed the blinking light. "Chris?"

"Yeah."

"What did you find out?"

"Not good."

"Tell it to me straight." How often had he heard his patients say that when he had bad news? He felt a twinge of guilt. Many of those times he'd sugarcoated the facts.

"He's asking for two million in actual damages for medical malpractice and ten million punitive for loss of affection/alienation of affection from his wife. He claims she's obviously seeing someone at the clinic."

Luc stared at the wall, wide-eyed.

"Luc, you there?" Chris asked.

"Yeah."

"I'm sorry, man."

Luc remained silent. The clinic was his life. As one of the owners of the clinic, he knew its assets would be subject to recovery. This case could destroy him. Totally. He could lose everything. Not just his reputation—but his license, his earnings, his future.

"Remind me. How much insurance are you carrying these days?" Chris asked.

"Only a million per occurrence. No coverage for punitive."

Chapter Two

AT THREE P.M. THAT MONDAY AFTERNOON, Marnie Sullivan's cell phone rang. Having just returned from a media luncheon, she still wore the expensive heels that brought her height to a perfect five feet eight inches. Her skirt whirled about her knees as she walked briskly back into the home office in her Northern Virginia estate. A trail of Chanel No. 5 lingered after her, though there was no one there to appreciate it. She had left her purse on the floor of her office and quickly fumbled inside it to find her phone. "Marnie Sullivan," she answered. A glance down at the caller ID told her it was her husband.

"Hey, Aurora." Tim hadn't called her that since she'd been pregnant with Emily, and it caught her by surprise. As a child, Marnie had loathed her last name, Boralis. The other kids had teased that her parents should have named her Aurora, after Aurora Borealis—the Northern Lights. But Tim liked the nickname and had used it as a term of endearment.

"Is there a problem?" she asked. Tim rarely called during the day unless it was to cancel their plans for the evening.

"I need to work late."

"So what else is new?" her voice, having softened in response to the old nickname, now had an edge.

"Are you gonna let me explain or just get mad?"

"Go ahead." Marnie sat down. She relented. Rubbing her eyes and pushing a brunette strand behind her ear, she readied herself to listen. She had no desire to fight.

"Some serious stuff's going down here at the clinic. Luc was served papers today. Somebody's filing a big enough malpractice suit to shut us down."

Marnie eyes widened. Tim actually sounded shaken. "So I have some stuff to do here," he continued. "I'll have to work late for the next few nights." By "working late," Tim meant midnight, even one in the morning.

She tried to sound supportive. Glancing at the calendar, she told him, "No problem tonight. There's only one event on the calendar this week—Dad's coming for dinner Wednesday. But he won't mind." Will Boralis normally ended up dining alone with his daughter anyway, and Marnie knew he wouldn't miss Tim as long as he got to see Emily. Will had an even softer spot in his heart for the couple's five-year-old than he did for his beloved daughter.

"I need you to handle something," Tim told her.

"What's that?"

"The insurance stuff."

"I thought you said you'd have lunch with the agent and get it straightened out."

"I was going to, but I have too much going on just now with this case."

"Fine," Marnie said in a tone that indicated it was anything but. "Is this case going to ruin us financially?"

Tim paused, then said, "Too early to tell. Gotta run."

Tim hung up before Marnie could say good-bye. She snapped the phone shut and threw it into her purse. Then she spent the next hour calming herself down, reminding herself that Tim Sullivan had a reputation as one of the world's top embryologists. *He could get a job in any city with a single phone call. As long as he's got his medical license.*

That night Marnie never heard Tim come in, but on Wednesday morning, he didn't leave for work at his usual 6:30 A.M. She found him sitting in the rocking chair in Emily's room, staring down at their daughter's dark curls as she slept. Even though he spent little time with Emily, Marnie knew that Tim adored her.

"You did good, Marn," he said, looking from the slumbering child to the mother whose features she bore. It was one of the kindest things he had ever said to her. Then he got up and kissed his wife with more affection than she'd felt from him in several years. Looking into her brown eyes, Tim started to say something, but then just hugged her and left for work. Marnie watched as he headed through the living room to the garage. *He must be really shook up over that lawsuit.*

That afternoon, Marnie groaned when she saw the right wheel of her husband's red BMW. "Not a flat tire! Not now!"

She checked to see if someone had slashed it. Then she remembered that the attendant at the service station had warned her, "Your back tire looks low. You'd better let me check the air pressure for you." But she'd been in a hurry just then and declined. *And that was a week ago, during the last ice storm. I thought Tim said he'd take care of it.*

She punched her father's number into her cell phone. Though Will Boralis had retired from government service the year Emily was born, his sixty-seven years hadn't slowed him down a bit. Marnie sometimes found herself wondering if her mother had really died of cancer last year, or if she'd simply collapsed from the exhaustion of trying to keep up with him. Today, he planned to take in Harper's Ferry with his buddy, a retired Army colonel. Marnie hoped the icy day had kept them in.

The phone rang three times. Just when she thought she'd get his machine, he answered.

"Dad!"

"Honey?"

Marnie's words ran together. "Yeah. I'm so glad you're there. I need you to bail me out. I have a flat. In this weather. . . ."

"Whoa. Slow down. Where are you?"

"Georgetown. Just got finished with an interview." She gave him the exact location.

"Let me change. Be there in thirty minutes."

Marnie locked her door and leaned back. She knew she could wait for him in the warm office she'd just left, but she felt uncomfortable asking anyone else for help. So she closed her eyes and took a catnap.

Will honked his greeting as his Jeep pulled into the lot. After parking in the closest space, he stepped out and walked over to the BMW.

"Having a hard day, hon?"

"Sure glad to see *you!*" She kissed his cold cheek and noticed that his face had the same scent it always had when he'd spent time outside.

"You're driving Tim's car today?" In the past Will had hinted that he found the Beamer a bit pretentious.

"Yeah, he insisted I take it. Better suspension than mine. Handles better on the ice."

Will looked surprised. "Well, that was decent of him. Now, let's have a look at that tire." He examined the wheel. In his red flannel shirt and khakis he was the very image of an outdoorsman. Finally, he turned with a grin and shrugged. "It's only flat on one side."

"You do amuse yourself, don't you Dad?" Marnie said with a smile. She turned and popped open the trunk.

Her father reached for the spare tire and said, "I'll need about twenty minutes. Why don't you take my Jeep and do whatever you were doing." He handed her the keys.

"Really?"

Her father waved her away. "Sure. Meet you at your place. It just means I'll get there a few hours early tonight. Oh—and I'll pick Emily up from preschool again." He knew where Marnie kept the house key.

"Thanks, Dad. I do have an afternoon seminar I'd like to make."

"Anything interesting?"

"Personal, not business."

"Topic?"

Marnie hesitated. "How to Have the Life You've Always Wanted."

"Mmm."

Though he'd never said as much, Marnie knew her father credited the loneliness in her life to her husband's workaholic tendencies. She kissed his cheek and stepped up into the Jeep. "You're the best."

After making it past the various levels of security, Tim had dined privately in the family quarters of the White House. He now stood with his uncle in his bedroom.

"Appreciate the curbside consultation," the president joked.

"My pleasure. *I've* appreciated all your support of my work, Uncle Cal," Tim said. "And especially this latest decision."

"Well, it's not exactly altruistic. But I wish I didn't have to know so much. When do you think it will become legal?"

"Hard to say. But with delays, red tape, lawsuits and countersuits, we need to press ahead now, regardless," Tim told him.

"You know a scandal could raise public awareness enough to place even more limits on the research, don't you?"

"Uh-huh."

"Not to mention the hammering I'd take from prolifers." He paused for a moment before adding, "And if I want to make it through a second election. . . ."

Calvin Sullivan was in the second year of his term. He carefully studied his nephew's response. The doctor swallowed nervously and sat down on an antique chair.

"Still," the president continued, "I've needed to stay involved and informed. It's the only way I can sleep at night."

"Shall we start?" Tim asked tentatively.

"I suppose."

"Been having any symptoms?"

"I'm not sure. It might just be stress. But I've had a general, uneasy feeling," the president replied.

Tim nodded. After a series of preliminary questions, he pulled out his pocket opthalmoscope and turned on its light. He found his uncle's pupils equal, round, and regular. They reacted well to the tiny beam. "Good," Tim said. "Now follow the light with your eyes." He moved the light from side to side, up and down, then placed it near his uncle's nose, watching for asymmetry or nystagmus. "Great," he murmured.

The president looked relieved.

"Now open your mouth. . . . Okay, stick out your tongue. . . ."

"Good."

"I've wanted to do that during a press conference," he joked, drawing a faint smile from his nephew.

"Now move it from side to side. . . . Okay. . . . When did you say you had your last medical exam?" Tim asked.

"About nine months ago. Passed with flying colors."

"Hmmm. Okay, say 'Ahhh.'" Tim looked into the president's mouth at his uvula to see if it would elevate or deviate to one side or the other. "Looking good.

Okay, if you would stand now, I need you to stretch out your arms." Tim studied his patient intently. "Fine. Now close your eyes." The doctor watched for signs of balancing difficulties. "Good. Okay, now stand on one leg keeping your eyes closed."

The patient wobbled a bit and tried nervously to cover his embarrassment with a joke. "Gee, Tim, it's not like I'm a drunk driver or anything."

"I think you're under the limit," Tim quipped. It was meant to sound reassuring, but his own heart had begun to pound—did he sound concerned? *Keep your professional tone,* he reminded himself. "Okay, now touch your finger to your nose."

The president complied.

"All right, now touch my finger." Tim moved his finger again—right, left, up, down—testing coordination by having the president meet it in midair. Then he had his uncle reach out and squeeze his hand with successive right and then left hands.

"How am I doing?" the president asked. Tim didn't answer.

"Okay, you can sit down now," Tim told him. He pulled his chair closer and sat with his knees nearly touching his uncle's. Placing the president's hands on his own thighs near the knees, Tim asked him to flip his palms down then up, one hand at a time—palm up, palm down, as fast as he could go. The right hand worked perfectly, but the left didn't.

Dysdiadokokinesis, an early sign of brain involvement. Tim glanced nervously at a picture of the president with his wife and two junior high-aged girls.

"You know a lot about me, Tim," Calvin Sullivan said

quietly, in a tone that Tim couldn't interpret as being either positive or negative.

"You know almost *too* much about me, Tim." Calvin Sullivan's voice sounded strange.

Under normal circumstances, his nephew might have chuckled, but the events of the past hour had been far too sobering.

⚜

After dinner that night, Will Boralis built a fire in the den and pulled his little granddaughter onto his lap. Marnie cleared the table and loaded the dishwasher. She came in just as he was saying, ". . . All the king's horses and all the king's men couldn't put Humpty together again."

Will glanced up to see Marnie's look of disgust.

"What? Did I say something wrong?" he asked.

"No, it's that nursery rhyme. Last time Tim read it to her, he ended it with, 'But if they'd called me, not only would Humpty be together—she'd be fertile.'"

Will rolled his eyes. Emily just tugged on his shirt, saying, "Again! Again!"

Will had started over when the doorbell rang. Marnie walked through the living room to the front door, wondering who would be out on such a cold night. Christmas carolers, perhaps? Through the glass side panels of the door she saw three men on the porch—two police officers and a man in a tan trench coat.

"May I help you?" she asked, opening the door with the safety chain still on its catch. The weatherman had predicted intermittent freezing rain, and a warning against traveling was in effect for the metropolitan area. Marnie could feel a blast of cold air through the small opening.

"Mrs. Marina Sullivan?" the older of the two officers asked.

She blinked and nodded. "Yes, that's me. Is there a problem?"

"Wife of Timothy Lane Sullivan?"

"Yes." Marnie felt her pulse quicken.

"May we please come in?" he asked softly.

"Sure." She shut the door, released the chain, and opened it again, gesturing toward the couch and chairs. "Have a seat." Will, seeing the officers' blue uniforms from the adjacent den, briskly ushered Emily into her own room to watch a video.

The men wore serious expressions and avoided eye contact with Marnie. The officers removed their hats. The man in the overcoat, a kindly gentleman in his sixties, said, "I'm Bob King, one of the staff pastors of Cherrydale Church. I ride along with the police as the precinct chaplain." He paused to find the words. "I'm so very sorry, Mrs. Sullivan. I'm afraid there's been an accident. Your husband's car apparently slid off the road along Rock Creek Parkway into the Potomac."

Marnie felt something heavy press against her chest. *I can't breathe*, she thought.

Her eyes widened.

"They've recovered the car, but divers are still looking for your husband."

Breathe!

"It's been two hours," the pastor said quietly. "Perhaps they've found him by now, but we wanted to notify you before you saw it on the news. I'm so sorry."

Uneven gasps forced their way past Marnie's lips. She shook her head. "You'd better repeat all that," she said barely above a whisper. "I'm not sure I caught it all. . . ."

Will Boralis emerged from the kitchen hallway. The chaplain looked at him and then back to Marnie, as if to ask whether she wanted this conversation to remain private. "This is my father, Mr.—uh, Pastor . . . I'm sorry, I've forgotten your name."

Marnie, the accomplished reporter, never stumbled over names. Will sat down quietly next to his daughter, knowing what he was about to hear couldn't be good. The police chaplain reviewed the scant details a second time. Marnie buried her head in her father's shoulder and began to sob.

"Are you saying Tim's *dead?*" Will asked, staring at the three men as if he hadn't understood in the least any of the implications.

"Don't know anything for sure, sir. But it's unlikely anyone could survive long in that water," one of the officers responded. "Where Dr. Sullivan's car left the roadway there's a short strip without a guardrail. The roads were icy. My guess is that he lost control. We've got the car. The driver's side door was open, so it looks like he managed to get out. But with the water temperature and the undercurrent . . ."

"You haven't found Tim." Marnie struggled to absorb what she'd been hearing.

"Not yet, but we're doing our best. The cold water and ice make it tough for the divers. That's a treacherous part of the river. We'll let you know as soon as we find the body. I'm sorry, ma'am. Really sorry."

Just then, Emily came to the door and urged,

"C'mon, Grandpa! Come back and watch it with me."
But after taking one look at her mother's tear-stained face, she ran to Marnie.

"What's wrong? Mommy! Why are you crying?" She quickly worked herself up into a frenzy. "Mommy? Mommy! Don't cry, Mommy!" she wailed.

Marnie stumbled to her feet and pulled her daughter into the next room, leaving Will to handle the visitors.

"Perhaps there is someone I could call for you?" After a long moment of silence, the chaplain repeated his question.

"No," said Will. "But thanks." He stood, signaling the end of their visit.

After the men left, Will found Marnie in the same place she had discovered Tim that morning—in the rocking chair in Emily's room. He lowered himself gently to the floor and listened helplessly to the mother and child sob. When the doorbell rang again, he rose to answer it, hoping for word of Tim.

Instead, a network news reporter was on the porch, asking for an interview with the widow of the president's nephew. Will, who normally would have expressed unrestrained fury at such callousness, noticed a cameraman was aiming a bright light and camera in the direction of the front door. He kept his cool. Marnie's work entailed dealing with the media, but not tonight! Stepping out into the icy chill and closing the door firmly behind him, Will issued a simple statement. "Nothing's certain yet. All we've been told is that there's been a terrible accident. We don't know anything else." With that, he excused himself and went back inside.

Marnie, who had managed to interest Emily in the

video again, emerged and slumped into a stuffed chair in the den. More reporters began to call and leave messages wanting to know about the service, the time, the place. Would the president and the first lady attend? Marnie was too stunned to speak. *Unbelievable. We lose husband and father and all they care about is where the next presidential sighting will occur.*

Emily wandered into the room carrying her blanket, and Marnie looked at the clock. It was past bedtime. Reading his daughter's thoughts, Will scooped up Emily to take her to bed, but Marnie touched his arm. "Thanks, Dad. But I'll settle her tonight. She can sleep in my bed."

As she sat rocking her pajama-clad girl, Marnie sang in a sweet soprano voice. "Mommy's here, Mommy's near, singing you a lullaby." She buried her nose in Emily's hair, smelling baby shampoo and Colgate. *How can this be? Tim said he had to work late. What was he doing out at seven o'clock? Coming home for dinner with Dad? He knows these roads like his own driveway.*

Then she remembered he had taken her '68 Mustang today. *Older. Not nearly the suspension the Beamer has. Maybe the difference in handling was too much. Why did he have to take* my *car?*

The possibility of suicide entered her mind as she thought about Tim's tenderness the last time she'd seen him. But she immediately dismissed the thought. *He was upset but not that bad.* Her mind wandered wildly to all sorts of scenarios. *Kidnap? Someone wanting to get to the president?* She wondered whether anyone involved in the court case might have reason to want him dead. But Tim had assured her that the embryo transfer had taken place while they'd been in Hawaii. *Whatever happened there was someone else's doing.*

After tucking in her daughter, Marnie walked back out to the den and sat in front of the fire on an over-sized pillow. Her father sat down beside her. They stared at the flames in silence, sipping the fresh coffee he had brewed. "I just can't believe it. I just can't." She kept shaking her head. "Can't!" Then she began to cry again. She wrapped her arms around her father's neck and buried her face, her shoulders heaving.

Once he had her settled down, Will began to think of relatives they needed to notify. It occurred to him that Tim's business partners needed to know immediately what had happened. He asked Marnie for the clinic's number and dialed. The answering service picked up. An operator, speaking in a monotone, asked, "Do you need to speak to the doctor?"

"Yes. Emergency."

"Dr. Morgan is on call tonight. At what number may he reach you?"

Will quietly gave the information to the operator who assured Will, "I'll page Dr. Morgan for you now. He should call you back shortly. If not, please call again."

Within ten minutes, the phone rang.

It was Luc. "This is Dr. Morgan," he said expectantly.

"Doc, this is Will Boralis, Marnie Sullivan's dad."

"I knew the name was familiar, but I couldn't place it. What can I do for you?"

"I don't know exactly how to tell you this," her father continued, "but Tim was in a wreck tonight."

Luc gasped. "Tim? How bad is it?"

Will filled him in on the details. Luc was so stunned he could only express his condolences and hang up, promising to call Benjamin McKay, the third partner in their practice.

Within minutes, the phone rang again. Will glanced at caller ID and said, "Ben McKay. Want to talk to him?"

"No, that's all right. The machine can get it."

After "please leave a message," they heard, "This is Ben McKay. What horrible news! I'm so sorry. Luc just called and told me. I'm praying for you. . . ."

On hearing this, Marnie shrugged and nodded to her father. Will picked up the receiver and soon found himself explaining to Ben what had happened. Marnie could tell by her father's responses that many of Ben's questions related to her.

"She's gonna be okay. . . . Yeah, to be expected. . . . Uh-huh, just a few hours ago. . . . Don't know. . . . No, they haven't found the body yet. . . . Yeah, makes it harder. . . . A few TV crews. . . . Yeah? Don't know. Might help. I'll ask." Her father turned to her. "Says he's a chaplain. Could handle the media for us and bring some sedatives if you need them. Want him to come over?"

Normally Marnie opposed the use of sleep medication. She'd watched too many of her husband's colleagues form addictions to substances that were so accessible. Yet at the moment the suggestion sounded so appealing. Still, she answered by shaking her head. "It's getting late—a nasty night out there. I couldn't ask him to do that."

Will repeated Marnie's words to Ben. After a moment, Will asked her again, "Do you have *anything* here you can take?"

Marnie replied by shaking her head. After a few more moments of conversation, she heard her father giving directions.

When Ben McKay pulled up to the Sullivan's house he noticed the news van parked outside. The doctor approached the vehicle, where he found the crew huddling to keep warm.

"Who are you?" they wanted to know.

"Friend of the family. And may I ask a favor?" he asked in a gentle voice. He looked at the guy in the driver's seat and motioned toward the house with his head. "If you'll give me your card and leave them alone, I'll call you when they find the body." The crew, even though they only half believed him, seemed happy for an excuse to leave. Exchanging shrugs, they took him up on his offer.

As the van pulled away, Will opened the front door and stepped out onto the porch. He had been watching through the window and appreciated what he'd just seen.

When Ben entered, Marnie stayed put on the floor in front of the fire. She looked pale and strained as she glanced up at him with gratitude in her swollen eyes. Ben sat down in front of her on the hearth and placed his elbows on his knees, holding his chin in his hands. "I'm so sorry," he quietly offered.

Marnie nodded, then stared at the ground. She had seen Ben at a few social events and remembered thinking he could have been a model. She knew he'd lost his wife about the same time she and Tim had met. Her husband had said it was "some sort of medical tragedy," and she had not asked for more information. A practicing OB/Gyn, Ben had been Tim and Luc's partner in medicine before he lost his wife. After a leave of absence, he had returned to the clinic as a part-time administrator and medical consultant. He was still a partner in the business, and he also worked at the hospital as a chaplain, but he no longer saw patients. Tim rarely mentioned him.

"I can't imagine how you feel," Ben continued.

She looked up through the tears and said, "Thank you." *That was thoughtful, considering that he lost his wife*. It always annoyed Marnie when people said they knew how you felt, when really they had no clue.

"If you don't mind, could I just sit here with you for a while?"

Marnie shrugged gently and nodded toward him with half a smile. He sat down on the floor next to her and fixed his gaze on the fire. "If you'd rather be alone, just say the word. This news is a shocker. Luc sends his deep condolences." After this, Ben sat comfortably silent, occasionally looking down at his folded hands.

The presence of her father and Ben, two men who had lost their spouses, brought Marnie a strange sense of peace. And something about Ben made her feel a little more secure.

"Kind of you to come out on a night like this, Ben," Will said. Despite his bias against "religious people" he instantly liked this one.

The doctor acknowledged the comment with a nod. They all fell silent, lost in their sadness. After many minutes, Marnie looked at Ben, studying his face until he raised his long eyelashes and their eyes met. He gave her a kind smile. "Want me to go?" he asked just above a whisper.

Marnie shook her head. Tim didn't have many friends, and the presence of one that cared enough to come over brought comfort, even if she barely knew him. They sat for a while longer. Then she watched him as he stood, rolled up his sleeves, and rebuilt the fire. He lifted the heavy logs with ease. Doctors Luc and Ben, who'd been friends since rooming together in med school, often went to the gym together and played competitive racquetball until the club closed at night. They had long ago stopped inviting Tim. He never went; athletics bored him.

Will had gone back to the living room to watch out the window, hoping someone would soon bring word. Comforting others was not his gift. He was a doer, a fixer, and the silence pushed him beyond his endurance. So now he stood in front of the window, using the cordless phone to notify family members. Only nine months had passed since he had phoned many of the same people to tell them of his wife's passing. He could do this much for Marnie.

After Ben settled back down, he again looked at Marnie. She was beginning to cry again. "They haven't found him!" she choked out, trying to whisper so Emily wouldn't waken. "Tim's still out there somewhere in that freezing water. And drowning in ice. What a horrible . . . I can't stand it! I want to go look for him myself." At this, she broke down completely.

Ben blinked hard, and a tear rolled down his cheek.

After a few minutes, Marnie looked up to notice the tear-stained face of Tim's kind friend. She reached over and put her hand on his knee, touched by his compassion. As she regained her composure, she began to talk. She told him in detail about the visit from the officers, about Emily's tears, where she'd been sitting, what the men had said. After another long silence, she started again. "It's crazy what you remember at a time like this."

Ben listened quietly.

"Like how he sneaked into my office and loaded a screen saver he'd designed when we were dating. A Shakespeare sonnet. He wasn't into poetry, but he knew I loved it, so he made it for me. I haven't thought about that in years. And there was the time we went to Lake Anna, and Emily fell in the water feeding some ducks. You've never seen a nonswimmer dive in so fast. He went right after her. It was one of our few family outings."

Ben's smile provided all the encouragement Marnie needed to continue. She wished Tim had not taken her car today instead of his own. She felt glad he'd kissed her this morning. She had a lot of regrets. Falteringly, she went on and on until the clock on the mantle struck midnight, and she knew she shouldn't hold Ben captive any longer. "But what do I do now?" she had to know. "I don't know much about ministers and picking out caskets." She felt a chill as she said this last word. In the absence of a body, who would need a casket? "We don't go to church or anything. When Mom died last year, Dad didn't even have a service. But I want one for Tim. And I don't want to cremate him and throw his ashes in the Pacific like he did Mom's," Marnie said, gesturing to the other room toward her father. Then she lowered her voice. "When they *find* Tim."

Ben answered in a barely audible voice. "Well, in addition to being a doctor, I'm sure you know I'm also a chaplain—an ordained minister. I'd be glad to help you through these days. When they find him, I'll help make the arrangements, if you'd like. You've got enough on your mind. I'll leave my phone and pager numbers for you to call, anytime, day or night, whenever we get some news. We can make plans when you feel strong enough."

"Thank you, thank you so much. You've been so kind." Marnie was glad that a friend of Tim's could perform the funeral, and his use of "we" made her feel less alone. Considering the politics involved, she knew a high-profile ordeal was ahead.

"It's a privilege to help. I like Tim a lot."

Somehow, Marnie felt glad that Ben had not referred to her husband in the past tense.

"One of the smartest guys I've ever met," Ben continued. "I just wish I could do more. If you want me to help with any arrangements, *please* call."

"Your presence here has already helped a great deal. Thank you again."

"You're welcome. I'll call in the morning to check on you."

Marnie nodded. As she walked Ben to the door, they could hear her dad snoring on the recliner. Then Ben reached into his pocket and pulled out a prescription for her. "Oops. Almost forgot."

She took the medication from him and gave him a grateful bear hug. It felt hard to let go. "Thank you again, Ben." She released her grasp and looked at the pills.

"It's Ambien," he said. "Pretty mild. Should help you fall asleep, but it stays in your system only a few hours. Won't make you wake up too groggy." Ben kept some on hand because he occasionally had trouble sleeping.

"Thank you so much."

"Good night, Mrs. Sullivan."

"Please! It's Marnie." Her red eyes met his. It felt strange for a man barely forty—only a few years older than she was—to speak to her so formally.

"All right. Good night, Marnie." Ben nodded deeply and walked out into the cold.

Chapter Three

ON THURSDAY MORNING, Dr. Luc Morgan entered Tim Sullivan's office before dawn and sat in his chair. Still reeling from the shock, both personal and professional, Luc looked around at all the reminders of Tim. *Can't believe he's gone. He was just here. So sudden.*

Luc spotted Leigh Rivera's chart on Tim's desk and breathed with relief that it hadn't perished in Tim's briefcase. Then he chided himself for thinking selfishly at a time like this. He looked with compassion at the family photo on the credenza. *The guy leaves a wife and kid, and I'm worried about my lawsuit.* He sat for a long time remembering his friend. Eventually his thoughts moved on, and he began to wonder how to go about replacing the man he'd considered the best embryologist in the country.

After a while, Luc made his way down the hall to Tim's lab. He found the computer files readily accessible. His friend's superb organizational skills had left everything well marked and easily identified. *He'll be a*

hard one to replace on many levels, Luc thought as he
sat and stared at the screen for a long, long time.

Ben sat with Marnie, Will Boralis, Tim's mother—
Mavis Beth Sullivan from New Jersey—Emily, and Tim's
three brothers and their families. From the pastor's office next to the chapel, they could hear the organ playing softly. Ben noticed that Marnie, more beautiful than
ever in black, hummed quietly with the classical pieces
but stopped when the familiar hymns that always accompany memorial services were being played.

They all sat quietly together, occasionally speaking in
hushed tones, as they awaited the hour. Seven days and
many tears after the tragedy the divers had called off
their search in the icy Potomac. Public interest in the
story had kept them looking for longer than usual. Finally, Ben had suggested to Will that it was time to move
ahead and get the media people out of Marnie's life.
Her father agreed. So here they sat, waiting for the
memorial service to begin.

Mavis Beth broke the silence. "I'm sure he'll be here."
She was referring to her brother-in-law, President
Sullivan. "I just know he'll come."

Sensing that her comment was more a question than
a statement, Ben stood and moved toward the door. "I'll
check to see if everything's ready." The press, allowed in
without cameras, vastly outnumbered the modest crowd
of friends, the entire clinic staff, a few colleagues, and
distant relatives. Dark-suited men with matching lapel pins
stood by each door, having conducted an intensive

security sweep just before noon. Nearing one o'clock—the scheduled time for the memorial—everything stood ready.

Ben looked around. *This sure feels weird. No body, no funeral home, no viewing visits. None of the normal stuff that helps prepare people for that last good-bye. Hard to get closure without it.* He returned to the family and shook his head when Mavis Beth looked up at him. She sighed her disappointment, and they all stood for Ben to lead the procession into the sanctuary. The chapel, adorned with Christmas wreaths and poinsettias even before the funeral bouquets had begun to arrive, now smelled of greenery and cut flowers.

Ben took his place on the platform beside the podium and signaled for the assembly of mourners to rise. At his sign, the organist stopped playing. In respectful silence, the crowd watched as the family entered the reserved section at the front of the church. During this solemn procession, Ben noticed some activity among the Secret Service agents, but he didn't immediately grasp the significance.

As the family settled in to the first few rows, Ben motioned for everyone else to be seated before he began. "The family would like to extend its deep appreciation for the outpouring of love demonstrated in the many flowers you see around me, a tribute to the impact of this man's life. Your presence here, a gift of your time, serves as a testimony to your heart for Tim Sullivan and his family. On their behalf, let me say 'thank you.'" He turned and took his seat on the platform, motioning for the musicians to begin.

The service opened with a solo rendition of "The

Lord's Prayer." Marnie, with handkerchief in hand, leaned to whisper something to Emily. *She seems very composed*, thought Ben. *An interesting combination of strength and vulnerability . . . such a terrible thing for her to endure.* As a physician, Ben had witnessed plenty of tragedy, and as a chaplain, he had done his share of funerals, but after Juli's death, he had an especially soft spot for those who didn't get to say good-bye.

Just as the organist concluded, the dark-suited man beside the door to the left of the platform quietly opened it. Two other men escorted the president and first lady to seats on the front row with the family.

Glad he's here—for Marnie's sake, thought Ben. *Decent of them. Tough to send the vice president to this one.* Amazingly enough, though many whispers and nods rippled through the pews, no cameras flashed. Before taking their places, the president and his wife exchanged warm embraces with Marnie and the family. Ben paused long enough to let everything settle; then he introduced Luc Morgan and sat down.

"We come together today to celebrate a life and to mourn the passing of a husband, father, son, colleague, and friend," said the distinguished-looking physician. As Luc spoke, Ben scanned the crowd for familiar faces and saw members of the staff nod their recognition. "Timothy Lane Sullivan of Westfield, New Jersey. Passed from this life on the third of December, at the age of thirty-eight years, eight months, and seventeen days. Preceded in death by his father, Horatio S. Sullivan. Survived by his wife Marina Boralis Sullivan, daughter Emily Ann Sullivan, his mother Mavis Beth Sullivan . . ."

On hearing her name, Emily looked at her mother

and whispered with a smile, "He said my name!" Marnie looked down and nodded.

"Born in Westfield, New Jersey, Timothy Sullivan graduated with highest honors from the University of Kentucky. There he specialized in biochemical research at the animal husbandry laboratory just outside of Lexington. He went on to attend the University of Texas Southwestern Medical School in Dallas, Texas, earning the double doctorate of M.D. and Ph.D." Relaxing his tone a bit as he came to the part most familiar to him, the doctor continued, "Tim served as my partner; he was an embryologist at the Center for Fertility Enhancement for eight years and was instrumental in discovering the Uterine Implantation Factor. Loving husband, father, son, and brother. And nephew of the U.S. president." Luc cast a sympathetic eye in the direction of Calvin and Elizabeth Sullivan. "He was a fine citizen and a brilliant researcher.

"On a personal note—'Humpty Dumpty sat on a wall.'" Luc continued, going on to give a glowing eulogy beginning with Tim's most recent "edited" nursery rhyme. Tim had a reputation for twisting Mother Goose, so this example brought a smile to the faces of all who knew him.

As Luc descended the platform, he looked to Marnie for assurance that what he'd said had been in line with her wishes. She nodded gratefully. Luc was known for his natural stage presence.

Ben reapproached the podium. "Please join me as we pray together." He bowed his head and the mourners followed his lead. "Heavenly Father, God of all comfort, hold us up now by your grace. . . ."

Marnie's thoughts drifted to the past week of waiting and waiting. At first, with each new ring of the telephone, she'd hoped for good news, that somehow Tim—always a survivor—had escaped the submerging car. Then she'd just wanted news, any news, so she could know for sure that Tim was gone. The uncertainty overwhelmed her. She remembered interviewing a man after the Oklahoma City bombings who'd said he'd found it harder not knowing what had happened to his wife than finally learning she was dead. At the time, the statement had struck Marnie as strange, but now she understood.

She felt tears well up in her eyes as her mind wandered back to the moment when the men had first arrived with the bad news. The sounds of Pachelbel's Canon brought her back to the chapel, as Chaplain McKay rose slowly from his seat and returned to the podium. Marnie hadn't even noticed he'd sat down after the prayer.

He began again, slowly opening his Bible. "Dear family and friends, you have come today out of respect for the life of this man and love for one another. You look for answers, a sure word, something you can trust. We can find that certainty, the true comfort that reaches to the soul, only in God's Word. Life and death, joy and mourning, are so familiar to us. Yet in such moments our footing seems unsure. We can't understand."

Marnie felt for a moment as though she were someone else, observing everything but not believing it was her own reality. She looked down at Emily and squeezed the child tightly against her side. Emily, who always spent Sunday mornings watching cartoons, had never been part of any kind of service before. She sat politely in her new navy-blue dress with full petticoat, her feet sticking out several inches beyond the edge of the pew. At the moment, the red-pencil picture she was drawing on her order of service paper consumed her attention.

"In Ecclesiastes 7:2," Ben continued, "Solomon, the wisest of all men, wrote: 'It is better to go to a house of mourning than to go to a house of feasting, for this is the end of everyone, and the living will lay it to heart. Sorrow is better than laughter, for by sadness of countenance the heart is made glad. The heart of the wise is in the house of mourning, but the heart of fools is in the house of mirth.'"

Ben continued. "How can Solomon say it's better to go to a house of mourning? What can we learn in the midst of such pain? The anguish, the tears of a wife who has lost her husband, a mother who has lost her son, a sweet child who has lost her daddy? How is a sad face good for the heart? How does this wisdom come? Where do we find anything positive in such tragedy?" Marnie looked up at the stained glass windows, self-conscious that Ben's words had directed the crowd's thoughts to her, trying to hold back her tears when Ben said the word "daddy." Luc was observing his partner and friend in the role of chaplain for the first time. He smiled proudly.

"When the Bible speaks of passing from this life into eternity, we see several beautiful word pictures," Ben explained. "Death is likened to three things: striking the tent to prepare for a journey, going to sleep, and going home.

"Now, most of us have a great sense of joy as we prepare to go on a journey, especially if we know our destination is a beautiful, safe place."

Again Marnie's thoughts drifted. She thought back to the wonderful days she and Tim had spent in Hawaii last Christmas. Lately she kept remembering, not the big events they'd shared, but the little things. Like that trip—how they'd been so amused to find the car they'd rented for buzzing around Maui was a red convertible, only then to discover that the cars the rest of the tourists had were exactly the same. They'd seen as many red convertibles there as yellow cabs in New York.

"Heaven is such a place. Beautiful beyond our imagination, heaven is a place where there is no death, no need for tears, no need ever to mourn again," Ben continued.

Marnie hoped such a place really existed and wondered whether Tim had made the journey there. She looked admiringly at Ben, feeling the compassion in his voice pouring over the crowd. Standing behind the podium, he looked strong, exuding confidence. *He really believes what he's saying.*

She realized that she was surprised. She had never heard someone as educated as a physician say anything like this, and she found comfort in his words. She hoped they were true. Emily's fidgeting interrupted Marnie's thoughts. Having covered the program with scribbles, the little girl had begun looking for a new project. Her mother reached in her purse and pulled out a note pad.

". . . and going to sleep at the end of a long, tiring day," Ben said. "Nothing sounds better. Dying, for the child of God, has been described—accurately, I think— as being like a child falling asleep in front of the television. She awakens the next morning in her own bed, not knowing how she got there, but rested, refreshed, and at home. Now, we know that her mother or father has gently picked her up and carried her to bed, pulling the covers over her and tucking her in securely. So it is when one of God's children passes from this life to awaken in the next. We can trust in the tender care of our heavenly Father to transport each one of us safely there, home with the Father in heaven."

Marnie dabbed her eyes as she remembered the last time she had seen Tim carry a slumbering Emily to bed, planting a gentle kiss on her forehead as he tucked her in.

"Perhaps the most familiar and beautiful picture of this life's end is that of going home. Is there any sweeter phrase? Going home. Ideally, home is a place where love and security abound, where they surround each family member."

Home. What am I going to do about the house? Huge payments. Insurance. Stocks. Bonds. Investments. Marnie felt her anxiety building momentarily. *Tim handled all that on his computer, and I don't even know his password.* Emily slid out of her seat to stand on the floor. Marnie gently patted the pew and shot her a stern look.

"Finally, Jesus said, 'In My Father's house are many dwelling places. If it were not so, I would have told you,'" Ben continued. "Some translate this as 'mansions.' But whatever the heavenly abode looks like, we will find it perfect for us." Ben continued reading, "'I go to prepare a place for you, and if I go to prepare a place for you, I will come again and receive you unto myself, so that where I am you may be also.' We have it on the authority of Jesus, the Son of God, that God has a place prepared, and safe passage promised for those who have trusted in Him, in Jesus, the Lord and keeper of our souls.

"Why does Solomon say to find wisdom in the house of the mourning? Because in the sad times, the hard times, we look into the faces of those we love who have themselves lost loved ones. In those times, we remember, and we consider our own frailty—our own mortality. The passing of Tim Sullivan reminds us that this life is a vapor. It's here and so quickly gone. Are we prepared for that journey? Are we certain of our heavenly home? You *can* be certain, secure that when the time comes for you to strike the tent, to slip into sleep, that you are going home to the promised, prepared place in the Father's house."

At this point, Marnie looked up in surprise. *Are you saying you can be sure you're going to heaven? I thought you had to live a good life and hope it all balanced out. Isn't it sort of arrogant to think you can know for sure?* Yet Ben didn't strike her as arrogant.

"We are here to mourn the passing of our friend Tim. Let us allow God to comfort us through his promises to us in Jesus Christ."

Marnie didn't know what promises he meant. Neither Tim nor she had ever given much thought to religion. To them, religious denominations had often seemed like just so many politically motivated groups. Tim's parents were Presbyterian. Hers were good people but completely unreligious. She looked over at her father, who was gazing up, admiring the windows.

Ben really believes this. She felt surprised at her own astonishment. Up until now heaven had always seemed so far off but, having lost her mother in the last year and now Tim, she'd begun giving it a lot more thought.

"Emily," she whispered firmly, grabbing her

daughter's arm, as once again she slid down from the pew and tried to inch away. The child pointed to Grandpa, indicating she wanted to go sit on his lap. When Will winked at her, Marnie shrugged and reluctantly nodded her approval.

"What greater tribute to Tim could there be," Ben concluded, "than for his untimely death to serve as the alarm that stirs your soul, that moves you to give your heart, your life, your eternity to God through Jesus Christ? Let us pray.

"Lord, we give you thanks for the privilege of prayer, which gives us free access to your mercy and grace in times of need. And this, Father, is just such a time of need."

Marnie, who was finding comfort in these words felt annoyed to be jarred out of her thoughts with "Mommy, I need to go potty!" Emily had whispered just loudly enough to draw a few muffled chuckles along the front row.

"In a minute, honey; it's almost over," Grandpa soothed her.

". . . in your precious name. Amen."

Ben returned to his seat, wondering whether Tim had ever placed his trust in Jesus. As he sat, the organist began playing "Amazing Grace," the final hymn. Ben felt relieved to have completed his part of the service, and he mentally sang along. He scanned the crowd, allowing his eyes to fix on the president who was sitting nearby with the first lady, surrounded by Secret

Service agents. *He's sure not showing any emotion today. Guess they weren't that close.*

Ben continued to look at the crowd, and finally his
eyes rested on Marnie. She nodded slightly at him and
gave him a grateful half smile. Ben nodded in return.
Wonder what she thought about what I said? He realized seconds later that he felt more concerned about
her impressions of his words than the president's.

Before the last chords of the hymn faded, the president stood up with his wife and, surrounded by his
Secret Service escort, departed the way he'd entered.
As Ben watched him go, he noticed a slight, almost im-
perceptible abnormality in his gait. His mind went back
to med school days when the instructors had told the
students, "Observe. Watch your patients walk, sit, stand,
even before they speak. Then, when you listen to what
they say, you'll get the right diagnosis."

Maybe his foot just went to sleep while he was sitting,
Ben mused as the hymn ended. With the presidential
party now absent, Ben stood at the podium to thank
the gathered friends for coming and asked that they
allow the family a few minutes to slip ahead to the fel-
lowship hall for the reception to follow.

Luc approached his partner, pulled him aside, and
said in a warm and quiet voice, "Living in the house
of mourning has made you wise, my friend. Good job."
Ben deeply appreciated this remark. Luc had never understood why Ben had chosen to stop seeing patients
in favor of chaplaincy work. But Ben didn't stay to talk;
he wanted to speak with Marnie. As he approached
her, she took his arm and started to say something.
But Emily looked Ben squarely in the eyes and said,

"I gotta go potty. Mommy says you know where the potty is."

Ben met her eyes, nodded seriously, and said, "No problem. Let's go."

When Emily boldly grabbed his hand, Marnie pressed her lips together to stifle a smile. The three moved out the side door, stopping at the ladies room, and then walked in silence to the reception.

"Can we talk later?" Marnie asked Ben in earnest.

"Sure."

Ben wondered what about.

Chapter Four

DR. LUCAS MORGAN WAS HAVING trouble sleeping. He walked from his bedroom into his study and pulled out a medical journal. He had spent the last two weeks searching for something, anything, that might suggest a reason why the Riveras would want to sue him. So far, he'd found nothing. After several hours, he headed back to bed, hoping to catch a few hours' sleep before tomorrow's early IVF procedure.

Puiiing the covers around him, Luc purposely stuck a cold foot against the leg of his sleeping wife, Janelle. She shot up and exclaimed, "Pizza! With anchovies!"

Ben's pager went off late Friday afternoon, the day after Christmas. He stared at the incoming number, which looked only slightly familiar. After pulling over to the side of the road, he punched it in on his cell phone.

"Yes, this is Dr. McKay," he said when the person at the other end picked up. "Someone paged . . ."

"Ben?"

"Yes?"

"It's Marnie Sullivan."

"Oh! Hello!" Ben tried to conceal his delight, then chided himself for thinking like a man instead of a chaplain.

"Um . . . uh . . . well . . ." Now she was having second thoughts about phoning.

"Is everything okay?" he asked, trying to coax out of her whatever it was she was having trouble saying. *I wonder if they found Tim's body.*

"You said to call if ever I needed anything?" It was a question, not a reminder.

"Absolutely," he assured her, happy she'd taken him seriously. After the funeral, she had invited him to come back to the house with the family. He had stayed late. Marnie had asked him questions about his sermon, and he had been only too happy to try to answer them. At the end of the night, she had prayed with him and placed her faith in Christ. Ben had called almost daily since then to check on her, but this was the first time she had called him. "How can I help?"

"I know it's sort of short notice, but Mavis Beth is expecting us to bring the memorial plaque for Tim up to the family plot in Westfield, New Jersey, tomorrow."

"Yes?" Ben concentrated on her tone of voice, trying to discern what her need was.

"Emily has a nasty cold, and I'd rather not take her out. Dad says he'll stay with her, and he thought perhaps you wouldn't mind driving with me up to Westfield to place the marker?" Actually, the four-hour drive had been Marnie's idea, not her father's, but she suddenly felt so self-conscious that she was too afraid to admit it. She figured Ben knew how to handle these things, and she dreaded having to do it alone. Mavis Beth said she had shopped for a special lunch, and her daughter-in-law hated to disappoint her. Besides, Marnie herself needed a sense of place in the absence of the body . . . some physical location where she could put her last memory of Tim. "I know it's really a last minute idea but . . ."

"I'd be delighted," Ben responded. "Let me make a call to open my schedule."

Marnie groaned. "You'll have to change your schedule? Oh, no. Never mind. Really! I never should have asked."

"Marnie, it's just racquetball. I can reschedule, okay? Nothing important—honestly. I'd like to go with you. You shouldn't drive alone with the ice on these roads anyway."

"It's so kind of you." Marnie sighed deeply, relieved that he didn't seem annoyed.

"No problem. Is there a minister up there I should contact? Or someone at the cemetery?"

"Yes. I have it written here somewhere." Marnie paused a moment. "Here it is. Reverend Jim Coleman. An old friend of Tim's parents."

"Got his number handy?" Ben fumbled for his pen.

Marnie asked him to hold on again, retrieved the number, and repeated it for him.

"Okay, I'll take care of everything. What time do you want me to pick you up?"

Marnie was glad Ben was going to handle the details. "I don't know. What time do you think's good? I can't make even little decisions like this these days."

Ben remembered how that felt. "Would seven be too early?"

"No, that's great. I'd like to get an early start."

"Great. See you in the morning, then. Dress warmly!" After he hung up the phone, Ben continued sitting by the side of the road for a few more moments, offering a prayer for Marnie and her family. He felt deep joy at the prospect of spending more time with her. Walking her through these difficult days had brought him a sense of calm. Yes, it had opened some old wounds but, in some ways, it had brought healing.

Leigh Rivera put her three-month-old twins down for the night and walked out onto the porch, sipping a glass of purified water with a lemon slice in it. She sank into one of the rocking chairs that dotted the terrace of the enormous ranch house, gazing at the stars and the silhouette of the mountain in the distance. A tear caught her by surprise, and she quickly wiped it with her shirt. Though exhausted from taking care of the twins, she fought sleep. She wanted to wait up for her husband, who had seemed so distant the past month. Here she had left her family and her country to live what everyone expected would be a glamorous life with a man she loved. But nothing had turned out as she had hoped, starting with the infertility problems.

In a few moments, the headlights of Carlos's Mercedes turned up the road. She heard his footsteps in the house and waited for him to come outside looking for her. When he didn't, she went in to find him. Sitting at his mahogany desk, he looked up to see her standing in the doorway. Without a greeting, he deliberately ignored her and looked back at the papers he was reviewing.

~c9e~

December 27 broke clear and cold. As Ben pulled into Marnie's driveway, Emily waved at him through the bay window. He came up the walk, and she opened the door to greet him. "I'm sick!"

Once he was inside and had shut the door against the cold, Ben stooped to look into her eyes and in his low, official-sounding "doctor voice" replied, "I'm so sorry to hear that."

"Do you like my jammies?" she asked, spinning around so he could see the bunny tail on the back of her flannel footy-pajamas.

"They're just beautiful," Ben said dramatically. "And so warm for a cold day." Before he finished, Emily had turned to announce his arrival with, "Mommy! Mommy!" But Marnie had been standing there all along, watching.

Ben and Marnie flashed smiles at each other, and then she blushed and looked at the floor. Ben's eyes followed hers. "Thanks for agreeing to come," she said quietly. "I know you don't know me very well but asking for help isn't something I do often."

Ben nodded deeply. "I'm glad you did. Really glad."

She looked up and smiled gratefully, then turned and walked to the closet to grab her black wool coat and red scarf. After pulling on a pair of black leather gloves, she hugged her daughter, now planted firmly in front of the television. Will emerged from the garage where he'd gone to get the memorial plaque. He carried it out to Ben's car as Marnie and Ben followed. While Marnie climbed into the passenger's seat, the men secured the memorial in the trunk.

"Thanks for taking care of my girl today, Doctor," Will said.

"You're welcome." Ben smiled and walked over to open his car door.

"All ready?" Will asked, leaning down to look in the car window at his daughter, all bundled up for the cold.

"I think so," she said. "Thanks for carrying the plaque, Dad. That thing weighs as much as Argentina."

"I'm not as old as you think, honey."

He waved at them while Ben pulled away from the curb, and Marnie thought he looked sad.

"You're the first preacher he's ever liked," Marnie said.

Ben raised his eyebrows in response. "Why? Because I'm also a doctor?"

"Actually, no. I think it's because you drive an SUV. It kind of messes with his categories. Doesn't fit what he expects. Since he drives a Jeep himself, he figures you can't be all bad."

Ben chuckled and they drove in silence for several minutes. "Been to Jersey," he said. "But whereabouts is Westfield?"

"No problem," said Marnie. "I'll get you there."

"Hmm . . . a woman with directions. Is that because you figured I'd never stop and ask?" Ben asked, smiling.

"Do you have a Y chromosome? Is Oprah on a diet?"

"OK. Touché." Ben was delighted that their trip had started on a less somber note than he'd feared.

"Trust me," she said, smiling broadly. "I'll get us there. No problem."

"Have I mentioned that you look great today?" As soon as Ben said the words, he wondered if Marnie would wrongly interpret them as a come-on.

The remark did catch Marnie by surprise. "Didn't think chaplains noticed that sort of thing."

Ben glanced quickly in her direction. "What?"

"I don't know. Like priests, or something. I guess I figured you're sort of like a third gender. Seems kind of dumb, come to think of it." Once challenged, Marnie wondered at the lapse in her own logic. "But take it as a compliment. When I'm with you, I feel like a person, not a woman."

"Nothing wrong with feeling like a woman, is there?" Ben voice revealed his struggle to understand.

Her red lips parted to reveal a full and perfect smile. "No. I guess there isn't, is there? But honestly, I meant no offense. And you look very nice yourself."

As they rolled along the Garden State Parkway, their conversation remained light. The ice had melted in the bright sun despite the cold, making the trip easier than Ben had expected. His CD player was loaded with soundtracks from popular movies, to the delight of his passenger. Background music from *Somewhere in Time*, *Titanic*, and *Zorro* made the drive time pleasant.

"I thought you'd listen to religious music," she jibed.

"I'm a man of many tastes."

"Apparently some of them romantic," she observed. She immediately regretted it. But the delight on his face in response to her remark alleviated her fears. *"Somewhere in Time* is one of my all-time favorite movies," she said.

"Mine, too." Ben looked over at her and smiled.

"Honest?"

"Uh-huh."

"I think Jane Seymour in that movie is one of the most beautiful women in the world."

Ben bit his lip to keep from saying what he was thinking: *Funny. I think you look just like her.* He had a soft spot for brunette heroines, but he kept this observation to himself as well. He'd planned to change the music if it evoked painful memories for Marnie, but she seemed happy.

They reached the Clark cutoff and turned down Rahway Avenue, following the signs to colonial Westfield. Marnie had visited there fewer than a dozen times. With Tim's work schedule, his mother usually came to visit them instead. But the town was small enough that it was hard to get lost. They passed the Rialto Theater on the right and turned up Mountain Avenue. "Wow," Ben whispered, when he saw the tall white spire of the First Presbyterian Church. "That is *striking.*"

His appreciation delighted his traveling partner. "Yes, Tim's parents attended there for three decades or more. Mavis Beth still attends. The original church was built in the 1700s. Tim said that, when he was a boy, they split it to preserve the entryway and the platform area. Pulled the two halves apart and built more room in the middle. Can you believe that? All to preserve the look and feel of the place."

"Certainly a magnificent structure."

After parking the car, Ben left Marnie listening to music. He momentarily went inside to find the Reverend James Coleman, who was sitting in his office waiting for Ben's arrival. The pastor directed Ben to the caretaker of the cemetery across the street. "He has the site prepared and will be available to assist you in any way," said Mr. Coleman in his best pastoral tone.

"Thank you. We'll probably just place the memorial plaque, spend a few moments, and then allow your caretaker to secure it after we leave."

"Fine," answered the minister. "And, may I say, I am sorry for your loss."

"Appreciate that," replied Ben, feeling no need to explain his role. He returned to the car and opened Marnie's door, offering his arm as she got out. After lifting the antique bronze plaque out of the trunk, he told her what the pastor had said.

"Thanks, Ben. I'm glad I don't have to meet strangers right now. This role of bereaved widow feels odd."

Together they crossed Mountain Avenue and walked up the steps of the cemetery. The old gate stood open, and Ben was immediately taken by the history of the place. Some of the markers dated to the late 1700s. *Interesting,* he thought. *Hundreds of years ago, families stood on this very spot to grieve the passing of their loved ones. And now, no one remembers them.*

The reality of their purpose and the quiet stillness of the place caught Marnie by surprise. Feeling the need to touch someone, she instinctively reached over and grabbed Ben's arm as he carried the heavy plaque in his hands. The caretaker waved discreetly to them, and they walked up to the prepared site. Marnie saw a stone reading "Horatio S. Sullivan," with the dates and particulars. "Loving husband and father. Rest in Peace," she read quietly. Right beside it was the vacant plot with nothing but the mounting plate for the memorial plaque. She shuddered, partly because of the frigid day and partly because this was it—the place. As she reflected on the events since her husband's death, her thoughts mixed into a jumbled ball of yarn. She appreciated Ben's calming presence and felt glad she'd worked up the nerve to ask him to come.

Ben, assisted by the caretaker, gently and reverently laid the plaque into place. They stood silently for a few moments, then the caretaker withdrew. "May I offer a prayer?" Ben asked.

Marnie, brought back to reality from deep thought, looked up at his eyes and nodded gratefully. *If Dad were here, we wouldn't do this. And I need it.*

They stood side by side in the cold, staring at the words on the stone. Ben reached over to put his hand on top of Marnie's as she continued to hold his arm. "Heavenly Father, we stand grieving the loss of Tim. We ask that his physical remains might be found so we can return to this spot with them, a sacred site where you will one day resurrect each of your creatures. Please extend your comfort to Marnie, to Emily, to Mavis Beth, to Will, and to their families. Walk with them closely through the days and months ahead. Grant us your peace now, even as we pray that Tim's spirit might rest in your peace eternally. In Jesus' name. Amen."

Marnie wiped the tears streaming down her face with the back of her free, gloved hand. She didn't remember ever hearing someone pray for her by name, and she wanted to keep holding on for a while. They stood together for a number of minutes until a bunch of laughing young teenagers, carrying skates over their shoulders, broke the silence.

Ben looked up. "Skates? Where do people skate around here?"

"Just down the hill," said Marnie. "Emily and I skated there last winter when I brought her up to see her grandmother. Want to see it?"

Ben understood—time to go. They walked out of the cemetery, continuing along between the big church buildings, down the hill into Mindowaskin Park. The snow on the ground kept Marnie hanging onto him, and neither of them minded.

"Interesting name," Ben said.

"I think it's Indian—or I guess I should say 'Native American' or 'indigenous.' This area has plenty of barely pronounceable names."

A hard freeze had created a center of great winter fun. People of all ages crowded the lake, skating around and between the small islands accessible now because of the frozen surface. Marnie relaxed as she watched the skaters, some skillful, others awkward, a few downright dangerous.

"I'll bet you and Emily had fun," Ben said.

Marnie nodded and pointed to a bench at the shore. They walked over to it and sat huddled together, Marnie still clinging to Ben's arm. For a few moments, as they watched life and joy speed past them on the ice, they forgot their pain.

Finally, Marnie looked at her watch and said reluctantly, "It's time to go to Mother's. She'll have lunch waiting."

"Think she'll want to come to the cemetery for the placing of the memorial? Maybe we should bring her back out after lunch."

"No, she stays inside during cold weather. We'll just tell her it looks perfect, and she can see it when it warms up. Until they find Tim, I don't think she'll give up hope anyway." Marnie paused to keep her voice from cracking, then continued, "Going out to the plot would make the finality of it all the more real."

Ben's look said he was sorry for her pain. "Okay, lead on," he said.

At Marnie's direction, Ben guided his Explorer down Mountain Avenue to East Dudley, took a sharp left, and traveled to the Sullivan family home at 41 West Dudley. Ben eyed an attractive, two-story colonial with a big pine tree in front. "The red one?" he asked.

"Uh-huh."

They walked up the steps to the front door, where Mavis Beth stood waiting. "Come on in," she motioned to them. "It's freezing out there!" She gave Marnie a hug and shut the door quickly. When Tim had married Marnie, Mavis Beth, the mother of four boys, made it clear to everyone that she loved finally having someone else in the family with estrogen. And Marnie had grown to appreciate that affection even more since her own mother's passing. Tim's mother epitomized the Southern charm of her Louisiana roots. She had impeccable manners, but she used them to create a sense of comfort, not to intimidate.

Ben realized that, with Marnie for company, he hadn't even noticed the cold.

"I'm glad you came ahead today," Mavis Beth said warmly in her soft Southern drawl. "I've really looked forward to your visit. Maybe you can bring Emily up in a week or two when she feels better."

Marnie shrugged lightly, by which she meant "yes, perhaps."

Ben glanced into the dining room as they passed on the way to the living room. Mavis Beth had laid a lovely spread, complete with china. *Marnie was thoughtful not to cancel on her,* he thought.

Entering the room Mavis Beth turned. "Come on in. Please make yourselves at home. Nice to see you again, Dr. Chaplain."

Ben smiled.

"What am I supposed to call you?"

"Most people call me Ben," he said. "And I'd be honored if you would, too."

"All right then! Welcome, Ben. Sit down and take a load off!"

Marnie and Ben removed their coats, sat on the sofa, and recounted the events of the morning. Mavis Beth seemed glad that the arrangements had been handled but was clearly even more pleased by the company.

"How's Emily?" she asked, sounding worried.

"Oh, she'll be okay. Just a nasty cold. Really. Nothing major. Wouldn't you say so?" Marnie looked at Ben for reinforcement, and he nodded confidently.

When the room grew silent, Ben remarked, "You have a lovely home."

"Thanks. Horace and I bought it back in the fifties, and I couldn't bear to leave it."

After more small talk, the women left Ben in the living room so they could pour the drinks and add finishing touches to the flawless spread. He stood as they got up to leave and then, since he was up, walked over to get a closer look at some of the pictures on the mantel. Tim's UK graduation photo. A family vacation shot. One of Emily as an infant. *She seems so tiny.* He thought Marnie looked beautifully maternal holding her and, with that, the pain of an old memory brought an unexpected mist to his eyes. He blinked and moved on.

There was a yellowing portrait of Horace and Mavis Beth. Another of Horace with his much younger brother, now the president. But Ben's eyes widened when he saw Tim and Marnie's wedding picture. *Absolutely enchanting,* he thought as he looked at the dark-haired bride, luminous in all her finery.

"Lunch is ready." Ben turned to see Marnie standing next to him. The look on her face made him wonder how long she'd been there.

Chapter Five

As LUNCH WAS SERVED, Ben reentered the conversation. Mavis Beth had been talking about her husband since the two women left the room together. Now she picked up where she'd left off. "He was a good man and a fine husband, at least until those last years."

"Really? " asked Ben, leaving room for Mavis to continue or to close that door.

"The final few years his body and mind played tricks on him and then finally gave out. Died one night in the sun parlor over there. When he couldn't get up the stairs any more, I fixed him up out there by the piano. He spent most of his last days right there."

Marnie had heard all of this several times. She looked with compassion at her mother-in-law.

"I usually sleep out there myself now, especially in the summer heat," Mavis Beth continued. "I feel his closeness. Gives me comfort. Anyway, it's an awful disease." She began to tear up a little.

"I'm sorry to hear that," said Ben. "A lingering illness?"

"No," she said. "Akenosis. He nicknamed it the Sleep of Death, or SOD—because you knew, once you had it, that before long they'd be laying you under the sod. When you were preaching that fine sermon, and you talked about sleep, I kept thinking how afraid Horace was to go to sleep at night. Afraid he wouldn't wake up—though when he got sick enough there at the end, his mind was too far gone to know it."

Ben couldn't recall any such disease from medical school. But his specialty in OB/Gyn had made him more interested in syndromes affecting women and small children than those of older men.

Mavis Beth went on, "I'm surprised Tim never mentioned it to you."

Marnie nodded her surprise, too.

"He worried constantly about it," Tim's mother continued. "Apparently, it shows up only in the men of a family. Not all of them, but most. First they walk funny. They shake. They talk strangely. Then their memory starts to go, from the recent stuff to the really old stuff. Emotions get out of kilter. When you see all that happen to them, you begin to wonder every night if that'll be the one when their brain will 'forget' to tell 'em to breathe, and they'll die."

Realizing she was rambling, Mavis Beth took a bite, but no one jumped in to change the subject, so she began talking again.

"Ever since Tim was old enough to understand, he set out to find a cure. For his family, for his father, and I guess for himself. You know, he did his doctoral dissertation on the subject. Something about genes and all. He was always afraid he would die that way." She stopped abruptly as the realization of his drowning again hit her.

They all ate in silence for a while. Regaining her composure, Mavis Beth picked up where she'd left off. "I think it was the potential for mental changes that scared him the most. He always had to be the smartest boy in the room."

For as long as Ben had worked at the clinic, he had never heard Tim mention anything about any of this. *Tim was one private guy.*

Mavis went to the bookshelf beside the old mantel, looking for her copy of Tim's research book, but couldn't find it. "Probably took it with him," she said.

Ben asked a few medical questions, which Mavis Beth answered as best she could.

Marnie told him, "If you're interested, there's lots about it on the Internet. Tim was always writing articles there."

"Interesting. I'll have to log on and check it out."

"When Tim wasn't working at the clinic, he holed up at home doing research on-line," Marnie said. "Are you into computers?"

"Not a hobby or anything, but it does come in handy for research," Ben offered.

He could see from Marnie's expression that she wasn't crazy about them.

"So does that look on your face mean you don't know the difference between pixels and pizza?" he asked her.

"No, it's not that. I use computers all the time for my work. I just didn't share my husband's interest in the latest hardware." She glanced over at Mavis Beth to make sure this comment had not come across as a criticism of Tim. But when her mother-in-law rolled her eyeballs and laughed, Marnie added, "It seems like the newest equipment gets outdated in a nanosecond, so it's a never-ending expense."

After serving an exquisite lunch, followed by chocolate mousse, Mavis Beth spoke more about Horace and Tim. Finally, Marnie discreetly pointed to her watch, signaling to Ben that they needed to be on their way. He nodded and took responsibility for their quick departure. "Thank you for a lovely meal, Mrs. Sullivan. You're a wonderful cook. I hate to say it, but I really have to get back now."

"So kind of you to bring her to me, Ben," she said, looking lovingly at her daughter-in-law. As Marnie made a quick trip to the rest room, Mavis asked him, "Do you think she's going to be okay?"

Ben reached out and placed his hand on the worried woman's shoulder. "I think she'll be fine. You're kind to care so much for her."

Marnie emerged and, after a few parting words and warm exchanges of affection, the couple pulled out of the driveway homebound for Washington, D.C.

Ben welcomed the silence of the first hour, content just to be with Marnie. When she finally spoke, she surprised him. "We weren't doing that well in the marriage area, Tim and I."

Ben listened, not knowing where this would go. "Sorry," he said sympathetically.

"Tim didn't want to have children because of the Akenosis. So he really went ballistic when I turned up pregnant after we'd been married about a year. He said I'd have to have an abortion, no question about it. He was really out there. We fought over it constantly. I wasn't trying to get pregnant. The pills just hadn't worked. I took some antibiotics for a little acne problem and—bam—pregnant. So we argued. No way I wanted an abortion. Since this family thing was only in men, I managed to convince him to wait until we knew the baby's sex. I told him if it was a boy, I'd have an abortion. I doubt that I would have, but it bought some time. When the amniocentesis showed Emily was a girl, things settled down a bunch. But the harsh words . . ." Marnie shook her head. "It was hard to forgive him for those."

Ben was accustomed to hearing women relate their reproductive histories, but somehow it caught him by surprise today. He was glad she'd opened up, though. It answered a few questions about the way she was dealing with her husband's death.

"In fact, in the years following Emily's conception, we virtually stopped being intimate. Hardly ever." As soon as she had said this, Marnie gasped. "I can't believe I'm telling you all this! I'm so sorry. It's really . . . it's not like me to just blather on. I've never mentioned it to anyone else."

"Don't worry, Marnie," Ben said. "Life gets messy for everybody sometimes. I'm honored you felt you could trust me. Really."

Marnie looked over at him, and he shot her a kind smile.

Tim must have been as blind as a mole, he thought. After a few moments, he realized she was still looking at him. He returned the glance.

"Just wondering something," she said.

He raised his eyebrows in curiosity. "What's that?"

"What it is about you that makes me want to tell you so much?" She looked back at the road, apparently lost in thought, while he let her compliment sink in. "Anyway, I would never marry a doctor again," she said, thinking aloud.

"Why not?" He tried to hide the sudden rejection he felt in this remark.

"Too busy. Awful hours. Tim always told me I was living in an ideal world, and maybe I was. But I always pictured marriage the way it was for my parents. Not perfect—but they liked having each other around. They did stuff together. It took an act of congress to get Tim to take a vacation last year. You know why Mom and Dad named me Marnie?"

Ben looked over at her and waited.

"It's short for Marina. The year I was conceived, they spent the summer sailing the San Juans together, so they figured it was appropriate. What I'd give to have had time with Tim like that! But when you're a doc, that's impossible."

"I dunno. I'm not so sure about that. Nothing wrong with a woman wanting the man she loves around. I know some doctors with happy marriages."

"You can't work seventy-hour weeks and have a marriage."

"Right. Absolutely. But who says you have to work that much?"

Suddenly Marnie wondered if Ben was defending "marrying a doctor" because he was one. She covered her lips with her hand and glanced over with a look of horror on her face. Seeing her expression, he knew for certain that her remark about doctors had not been aimed directly at him. In his relief, Ben burst out laughing. She breathed a huge sigh and shook her head. "I think I'd better just be quiet and listen to music the rest of the way home. That is, unless you have some chocolate syrup."

Ben looked puzzled.

"For me to pour on my foot, so it'll taste better the next time I stick it in my mouth! I'll shut up now."

Ben smiled and shook his head gently. "If you shut up, the loss will be mine." He reached over and patted her hand. She admired his uncanny ability to smooth over the awkward moments she kept creating. The CD player clicked and began to play a new CD of oldies they both knew. At first they hummed together, but eventually they loosened up enough to harmonize all the way to the Washington Beltway. At one point, Ben even got Marnie laughing with his deep bass voice on "Duke of Earl."

"Want to stop for a bite to eat?" Ben asked, trying to make the day last. It had been the shortest eight hours of driving he could remember.

"No, thanks. You've given me your whole day, and I'm really, truly grateful. But I should get back to Emily."

Ben said nothing but nodded when she tacked on, "Maybe some other time."

Later, as Ben escorted Marnie up the walk to her front porch, Will met them at the door. "You just missed talking to the FBI," he announced. Ben, who had turned down Marnie's invitation to come in, suddenly changed his mind.

Chapter Six

"I THINK MY HUSBAND IS HAVING AN AFFAIR," a weepy Leigh Rivera told her friend long-distance. "He hasn't touched me for three months—not like him at all. We were so close. And now he seems so *angry*."

"Maybe that's not it, Leigh. Some men are sort of funny after delivery. Takes them a while to get over that experience and view their wives as objects of romance again instead of baby factories," her friend said.

"Sorry, but that's just not it. He stayed away from the room during the delivery. Said it wasn't macho. Besides, this lack of affection started after the twins were already a few months old."

After two months of sleepless nights, Luc felt strangely relieved to receive the interrogatories—basic background questions from the opposing side's lawyer, which the doctor was to answer in writing, under oath.

Luc wanted quick resolution, but he knew that wouldn't happen. The next best thing was doing something—anything—to move the case forward.

He answered each question honestly. Yes, he'd kept his license current. He'd received his training in high-tech procedures in Norfolk, Virginia.

"What do they mean when they ask about my corporate connections?" he asked his attorney.

"Do you serve on the board of General Electric? Anywhere else they can get money out of this?"

"Yeah, right! Who has time? Hate to disappoint them, but that list is pretty short. I do have some blue-chip investments."

"Nope. Not what they're looking for."

Luc provided the organizational structure of the clinic, listing himself as the man in charge. He described each employee and his or her responsibilities. He attached a list of articles he'd published, said he'd never had his license revoked, and that no hospital or medical board had ever brought disciplinary action against him. And he specified that he, Ben, and Tim had each shared one-third ownership until Tim's death, at which time Ben and Luc each became half owners. He sent his answers to Chris for review and began his long wait again.

Dr. Allan Brown sat in his Dallas office and took a sip of coffee before logging onto the Internet to read the *Washington Post*. He had followed with interest the events in the nation's capital. Part of him felt smug sat-

isfaction knowing that the filing of a lawsuit and result-
ing publicity had hurt the reputation and referral base
for the Center for Fertility Enhancement. *Luc Morgan
had it coming. That pompous jerk—it's about time he ate
humble pie.* Most researchers referred to the Uterine
Implantation Factor as UIF, but Dr. Brown preferred
FUI or "fooey."

Though he gloated over Luc's difficulties, he actually felt relieved each time he found nothing about the
suit in the news. It had all the elements for drawing
publicity—big clinic, rich doctors, rumors of scandal.
Still, the less publicity the case received the better for
Allan. *People get so nuts. Anything involving in vitro clinics, cloning, or fertility docs. Funding gets threatened.
Ethicists start spouting off about stuff that's way over their
heads. Ridiculous.*

Finding nothing that day on the case, Allan skipped
over to read an on-line neurosurgical journal. Early on,
he'd learned the techniques for micromanipulation under the mantle of animal research. Among his colleagues,
he'd always had a reputation for trying to "build a better cow, develop a faster racehorse, create a sheep with
the best wool." Armed with his microscope and
micromanipulating tools there was little he couldn't do.
Now he had the best lab, the brightest research students, and virtually unlimited funding for the project
he headed. Taking unused frozen embryos left over from
in vitro patients, his team worked around the clock to
find a cure for diseases that affected kinetic activity of
nerves, such as Alzheimer's, Lou Gehrig's disease,
multiple sclerosis, and multifocal hypermyelination syndrome, or MHS—also known as akenosis.

A knock on his door brought him back from the world of medical terminology. As he looked up, his new young researcher peeked in. "Dr. Brown, there's a call for you on line three from a Dr. Steven Harrison. Says the surgeon general's office told him to call."

Marnie and Emily stood in the foyer after the Sunday service at Cherrydale Church and waited for Ben. For the past four weeks, Ben had been bringing the Sullivans to church as his guests. Marnie already loved the singles Sunday school class. After her first visit, she had received food, cards, and calls from its members. Their missions pastor, Bob King, had been the one to inform Marnie of her husband's death, so the church had heard about her both from Bob's prayer requests and from Ben's. In fact, Pastor Bob had called Ben with the news of Tim's death shortly after Luc had phoned. When Ben expressed a desire to visit Marnie, Pastor Bob encouraged him to follow his impulse. Seeing Marnie and Emily standing alone, he approached them, extending his hand. "I've been praying for you, Mrs. Sullivan."

"How kind, Pastor," she said with genuine gratitude. "Thank you so much. And please—call me Marnie." Having people say they were praying for her was a new experience, and one she appreciated. As they talked, Marnie again thanked the pastor for coming the night of the accident, and she told him some of the details she'd learned since then as well.

Amazed that she would be willing to discuss the accident so soon, Pastor Bob said, "I read in the *Wash-*

ington Post this week that the FBI determined the cause to be brake failure."

"Yes," Marnie replied. Her voice was steady. "The FBI felt compelled to investigate because of Tim's relationship to the president, but they found nothing out of the ordinary. He probably hit a stretch of ice, and the brakes locked. You can bet they'll be installing a guardrail there now. Apparently he managed to get the car door open, but the current probably swept him under. We've known for about six weeks." Marnie always felt better when she talked about it, which surprised many of her friends, but also satisfied their curiosity.

She kept the more personal facts to herself. She had cried when she'd learned that the FBI had found a bouquet of flowers floating in the car with an envelope addressed to her. These details, combined with Tim's actions the morning of his death, suggested that he'd planned to surprise her by coming home for dinner that night.

So far she'd felt the most grief over words left unsaid and the lost dreams of a less-than-perfect marriage. Knowing Tim's gestures, then, brought comfort. Life might have been different had he lived.

Luc Morgan sat uncomfortably on the heavy leather sofa in Chris Winston's office, waiting for the deposition hearing to begin. Four months after he'd first received the intent-to-sue documents, the day had finally arrived. At last he would have a chance to tell his side of the story.

He stood and stretched, then reached with his left hand to massage a kink out of the side of his neck as he walked over to examine his friend's credentials on the wall. Turning back toward the desk, he drummed his fingers idly on a stack of files. He was ready. With the help of Chris Winston and his staff, he'd gone over the case from every imaginable angle, working through the questions he might face. And even though he felt confident in himself and his professional conduct, his sweaty palms revealed that Luc had no suitable explanation for why Carlos Rivera would want to sue him.

Chris Winston walked in the door and greeted him with a warm handshake. "Ready?"

"Guess so," Luc shrugged.

"Everyone's here. They've asked to videotape the testimony, which is normal procedure. Remember—answer the questions truthfully but don't volunteer anything. As for the video, just talk as you would in your office explaining procedures to your patients. Be an educator. Don't let the attorney throw you off track or get you stressed. That's his job. He will try to get you to say something that contradicts what you've already written in the interrogatory questions."

Chris placed his hand on his friend's shoulder and ushered him toward the door. "Don't try to convince him you did everything right. He succeeds in his job by disbelieving you, so expect it. If he asks you anything that isn't completely clear, ask him to rephrase it. Then pause for a second or two after he finishes the question. That gives me time to object if necessary, and it creates the impression that you're thinking about the answer. We don't want your responses to look rehearsed.

"He'll ask if we've discussed the case, and what I've told you to say," Chris went on. "They *all* ask that. Don't worry. Answer honestly. Of course you've discussed the case with your attorney, and I've told you to answer the questions truthfully. Got it?"

Luc buttoned his suit jacket. "Let's do it."

Luc took a quick look around as he and Chris walked into the conference room of Blackman, Lonas, and Winston, Attorneys at Law. The burnished wood paneling and rich furnishings were right off the pages of *Architectural Digest*. Chris introduced Luc to the plaintiff's attorneys, and everyone settled into the large, leather, high-back chairs surrounding the massive mahogany conference table. The court reporter sat at one end with her keyboard, while the video operator switched on his camera at the other.

Luc was disappointed to see that Carlos Rivera had chosen not to attend the deposition. He'd hoped to assuage the mayor's anger and suspicion with a forthright testimony.

The two attorneys "representing the plaintiff in action No. 88-91578-G, Carlos Rivera vs. Lucas Morgan, M.D." were formally introduced so they could begin the proceedings. Luc calmly looked each man in the eye and nodded. He knew he faced a long day, but he was hopeful that the ten o'clock starting time would allow the entire deposition to be wrapped up in one day. He wanted to avoid having to gear up emotionally for another round.

The doctor raised his right hand and agreed to "tell the truth, the whole truth, and nothing but the truth." The first attorney, Arthur Hernandez, opened his files and addressed Luc in a barely civil tone. He said he wanted to be sure that Dr. Morgan understood each question posed, and that he would be happy to rephrase any question the doctor found vague or unclear. Then he began his formal questioning: "Please state your full name for the court and jury."

"Lucas Hamilton Morgan."

"And what is your home address?"

Even as Luc gave his answer, he was sobered by the solemnity of the proceedings. Chris had explained that his testimony this morning bound him just as much as anything he would say in court.

Mr. Hernandez asked him about his partners, following up with several specific questions about his relationships with Ben McKay and Tim Sullivan. Luc answered in an even voice, careful to avoid adding anything beyond the scope of each question. After responding to inquiries about his training, his residency, his specialty work, and the founding of the clinic, Luc wondered if they would ever get to the case. Still, he began to relax, lulled by the litany of seemingly harmless background questions.

Finally, after an hour of questioning, Arthur Hernandez got to the specifics of the case. "When did you first see Mrs. Rivera?"

Luc glanced at the chart on the table and recited the date.

"What was the nature of the visit?"

"Mrs. Rivera presented as a new patient for evaluation of infertility. She had been attempting conception for approximately eighteen months without success and was referred to our clinic by her personal physician."

"What type of evaluation did you perform?"

"Our new-patient visit involves a detailed history, a thorough physical examination, and laboratory tests as indicated."

"What was your diagnosis, Doctor?"

"My records show that Mrs. Rivera was a healthy twenty-five-year-old female. No prior history of pregnancy. She had a history of regular, predictable menstrual cycles. However, she had exhibited some change in the level of discomfort during the cycles preceding her initial visit."

"What is the significance of such pain?"

On and on the questions dragged for another two hours. Luc maintained his composure, answering each question accurately and without embellishment, even though none of the attorney's inquiries seemed particularly pertinent to the lawsuit. By the time Luc's stomach began to growl, he was wondering why the questions had ventured nowhere near the in vitro cycle in question. Instead, it seemed to Luc that Hernandez was content to slog meticulously through material of no consequence.

He glanced over at Chris Winston. The briefest of nods assured Luc that he was doing well. Only on occasion did his attorney interrupt to object to the form of a question, or to say, "I believe we've already answered that."

Finally, at one o'clock, Chris asked, "What say we break for lunch?"

All parties agreed, and they scheduled to resume Luc's "inquisition" in an hour.

As they retired to Chris's office for turkey sandwiches

and chips, Chris told Luc, "You're doing fine. Just keep your cool and tell them what happened. We've got nothing to hide here. How you holding up, buddy?"

"Not bad. Do these things ever end?"

"You kiddin'?" Chris laughed. "We get paid by the hour. At two hundred per, nobody's in a hurry!"

Chapter Seven

SHORTLY AFTER TWO, all the players settled into their seats in the conference room, and the deposition resumed. Arthur Hernandez reread the final question and answer aloud, then proceeded with his interrogation.

"You stated, Doctor, that the egg harvest succeeded?"

"Yes. Correct."

"How many eggs were obtained?"

Glancing at the record, though he knew the answer, Luc answered, "Twenty-two."

"And that would be normal, sir?"

"Yes."

"How many of the eggs were fertilized, Doctor?" Mr. Hernandez's inflection on the word *doctor* made it sound like an obscenity.

"Thirteen were reported as high-quality eggs and were exposed to the semen sample obtained from Mr. Rivera. Of these, ten showed evidence of fertilization." Chris sat up straight and locked eyes with Luc: *Quit adding more to the answer than was asked.* Luc held his tongue, and Chris leaned back into his chair.

"Who was responsible for the harvesting of the eggs?" Hernandez intoned.

"I was."

"And who was responsible for the eggs after they were retrieved?"

"The late Dr. Tim Sullivan."

"Dr. Sullivan, your partner?"

"Yes, sir."

"Dr. Sullivan took responsibility for the eggs?"

"Yes, sir."

"Who was responsible for handling the semen produced by Mr. Rivera?"

"The semen was given to our nurse, Kathy. She prepared it, then gave it to Dr. Sullivan."

"Would you state the full name of your nurse?"

Luc answered the question and stifled a yawn, beginning to feel the need of a post-lunch siesta.

"What happened to the eggs in Dr. Sullivan's care?"

"Dr. Sullivan evaluated and graded each egg. Then he exposed the eggs of the highest quality to the sperm."

"What became of the eggs exposed to the sperm, the way you've described?"

"Dr. Sullivan, our embryologist, carefully watched the eggs for evidence of fertilization and division."

"Where were the eggs kept?"

"In Dr. Sullivan's laboratory."

"Who had access to this laboratory?"

"The laboratory is locked with a security access code."

Fernando Guitterez, the other attorney representing Carlos Rivera, interrupted. "Objection. Nonresponsive."

"I believe he answered the question," Chris Winston said.

Arthur Hernandez asked the court reporter to repeat the question, which she did.

"Yes, Doctor," said Hernandez. "Who had access to this laboratory?"

"Dr. Tim Sullivan, Dr. Ben McKay, and myself."

"No one else had access to this room?"

"Correct."

Mr. Hernandez delivered his next sentence slowly and carefully. "Is it your testimony, Doctor, that no one except you, Dr. Sullivan, or Dr. McKay could access the material in this laboratory?"

"That is correct."

"And, Doctor, what happened to the eggs exposed to the semen?"

"Ten eggs exposed to Mr. Rivera's semen showed evidence of fertilization and division."

"What was done with the ten fertilized eggs?"

"At the appropriate time, with the patient's full understanding and consent, three pre-embryos were transferred into Mrs. Rivera's uterus, and the remaining seven were cryopreserved—uh, frozen."

"*Pre*-embryos, Doctor?" Hernandez pressed.

"We refer to fertilized eggs as pre-embryos in the early hours following fertilization."

"I see. And again, what about the remaining seven?"

"Frozen for later use." Luc wanted to explain more but held his tongue.

"What became of the other eggs that were harvested?"

"Eggs found unsuitable for fertilization are discarded."

"Who is responsible for the discarding?"

"Dr. Sullivan was—up until the time of his death."

"Doctor, is it your sworn testimony that the remaining eggs taken from Mrs. Rivera, those not exposed to the semen of my client, Mr. Rivera, were discarded?"

"To the best of my knowledge."

"Objection. Nonresponsive," Mr. Guitterez interjected.

Luc paused, uncertain what "nonresponsive" meant in this instance. He'd answered as honestly as he could, but he realized that Tim had had total control over the eggs. He hadn't actually witnessed what Tim had done with them.

"Doctor, what became of the three pre-embryos that you transferred on October 23?"

"There was chemical evidence of pregnancy, but in the end none resulted in a viable pregnancy."

"What is chemical evidence, Doctor?"

"A blood test for a hormone produced in early pregnancy suggested that one or more of the transferred pre-embryos had implanted, but a successful pregnancy was not achieved."

"Your testimony is that a successful pregnancy was not achieved?"

"Correct. Not during this first cycle."

"What did you recommend to Mr. and Mrs. Rivera at that time?"

"I suggested that we transfer some of the frozen embryos during a later cycle."

"And did they agree?"

"Yes."

"Did the Riveras ever refuse to follow your medical recommendations?"

"No, sir."

"Would you say they were compliant patients?"

"Yes, sir. They were good patients." Luc wondered if the "storm" was over, even as Arthur Hernandez pressed on relentlessly with his questions.

"Who was responsible for the eggs?"

"Dr. Sullivan was responsible."

"Who was responsible for the embryos?"

"Dr. Sullivan was."

"Who exposed the eggs to the semen?"

"Dr. Sullivan."

"Doctor, is it your testimony that these eggs, the responsibility of Dr. Sullivan, were, for a fact, exposed to the semen of Carlos Rivera?"

"Objection!" Chris Winston interjected loudly. "Form of the question."

Luc took this as a cue. *Loaded question. Walk carefully.*

"I will rephrase," offered Hernandez with a smirk. "Doctor, please answer yes or no. Do you know that the eggs of Mrs. Rivera were exposed to the sperm of Mr. Rivera?"

"To my knowledge, sir. That is the procedure of the clinic."

"Objection." This time it was Fernando Guitterez. "Nonresponsive."

Luc saw Guitterez's point. His answer *was* nonresponsive. The medical step in question had been totally Tim's responsibility. Luc could not say for sure whose sperm he had used. *But Tim wouldn't make any mistakes. There is no way he would have used the wrong sperm.* Yet even as the thought registered, doubts began to surface.

"Doctor, do you know for sure that the eggs of Mrs. Rivera were exposed to the sperm of Mr. Rivera? Yes or no?"

Luc paused and looked at Chris, who leaned forward and said confidently, "You may answer the question."

So Luc answered. "No, sir, I do not."

Luc now felt off balance. His energy seemed to be draining out of him. And it wasn't over yet.

"Did Mrs. Rivera come back to see you again, Doctor?"

"Yes, sir, on December 26."

"What was the nature of the visit?"

"We had talked several times by phone and had arranged for the transfer of more frozen embryos, timed hormonally with the assistance of her physician in Mexico."

"And did Mrs. Rivera come at the appointed time?"

"Yes, sir."

"You performed the embryo transfer?"

"Yes, sir."

"You used three more embryos?"

"Yes, sir."

"Was Dr. Sullivan involved at this appointment?"

"No, sir." Luc felt a lump rising in his throat.

"Who selected the embryos for transfer on December 26?"

"I did."

"You entered the secured area and obtained them?"

"Yes."

"How did you know they were the correct embryos?"

"Dr. Sullivan devised a very precise system of cataloging, identifying, and storing."

"And you are familiar with this system?"

"Yes."

"You entered the secure room and selected the embryos that you transferred into Mrs. Rivera?"

"Yes."

"What was the result of this procedure?"

"Mrs. Rivera conceived and later gave birth to two healthy female infants."

"Was anyone else present at the office appointment during the transfer?"

"My nurse, Kathy."

"Is it your testimony, Doctor, that the twins conceived by Mrs. Rivera were the direct result of an embryo transfer which *you* performed on December 26?"

"To my knowledge, yes."

"There were no other doctors involved?"

"No, sir."

"These embryos were the result of the egg retrieval and sperm exposure from the office visit of October 30?"

"Yes, sir."

"Who had access to these eggs between the office visits?"

"Dr. McKay, Dr. Sullivan, and I did."

"You testified that you did not know that Mrs. Rivera's eggs were exposed to the sperm of Mr. Rivera."

"Dr. Sullivan handles the eggs and sperm."

"Objection. Nonresponsive," Mr. Guitterez chimed in.

"You cannot be certain, Doctor, that Dr. Sullivan exposed Mrs. Rivera's eggs at any time to the sperm of Mr. Rivera, can you?"

"No, sir."

"Reserve further questions until time of trial," concluded Hernandez, relaxing confidently in his chair. "Pass the witness," he finished.

Fernando Guitterez followed with a few more questions about training and background, and then presented Luc with a document labeled Exhibit A.

"Please read this document, Doctor," he said as he handed notarized copies to each of the attorneys. Chris scanned it, expecting bad news.

"You have in your hand laboratory test results and interpretations from Gaines/Kirkpatrick Labs of Los Angeles, California. Correct?"

"That would appear to be correct, sir," answered Luc, only now grasping the document's significance. He read the report and felt the blood drain out of his head. He sat in shock, looking at the chromosome study of both Mr. Rivera and the girls. The paper declared, "With 99.9 percent certainty, Mr. Rivera is not the genetic father of the identical twin daughters."

"Are you familiar with DNA, Doctor?" Guitterez probed.

"Yes, though I'm not an expert in genetics."

"No, sir, of course not. But do you understand this report?"

"Yes, sir."

"Do you agree with these findings?"

"Objection," Chris interjected. "I'll not allow my client to answer the question. We would require independent testing by a mutually agreed upon laboratory and further expert opinion on this matter."

"Yes, I'm sure you would," Guitterez smiled smoothly. "No further questions."

"Reserve questions until time of trial," said Chris.

"Thank you, Doctor." Both Hernandez and Guitterez stood and extended their hands. Their smug smiles confirmed they thought they had "bagged" their doc for the day.

Luc stood, weak-kneed and exhausted. The clock read 8:04 P.M. The day had evaporated. He returned to Chris's office without uttering a word. Once the door had been closed, Chris put his arm around Luc's shoulders and said, "We've got some work to do, my friend."

"They got me, didn't they?" murmured Luc.

Chris smiled. "Any lawyer that can't get you to say something 'iffy' during a deposition isn't worth his salt. But we do need to talk about the DNA evidence. If that holds up, and the kids aren't Carlos's, we're in for a long, costly go of it. It's a real shame about Tim. We could use his testimony. As it is, you're kinda hangin' out there by—"

The fear in Luc's eyes stopped Chris in mid-sentence. "Okay, not by yourself. I'm with you, buddy!"

"Thanks, Chris. I'd hate to do this without you."

"Go home. Get some rest. Take in a show and put it out of your mind for a while. You've earned it. You did great today." Chris tried to reassure his friend as he draped Luc's coat over his shoulders and headed him toward the door. "We'll get our turn, too. Just wait."

Chapter Eight

THE NEXT DAY, LUC ARRANGED an afternoon meeting with Ben McKay to tell him about the deposition hearing. After talking with his partner for forty-five minutes, Ben returned to his office and sat down at his desk, his mind turning over the details of all Luc had said. Leaning back in his chair, he stared at his computer, his eyes following the motion of the screen saver. After dodging two calls, he grabbed his coat and told Lisa he was leaving for the day.

Ben drove slowly over to the hospital, made his way to the chapel, and spent an hour in silent reflection. In the years since Juli's death, he'd found the small room a place of solace. But on this day, it was Marnie Sullivan, not Juli, who occupied his thoughts. After deliberation, he decided to inform her about Luc's deposition. Breathing a prayer for wisdom, he pulled the cell phone from his pocket and punched in her number.

"Hey, Ben! What's up?" Marnie sounded tired but happy to hear from him.

"How are ya?" he asked gently.

"Okay. Had a bit of a rough night last night. I didn't sleep real well."

"I'm sorry to hear that."

"Thanks." Marnie fell silent.

"Something in particular on your mind?"

"Oh, I'm just getting to the next layer of people who need to be notified about Tim's death. I've gotten past the credit card companies, the bills in both our names, the car title, those sorts of thing. Now it's the more distant friends. Tim traded e-mails with a lot of colleagues, but I don't know his password, so I can't notify them. A few have phoned—you know, to find out why he hasn't responded."

"They didn't see it on the news? I mean, he was the president's nephew! That made national news, didn't it?"

"Sure, if he told them. But Tim usually avoided mentioning his relationship to the president if his colleagues didn't already know. You never noticed that?"

"Guess I never paid attention. . . ." Ben lapsed into silence.

"I'll bet I know what you're thinking," Marnie prodded.

"What?"

"You didn't think Tim was ever that humble."

Ben chuckled. "You're right."

"It wasn't humility. Tim really hated it when people thought he'd achieved what he had because of his name. He worked hard for his M.D. *and* Ph.D. to establish a name for himself. He was touchy about people thinking he'd had everything handed to him."

"Yeah, I could see that," Ben, ever the problem-solver, clicked onto a different track. "What Internet provider did he use?"

"America On-line."

"Did he ever do flash sessions?"

"Flash sessions?"

"That's where you program AOL to sign on automatically and download your e-mail and other files for you."

"Never heard of it."

"Okay. Well, I'm on AOL too. How about if I come over for a while tonight and see if I can get into Tim's message file?"

Marnie sounded grateful. "You think you could?"

"Possibly."

"That would be great."

"I'll be tied up at the hospital until about eight-thirty, but I could come by after that."

"That works for me," Marnie said. "Emily goes to bed around eight-forty-five." She paused for a moment. "You'll be famished by then. Why don't you come for dinner, around nine?"

"Honest?"

"Sure!"

"That'd be great."

"I hope you like squid and escargot."

"Uh-oh!"

"Just kidding." Marnie's playful tone told Ben that he'd succeeded in easing her mind. "See you at nine," she said.

"Wait!" Ben stopped her.

"What?"

"The reason I called."

"Oh! Sorry. What's up?"

"Luc and the clinic's attorney met with the Rivera attorneys."

"Uh-huh."

Ben paused. "It's worse than we imagined."

"What? What is it, Ben?" Marnie's voice revealed her mounting anxiety.

"Mrs. Rivera had her blood tested. Turns out her husband is not the genetic father of the twins. That's a 99.9 percent certainty."

"So he's blaming the clinic because his wife had an affair?"

"Well, her husband has suggested that she and Luc had a thing going. *Highly* unlikely. Besides, Luc's nurse helped with the procedure."

"So what are you saying?"

"It doesn't look great. Possibly a sperm mix-up."

"No way! With *that* system? That's really hard to imagine. But Tim and I were out of town at the time, right?"

Ben softened his voice. "That's just it, Marnie. Luc used frozen embryos. So whenever the accidental switch took place—if that's what happened—it had to have occurred at the time of the first transfer, in October—*before* the eggs were ever frozen. And Tim did that procedure."

Marnie gasped.

"I'm sorry to have to tell you that," Ben said gently.

"So you think he used the wrong sperm? Will they sue his estate?"

"Oh, I doubt it." Ben regretted telling Marnie over the phone. She sounded as though he had dumped a load of concrete on her shoulders.

They talked for a few more moments, and Ben finally suggested, "Let's discuss this further over dinner. I probably should have waited to say anything."

"I'm not sure there's anything left to say about it," Marnie told him.

When Marnie opened the door at eight-fifty-five, Ben McKay stood on the step, wearing Dockers and a sweater and holding out a bouquet of flowers. "A peace offering," he said, bowing his head.

Marnie looked puzzled as she motioned him in from the cold.

"I'm sorry. I picked a lousy way and a lousy time to tell you about the case," Ben explained.

Marnie sighed. "That's okay. I guess I just don't see how it could happen, that's all. But it's not like I've given it a lot of thought. Even this e-mail thing is more a nuisance than anything. What's really driving me crazy is wondering when I'm going to get the call that they've found his body. I need closure. I can't sleep. Can't concentrate. Can't make decisions."

"I'm sorry," Ben said, holding out the bouquet.

"Thank you, Ben. How kind." Marnie lifted the flowers to her nose to enjoy the sweet scent.

"I don't expect the mix-up will affect you, really. Certainly not financially. It's just such a mystery. We have so many checks and balances in our system."

"And it hardly seems fair that Tim's not here to defend himself." Marnie's voice revealed her frustration.

"You're right. Again. I'm sorry. I was—and am—a slug."

This brought a smile. She looked him straight in the eye. "You're forgiven."

Ben grinned back, and Marnie momentarily admired the lines of his face. "Hungry?" she asked.

"Indeed! And whatever you've got cooking in there sure smells good."

"Well, I got a late start. The sauce still needs to simmer another twenty-five minutes. Can I get you something to drink?"

"A glass of water sounds good," Ben replied. "You want me to try to get into the computer before we eat?"

Marnie guided him back to Tim's office, still holding the flowers. She pointed to the terminal on the desk. "I fired it up for you. Just let me get these flowers in a vase—and I'll be right back with your water."

"No hurry." Ben pulled up a chair. He sat down, grabbed the mouse, and clicked to select automatic mail. In seconds, he had a connection. About eighty-five messages came up on Tim's "in" box. Ben began sorting, weeding out the usual assortment of advertisements and pornographic solicitations. When Marnie returned, she was amazed to see how quickly he'd been able to access Tim's mailbox.

"How'd you do that without a password?"

"I used that flash session feature I was telling you about. I was hoping that Tim had stored his password and, sure enough, I'm in. I've already dumped all the junk mail. What do you want to do with the rest?"

Marnie shrugged. "I guess we should try to answer them."

Wanting to spare her whatever pain possible, Ben suggested, "How about if I write a generic reply with the news of Tim's accident? You shouldn't have to worry about that."

Marnie nodded gratefully. "That would be wonderful. I'll leave you to it while I check on dinner. Be back in a few minutes."

Ben turned his attention back to the screen. The remaining mail came mostly from researchers. Apparently, Tim had written a letter to the editor of a neurosurgical journal that had evoked quite a response from the readers. From what Ben could piece together, Tim had disputed the findings of some group, claiming that their model for the disease they were studying was flawed. One message made reference to a journal article Tim had contributed about nerve regrowth in rats.

Reflecting back on his med school education at the University of Kentucky, Ben thought of Dr. Gilliman and the months she had spent teaching him and his fellow students neuroanatomy diagrams and pathways. *That stuff never really stuck. I can't remember much of anything!*

It didn't take long to draft and send the same reply to each query. About the time he was finishing, Marnie returned.

"Anything important?"

"Most of it wasn't. Several messages asked about a letter he wrote in response to a neurosurgical article."

Marnie nodded. Ben wasn't sure how to interpret her response. "Pretty strange to have such an interest in neurosurgery when you're an embryologist, don't you think?" he asked.

Marnie raised her eyebrows.

Ben searched her face for a response. His question wasn't rhetorical. Finally, Marnie raised her palms and shrugged. "Yes, it does."

"Mind if I have a look at Tim's letter and some of the articles he's posted?"

"I have no clue where to find anything. He never mentioned it," Marnie said.

"Do you mind if I search the Web?" Ben asked.

Marnie shrugged again. "Be my guest."

Ben accessed the Web browser and went to the medical research section. After typing in "Sullivan," he scanned the articles, looking for anything Tim might have written. He was quiet for a while and then said, "He sure knew a ton about the nervous system. Lots of research articles on rat brains."

"Hmm," Marnie said.

Ben mumbled his way through the topic options: "Causing injury . . . trying to cause injury to heal with medications . . . electrical stimulation . . . nerve cells taken from newborn rats. . . . You'd have to really love this stuff—or hate rats!"

"Those must be from his doctoral studies," Marnie said. "As far as I know, it's been awhile since he worked with rats."

Ben started noticing publication dates and saw that Marnie was right. The research extended back to Tim's doctoral training days. So he typed in the keyword "akinosis." Nothing.

"Try a-k-*e*-n," Marnie suggested.

When Ben typed in "akenosis" and hit the return key, the computer whirred and then listed eight articles.

Ben reviewed the literature. "There it is: 'Akenosis—Multifocal Hypermyelination Syndrome.' You know I'd never even heard of it until that day we went to Tim's mom's house in Jersey."

"I still find that amazing." Marnie looked concerned.

Ben scanned the abstract. "Reported first by Alexei Vorobyov, Kiev Ukraine, 1912, publicized by Demetri Somatos of Greece in the 1940s. Hmm, Y-linked recessive gene. Interesting. 'Variable penetrance, symptoms present in fourth decade or later. Often characterized by peripheral neuropathies, fine motor weakness and tremor, short-term memory loss, emotional disturbance, sleep apnea, terminal event respiratory arrest. Progressive over three to fifteen years from onset of symptoms.'"

Marnie pulled up a chair and sat next to him.

"No wonder Tim was interested. It's a Y-linked recessive gene," Ben said, and Marnie nodded. "If his dad had this, and he's got three brothers, and his uncle's the president—that's a lot of men in the family at risk."

He read on: "'Pathogenesis—abnormality of myelin production centrally. Nodules of myelin encircling nerve fibers causing intermittent compression initially, progressing to nerve atrophy and death of nerve cell.' Oh maaan! Get me back to my own specialty."

Marnie laughed.

"I'm used to the clinical terminology, of course, but that doesn't mean I understand all the jargon in other specialties. This stuff here is totally foreign to me."

"Well, that makes two of us," said Marnie. Although she often wrote on medical topics, she found her eyes glazing over from the barrage of strange, polysyllabic terms.

As Ben pulled up successive articles, he noted that all the basic information remained the same. "'Newer research—scant as it is,'" he continued reading out loud, "'suggests a failure in the cell-cycle mechanics, permitting an overgrowth of myelin cells in a cancer-like fashion focally. Could eventually be picked up on CT scan or MRI.'"

Ben scrolled through the article. "I wonder if it's treatable?" he murmured, more to himself than to Marnie. "Let's see. Chemotherapy trials have proven fruitless. To get dosages high enough to affect the bad cells, unacceptable damage resulted to healthy areas. Trials of radiation therapy also proved unsatisfactory. Akenosis is a bummer of a disease. Nobody has a clue."

Ben called up another article and read silently for a few moments before he said, *"This* is interesting."

"What's that?" Marnie arched her neck to read over his shoulder.

"Slow spread, incidence estimated at one in two hundred thousand. Incredibly rare," Ben said.

Marnie nodded. "That much I knew."

Ben scanned the references cited in the articles and noticed that most of the research dollars were being funneled into research for Alzheimer's, MS, Lou Gehrig's, and Parkinson's.

That makes sense, Ben thought as he contemplated what he had just read. *All those diseases are degenerative. But akenosis seems a bit different. Rather than degenerating the myelin sheath—and causing the nerves to misfire—the sheath starts to "pile up." In effect, it chokes off the nerve after detouring the messages for a while. But Tim wasn't even forty yet. And there were certainly no symptoms of mental or emotional change! He was the sharpest guy I ever knew.*

Ben still hadn't found the article he was looking for. Nothing he'd seen so far had any direct correlation to an embryologist at an in vitro fertilization clinic. He was about to sign off when he remembered to check "favorite places" on the screen menu. *Maybe that'll tell me what sites Tim last visited.*

The machine whirred, and a list appeared. Ben scanned through a string of articles from the month preceding Tim's death. Every item came from one neurology journal or another. The titles were all unfamiliar to Ben. "Hmm. *The Journal of Neuroscience—The Official Journal of the Society for Neuroscience.* Yeah, like I'll bet there are dozens of 'unofficial journals' for this bunch."

Marnie laughed.

He scanned through one article then another. Most were studies where researchers had inflicted surgical damage on the spinal cords of rats. "Fetal cells to treat spinal injury . . . restoring, repairing damaged nerve cells . . . still not exactly what akenosis does, but . . . Marnie!"

"What?"

"It's got to be related!"

"What's related? What do you mean?" She scooted her chair closer and peered at the computer screen.

"This article says they can use a CT scan to localize the area of myelin buildup in akenosis, and they can use this technique to place electrodes into the precise area of the brain that they want to treat."

He read for another minute, then looked at her. "I'll bet Tim was thinking he could inject or implant something into the damaged area of the brain to correct the problem. But using electrical current to destroy the hypermyelinated areas would have destroyed the nerve.

Was he hoping to rebuild the nerve?" he asked rhetorically. "Nobody has reported any animal models being used for akenosis, so how could Tim research it?"

Ben rubbed his jaw and looked at Marnie. "Where are his records?"

"I have no idea."

"Hope somebody else was involved in all this so that Tim's work isn't lost. Maybe his old professor at UT Southwestern in Dallas was in on it."

"I wish I knew," Marnie said.

After a moment of reflective silence, Ben scooted back, still looking at the screen with a satisfied expression on his face. "Well, that's enough for one night, but very interesting. You're a mystery, Dr. Tim!"

"You can say that again," Marnie replied, looking at her watch. "Hey, if you're finished here, we can move on in to the dining room. Dinner's ready whenever we are."

"Great. I'm starving." Ben shut down the computer and followed Marnie out the door. On their way through the den, Marnie put on a CD and Ben recognized a Rachmaninoff tune from the movie *Somewhere in Time*. Marnie didn't see his gentle smile as he followed her into the dining room.

Chapter Nine

As MARNIE AND BEN WERE finishing the last of the dinner, the music in the background moved into a beautiful violin solo. Ben closed his eyes momentarily then looked at Marnie. "Nice music."

"Thanks."

"Always makes me want to dance."

From this, their conversation wandered into memories of their high school proms. After laughing about how the hairstyles and Top 40 hits had changed, Marnie found her thoughts drifting. Finally she said, "I loved my senior prom. It was a fabulous night. In fact, I was so sorry to see it end that I left before the last dance."

"Why?"

"I told my date I wanted to go home. I didn't want to cry all the way through the last song."

Ben looked at her for a long time with a puzzled expression. "The way I see it, you should always stay for the last dance, even if it means you cry all the way through it."

"Nope. Too hard."

"But you'll miss most of life's sweetest moments."

Marnie shrugged. "I don't know. I'm not sure it's worth the pain."

"Interesting," Ben said, his thoughts suddenly shifting to a far-off memory. "In my mind, there's not a shred of doubt. It's definitely worth the pain."

After a few moments of reflective silence, Marnie excused herself to clear the table and make some hot chocolate. Ben wandered into the den and stoked the fire while he waited.

When Marnie returned with two steaming mugs of cocoa, Ben made himself comfortable on the couch and motioned for her to join him. Marnie set the mugs on the coffee table and settled onto the middle cushion, drawing her legs up underneath her. For a few moments they sat staring at the flames with only the sounds of crackling wood punctuating the comfortable silence.

Finally Marnie wondered aloud, "Ben?"

"Yeah?" He turned his head to make eye contact.

"Since you say you're not afraid to embrace pain, may I ask—?" She stopped herself.

Ben's eyes searched hers. "What, Marnie? Go ahead."

"What's the 'secret sorrow' hidden behind those eyes?"

Ben smiled briefly and stared at the sliding glass doors leading out to the patio. Marnie thought he looked like a lost child. Finally, he rubbed his chin.

"It was seven years ago. I try not to revisit it too often."

"I'm sorry. I shouldn't pry." Marnie feared that her curiosity might have ruined the pleasant evening.

"No, no, I don't mind your asking. I'd like you to know." Ben touched her arm gently.

Marnie picked up her mug of hot chocolate in her hands. She looked at Ben expectantly.

"I was driving home early after a full day at the clinic. I'd done a smooth full-term delivery, but the day was otherwise uneventful. I was feeling pretty good, driving along, when my pager went off. I knew it was Juliet—my wife, but when I looked down, I saw she'd typed in our distress code along with the phone number. I called her immediately from the car. She didn't answer the phone. I was still a few blocks from home, but I got there in a couple of minutes, parked the car, and ran into the house, calling her name."

Marnie swallowed hard and set down her mug.

"No answer." Ben spoke slowly. "I raced back to the bedroom. I knew I'd find her there. We were about seven months pregnant, and she was on strict bed rest and medication to prevent premature labor."

Ben looked at Marnie. Her eyes told him he could take his time.

"She was lying motionless on the bed—on her left side. Her eyes were closed, and her face had such a peaceful expression." Ben's eyes started to fill with tears. "She didn't respond to my voice. I shook her gently, called her name, squeezed her arm, but there was no response. She'd stopped breathing.

"I pulled her off the bed and started CPR." Ben was breathing audibly now, and his words were tumbling out. "She was completely limp. Between chest compressions I grabbed the phone off the nightstand and called 9-1-1. Juli's pupils were widely dilated, a terrible sign. I don't know when it had started, but it hadn't been very long between her call and my arrival home. I hollered at the phone between breaths. 'Emergency! I've got a pregnant woman in cardiac arrest! I'm doing CPR, but I'm all alone!'"

Marnie stared in disbelief.

"It seemed like about twenty minutes, but they told me the ambulance got there in three. I heard the siren, but I couldn't leave Juli. Anyway, the paramedics arrived and took over the CPR. They started a quick IV line and hooked up EKG, but we were flat lining. A couple of jolts with the defibrillator didn't change a thing, so we decided to transport while maintaining CPR. They lifted Juli onto the stretcher. . . ."

Ben paused for a moment to wipe his eyes. Marnie reached for the box of tissues on the coffee table and handed it to him. She had felt sorry that Tim hadn't died in her arms, but now she questioned whether that was such a romantic notion.

"I rode in back for the ten-minute run. I assisted the paramedic with the CPR while the driver radioed the hospital. I heard him say, 'Blown pupils, no response, multiple efforts at defib, drug therapy, down at least ten to fifteen minutes. Call OB, have them ready.'"

Ben made no effort now to fight the tears streaming down his face. His voice softened. "When we got there, staff, friends—men and women I worked with daily—swarmed the ambulance and moved her into one of the trauma rooms.

"I remember the surgeon on duty saying to me, 'Doc, OB's on the way, but we gotta go for it. We need to try for the baby, then maybe the resuscitation will have a chance.' I knew they really didn't think so, but we had nothing to lose."

Marnie placed a comforting hand on Ben's shoulder, but he was unaware, caught up in the immediacy of his memory. "My tears kept getting in the way, but I grabbed the scalpel and began the operation I knew all too well. Skin incision through the fatty layer to the fascia, one stroke. Fascia to the peritoneum, one stroke. Big midline incision in the uterus, one stroke. In seconds, we were to the baby. There was no real bleeding, just dark pooling. It's hard to compress the chest in a pregnant woman, but they tried."

Marnie squinted, living the pain. She pressed a tissue into Ben's hand. He nodded and wiped his face. Marnie grabbed another tissue for herself and rubbed Ben's arm gently as he continued.

"I popped the amniotic sac. The fluid was deeply stained with fresh green meconium. Then I reached in and grabbed my daughter's legs."

When he said the word "daughter" his voice cracked.

"She was limp. Lifeless. I passed her to the waiting pediatrician. By then the OB had arrived. Thank God, they'd called Luc. He stepped in front of me, and he knew right away, I could tell. He didn't waste any time. He started closing the incision.

"I backed up until I hit the wall. When I reached to pull off my surgical gloves, I realized that I hadn't taken the time to put any on. Juli's blood was drying on my hands and my arms—it was all over my shirt. I sank to the floor and just sat there, waiting for some encouraging word from somewhere. But they were still trying to revive her.

"I listened—waited—strained to hear a cry, a squeak, a fetal heart monitor—*anything* from the overhead warmer where the team was working on our daughter. But—nothing.

"Finally, one of the OB nurses who'd come down with Luc brought me a surgical towel to wipe off my hands and arms. She handed me a fresh scrub top, and took me to the *special* chaplain's waiting room . . . the one where they take families when the news is going to be bad. I didn't have the strength to resist. . . .

"I knew what they were doing. They didn't want to call the code with me in the room. They didn't want me to hear them pronounce her dead. It was a pulmonary embolus . . . massive blood clot. Nothing I did made any difference."

Marnie's hand covered her trembling lips.

"I sat. Waited. Too stunned to think. Then the chaplain came in with Luc. They sat with me for a long time. It's the only time I've ever seen Luc cry."

Marnie moved closer to Ben.

"Finally, I managed to ask about the baby. The chaplain hadn't been brought up to speed. He looked at Luc. So I looked at Luc. Then I knew. Before he even shook his head. I'd lost my Juli and our little girl. Our only child. Lost before we ever met. Conceived on earth. Born in heaven."

Marnie wiped her nose and eyes.

Ben sniffled. "I don't know why, but I had to go back. So I took 'the walk.' A nurse on one side, Luc on the other. Back to Trauma One. They'd removed all the medical paraphernalia and covered Juli with a sheet. The resuscitation efforts had distorted her face a bit, but she looked peaceful. Very peaceful really. She loved the Lord. She had entered His presence. I asked to be alone, just for a while. So they left me with her.

"I sat and stared at her beautiful face. We'd had breakfast together that morning. I'd called her at lunch to see how she was doing. 'Love you, Jewel.' That was the last thing I'd said to her. 'Love you, Jewel.'"

Ben broke down and sobbed. Marnie rubbed his back gently and finally pulled his head over and rested her cheek against his. "I'm sorry. So sorry," she whispered. "So sorry."

"That was one of the first things I tried to remember. What was the last thing I said to her? Did she know how much I loved her? I was glad I'd told her. She must have been so frightened, and I wasn't there. . . ."

Ben leaned back and looked up at the ceiling. "I kissed her good-bye. Then I just sat there. Stared at the wall. Couldn't even breathe."

Marnie and Ben sat, surrounded with tissues, and wept together for several minutes. They had taken the last tissue. Marnie went to the next room and found another box. From behind the couch she set it down. She placed her arms around Ben's neck, resting her cheek on his and rocking gently. She held him while he continued.

"I went over to the warmer where they'd wrapped our daughter." His voice softened again. "They had her in a yellow receiving blanket. She had the most beautiful face. Just under three pounds, but perfect in every way. We were going to name her Amanda—Mandy for short. I picked her up. Held her. Rocked her." Ben looked down at his empty arms. "I told her I loved her. Told her I'd hold her again one day in heaven. I carried her over to

Juli and sat holding on to my precious wife with one hand and cradling our daughter in the other. I couldn't take my eyes off Juli's face. She was so sweet, so innocent. I didn't want to leave her. Yet part of me wanted to run. Hide. Scream. I've never felt so helpless.

"I don't remember how I got home. I think Luc must have driven me. The chaplain said he'd take care of the arrangements. I'd heard that said dozens of times, but it seemed so cold. So final.

"When I got home, I went back to our bedroom. The phone was still lying on the floor, off the hook. Blankets and sheets were all over the place. I collapsed on the bed and cried out to God. With all my training, skills, and experience, when it really counted, I failed. Failed my wife, my child, myself."

Marnie shook her head, ready to argue that he shouldn't blame himself, but she knew better than to interrupt. Right or wrong, he was entitled to his feelings. She'd wanted people to let her express her grief when Tim had died, but so many had tried to talk her out of simply feeling how she felt.

"I decided I'd never again shoulder the weight of being 'the doctor.' My life was over. Yet—'life' inexplicably went on. I'd be driving down the street, and I'd want to yell at everybody that they needed to stop what they were doing and mourn. Like it was the end of the world. But they just kept driving by."

Ben reached back, put his arm around Marnie's neck, and held her close. For a long time they stayed like that, rocking softly, staring at the fire.

Finally, Ben broke the silence. "It is for fear to wet a widow's eye," he whispered. It was the opening line to

Shakespeare's ninth sonnet. "As if your wounds aren't already raw enough. I'm sorry. Hope I haven't brought back too many hard memories for you."

"No." Marnie walked around the couch and sat on the arm, next to Ben. "Thank you for telling me, Ben. I love you for it." She immediately regretted having used those words, but he didn't seem to mind. "I feel less alone," she added.

They sat quietly again for several minutes before Marnie spoke. "When Tim died, I wondered why the phone company felt the need to fix the broken lines outside our house the next day. I wanted everyone to stop. I wanted the world to change with me. Nobody's ever put it into words for me the way you just did.

"I'm sorry for your loss, Ben. And I'm glad you told me. I already said that, didn't I?" Marnie began to feel awkward, afraid she might start stammering and say the wrong thing. But Ben stood and drew her to him. The fire had almost burned itself out, and they stood in the dark, holding each other until the crackling wood grew silent.

Chapter Ten

AFTER A LATE MORNING LECTURE, Luc glanced through the mail on his desk. His eyes grew wide when he saw the return address on one of the envelopes: Leigh and Carlos Rivera, Culiacán, Sinaloa, Mexico. The shape of the envelope looked more like that of a greeting card than legal correspondence. He tore into it, and a photo dropped onto his desk.

He read the handwritten note:

Dear Dr. Morgan,

How can we ever express our appreciation for what you've done for us? I've enclosed an updated photo of the twins. They're even more beautiful in person, if you'll excuse my sounding like the proud parent. My husband doesn't like me to take them out in public anymore, probably because they draw such a crowd. They really stand out in this part of the world. We couldn't love them more. Thank you again for helping to make our lives so full. You're a wonderful doctor.

Gratefully,
Leigh Rivera

Luc sat with furrowed brow, staring at the photo. Two light-complected, identical-looking babies—their heads each covered with a fuzz of blonde hair—lay together on a blanket. *They* do *seem pale to be Carlos's kids,* Luc observed. Then he reread the note.

Yeah, right. You're so grateful; that's why you're suing me. Didn't your attorney tell you not to contact me like this?

Then it occurred to Luc that maybe she *didn't* know—not just that it was inappropriate to contact him, but about the suit itself. After all, she appeared to be uninformed about the paternity findings—at least at the time she'd written the note. He glanced at the postmark, wondering if something had delayed its arrival, but it said April 26. *Four days ago.*

As Luc sat pondering what this meant, he remembered what his attorney had said the day the first legal papers had arrived: "They're asking ten million punitive for loss of affection/alienation of affection from his wife, whom he claims is obviously 'seeing' someone at the clinic." *No wonder Carlos thinks I'm that "someone."* Luc looked again at the children in the photo. *I'm the only blond male here.*

Just then, Ben poked his head in the door. "G'day, mate!"

One look at Luc's ashen face changed his mood. He stepped inside, closed the door behind himself, and sat down on the chair in front of Luc's desk. "What is it, man?"

Luc handed him the card. "Read this."

Ben read the note and grimaced. "I don't get it."

"Me neither," said Luc, "but I think I may be starting to figure out some of it." He handed Ben the photograph.

Ben looked at it, then handed it back. "What do you make of it?"

"Seems like a sperm mix-up is the only logical explanation. But that's hard to imagine," Luc said.

"Yes. Very. But I think Tim was researching something up here after hours. Maybe a mix-up happened then."

Startled, Luc pressed his friend. "What? What kind of research?"

"I don't know yet. But that's what he told his wife."

"He did?"

"Uh-huh."

"When did she tell you *that*?"

Just then Luc's private line beeped. He held up his index finger, motioning for Ben to remain, and picked up the phone. After talking to the caller for a minute, Luc pushed the hold button and told Ben, "I need to take this call, but I want to discuss this further with you."

Ben said, "I have a suggestion."

"What?"

"Why don't you, Marnie, and I get together and pool our ignorance? We know stuff she doesn't know; she knows stuff we don't know. Let's see what we can come up with together."

"Good idea. When's good for you?"

"My Saturday night's free. But I don't have any family responsibilities like you do."

"I think Saturday's okay. But let me check with my

wife," Luc said. "Tell you what—let's plan on it, unless you hear otherwise. See if Marnie can meet you and me at the club at seven. Tell her I'm buying dinner."

All the way to the club on Saturday evening, Marnie asked Ben questions about the Gospel of John, which she had been reading. Ben was sorry the conversation had to end as he pulled into a parking space at the Arlington Heights Country Club. He got out, walked around the car, and opened the passenger door for Marnie. As they crossed the parking lot, they saw Luc's Jaguar pull in and waved. When they got to the door, they waited for Luc in silence.

Finally Ben spoke. "Have I mentioned how lovely you look this evening?"

"Why, thank you," Marnie smiled. "You're looking pretty dapper yourself."

Ben nodded his appreciation as Luc walked up. After greeting each other, the trio entered the clubhouse restaurant.

Ben guided Marnie to the seat with the best view, then took the chair to her right. Luc settled on her left. He hadn't seen Marnie since the memorial service, and he expressed his condolences to her. She thanked him again for his participation. "You did a great job of capturing Tim's personality in your eulogy, Luc. That Mother Goose reference nailed it."

"Thank you," Luc said, looking genuinely pleased with her approval.

Marnie proceeded to tell a few of Tim's favorite "twisted nursery rhymes," and the men nodded and laughed, remembering times they'd heard Tim recite the very same versions.

The waiter brought menus, and the three friends discussed what they planned to order. Then the conversation returned to Tim.

"I remember one time about six months ago," Ben reflected. "I quoted Tim a line from C. S. Lewis: 'No clever arrangement of bad eggs will make a good omelet.' Man, was he quick. He popped back with, 'Yeah, but *I* could take the omelet and make good eggs!'"

The two doctors laughed and shook their heads, but Marnie rolled her eyeballs and said, "Oh, please! Tim definitely never lacked for confidence, did he?"

They all shook their heads.

"Tim probably wouldn't have known C. S. Lewis from Jerry Lewis, though," Marnie said.

"True," Ben said, still chuckling.

"Ben, you're the theologian," Marnie suddenly looked serious. "Tell me if this could happen. I've heard that a doctor went to heaven. He got to the pearly gates and St. Peter let him in. When he saw a guy walking around in a white coat, he asked who it was. And Peter answered, "Oh, that's God. He likes to pretend he's a doctor."

They all laughed. Then Luc added, "Yeah, M.D.eity!"

"Sadly, that's the way a lot of docs think, isn't it?" Ben said. Delighted with Marnie's wit, he watched her as she continued talking with Luc. *So beautiful. And animated*. He didn't hear a word she said. After a few minutes, she glanced over at him and smiled. He caught himself and determined to rejoin the conversation.

He tuned back in time to hear Marnie tell Luc, "No, Tim wasn't crazy about people—said he hated the patient contact rotations in med school—but he sure loved his research."

"You're such a people person," Ben observed. "How did the two of you link up?"

Luc, who was more interested in the research part than the relational stuff, forced himself to be patient. "You were on leave from the clinic at the time," he told Ben.

Marnie said, "I was freelancing for the *Washington Post* when Tim and Luc discovered the Uterine Implantation Factor."

Luc added, "She was the hotshot investigative reporter who came to check us out."

"Well, not exactly," Marnie interjected. "But I was the reporter on the scene. Tim had done the research on UIF while he was doing experimentation on embryos. He actually discovered UIF by looking for something else. Really, his focus was akenosis research."

"What are you talking about?" Luc said sharply. "Akenosis research? What's akenosis?" Marnie had startled him, and his urgent response in turn shocked her. Just then the waiter interrupted to take their orders but, as soon as he left, they quickly returned to the conversation.

"You think he was using our lab to research some disease?" Luc sounded skeptical, as though Marnie must have misunderstood something.

"As far as I know, he was," Marnie insisted. "He was never home—always up at the clinic. And about a month before he died, he told me he was making great progress. I assumed you guys were all involved."

"Whoa, whoa," Luc responded with his hands up-raised in a gesture that said "stop." "Let's go back to the beginning. What in the world is akenosis?"

With Ben occasionally supplying the appropriate medical terminology from his own research, Marnie explained Tim's family history of akenosis. "I did a follow-up interview with him after we started dating. He kind of got my sympathy when he told me off the record about this disease, that it might someday kill him and his male relatives if he didn't find a cure. He told me—again, strictly off the record—that the big IVF discovery came as a side-benefit of research he was doing on his own for akenosis. And since akenosis is similar to MS, Alzheimer's, and Parkinson's, he seemed pretty elated about the possibility of improving the quality of life for a lot of people. As far as I know, he was still working on that research when he died."

Luc leaned over to pick up the fork he had dropped midway through Marnie's revelation. Her explanation about Tim's research didn't sound like a minor husband-wife misunderstanding. Putting the pieces together, with Ben's input from his Internet search, it seemed clear that Marnie's information was true.

"If Tim was fooling around doing research in our lab, he may have had more than just fertilized eggs in the fridge," Luc realized, thinking aloud. "I assumed I had the Riveras' embryos when I did the transfer, but now I don't know what I had. Not exactly."

"I wonder what Tim knew?" Ben said. "And who else knew what he knew. And if there's any danger involved."

He immediately regretted sharing this thought aloud when he saw the look on Marnie's face. He stopped himself before wondering out loud whether Tim's accident had been an accident after all.

Luc paid no attention to Ben's comment. He had thoughts of his own. "Why in the world wouldn't he tell me what he was doing? What *was* he doing?"

Outside the clubhouse, Victor crushed the butt of his cigarette with his heel. He had followed Luc's Jaguar to the country club, but he waited for the cover of darkness before acting. As he pulled on a pair of leather gloves, he looked around the parking lot to make sure he was alone. Walking casually and confidently over to the doctor's sleek green car, he stooped down, popped the lock easily, and slid into the driver's seat. Pulling a plastic zip-lock bag out of his shirt pocket, he opened it and set it on the passenger's seat. The dome light remained on long enough for him to search the driver's headrest for a strand of blond hair. Finding several, he grinned. *Piece of cake.* He lifted the samples and placed them carefully in the plastic bag.

For the next hour, Marnie, Ben, and Luc sipped on their after-dinner coffee, ate chocolate cheesecake, and combined their knowledge about Tim. They built a profile of what they knew, starting with Tim's training.

"Did either of you do any work at the animal husbandry laboratory in Lexington?" Marnie asked the two doctors.

Both men shook their heads.

"Well, I guess you know Tim loved it there. He gained lots of experience cloning sheep, goats, pigs. And he sure came out of there with some creative ideas."

"That's why we hired him," Luc said. "Some of those ideas were brilliant."

"So, we know he loved cloning," Marnie said, "and we know he was doing research you didn't know about." She paused for a long time. "You don't suppose?" She stopped and stared at the candle on the table as though mesmerized by it.

"What?" Luc wondered.

She looked up at him. "Do you think maybe he cloned human embryos in the lab?"

"Doubtful." Luc didn't even have to think about it.

"What makes you so sure? I mean, what if cloning is at the heart of the Rivera mystery?" Marnie asked.

Luc shook his head. "That's impossible. If the Rivera twins came from a cloned embryo, they would have matched both parents genetically."

Marnie looked puzzled.

Luc continued, "Mr. Rivera's DNA failed to match his daughters'. So we *must* be looking at some sort of sperm mix-up."

"Maybe we should look at it this way," Ben said thoughtfully. "If Tim was doing some research on the side that we *didn't* know about, maybe there are some clues in the research that we *do* know about."

He looked at Marnie and Luc, and Luc waved his hand as if to say, "Go on, we're listening."

"Remind me of how the big discovery came about," Ben continued. "I was pretty out of it back then."

Luc quickly warmed to the task of recounting the events leading up to the discovery of the Uterine Implantation Factor. "We assumed the lining of the fallopian tube cells released some kind of chemical factor that prepared the embryo to implant and survive in the uterus. Tim thought maybe the missing factor—what was limiting our IVF success rates—resided in a substance the tubes secreted. He developed cell cultures of these unique fallopian tube cells and used them for incubation."

"And that did it?" Ben asked quizzically. He didn't remember the breakthrough being related to fallopian tube research.

"No. But when that didn't work," Luc explained, "Tim told me, 'If it's not from the egg or from the tube, maybe it's from the sperm.'"

Ben nodded. This version was closer to what he had understood as the solution.

"Ordinarily," Luc continued, "in natural conception, millions of sperm travel through the uterus before finding the egg inside one of the tubes. With all the high-tech procedures we use in IVF, though, we bypass this normal pilgrimage. Tim thought that maybe something in the sperm—the ones that never made it to the egg—might give us a clue. We knew that certain enzymes reside in the head of the sperm. He thought maybe the sperm that crash into the uterine wall released enzymes that initiated a reaction. And if so, maybe that reaction was key to helping the embryo that would come along later."

"And that was the key, wasn't it?" Ben said with a nod.

"Yep, the secret was locked in the enzyme complement of the sperm. Far from being 'lost' en route, the sperm that didn't fertilize the egg provided an important part of the process. In retrospect, it seemed so simple."

"So, what seemed like wasted sperm, turned out to be the key to conception," Ben said. "What a great design—and right under our noses!" He leaned back, a look of satisfaction on his face.

The couple at the next table looked over at Ben, who had said the word "sperm" a little loudly. He and Marnie smiled a mutual "Oops" as Luc resumed his story, oblivious to the curious glances.

"It took a while for Tim to extract the enzyme components in the sperm head," Luc said. "But eventually he got it right. First, he used this material in primate experiments, and we went wild when he achieved a nearly 90 percent successful implantation rate. That was thrilling beyond words. Not only did I see the potential for successful human pregnancies, but I also wondered if this 'crash' process might also prepare the uterus in a way that decreased the risk of miscarriage from immunologic causes.

"Our pregnancy rates soared. And when we published our discoveries, the media picked it up, thank you." Luc motioned toward Marnie. "It brought couples from all over the world to see us."

Marnie noted with interest, "So Tim's research was the breakthrough, but it was your application of the information that brought it to worldwide attention."

"Well, I guess you could say that," Luc shrugged.

"I don't think that's how Tim saw it," Marnie said gently.

"What do you mean?" Luc and Ben said in unison.

"I'm not sure how to put this kindly, but Tim resented you," Marnie told Luc. "He said you took the credit for his big discovery."

Marnie's disclosure knocked the wind out of Luc. "I don't know what to say. I mean, I doubled his salary, for starters. That's the sort of credit most people appreciate."

"Yes," Marnie smiled, "you did."

"And I believe it was you who recommended that I serve as sole spokesman for the clinic."

"Yes. And I still agree with that decision. But it was a sore spot for Tim. No question—you were more articulate, had more of a sense of media presence. The cameras loved you. Of course, he thought I just defended you because I didn't want him to be angry at you. But it really chapped him when *20/20* focused on you and not him."

"As I recall, I told them to interview him, but they never used that part of the footage," Luc said, feeling defensive.

"Right again. I'm not saying you did anything wrong," Marnie insisted. "I'm just saying Tim had a beef about it."

At six-thirty P.M., Leigh Rivera picked up the ringing phone before her husband could get to it. But when she said, *"Hola?"* she heard a click.

Fifteen minutes later, Carlos walked outside to his car, claiming he'd left important papers in the passenger seat. He picked up the phone and called Victor's number.

"Did you call?" Carlos asked.

"Yes. I just wanted to tell you—I got what you needed."

"Excellent." The mayor's lips curled into a sly grin.

Later, a weeping Leigh Rivera called her friend. "I think she phoned here this evening. And Carlos called her back from his car."

After Marnie's revelation about Tim's resentment of Luc, the conversation changed course. Luc seemed distracted. "I've been trying to remember the name of Tim's mentor at UT Southwestern in Dallas," he said.

"Can't help you there," Marnie said. "I don't remember either. I never met him. Tim did keep in touch with him by e-mail. We might be able to check his address book." She cast a glance toward Ben, who nodded.

"What do you think he could tell us?" Ben asked.

"I don't know. It's probably a long shot," Luc said. "I'm just trying to think of anyone who might know more than we do."

"Like what?"

"I don't know. Never mind. Forget it."

"It's really bothering you that Tim thought you took credit, isn't it?" Marnie said.

Luc didn't respond to her question, and everyone at the table was silent for a few moments. Finally, Luc changed the subject. "It's sure hard to find a good embryologist. The new one—she's doing okay—but Tim's a tough act to follow."

An hour later, Ben walked Marnie to her door, said good night, and gave her a hug.

"Even though what we're learning makes me a little scared, that conversation provided some great therapy," she told him.

"What do you mean?"

"You know how it is after you lose someone. Everyone avoids the subject. No one mentions the deceased—certainly not by name. But tonight, I sat with Tim's friends and reminisced about him—'warts and all.' It helped a lot."

"I'm so glad," Ben smiled down at her brown eyes. "May I pick you up for church again in the morning?"

"That would be great."

Ben strolled back to the driveway, enjoying the crisp night air. When he slipped into the driver's seat and closed the door of his car, the lingering fragrance of Marnie's perfume caught him by surprise. He grabbed the steering wheel with both hands and rested his head on it for a few moments. Then he turned the key in the ignition, backed into the street, and drove slowly away.

Chapter Eleven

As DAWN BROKE, STREAKING THE SKY with violet-tinted light, Marnie slid open the glass door leading to her back yard. Her father, who had stayed overnight after baby-sitting for Emily, lay snoring in the guest room. With newspaper and coffee mug in hand, Marnie slipped into the porch swing. Balancing her coffee on the slatted seat, she peered at her watch. Six-thirty. Two hours before she and Emily would need to leave for church. She prayed for a few moments, then leaned back to enjoy the morning's incandescent glow and the scent of honeysuckle. When she had finished her coffee, she opened the newspaper.

Dancing President Falls, Dislocates Shoulder. The front page headline jumped out at her, and her heart rate instantly accelerated. She scanned the story for the key facts. At a White House black-tie dinner last night, while dancing with the first lady, the president had apparently tripped over her foot. The White House press secretary had issued a statement saying that the president, normally a graceful dancer, was in some discomfort, but expected an uncomplicated recovery.

Maybe it's nothing, Marnie told herself. But before she could completely dismiss the thought, she remembered Ben's question from the night before about the president and his suggestion that there might somehow be some danger. At the time, she had told herself Ben was wrong.

"Morning, honey." Will slid the door open a crack and waved to her. "Need a refill?"

"Sure, Dad. But I'll come get it." She stood to go into the house. Emily would be up soon, and she wanted to read the on-line news first to see if it gave her any additional information about the president's mishap.

She found Will sitting at the kitchen table, his hands wrapped around his mug as though they needed warming. A pot of coffee sat parked beside him. She held out her cup for a refill and asked casually, "Dad, would you like to join us for church sometime?"

"Nope. Thanks, dear. You know that's not my cup of, uh, coffee. But I'm happy for you. I can see it's helping you a lot. That's real nice."

She slid into the chair across from him at the table. "Okay. But I want to ask a favor." She put her hand on his arm.

"What's that?"

"I'm getting baptized in two weeks." Her voice shook a bit as she told him. "Would you come? It would mean the world to me to have you there."

"Sure, honey, if it means that much to you." Will shrugged. "Where?"

"Here." She pointed to the back yard. "In our pool.

I'm inviting some neighbors and friends. You'll know a lot of them."

Will looked intrigued. "Really? Well, okay. Who's gonna dunk you? Some neighborhood kids?"

"Ben's performing the baptism."

"Swell! You went to dinner with him last night, and he's picking you up this morning, too, eh?"

"Uh-huh."

"Sounds serious." His eyes twinkled.

"No, Dad, it's. . . ."

"You have a nice Beamer, sweetheart. You're capable of driving yourself to church, aren't you?"

"You don't like him?" She sounded concerned.

"You bet I like him," Will grinned. "I was merely trying to make a point, that's all." His eyes sparkled again. "Now, about this dunking. Shall I bring my swim trunks?"

"Sure!" Marnie walked around and gave her dad's shoulders a squeeze. She leaned down next to his ear. "Thanks, Pop."

Her spirits lifted, she headed down the hall to the office. She logged on and heard the familiar electronic voice tell her, "You've got mail." She smiled when she saw that the message was from Ben. He had written almost daily this week, and his messages usually amused her. It was a side of him that came out on-line, rarely in person, and she liked it.

She clicked "read" and noticed that the message had been received late last night. "Marnie, I sure enjoyed your company tonight," she read. "Thanks again for meeting with Luc and me. As I was driving home, I noticed that some of the houses in your neighborhood have security system signs. I didn't see one at your place. Now that Tim's gone, do you have any kind of security system? See ya in the morning. Sweet dreams. Ben"

"Good morning." Ben leaned down to shake hands with Emily, who had answered the door. She spun around to show him her new dress. "Wow, that's pretty, Emily."

Marnie emerged in a sky-blue linen spring suit. "Good morning, Ben," she smiled. "Or should I call you Mother Hen?"

"My, aren't you both looking photogenic this morning," Ben said, ignoring her remark. Marnie cocked her head and thanked him.

Smiling broadly, Ben bent down to Emily's level. "I brought you something this morning. It's in my car. It's a book about a man named Daniel. Do you know the story about Daniel in the lion's den?"

"No," Emily told him, wide-eyed.

"Sounds violent to me!" Will said, emerging from the next room to greet Ben.

"Not if the lions aren't hungry," Ben said. "Good to see you, Will," he grasped the older man's hand and shook it.

"I'll be gone when you get back, honey," Will told Marnie. Hearing this, Emily rushed over to give her grandpa a hug and a kiss.

"Drive carefully with my precious cargo," Will told Ben. "They're all I've got in this world."

"Yes, sir." Ben helped Emily on with her coat, and the three churchgoers headed for the door.

"He said he'd come to my baptism," a delighted Marnie told Ben when they were out on the porch.

"Marvelous! Hope we get some warmer weather between now and then."

Emily sat quietly in the back seat, looking at her new picture book. Ben and Marnie drove in silence as well. Finally, Marnie spoke. "I got your message this morning. And yes, we do have a security system."

"Do you activate it at night?" Ben glanced over at her.

"Uh-huh."

"Good." He was silent for a few more minutes, but about a mile before they reached the church he asked quietly, "Have you read the paper yet this morning, Marnie?"

"Mmmm, yes, I did."

"Sobering, isn't it?" Ben turned on the radio so Emily could not hear their conversation.

"I was hoping you'd say it was nothing," Marnie said.

"I just wish I could convince myself."

"You know what's worse, Ben?"

"What?" he looked at her with a puzzled expression.

"I read on the Internet that several people who were there said he stumbled over his own foot, not his wife's."

Ben slowly shook his head. Then he looked over at her. "Marnie, do you ever have an uneasy feeling about Tim's disappearance?"

"Of course I do. But journalists are trained to be suspicious. I have a bad feeling he was working on a possible cure for the president before he . . . uh . . . disappeared."

"Ben! You haven't introduced me to your new girl-friend!" Ben spun around as Mrs. Roberson made her way toward him after the service, a cane aiding her progress. One of the pillars of the Young at Heart Sunday school class, Mrs. Roberson prayed daily for Ben and his ministry. Every Sunday she sought him out to get her week's assignment. Ben deeply appreciated this, but her remark and the assumption behind it brought color to his face. He had no idea how Marnie would respond.

Marnie smiled warmly at the woman and extended her hand. "No, I don't believe we *have* met. I'm Marnie Sullivan. Any friend of Ben's is a great friend of mine."

Ben recovered enough to finish the introductions. When they'd finished talking, he pulled Marnie aside and said, "She's always trying to fix me up with someone. Maybe she'll stop now. But I'm so sorry about what she said."

"Sorry? Don't be," Marnie said. "It makes sense. She's seen us here together for weeks now. How could she know we've never even had a date?"

"Just didn't want you to be offended, Marnie."

She looked surprised. "Offended? More like flattered, Ben! Doesn't everyone want to be seen with a doctor?" Marnie smiled and winked. Without awaiting a response, she started off down the hall to pick up Emily from her classroom.

Ben stood staring after her, shaking his head with a huge grin across his face. He had hoped Marnie's affection was more than a grieving widow's appreciation, and this was all the encouragement he needed to find out.

Early Monday morning, Luc went to the refrigerator in the lab. Jennie, the new embryologist asked, "Looking for something?"

He ignored her question. "What can you tell me about Tim's filing system? Did you find anything strange about it when you set up the lab?"

She gave him an odd look. "No. It was great." Pointing to the vials, she said, "They all have names, numbers, and color codes. In fact, the system was so good, I adopted it."

"Names, numbers, and color codes?"

"Uh-huh."

The ones I transferred definitely had no color codes. "Did you make any changes? Adding the color codes or anything?" Luc wanted to know.

She shook her head. "Didn't need to. Why?"

"Thanks," he said. Walking back to his office, Luc felt like someone had punched him. He knew he probably bore sole responsibility for a horrible mix-up.

When Marnie saw Ben's name on her caller ID on Tuesday morning, her heart skipped a beat. "Hey, Ben!" He usually didn't call during the day, and she tried to sound nonchalant.

"Hello, Marina."

"Wow. Mighty formal this morning, aren't we?"

"I like Marina. It's a good name. And I love how your folks came up with it."

"Well, thanks. What's up?"

"I figured I needed to remedy a situation."

"Really? What situation is that?"

"Well, you were talking about Mrs. Roberson on Sunday, and you said—and I quote—'How could she know we've never even had a date?'"

Marnie waited silently for him to finish, unconsciously blinking rapidly.

"I thought about it—and you're right. So what do you say we live up to her assumptions there?"

Marnie sat down. "What did you have in mind?" She realized that her voice was doing nothing to conceal her delight.

"Ever seen *Les Miserables*?"

Marnie thought for a moment. "I think I saw the movie a long time ago. But I don't even remember the plot, sorry to say. What's it about?"

"If you see the musical, I think you'll remember it. It's about grace."

"Ah, my favorite theme."

"Indeed. So may I have the pleasure of your company this Friday night? Dinner and a play?"

"How thoughtful, Ben. I'd love it. Let me ask Dad if he can keep Emily again."

Marnie had feared that Ben's interest in her was purely that of a chaplain making sure the widow was working through her grief process, or a Christian brother seeing to it that a younger sister got grounded in her faith. Perhaps she had been wrong. She certainly hoped so.

⤚❧⤙

In his Dallas clinic, Dr. Allan Brown had methodically created brain injuries in a group of live mice, then injected a line of cells into the injured areas. After waiting seventy-two hours for the process to take hold, he'd tried to contain his excitement when he saw that the cells had actually attached themselves to the damaged nerves. *Maybe it doesn't show signs of restoring the damage, but at least the cells survived and attached to the right area!*

With growing confidence, he'd requested three chimps so that he could proceed to primate studies. The medical supply company had sent him Larry, Moe, and Curly. Allan generally gave little thought to the animals he used in his research, but the secrecy of this particular project and the innumerable hours they spent together in the laboratory had spawned a bond between man and primates.

Now several months into his work with the chimps, Allan reviewed the meticulous methods he had used, trying to find anything he might have missed. First he had isolated stem cells using the chimps' blood and other organ cultures. Then he'd injected the cells into their bloodstreams. Even if it did no good, at least it had caused no harm. Next, he'd tried brain injections, which showed no discernible effect. He'd noted one encouraging difference, though: The cells survived longer.

In preparation for the next phase of his study, Allan had invested a few weeks of intensive training in the microsurgical lab, buttressed with studies in animal anatomy and physiology. Once he had mastered the necessary skills, he was ready to proceed.

Selecting Moe as his next research subject, Allan used

electrical current and precise microscopic guidance and techniques to destroy the area of the brain that controlled the lower portion of the chimp's left leg. He was able to monitor the chimp's response to the nerve injury by MRI scan. Next, he injected the cell line specifically into the affected section of the brain. To his delight, the cells adhered to the damaged nerve.

Ben said nothing when Marnie emerged for her evening out with him but, as he held the passenger door open for her, his eyes betrayed his thoughts. He slid into the driver's seat of the Explorer, looked over at her, and said, "What a joy—to be with such a beautiful woman, and who has depth of character and a compassionate heart as well."

Marnie looked at Ben with a sparkle in her eye, "You've obviously been taking your Vitamin B lately."

He looked at her with a puzzled expression.

"Vitamin B, for 'baloney,'" she explained.

Ben feigned a deep wound to his dignity then replied with great dramatic flair, "Are you suggesting, madam, that I would exaggerate? I'm crushed!"

They both cracked up as Ben put the car in gear and pulled out of the driveway. After driving in comfortable silence for a few blocks, Ben thanked Marnie for the delicious hors d'oeuvres she had served before they left the house. They would certainly keep them going until their late dinner. The two continued chatting amiably as they drove into Washington, D.C.

They continued their conversation as they settled into

their seats at the theater. When the opening curtain went up, both Marnie and Ben became enthralled by the unfolding drama, until the play reached a scene where a young mother dies. Ben had forgotten about this part and, in spite of himself, tears began to stream down his face. He whispered an apology to Marnie. Understanding his response, Marnie discreetly handed him a tissue and laid her hand on his arm. Before long, she felt her own tears welling up. Both she and Ben wept through most of the second half of the play.

After the show, Ben and Marnie walked to the car without saying a word. But once they were inside, Ben broke the silence. "I'd forgotten what a tearjerker *Les Mis* is. I saw it in London years ago, and I cried then, but nothing like tonight."

"But it was wonderful," Marnie assured him. "I loved it!"

He looked over at her. "Honestly?"

"Oh, yes!"

"You're not upset I didn't warn you you'd get your heart torn up?"

Marnie shook her head. "Not at all. I'm just glad I wore waterproof mascara!"

"Good. I'm so glad you liked it."

They drove toward home, listening to Mozart and drinking in the lights of Washington, D.C., reflecting on the Potomac as they crossed the bridge back into Virginia. As Ben pulled into the restaurant parking lot, he told Marnie, "Good thing you fed us before the show. It's nearly eleven. You must be famished, Marnie. Or I guess after a play based in France I should call you Marn-yay. Or better yet, Grand Marnier."

Marnie laughed and faked a French accent. "Oui, Monsieur McKet. I am most hungry."

"Me, too. And since we are being so international tonight, what would you say to Italian food?"

"I'd love it," she nodded.

"Good." With a purse of the lips, he brought her hand to his mouth. "This place is *fantastico!*"

Once they were seated inside the restaurant, Ben looked into Marnie's eyes with concern. "I need to talk to you about something."

"What? What is it?"

"The weekend after your baptism I'm leaving for Russia for a week."

"Really? Why?"

"It's an administrative trip to set up an international medical conference I'm coordinating in a few months."

"Oh my, Ben. I had no idea you did anything like that!"

Over a superb dinner of veal, Marnie listened intently as Ben described the conference and his heart to see lost doctors come to Christ through it. "It's not a Christian conference, *per se*. But the presenting physicians are both top-notch experts in their specialties and they have a genuine faith."

Marnie listened with admiration as Ben talked. *He's amazing. I've never met anyone with such a good, strong heart. And a great face to go with it.* She studied his countenance, trying to memorize every detail.

"It's the fulfillment of a dream for me," Ben continued with conviction, "to share both medical insights and spiritual truth with colleagues from the former Soviet Union. Initially, I planned for several hundred to attend, but it looks more like we'll have fifteen hundred physicians from across Ukraine. The speaker list has expanded. I now have sixteen American, Australian, and British physicians."

"Wow, that sounds fabulous," Marnie said.

"Now, I want you to think about something—something to consider doing while I'm gone."

"What's that?"

"I want you to think about staying at your Dad's place."

"What? Why?" Marnie didn't really object. But Ben's request caught her totally off guard.

"I'd just rest better, that's all. I can't really put my finger on it, but I'm concerned for your safety. I don't want to scare you. I'm really sorry."

"Ben, honestly, I'll be fine. But I appreciate your concern." Marnie didn't want him to know the fears she'd been entertaining. She knew that Tim had kept records that she didn't know how to access on his computer. She sometimes wondered, late at night, whether someone out there might want something she had.

Marnie lay staring at the ceiling in her bedroom, her heart overflowing. She wanted to remember as much about the evening as she possibly could. The play. The music. The dinner. The scent of Ben's cologne that lingered on her hair after his good-night hug. How it felt to have someone strong guiding her by the elbow. She wondered what it would have been like if he had kissed her.

She had loved the story of Jean Valjean. And the way Ben had looked at her when she'd emerged from the back of her house, ready for an evening out. She thought of how it felt to have a date with someone who prayed before dinner. And the look on his face as he shared his passion for reaching Ukrainian doctors. She couldn't sleep, and she didn't want to. So she got up and went to her computer to see if she had any e-mail messages. But there was nothing. Instead, she decided to send one of her own to her favorite doctor. He'd often written to her, but she had never initiated contact. *Better keep it short.*

"Dear Ben, Thanks again for a great evening. I laughed; I cried; it was better than *Cats*. — 'Marnier'"

The following morning, when she checked her e-mail, Ben had replied.

"Dear Grand Marnier, Glad you had a great time to-night. I did, too. The company was superb. I laughed; I cried; it was better than a CAT scan."

Marnie threw back her head and laughed.

Chapter Twelve

BY MID-MAY IN CULIACÁN, the sun already beat down fiercely during the day. But tonight a cool breeze drifted through the open windows of the hacienda, lulling Leigh Rivera into a deep sleep. A crying baby jarred her out of her slumber. Vaguely aware that her husband had not yet arrived home, Leigh bolted out of bed to calm the one twin before the noise woke the other. Combing her long blonde hair back out of her face with her fingernails, Leigh covered the distance to the nursery before she had fully awakened. Her dog followed on her heels.

Leigh leaned down to lift Liliana out of her crib. "Hey, sweetie," she whispered. "Mommy's here now. Shhhh!"

She had a raging fever!

Leigh tried not to panic as she reached over and turned on a table light. Little Gabrielle, awakened by her sister's cry, now began to fuss when she saw her mother. Leigh balanced Liliana's hot little body on one hip while she reached into the crib and patted the other child's back with her free hand. "It's okay, it's okay," she assured both girls softly.

Once Gabrielle was quiet, Leigh laid her sister on the changing table and reached for the fever thermometer. Placing it gently into the child's ear, she waited for it to beep. When the LED readout showed 104 degrees, Leigh gasped. But before she had time to think about what to do next, her tiny daughter convulsed in a febrile seizure.

Terrified, Leigh yelled for a member of the ranch staff to assist her. Maria, the cook, appeared at the nursery door in her bathrobe. Quickly assessing the situation, Maria launched into a torrent of instructions in Spanish too fast for Leigh to understand. When Leigh's confusion became evident, the cook threw up her hands and ran to get a damp towel.

After several minutes swathed in cool, wet terry cloth and cradled in her mother's arms, Liliana finally relaxed. Gabrielle had been reawakened by all the commotion with her sister and was screaming at full voice. Leigh, who was still frightened, asked Maria to get the phone and her address book. She called the doctor's office, informing the answering service that she had an *emergencia*, while Maria tended to the squalling Gabrielle.

When he learned that it was the mayor's wife who needed assistance, Dr. Armando Morales called back immediately. Leigh fought in her panic to find the Spanish words to tell him what had happened. The doctor asked a few background questions, and Leigh assured him, "When I brought the twins in last week for their monthly check, they were growing normally, eating and feeding well. And they had reached the expected milestones for length and weight."

Dr. Morales said he suspected that Liliana had a typical childhood viral infection. He suggested ways to lower the girl's temperature. After assuring the frightened mother that the seizure should not recur, he changed his mind and said, "All the same, to be safe why don't you meet me with her at the emergency room."

Leaving Gabrielle with Maria, Leigh took Liliana to the hospital immediately.

When Leigh arrived, the medical staff recognized her as an important woman and made sure she received expert care. Dr. Morales checked Liliana's throat and ears, which looked normal, but the abdominal exam showed a strikingly enlarged liver and spleen. He asked the nurse to draw some blood and requested that Leigh wait for the results.

When the lab sent up its report, the doctor grew somber and shook his head. "Señora Rivera, your daughter has a dramatically elevated white blood cell count."

"What does that mean?" Leigh asked, alarmed.

"I'm not sure yet. I need to run more tests. But we must admit the baby into the hospital."

"Is it contagious?" Leigh asked with wild eyes. "Do you need to check Gabrielle, too? I could have her brought here for you to examine."

"The initial test suggests a blood abnormality. Nothing contagious," the doctor reassured her gently.

"What? Like leukemia?"

Dr. Morales had hoped that Leigh might not realize the implications until he knew more. He hesitated, then told her, "I won't know anything until I have the test results—and check the bone marrow as well."

"What about Gabrielle? Could she have it too?"

"Mrs. Rivera, I assure you, leukemia and blood diseases of that type are not contagious. But we'll test your other child too if you'd like."

When Carlos arrived home several hours later, he called Leigh on her cell phone. So distraught she sounded hoarse, Leigh told him that Liliana had been listed in serious condition and asked Carlos to bring Gabrielle in for evaluation.

Dr. Morales examined the other twin and was amazed to discover that Gabrielle had an enlarged liver and spleen as well. When the blood work lab results came back, the doctor found that Gabrielle had the same diagnosis as Liliana. It suggested an atypical leukemia. Gabrielle was soon admitted to the hospital, and Dr. Morales ordered a battery of tests on her as well.

When Luc received a typed copy of the deposition transcript, he quickly scanned through it, signed it, and returned the document to Chris Winston. "I'll need fresh tissue samples to confirm the claims made by the Riveras' lab," Luc told his attorney.

Chris, in turn, contacted the Riveras' attorney asking for tissue samples from Carlos, Leigh, and the twins. He also asked that a representative of his choice be allowed to serve as witness when the samples were obtained. He wanted his own investigation, with a full report from the lab, hoping to find some sort of discrepancy in the previous results.

Carlos, hearing of the defendant's request, ranted his way into a tirade about "this unethical doctor in Virginia who inseminated seventy-five patients with his own sperm back in the 1990s." In his outburst, he lambasted every physician who'd ever practiced IVF, claiming they were all "obsessed with their own genes." When his attorney persisted in saying a sample would have to be drawn, Carlos flatly refused to cooperate, claiming he would never agree to provide any tissue samples. He softened his hard-line stance, however, when his law-yer—convinced that the facts would prove malpractice—explained that the results could bring an immediate offer for settlement.

Once Carlos had simmered down, he apologized for yelling at his attorney, explaining that he had been un-der a lot of pressure—which had only been made worse by the twins' grave illness. Because of all the medical tests, he felt like they'd already given enough blood to open a blood bank, and the last thing he wanted was more of "those kinds of tests."

"I think hair samples will work," his attorney assured him. "Let me check."

After hanging up with his attorney, Carlos picked up the phone again and called Victor.

"Didn't you get a hair sample on that doctor?"

"Yes, señor, I did."

"What did you find out, Victor? What did we learn from it?"

"I am sorry, señor. The lab lost what I gave them. I have provided another, but it will be another day or two before I know."

Carlos cursed.

"I will call you the moment I hear," Victor lied. He already knew the results, but he wanted more time to figure out what to do next.

"I will work with the lawyers until I confirm the identity of the *papá*," Carlos told him. "After that, I expect you to handle it."

"Of course, señor. You know I will."

That evening, a U.S. government agent placed a bugging device in Victor's home phone. During the night they did the same in his Audi.

When Chris met Luc at the club that night for a game of tennis, he told his friend about the twins' latest development. He'd heard about it late that afternoon from the Riveras' attorney, who had called to confirm that hair samples from all four Riveras would be forthcoming.

Luc, who was changing his shoes at the time, was stunned by the news and had to grab onto the bench to keep from pitching forward onto the floor. He placed his elbows on his knees and buried his head in his hands as he asked a few questions. Then he sat for a long time staring at the floor.

"Do you know the odds of that, Chris?" he asked. "Are you sure he's telling you the truth? Do you realize that's nearly impossible?"

~~ ❧ ~~

Marnie's phone rang at ten in the evening. The caller ID identified the source as "unknown," so she let the machine pick it up. She waited to hear if the caller would leave a message, and when she heard Ben's "Hey, Marnie!" she grabbed the receiver.

"Ben, how are you?" He was still on his trip to the Ukraine, and she had not expected to hear from him until he returned.

"Not great. The week got off to a rough start. It improved slightly today, though. I was hopin' you could cheer me up."

"I've been praying for you. What's going on over there?" She stretched out on the bed. Ben had flown out the previous Monday, and it had only taken a few days for Marnie to realize how much she had come to rely on his daily contact, and how much she missed him.

"Aw, you don't want to know."

"Of course I do!"

Ben sighed. "When you dropped me off at Reagan National, I flew up to New York to catch my flight to Frankfurt."

"Uh-huh."

"Well, so far that's the only part that worked out as planned. After I left New York, everything went downhill. We were battling headwinds all the way across the Atlantic, so my flight got into Frankfurt late. I only had forty minutes before the flight to Kiev. Of course, by then I'd been flying all night. That flight's a bear, so I was beat."

"Oh, that sounds awful," Marnie said sympathetically.

"They parked the 747 out on the tarmac," Ben continued, "and bused us to the terminal, then brought us through customs and security. I hustled and made the gate to Kiev with what I thought was ten minutes to spare. But when I got there, they told me, 'Door to jet has been closed.'" He put on a mock German accent for this last part.

"Oh, no!"

"Oh, yes. They told me I had to go to a Lufthansa desk over in the next terminal. I tried pleading my case at the gate, but the lovely agent was unmoved by my plight. She kept repeating that I'd need to go to the booking desk and arrange for another flight."

Marnie groaned her empathy, and Ben interrupted his tale of woe. "Hey, I didn't call to bore you with the travails of my trip. How are *you?*"

"I'm not bored," Marnie insisted. "Go ahead. I want to know what happened."

"I'll skip the details."

"No, I want to know the details."

"All right. If you're sure."

"I'm sure."

"Okay. I arrived at the information desk in time to see my plane push away from the gate. Then I stood in line for forty-five minutes with everybody else who'd missed their connections, only to find out there were no more flights to the Ukraine that day. I was supposed to have met up with a small group of docs in Frankfurt, but they were now on their way to Kiev. The agent told me I had two options. I could wait until the next day, or I could catch a flight to Berlin, leaving in four hours, and connect with Air Ukraine, arriving in Kiev at eleven-thirty that night."

Marnie remained silent for a moment, waiting for him to continue, but when he didn't, she asked, "So did you choose option one or two?"

"Two. I wanted to get there ASAP. The booking agent gave me his solemn vow that he'd get a message to my colleagues about the change in plans. He also assured me that he'd send word to Kiev as well, so the other docs would know my arrival time. So I booked the alternate route." He was trying hard to be good-natured, but his voice had a bit of a sarcastic ring.

"Why do I get the feeling they never notified anybody?" Marnie asked.

"You got it!" Ben continued. "Did they tell anybody? Nooooo. After the four-hour wait, I flew from Frankfurt to Berlin, arriving on time. But—to the surprise of no one—my luggage did not arrive with me. The friendly desk agent in Berlin assured me that Lufthansa would transport my bags straight through to my final destination, Kiev. I had nothing with me—no toothbrush, no change of clothes—zip—because I had brought my laptop instead of my usual carry-on. I wanted to be able to create any documents we might need during the planning sessions for the conference."

Ben took a deep breath. "In line behind me was a Ukrainian couple who spoke little English and no German, so I hung around to help them deal with tracking their missing luggage."

"That was nice of you."

"A deed which they more than repaid, I might add. Ninety minutes later, we boarded the Air Ukraine flight to Kiev, arriving on time at eleven-thirty to a dark air-port. Marnie, this was no Dulles or O'Hare. The airport looked more like a deserted bus station. Only dirtier."

"Oh, my."

"Dingy. Dark. And nearly empty at that time of night. Nobody around but some *very* shady-looking taxi driv-ers. I looked for my medical buddies—those low-life dogs!" Ben laughed. "I didn't realize they'd heard noth-ing of my change in plans. I figured they'd stood me up. Meanwhile, they were thinking I'd abandoned *them*. Anyway, I had nowhere to go, and no way to get there. I wasn't about to get into a cab with one of those driv-ers. There I was, standing in my rumpled sport coat and slacks, clutching my expensive computer, and tot-ing a lot of cash. I should've just painted a red bull's-eye on my forehead; I had 'easy target' written all over me."

"How scary! What did you do?" Marnie heard the alarm in her own voice.

"In a remarkable act of kindness, the Ukrainian couple I'd helped in Berlin asked if I needed assistance. They explained the problem to a security guard at the airport and described the missing luggage to her. Meanwhile, in my wallet I had the home phone number of a family in Kiev whose daughter and son-in-law attend seminary in the states—in fact, I had some letters and gifts for them packed in my luggage. The Ukrainian woman—she was so helpful—took the number from me and called them. And can you believe it? These strangers came to the airport in the middle of the night, picked me up, and took me to their home."

"How kind!"

"Very! And the Ukrainian couple stayed with me until my ride got there, to make sure I'd be safe. If I hadn't believed in angels before this trip, I would now."

"Wow. Amazing! Ben, I'm so sorry you've had such a rough time, but I'm glad you're okay now."

"Yeah. After subsisting for two days on airline peanuts and the Hershey bar I had with me when I left D.C., I got a pretty big thrill when they offered me spaghetti and canned asparagus for breakfast."

"Gross!"

"Hey, I've never liked asparagus, but it tasted just fine in the face of that kind of hunger. Perspective, don'tcha know?"

"Did you ever find your team?"

"Yeah. But even that took a while. When I got to the hotel the next day, they had checked out. Something about a discrepancy over the price they'd been quoted. I eventually located them in another hotel, and we were able to set up an appointment with the Ukrainian equivalent to our surgeon general."

"Yay!"

"Really!" Ben laughed. "Now, aren't you sorry you asked about all that?"

"Not at all. So where are you now?"

"At the hotel with the team. Late yesterday we managed to work out the details for a pretty cool conference."

"I should hope so, after all that!"

"Yeah. I'm guessing with that kind of opposition going in, God must be up to something big. Keep praying for me, okay?"

"That goes without saying. I'm sure glad to know you're okay. I've been thinking about you a lot. When

I get up in the morning, I think, 'Wow, it's already mid-afternoon in Ben's world today.'"

That was all the encouragement Ben needed to stay on the phone for another forty-five minutes. It made him late for his first appointment.

~~∘≈∘~~

Sitting outside Marnie's house in his Audi and listening through earphones, Victor had found this conversation so boring that he'd fallen asleep.

~~∘≈∘~~

At the Arlington Heights Country Club, Luc and Chris were seated for lunch. After the waiter left to get their beverages, Chris handed Luc the lab report he'd received in the mail.

"Tell me what it means, buddy," the attorney told his friend.

Luc began reading the report, then paused and stared out the window at the eighteenth green for a minute or two. Glancing over at Chris he said, "Interesting." He read more. "Says here Mrs. Rivera is definitely the mother. And the first run-throughs confirm no paternal genes from Mr. Rivera linking him to the twins." Luc shook his head.

He continued. "What's also interesting is that the babies are identical twins. Apparently one of the implanted embryos divided and formed twins in the usual manner of twinning. It's not unheard of in IVF cycles, but it's certainly unusual."

"How common?" Chris asked.

"Incidence would be similar to the general population with no family history of twins. Say, around one in every eighty-eight births. Unusual in an IVF cycle—but the same incidence as in the normal population."

Chapter Thirteen

"CARLOS RIVERA HAS A CASE," Luc conceded. "There must have been some kind of mix-up. So what's the right thing to do, Chris?"

The attorney looked at his friend thoughtfully. "I think some type of settlement would be in order. We can spare everyone the expense of a trial. They'd be well served with an out-of-court monetary settlement. But we do have a bargaining chip, Luc. Fact is, Tim made the mistake, and he's dead. Nobody gets much sympathy suing the estate of a dead guy. So a quiet settlement would be preferable."

"So what do we do next?" Luc hated "losing," but relished the thought of ending this ongoing saga.

"I'll contact Rivera's attorney to schedule a settlement conference. We'll work out the details of how much and how we pay it—whether they want cash, trusts for the kids, that sort of thing. As for the amount, I'll try to get them to drop the punitive damages. They have no evidence of any intentional effort to cause pain and suffering. We'll try to get the actual damages down to policy coverage and spread it over the life of the children."

"So what are we talking here?" Luc asked.

"Easily a million. Maybe two."

Carlos Rivera sat behind the great mahogany desk in his office in downtown Culiacán. He had waited all day for a call from Victor. He shut his door, picked up the phone and punched in the numbers to Victor's cell phone. It had been three days since they'd spoken. *I've waited long enough. Time for an explanation.*

Recognizing the agitation in Carlos's voice, Victor anticipated the reason for the call. He answered the question before Carlos had a chance to ask. "Señor, how did you know I have news for you?"

Carlos raised his eyebrows and braced himself for the blow. "What can you tell me?"

"Dr. Lucas Morgan is *not* the father of your wife's children. The DNA does not match."

"What?"

"He is not the father."

"Are you sure?"

"Ninety-nine percent sure, señor."

Carlos had fully expected the opposite answer. He sat staring at the desktop photo of his wife, who had borne his silent rage for the past few months. "If not him, then who? Someone else at that clinic must be responsible!"

"The deposition says that Dr. McKay and Dr. Sullivan were the only other ones with keys to the area in the clinic where the embryos were stored. Dr. McKay's work for the past five years has not required him to handle embryos. That leaves Dr. Sullivan as the prime candidate. And he's dead."

Carlos thought for a moment. *Leigh never mentioned a Dr. Sullivan.*

"Dr. Sullivan's death seems a bit too convenient," Carlos murmured. Victor waited silently for Carlos to guide his next move. Finally, the mayor spoke again. "I want you to find out what you can about Dr. McKay. And also about Dr. Sullivan. See if anything turns up. Somebody is the father of the twins, and somebody will pay. If not Dr. Morgan, then the entire clinic. Someone will *pay*."

"Señor, I can tell you this. Mrs. Sullivan and Dr. McKay are in contact with each other."

Carlos squinted. *"Very* interesting." He sat silently for a few moments. Then he spoke. "I wonder if Dr. Sullivan's disappearance was related to a romantic involvement different from what I suspected. Something will turn up; I know it. Perhaps Dr. McKay had something to do with his partner's death?"

A few nights later, when Marnie's phone rang at ten again, she didn't wait to identify the voice. She knew it would be Ben. He had run up several hundred dollars' worth of calls to her during his absence.

"Hello?" she said expectantly.

"Hey, wish you were here, Marnie!"

"Yeah, me, too. How are ya' tonight?"

"You mean this morning?"

Marnie chuckled. "Yeah, I guess I do."

This time, Ben told her about the cathedrals, the monuments, the subways, the people, and the food.

"How are the conference plans coming along?" Marnie wanted to know.

"I'm glad I brought my computer. Yesterday it paid off. We were supposed to meet with Dr. Pereideri, their surgeon general, but we were dismissed out of hand because we had no official proposal. So we rescheduled a meeting for the afternoon, I typed up a proposal, and then we launched into a search-and-destroy mission to find an IBM printer. An American missionary's office had one. From there, I went to the med school and got a Christian physician to translate our proposal. With about an hour to spare, we were ready for the meeting with Pereideri. And I think it went off well. We may end up with top government endorsement for this conference."

Outside Marnie's house, listening in his car, Victor wished they'd get down to the good stuff.

Two days later, Marnie and Emily stood at the terminal in Reagan National Airport, eagerly awaiting Ben's flight in from New York. Thunderstorms had delayed the plane, adding to their anticipation. Finally, the jet nosed its way to the gate in what seemed to Marnie like slow motion. Now they waited for the jetway door to open and the passengers to begin filing out. It took only a few moments but it seemed like an unbearably long wait. Emily stood on the tips of her toes, trying to see Ben's face among the flock of passengers.

"I don't see him yet," Marnie said. "He must have been sitting in the back of the plane."

From across the waiting area, Ben stood watching, a look of sheer delight on his face. Finally, he came up behind them and said, "Hello, Marnier!"

She spun around. "Ben! Where did you come from?"

He swept her into a strong embrace. When he finally let go, he knelt down and hugged Emily. Marnie, fighting back tears, asked again. "When did you get here?"

Ben looked at her eyes, saw her happiness and smiled. "I caught an earlier flight on standby. I was dying to get home. But then we got delayed in the bad weather, so I got here about ten minutes ago. I was going to call from the plane, but when it got close to the same time as the other flight, I figured I'd just meet you here."

Marnie stood back and surveyed him. "Gosh, it's wonderful to see you. I'm so glad you're home."

"Great to see you, too. You've never looked better. Let's go get my bags."

"They caught up with you, huh?" Marnie asked.

"Yes, finally!"

"Did you bring me somethin'?" Emily wanted to know.

"Emily!" Marnie scolded. "You shouldn't expect Ben to bring you something every time you see him!"

Ben knelt down to Emily's level. "Hmm. How about a piece of butterscotch candy?" Ben looked up at Marnie for approval, and she nodded.

As they walked to the baggage claim, they talked about the weather and the flight home. Before long

Ben's luggage arrived. He grabbed the suitcases off the conveyor and set them on the ground. Marnie lifted one and set it down again in surprise. "It's empty! Where's your stuff?"

"Gone."

"What happened? Stolen?"

"Uh. No." Ben looked a little sheepish. "I gave it all away." He paused, then defended himself. "I just couldn't bring it back, Marnie. You should have seen those children at the orphanage. What doesn't fit the high school boys, they can sell for good money." He picked up the bags and headed for the door. "A pair of jeans can bring a hundred fifteen bucks over there. And a pair of leather boots? A month's wages!"

Marnie shook her head, smiling in pleasant disbelief. *Nothing looks better to me than a guy with a heart for kids.* "Some day I'd *love* to see those kids."

Ben stopped in his tracks and looked at her. "Would you?"

"Well, sure." She shrugged, surprised at his surprise.

Ben stared at her for a moment. "Everything's set for the trip back next month. Why don't you and Emily come over with the team?"

Over in the adjacent baggage claim area, Victor lit a cigarette. Oblivious to the "no smoking" policy inside the airport, he leaned against a pillar and took a hard puff as he watched the trio walk away.

Although Luc had initially denied any possibility of cloning, doubts had begun to arise as he thought more about Tim's "creativity." Determined to know what did and didn't match genetically, he sent the Riveras' tissue samples back to the lab and told his contact, "We have some considerable confusion over parentage. I want you to rule out as many options as possible. See what types of genes do and don't match with Leigh's. That is—find out what type of paternal genes are present."

Chapter Fourteen

Dr. Steven Harrison was holding Dr. Allan Brown's request for human research subjects. Though the apparent progress of the research encouraged him, it also made him nervous. He had some questions, but he wanted the answers to remain undocumented; he needed to avoid the risk that someone would circulate them. So he had picked up the phone to schedule a time when he and Senator Washburn could see the chimps for themselves. Now the doctor and senator took their seats in first class on American Airlines. In the near-empty plane, Dr. Harrison adjusted his long legs and sighed, "You need a femur-ectomy to sit in these airline seats. Glad we're not in coach."

Senator Washburn looked at him questioningly.

The doctor pointed to his thigh. "The biggest bone in the body. You'd have to have it removed to sit comfortably in the airplane."

The senator chuckled, "Ah! Ain't that the truth!"

Once they were airborne, and had glasses of wine in

hand, the doctor began to brief his guest. He aimed to provide the medical information necessary for the senator to make a favorable decision after his visit to Dallas. Dr. Harrison took a sip and began. "Back in 1998, scientists successfully isolated and cultured human stem cells—a feat which had eluded us for nearly two decades. These cells allow us to grow tissue that has good results in treating Parkinson's, Alzheimer's, heart, and diabetes patients."

The senator nodded. "You'll have to remind me—what are stem cells?"

Back in the early 1990s, the senator had served on a committee that reviewed the National Institutes of Health's recommendations to the government concerning embryo research. At that time, the politician had received scores of letters against such research. Most of those who wrote objected to what they considered the destruction of human life, claiming that the embryo had the full status of personhood.

The senator had seen it differently. He had claimed it was wrong to protect unborn "pieces of fetal tissue" if it meant delayed treatment for a much larger number of people with life-threatening diseases. When he stated his views publicly, letters comparing medical experiments with Nazi Germany had begun to arrive. Many considered it unethical to "do evil with a good result in mind." Nevertheless, the senator believed that the worthy goal justified the less-than-perfect procedure.

Due to sharply divided public opinion, the government had opted to stay out of the business of funding experiments with embryos. It was determined that such experiments were legal as long as no one used the taxpayers' money to fund them. Private donors and businesses had immediately stepped forward to back the researchers' efforts. After the decision had been made to keep the government out of such research, the senator had lost interest in the issue, focusing instead on what he considered more pressing concerns.

"Stem cells are the cells from which every one of the 210 different kinds of tissue in the human body originate," the doctor answered.

"But they're different from embryos, right?"

"Right. Although a stem cell can give rise to more specialized cells, it can't form an entire human being. So it's not equivalent to the human embryo."

"Yes, I remember now."

"Still, as you know, Dr. Brown's approach to obtaining stem cells *does* involve the destruction of human embryos."

"Where does he get them?" the senator wanted to know.

Dr. Harrison didn't know for sure, so he speculated. "I believe most come from fertility clinics that donate unused embryos slated for destruction. Others may come from aborted fetal tissue. And he may create some from frozen sperm and eggs."

"I see," Senator Washburn nodded.

A few years after his involvement with the issue, the laws had changed somewhat. It had become legal to use federal funds for research on stem cells derived from human embryos. While no one could use taxpayer funds for research involving the destruction of embryos created to obtain these cells, researchers easily got around this technicality. The part of the process that involved destroying embryos was funded privately, and then the cells obtained from the embryos were turned over to federally funded centers for research.

Dr. Harrison knew he would find a sympathetic ear in Senator Washburn. Dr. Harrison was overseeing research on akenosis at the president's request. And though he was supposed to keep the project confidential, he also had a financial interest in it. He had committed his own funds to help the president, in hopes that when Dr. Brown developed a cure, the pharmaceutical companies would provide enormous payoffs.

His present aim was to enlist support for the loosening of the approved guidelines for genetic therapies. This would virtually guarantee the widespread acceptance of whatever "cure" was developed. He thought the senator might help.

Dr. Harrison continued. "Many diseases, like those I mentioned, result from the death or dysfunction of a single type of cell. We believe the introduction of healthy cells of this type into the patient can restore lost or diminished function. Researchers now isolate and culture stem cells. And we're at the stage where we're figuring out how to coax these cells into becoming the specialized cells and tissues needed for transplantation into patients."

The senator nodded again. His first wife had died of cancer, and the thought of preventing such emotional agony for someone else brought him a sense of comfort. It satisfied him when he was able to use his position to do something truly noble for humanity. And of course, secondarily, he hoped the whole thing would translate into votes.

Dr. Harrison took another sip of wine. "We all hope this will lead to the prevention and treatment of birth defects and cancer. Also, with a virtually unlimited supply of human cells and tissues in the lab, pharmaceutical companies could develop and test new drugs in a way previously impossible."

"Exciting possibilities," the senator said.

"Yes. But we need to get rid of all the governmental red tape."

Once in Dallas, the two men wished to remain inconspicuous, so they rented a dark-blue midsize car and sped to the Doctors' Surgical and Research Center. After the necessary introductions, they sat facing Dr. Allan Brown himself in his office.

Dr. Harrison got right to the point. "So you're encouraged enough to move ahead with human test subjects?" His voice sounded hopeful.

He leaned back in his lab chair, smiling as he reviewed the latest data. "I have three laboratory chimps—Larry, Moe, and Curly. Each has shown signs of progress. They've exhibited no chemical evidence of rejection and their MRIs haven't shown any signs of abnormality. So I have every reason to conclude that the transplanted cells are alive and growing."

Dr. Harrison smiled. "Would you mind reviewing the research you've done to this point?"

Dr. Brown gladly complied. He described the past few months of accelerated lab work, beginning with the specially bred strain of hairless mice. "First, I did the injections of the cell line, which I labeled LG. When I injected the LG cell line into the mouse bloodstream, I saw no negative effects, though the spleen apparently destroyed them. General injections made directly into the mice's brains again demonstrated no negative effects. The LG cell line didn't take hold, but at least it caused no damage. No seizures. No twitches. Nothing. Then I easily transplanted the LG cell culture. It was remarkably straightforward." *Amazing no one else has been as successful. But then I suppose the legal barriers would have been insurmountable in any other lab. And if these guys knew the whole score, I suppose I'd face more barriers, too,* he thought.

Both visitors now listened intently.

"Then came nerve studies. I cultured the cell line with normal nerve cells first. Then I extracted electrically damaged nerves and preserved them." He read from his notes: "No interaction demonstrated." He looked up and explained, "After seventy-two hours, I discovered that the LG cell line had attached to the mice's damaged nerve area. It didn't show any signs of restoring the damaged nerve, but still, at least the cells survived and attached to the right area."

"What did you make of that?" Dr. Harrison wanted to know.

"It was progress. Perhaps human cell line genetics are different enough from the mouse chromosome. It recognizes damage, but there's no signal to differentiate the embryonic LG stem cells to facilitate healing in the mice."

Dr. Harrison nodded.

"That's when I asked for the chimps." As he went on to explain how the cell line lived longer in primates, Allan had their undivided attention. "But the LG didn't do anything. It was not a total failure. I decided I needed to inject it more specifically into the correct area of the chimp brains. I felt pretty nervous when I operated for the first time on Moe."

"Yeah, I'll bet." Dr. Harrison was impressed.

"The first time I used the microtechnique to place a 'transplant' of the LG cell culture in the precise region of the injury—pow! The cells stayed. They survived. And they began to grow at the site of the damage. It was amazing!"

Both visitors now looked clearly pleased.

"Very interesting." Dr. Harrison worked to suppress his excitement.

Dr. Brown smiled.

"But if the cell lines aren't *repairing* the primate subjects' injuries, what makes you think we should move to human subjects? Do you realize the risk you're asking us to take?" Dr. Harrison was hoping that Dr. Brown had good reasons. An earthshaking medical discovery seemed to be within reach. The senator leaned forward, awaiting the doctor's reply.

Allan Brown nodded. He delayed a direct answer to this question for a moment and gave them, instead, what he wanted them to hear. "You know that nerve fibers have different diameters and types, right? They mediate different types of pathways. I think we may be on the verge of unlocking a mystery that has baffled medical science since the first case of nerve injury failed to heal. I watched Moe for days. He completely recovered from surgery, but he still exercised no motion in the injured leg. Repeat MRI scans showed that the new cells were alive and attached to the damaged nerves. But the cells failed to mature or develop into healthy nerve myelin that could restore the 'electrical transmission' in the nerve to get that leg moving again."

"So what happened?"

"At the least, I was encouraged by Moe's progress. We had clear evidence that he suffered no harm. True, the damage hadn't been reversed, but the new cells hadn't killed him, either. So I decided to give it a try on the other two."

Dr. Harrison raised his eyebrows.

Dr. Brown stood up from his desk. "Why don't you come see for yourself?" He directed them to the lab where he kept the primates caged. When the three men entered, Moe and Curly went wild showing off, while Larry tried to continue a nap. The humans spent a few minutes allowing themselves to be entertained.

"They're limping," the senator observed.

Allan was eager to get back to his explanation. "The chimps recovered well. And the laboratory and test results paralleled each other. The new LG cell line surrounded the damaged areas, attached to them, and survived. They didn't go so far as to differentiate—they did nothing to relieve the surgically induced nerve damage that injured their legs. But here's my question. To me it is key: Could it be that the tiny differences in the genetic material between chimps and humans was sufficient to prevent a positive response?"

The two visitors exchanged impressed glances.

"What might not work in a human-clone-to-animal experiment might well work on human subjects. Maybe these new cells can 'fill in the gaps.' Maybe they can restore nerve function and muscle response."

"You might have something there." Dr. Harrison knew

a test group of three chimps was hardly a large enough number to go on—not in any other sort of study. But this situation was very different from most.

"Still, to be honest, there is one problem," Dr. Brown said.

"What's that?" The senator did not like the sound of this.

"This 'disease' I'm creating with the microelectric current in the chimps' brains is *destroying* the myelin nerve sheath. Even if the LG cells restore the nerve function, it doesn't mean they will help in akenosis. MHS is a hypermyelinating disease. That is, with akenosis the myelin clumps up—it doesn't deteriorate. So it destroys nerve function the opposite way."

Dr. Harrison nodded. "True."

The senator stood silently, trying to assess Dr. Harrison's reaction.

Dr. Brown continued, "If I can get the LG cells to grow and heal the nerve sheath that's been damaged, even if they don't work on akenosis purely, perhaps I can vaporize the 'built up' areas with laser or electricity in akenosis patients and *then* the LG cells can go to work."

Dr. Harrison smiled. "Brilliant." It seemed that Dr. Brown had already considered every possibility.

"If only the chimps would get some function back in those legs!" Dr. Brown sounded both enthusiastic and frustrated. The chimps had learned to compensate for their partial paralysis, but they'd had no return of lost leg function. Yet the LG cells were still "on site" and alive. They just didn't seem to help the problem.

"I'll see that you get your human subjects."

"Excellent!" Allan Brown didn't even try to shield his enthusiasm.

"We don't have a lot of time, you know," Dr. Harrison said.

Dr. Brown agreed, and his mood changed.

Chapter Fifteen

MARNIE, BEN, EMILY, AND WILL emerged from the evensong service at the Washington National Cathedral. The *Washington Post* had commissioned Marnie to freelance a piece on Eleanor Roosevelt for a series they planned to run on great women of the last century, and the famous first lady's interest in the cathedral required that Marnie make an on-site visit. She had decided to take Emily along, and Ben had said he'd accompany them. In the interest of culture, Will had decided to go, too.

Afterward, they all strolled down to the Bishop's Garden to admire the blooms. The scent of roses permeated the air, and the bells of the carillon were playing some of Ben's favorite hymns. A comfortable evening breeze encouraged them to sit in the gazebo and linger a while. Emily, who quickly grew tired of sitting and visiting, pulled on Will's arm. "C'mon, Grandpa, let's go exploring."

Will rarely denied her a request that was within his

power to fulfill. "Okay," he told her. "Maybe we'll find a mystery hidden behind that gate," he said pointing off in the distance. He winked at Marnie, and the two disappeared out of sight.

"Do you have a lot of deadlines coming up next month?" Ben asked Marnie once they were alone.

"A couple, but not bad. It's actually looking pretty free."

"Then I have an idea."

"What's that?"

"I have an assignment for you."

"Oh?"

"We talked of it before. Why don't you come with the team to Kiev? You'd find lots to write about there."

"Mmm. Subtle, aren't you?" she laughed.

"I mean it."

Marnie thought the expression on his face made him look like a puppy, but she didn't dare say so. "I've been considering it ever since you mentioned the possibility at the airport. I figured maybe you were just being kind. But since you brought it up again, tell me more."

"Just being kind? No way! I meant it. Absolutely!" Ben could hardly believe she was so open to the possibility.

"It would be a great education for Emily. And it's a part of the world I've always wanted to see. I could probably interest the *Condé Nast Traveler* in a piece on Kiev. If so, they'd pay my way."

❧

Dr. Armando Morales emerged from the pediatric intensive care unit of the Culiacán Municipal Hospital, pulling off his gown and mask and walking slowly toward Leigh Rivera.

"What, doctor?" the twins' mother sprang out of the chair where she had been sitting, accompanied by a friend who'd come to translate. Leigh spoke Spanish fluently, but she didn't want to miss anything the doctor said. She searched his face for reassurance.

"I've never seen anything quite like this. Certainly never in twins."

"What is it?"

"Your babies are ill—critically ill, I'm afraid."

Leigh motioned for her friend to join the conversation. The doctor spoke a sentence or two at a time and then waited for the message to be relayed.

"They seem to have a blood disease similar to acute leukemia, but the cell types involved are certainly not typical."

Leigh nodded that she understood so far.

"The white blood cells, particularly the lymphocytes, are proliferating at an increasing rate. Yet because they're abnormal, the spleen is trying to filter them all out. We have a very serious problem here."

Leigh shook her head. "I don't understand. Can you treat them?"

"I've ordered strict isolation. We'll need to try a chemotherapy approach, perhaps even remove the spleens. Both babies are very similar in their status at the moment." The doctor shook his head in bewilderment. "I have a call in to Dr. Miguel Dunham in Mexico City. He's an oncologist with great experience in childhood diseases. I expect him to call back any minute. But I don't think we can transfer the babies to him."

"You mean they could die?" Leigh asked, tears welling up in her eyes.

Dr. Morales remained silent. He reached out and put his arm on Leigh's shoulder. The sad look in his eyes told her the worst was possible. After a moment he said, "Let me talk to my colleague. And let's give the medication a chance to work. Your beautiful babies are strong. Let's not get ahead of ourselves."

"May I see them?" she pleaded.

"Certainly. But as a precaution, let the nurse help you put on a gown, mask, cap, and gloves."

"You mean, they're contagious?" she asked, barely able to speak.

"Oh no," the doctor replied. "But with the combination of the disease and chemotherapy, we're concerned that the babies will lack resistance to outside germs. It's for their protection, not yours."

"I understand," Leigh gasped, trying to suppress a sob. As the doctor disappeared, she turned to her stunned friend. The two women held each other and cried. When Leigh had regained her composure, she slowly walked to the door of the pediatric ICU.

Once inside, after dressing appropriately with the nurse's help, she took a deep breath and purposed in her heart to be strong for her children. She approached the overhead warmers that held the tiny girls. Reaching out, she stroked Liliana's cheek. "Mommy loves you, sweet girl," she whispered. Then she did the same with Gabrielle. Leigh longed to hold her children, but tubes and wires were fastened to them from every angle. So she touched them as best she could. She let them wrap their little hands around her index finger and, as they did, she stood marveling at their miniature fingernails. She stroked their backs and caressed the tops of their heads. "Mommy's here, niñas," she sang softly, dreaming of the future she wanted with her girls and begging God to give them a chance.

Having completed his evening rounds at the hospital, Luc made a quick swing by the outpatient surgical center to discharge the day's laparoscopy patients. Then he returned to the clinic to review in detail the contents of the FedEx package he'd received from Chris. *Finally!* he thought. Ever since he had signed for the special delivery envelope that afternoon, he'd been eager to study the report.

Walking into his plush, wood-paneled office, he glanced up at a huge portrait of his wife and children over the mantel. *Better not stay too late,* he reminded himself.

He pulled out the lab results from Genetek Corporation as he settled into his leather chair. Propping his feet up on his desk, his usual manner of contemplating life's serious issues, he looked down at the papers with furrowed brow. In addition to the summary report, he held digital photos of the chromosome studies and the gel study reports for the major gene sites.

He read through the findings. *The twins are indeed identical—no doubt about that—one hundred percent match. And nothing, not even a hint that Carlos is their father.* Luc stroked his chin, looking up at the wall. He picked up the remote for his CD player, punched in the selector number for a familiar disc of soothing nature sounds, and returned to his reading. He looked at Mrs. Rivera's studies and noted the areas of genetic match. *No real surprise, but I still don't get how there could have been a mistake.*

Luc set the chart down and stood to retrace his steps once again, only this time he accepted that an error had indeed occurred. He walked silently down the hallway, the deep carpet muffling the sound of his footsteps. He entered the spacious procedure room. Though it was equipped like an operating room, thanks to a decorator's touch it also had some color to go with the exam table and sonogram machine. Beautiful cabinetry discreetly concealed the bulk of the equipment. The sliding glass window that led to the laboratory was closed and clean.

Luc flipped on the light, walked over to the wheeled stool that he used when he harvested eggs and sat down. He remained there thinking, looking around, and re-membering. *Egg harvest, embryo transfer, no problem.* After a while, he stood up and unlocked the door to the lab located between the procedure room and his consulting room. As he flicked on the lights, he only vaguely remembered looking for the Riveras' embryos.

He rarely entered the laboratory, but here he was again—coming back to the place where it had happened, trying once again to figure out how. It had been Tim's domain, and now Jennie, the new embryologist, had made it her private kingdom. As Luc looked around, a dejected expression on his face, his eyes rested on the cryofreezers. Instinctively, he went over to have a look. Finding nothing new to jog his memory, he shook his head and walked back to his office.

Back at his desk, he picked up the papers again and reread the summary note more carefully this time. Then he glared at the paper. *What?* Luc looked at the tests, back and forth. *Every gene in the makeup of the twins matches the mother, but not all of the maternal genes have a matching component in the twins. . . .*

He leaned back, hands on his head, closing his eyes, trying to make sense of this odd finding. *It couldn't be a sperm mix up. There aren't any genes in the babies that don't have a correspondence with Mrs. Rivera. Impossible! Not a single gene that doesn't come from the mother. Yet, not all of their mother's genes correspond. Of course, that couldn't happen unless they were . . . oh Tim . . . you* cloned *Mrs. Rivera. You cloned only Mrs. Rivera!*

Even as the thought was registering, he realized it couldn't be true. *He would have needed a tissue sample of mature cells and somehow cloned the adult cell and started a whole new embryo with the identical genome of the "original." That can't be. The only tissue he had to work with was the . . . the egg. The egg! Tim the "egg man." Could he have somehow cloned the egg? Half the mother's genome—and then somehow duplicated that? Never been done. But that would give a pure cell line and would not "technically" be cloning an embryo. Not "exactly" against the law. So this was the experiment. This is how you were going after akenosis!*

"I got the wrong embryos," muttered Luc aloud. *Tim must have known when he found my note and discovered the missing embryos. When the pregnancy "took," he must have been amazed. Or so full of pride that he didn't know what to do. Oh man, it's unbelievable. A cloned egg. This is a disaster! It's as though Leigh Rivera is the twins' mother* and *father genetically. No discernible paternal ge-nome? What in the world? Tim! What have you done?*

⟥⟤

The next morning, Luc phoned the lab. "Ever seen anything like this?" he wanted to know.

"No. We're still trying to explain it—no genes that fail to match the maternal profile! Amazing. We ran the tests twice. But the technicians say they couldn't isolate any distinct paternal contribution. All the trackable genes match the maternal profile."

"Thank you," Luc said as he hung up. Then he grabbed up the receiver again and punched in his attorney's number. He sat on hold for a while, but finally got through to Chris Winston and told him what he'd found out.

After several minutes of conversation, Luc ended with, "I can't believe Tim would do such a thing. I'm not exactly sure what he was up to, but based on what Ben told me about akenosis, my guess is that Tim was working on a cure for the disease. I suspect that if President Sullivan has it, Tim knew and was trying to help his uncle. First-term president, mid-forties. What a tragedy!"

Chris tried not to sound too alarmed, but he took the news quite seriously. "Luc, I think we'd better keep what you know under wraps until I can talk with somebody at the Justice Department. This may go all the way to the top. And since we've got a presidential connection here, we probably need to get some clearance before any of this becomes public knowledge. Sit tight, okay?"

"Sure," Luc told him. "No problem. Ben's the only one I'd want to tell, and he left this morning on a ten-day trip to the Ukraine."

That evening, Victor sat listening to the day's recorded conversations from the clinic's outgoing phone lines. After hearing the conversation between Luc Morgan and Chris Winston, his eyes widened. He made an urgent call to Culiacán and informed Carlos Rivera that Dr. Lucas Morgan might be involved in a high-level conspiracy involving the president of the United States.

Chapter Sixteen

"IT IS EEMPOSSIBLE!" THE WAITER TOLD Ben when the group of eight Americans emerged for their breakfast in the hotel restaurant and wanted to shove two tables together.

"What do you mean, it's impossible?"

"It cannot be done. It is eempossible."

The waiter pointed to the two tables and left, evidently assuming the Americans would divide up and seat tnemselves. Ben and another man in the group looked at each other, moved back the chairs, and slid the two tables together. "Astounding!" Ben said, raising his arms in the air in a victory sign. "We've done the eempossible!"

Once seated, the group waited for the waiter to return with the food they'd ordered. "He'll probably make us wait three years now," Marnie said.

"No, he won't. Just watch. He won't give a rip," Ben assured her.

Sure enough, the waiter soon returned with full plates

and said nothing about the tables being moved, as though it had never happened.

Marnie stared down at her breakfast of fat-filled sausage, fried sour cream and cottage cheese. "Yum," she said, trying to coax Emily into nibbling on something.

"At least they didn't bring cabbage this time," her daughter mumbled. She was struggling not to complain.

Before this trip, Marnie had known she'd been spoiled, but she hadn't realized how much. She had written in her journal that their hotel room had come straight out of the 1950s, with unmatched, threadbare towels and toilet tissue the consistency of wallpaper. One of the team members had even joked about the grade of sandpaper it might be made out of.

"How did your dinner with Natasha go?" Ben asked. Natasha, their translator, had invited Marnie and Emily out to dinner the previous evening.

"We had a great time. Although language sometimes creates a challenge."

"Really? What happened?"

"When I asked her about her family, she said her brother had had a tragic accident. He literally lost his head. So I said, 'He died?' And she told me, 'Oh, no. He's still alive.'"

Ben looked startled.

"So I asked, 'Without a *head*?' And she said 'yes.' So I argued with her a bit, and she began to be annoyed with me, insisting, 'Surely you have people in your country who have had their heads removed.' And I said indeed we did *not*."

Ben was shaking his head in confusion.

"'No! This can't be true,' she said. And I insisted,

'Yes, it is.' Then pointing to my head, I said, 'No one in our country who has no head has survived.' Well, when I pointed to my head, she gasped, covered her mouth and said, 'Oh, no! I mean 'foot.''"

Everyone at the table laughed. And then others launched into their own stories about various language bloopers. In time, the laughter and storytelling ended, and the people around the table returned to their own conversations. Ben leaned over and asked Marnie and Emily, "So what did you two do yesterday?"

Emily looked at her mother, so Marnie answered. "Wow. We stayed very busy. We broke into two groups in the morning. One went to the school and the other to the hospital. I toured the women's ward. Pretty sad— they really have no medications, no equipment. It reminded me of something you'd see in a really old movie. And the hospital had a distinct scent. A lot like boiled macaroni, only much stronger."

"I know the smell well," Ben told her.

"Then, in the afternoon, we visited a community of displaced Chernobyl victims. We gave the elementary-age kids some toothbrushes, pencils, and stickers. They were thrilled."

Emily added, "I liked that the best. They said 'thank you' over and over."

"Well, good!" Ben smiled at her.

"Yeah," Marnie told him. "They seemed overwhelmed by our generosity. A priest who lives in Kiev told us that the women affected by Chernobyl have a hard time marrying because of the risk of cancer and deformities in their offspring. Everyone in this community, no matter how intellectual, will probably end up working at menial tasks. They've been labeled for life, and they suffer from low self-esteem. I'd given one of the girls from the classroom—Lena was her name—a little hug. She wanted my autograph and followed us around. Before I knew it, Emily and I had a crowd of thirty kids surrounding us. So we gave them all gospel bracelets, didn't we?"

Emily nodded. "Yeah. And then we visited an orphanage."

"My, you *did* have a busy day!" Ben said.

"We spent an hour or so with a group of fourth-grade boys," Marnie told him. "When we got ready to leave, they lined up together, threw out their little chests, and sang a Ukrainian blessing at the top of their lungs." Marnie swallowed hard. "Most of the children have at least one parent living. But they've been removed from their homes because of alcoholism."

Ben shook his head sadly.

Emily added, "Natasha said it was hard for her to help us give stuff away. She wanted to keep some bubbles and English books for her own children."

"But not to worry," Marnie smiled. "We loaded her up with plenty, didn't we?"

Emily beamed up at her, "Uh-huh. She was happy!"

"Natasha calls me Marnichka now. I guess it's a term of endearment," Marnie said.

"And she said you're Benichek," Emily smiled up at Ben.

"Benichek, huh? And you, Emily? Does she have a name for you?"

"I'm Emilichka."

"Wow, that's a mouthful!" Ben laughed.

"We came back to the hotel and ate at the restaurant," Marnie continued. "Natasha said the purpose for dining in the Ukraine is fun, fun, fun. And we certainly were surrounded by jolly people. She pointed out a wedding party that was singing away and then told us what the words meant—'Columbus should have stayed in the place where they drink beer instead of discovering America.'"

"Oh my!" Ben grimaced. He gave Marnie an "Are you sure you're safe?" look.

"Don't worry. I don't think they realized Emily and I were Americans. Anti-American sentiment does seem to be a problem, though," Marnie said. "But I'm glad to be here and glad for Emily to see it, too."

The others at the table—two couples and a single doctor—drew them into their conversation. "Your wife's going with us today to meet with the Ukrainian National Women's Group," one of the women told Ben. Since Ben, Marnie, and Emily usually sat together for breakfast and dinner, others in the group had made certain assumptions, which no one—not even Emily—bothered to correct.

Marnie had written in her journal, "I am seeing a whole new side of Ben here. He's the man in charge, the speaker, and even the life of the party. That he is dashingly dark and handsome is merely a bonus."

Having completed his late-morning lecture on the sanctity of life, Ben stood amidst a sea of inquiring physicians and professors, all wanting to ask more about his topic. He felt his stomach growl.

"Dr. McKay?" A deep voice, with a strong Ukrainian accent, addressed him from behind. He turned to find

Dr. Gennadi Pereideri, the Ukrainian director of health—the equivalent of the U.S. surgeon general.

"Gennadi!" Ben extended his hand, but the doctor pulled him into the traditional Russian bear hug, complete with stereo cheek kisses.

Through Vladimir, his translator, Dr. Pereideri said, "I am sorry I could not hear your lecture—I'm sure it was excellent. But I had one of my own to deliver." The two physicians had met on Ben's prior trip to organize the conference.

"*No* problem," Ben assured him. Ben excused himself from the crowd of disappointed physicians and stepped to the side of the room with the health director. "I was hoping I'd see you today!" he told Dr. Pereideri, who had been out of town for the first few days of the conference. Ben waited for Vladimir to relay his message, then added, "I've brought some supplies for you. If we could go by the front entrance, I've checked the bag there." Ben had brought a suitcase full of pharmaceuticals to give to Dr. Pereideri, but he hadn't expected to deliver them personally.

The Ukrainian doctor smiled and nodded gratefully. "Then, please, I want you to visit the First Clinic. It is downtown!"

Ben had a few free hours before his afternoon session and very much wanted to see the clinic, but he needed a good meal first. Anticipating this, Vladimir the translator assured him, "We have lunch in Dr. Pereideri's office at clinic. They expect you. Car is outside."

The three men walked down the hall to the front of the Polytechnic Institute building, where Ben had left the suitcase of pharmaceuticals. Once Ben had retrieved the case, Vladimir took it from him to carry. The young translator showed no signs of strain, but Ben empathized as they made the long trek back through the building to the car.

"Sorry. That bag's about seventy pounds," Ben apologized.

"Oh! Expensive luggage!" Vladimir exclaimed.

Ben looked puzzled. Then he realized that Vladimir had learned the Queen's English and heard "money" instead of "weight" when he'd said "pounds." Concerned that Vladimir might think him an arrogant American bragging about his costly luggage, Ben cleared up the misunderstanding, and both men laughed. Then Vladimir turned to explain to his puzzled boss what they had found so amusing.

On the way to the clinic, Vladimir seemed eager to keep the conversation alive, obviously enjoying his role as the only one present who understood everything said by both the important doctors. Ben wanted Dr. Pereideri to focus on his driving and steered the conversation toward Vladimir. Still, more than once, Ben looked down at his own white knuckles and prayed for protection as the car zoomed through the streets of Kiev.

After fifteen minutes, Dr. Pereideri pointed to a large building, and Vladimir said, "Our clinic." The pride on both men's faces made Ben take a mental note to express appropriate gratitude to his hosts before the end of the afternoon.

Once inside, Dr. Pereideri took the suitcase from his translator. Standing almost too close to Ben, he looked up at him and humbly said, *"Spaciba."* Then he disappeared momentarily with the bag.

Ben gazed at the high gray marble walls and wide hall-
ways. "Very impressive." Vladimir smiled and nodded.

Dr. Pereideri rejoined them, and they began their
tour. Along the hallway, they passed several physicians
wearing the tall white hats that identify Ukrainian doctors. Some of the nurses wore colorful caps, a cheerful
contrast to what Ben had seen during his previous visits in other parts of the former USSR. As they walked
through the huge facility, Ben saw small light bulbs
hanging from cords here and there. He wondered how
anyone could practice medicine with such poor light-
ing. It was clear the workers were completely dedicated.
They walked from ward to ward, and Ben was struck
by the absence of equipment that would be readily visible and audible back home.

The supply area was lined with near-empty shelves,
and what equipment he did see was clearly antiquated.
At one end of the room stood a large glass cabinet, similar to those many Americans use to store china. "Our
pharmacy," the health director said, following Ben's
gaze. *Most Americans have more medication in their own
medicine cabinets than they have for this entire clinic,* Ben
observed. "For your gift—how can I thank you?" the
doctor spoke again through Vladimir.

"You are most welcome. God is big," Ben said, pointing upward.

This the doctor understood without help and smiled.
"Da. Bolshoi."

Vladimir excused himself to use the rest room, and
Ben and Dr. Pereideri struggled to discuss different treatment options through a bilingual physician who had
stopped to introduce himself. Ben had studied Russian,

but the highly complex vocabulary of medicine proved beyond his grasp. However, he did notice a similarity in many of the medical terms because of shared Latin roots.

On Vladimir's return, Dr. Pereideri told Ben, "And now to the women and children's building." Ben smiled. His friend had known what would interest him the most as an obstetrician and had saved the best for last.

Vladimir continued his running translation as the three men stepped into the dimly lit rooms. Dr. Pereideri began, "This is our obstetrical ward. We deliver four to five hundred babies per month. A very active service," he said proudly. As they moved into the labor and de-livery area, they donned scrub gowns and the required shoe covers, cloth boots that reached to the knee. Then Dr. Pereideri solemnly presented Ben with one of the starched white hats. It looked a bit like Abe Lincoln's stovepipe, but Ben appreciated the gesture of respect and professional courtesy, even if he felt a little silly.

The men approached the door of an operating room, where Dr. Maria Kutzenkova, chief of the obstetrical department, had begun a scheduled C-section. "For pregnancy-induced hypertension," the translator relayed from the surgeon. Ben noticed that the main operating room had two operating tables, side by side. Wide-open windows allowed in smoke from the outside. Ben looked around but saw no disposable paper draping or tow-els—only white cotton, some of which was now stained with the patient's blood. The nurse had carefully counted the used sponges and was now stretching them out on the floor.

Dr. Kutzenkova was meticulously incising the patient's

abdominal wall. She looked up only briefly to extend her greetings.

As the men returned to the hallway, a nurse burst out of a nearby room shouting and gesturing so fast that Ben could only look on in amazement. She ran past the small group and pushed into the operating room they had just left, calling loudly to Dr. Kutzenkova. Ben caught Vladimir's eye and raised a questioning eyebrow.

The translator pointed toward the door of a room just down the hall and whispered, "Trouble with delivery. The junior physician cannot get baby delivered. All other staff are attending conference. They need help, but Dr. Kutzenkova cannot leave her patient."

Pereideri's an internist! Ben recalled. *He's unlikely to offer much help in an obstetrical emergency.* "Would you ask Dr. Pereideri if I might be of some assistance?" Ben spoke quietly to Vladimir. He felt his heart rate elevating.

As Vladimir translated, Ben could read the health director's reluctance. Meanwhile, the nurse kept shouting in desperation that the doctor needed help.

Finally, Dr. Pereideri shrugged, then motioned to Ben, explaining quickly to the nurse that Ben was an American doctor, an "expert" in obstetrics. The nurse grabbed Ben's arm and escorted him into the delivery room, with Dr. Pereideri and Vladimir close behind.

Inside the delivery room, Dr. Sergei Bogdanov greeted the newcomers with a panicked look. It took Ben only a few seconds to recognize the "turtle sign"— when the baby's head has delivered but "sucks back" up against the woman's bottom because the shoulders won't fit through the bony pelvis. The patient, a large woman, was trying with all her might to push. Despite verbal encouragement from the anesthesiologist, the woman's efforts did little good. As Ben approached the side of the table, Dr. Pereideri stepped up on the other side and started pushing hard on the woman's abdomen above the navel, while Dr. Bogdanov manipulated the baby's head from below.

Ben knew that this intervention would make a bad situation worse. He glanced at the baby's face. Blue. *We're in trouble here. Oh, Lord, have mercy! This is going to be a big, big baby.* "How long's the head been out?" he asked.

Chapter Seventeen

VLADIMIR, COMPLETELY UNACCUSTOMED to such a scene, stood in the corner staring. When his wife had given birth, he'd remained outside, as did most Ukrainian husbands. Because of overcrowding inside the hospital, fathers would actually be waiting out on the sidewalk until they heard "It's a boy" or "It's a girl" shouted out the window. Suddenly realizing that Ben was depending on him for an answer, Vladimir repeated the question in Russian and then translated for Ben. "The head has been out three or four minutes already."

Nodding that he understood, Ben gently removed Dr. Pereideri's hands from the woman's abdomen and motioned for him to lift the patient's leg from the stirrup and rotate it back toward her shoulders, while Ben lifted the woman's other leg. Having rotated the mother's pelvis as far as they could, Ben applied firm pressure above the patient's pubic bone, while Dr. Bogdanov tried again to free the baby's forward shoulder in the birth canal.

For a moment, Ben thought he saw a flicker of relief
in Dr. Bogdanov's eyes, but then the young obstetrician
shook his head. Ben's heart sank, but he nodded his readi-
ness to move to the next option. Still holding the mother's
legs way up to her chest, he tapped on Dr. Bogdanov's
arm with his finger, then pointed to the trapped baby.
The Ukrainian doctor began trying to free its posterior
arm. Ben knew that if the doctor could free the baby's
shoulder, he could then rotate the infant in corkscrew
fashion to relieve the shoulder dystocia.

Unfortunately, they had little time. A quick listen with
the handheld Doppler instrument showed that the
baby's heartbeat had fallen to around sixty beats per
minute—less than half of normal. Although the technique they were trying risked fracturing the baby's arm
or clavicle, the consequence of further delay in the delivery could be permanent brain damage or even death.

Dr. Bogdanov stood in a full sweat now, his hands
shaking from the pressure and the tight fit in the birth
canal. "Nyet," he muttered, shaking his head. His eyes
betrayed his terror. With a note of urgency rising in his
voice, Dr. Bogdanov looked at Ben and spoke a single
word. Ben looked at Vladimir, but the young translator
shrugged and simply repeated the Russian word. He
didn't know the English equivalent. Ben glanced quickly
back to Dr. Bogdanov and the Ukrainian doctor pointed
to the patient's pubic bone and made a motion with
his finger.

"Oh!" Ben understood. "Symphysiotomy." He knew
that the other doctor was suggesting a procedure in
which the surgeon makes a small incision and uses a small
saw-like knife to divide the ligament that attaches in the

middle of the pubic bone. Ben looked at the clock on the wall, then back to the baby's blue, swollen face. He shook his head and said, "Zavanelli."

Unfamiliar with the word, Dr. Bogdanov looked at Vladamir, who sighed and shrugged again. Ben repeated the word "Zavanelli" slowly, then motioned for Dr. Bogdanov to push the baby's head back into the birth canal. Ben could tell by the young doctor's eyes that if he'd ever heard of the procedure, he'd never seen it done.

Just then, too exhausted to go on, the mother stopped pushing. The fetal heart rate had grown even slower. Both doctors knew that time was running out.

Ben felt the perspiration drip down his neck. *Jesus, please! Please, Lord!* It was the only prayer that came to mind. *We're almost out of time.*

Dr. Bogdanov stepped around the table, taking Ben's place holding the mother's leg while motioning for Ben to try anything he could.

It may be too late anyway; the baby looks gone. I've never tried this, but. . . .

Without mask or gloves, Ben moved to the baby. Gently but firmly grasping it on both sides of its head, he rotated it so it faced straight down again. Then he flexed the head so the chin tucked under. With a steady, firm pressure, he pushed the baby back up into the birth canal, reversing the normal descent and rotation.

Still holding the patient's legs, Dr. Bogdanov and Dr. Pereideri watched wide-eyed as Ben held the baby's head in place inside the birth canal and motioned for the Doppler. The nurse searched briefly and found a heartbeat.

Ben listened.

No more than 40.

He closed his eyes and pleaded with God again. Then he waited to hear whether the baby's heart rate would respond. The seconds seemed eternal, but gradually the heart rate picked up. Ben smiled as the readout showed 50, 60, 80. Finally, it inched back over 100.

Dr. Bogdanov spoke crisply to the nurse and anesthesiologist. Ben understood that he wanted to perform an immediate C-section. The obstetrician then spoke to Vladimir, who heaved a sigh of relief and relayed the doctor's question to Ben. "What size gloves do you need?"

Ben smiled. "Seven and a half." Vladimir translated this request to the nurse, who moved quickly to open instruments for the operation.

This story's not over, thought Ben. *That's a long time to be out to the shoulders.* Still, the heart rate gave everyone hope as they prepared.

After the nurse poured some soap on the abdomen, the two obstetricians began operating full speed. Dr. Pereideri stepped back, available if needed. He knew his limitations outside his specialty. The scrub nurse handed the scalpel to Dr. Bogdanov, who looked Ben in the eyes and, without a word, handed him the knife.

Ben hesitated. A brief flashback to that day in the emergency room with Juli made his heart jump to his throat. He swallowed hard, took the knife, and looked at the anesthesiologist, who had just injected the pentothal and the paralyzing medication. She nodded and motioned with her hand to go ahead.

Ben made the incision with the confidence of an athlete at the top of his game. Immediately he found himself on familiar ground: skin, fat, peritoneum, and then the uterus, which appeared blue and swollen and slightly rotated to the right. As he sliced through the uterine wall, he could see that the fluid within was a deep green, meconium-stained—evidence of acute distress, but nothing more. Dr. Bogdanov relayed this information to the nurse and to the pediatrician who had been called to the operating room.

Ben reached in, cradled the baby's huge head in his hand, and delivered it through the incision. Dr. Bogdanov quickly used the suction bulb, trying to clear any secretions, but they had no time to waste. With the Ukrainian physician pushing on the top of the uterus and Ben guiding the baby out, they accomplished the delivery.

Cord clamped. Cut. They heard no sound from the lifeless blue baby. The room fell silent. Ben placed his hand on the infant's chest and felt the heartbeat.

"Heart good," he said in fractured Russian as he handed the baby to the pediatrician. As the baby changed hands, Ben glanced down and noticed the sex.

It's a girl! He gasped slightly, then swallowed hard, fighting back tears.

Dr. Kutzenkova, who had completed her operation in the other room, now pushed through the doors to assess the situation. Dr. Bogdanov gave her a report while the resuscitation efforts on the baby moved ahead with full force. The senior surgeon's eyes met Ben's, and they exchanged the knowing look of warriors who have fought the same battle. Ben smiled at her and spoke to Vladimir. "Tell her Dr. Bogdanov was great."

From the other side of the room, a faint sound caught their attention. It developed into a slight whimper, then a cry, then a lusty wail. The baby had responded. She was alive!

Dr. Kutzenkova did a short scrub, regowned, gloved, and stepped in to relieve Ben, who had continued to assist Dr. Bogdanov with the mother. Having controlled the bleeding, Dr. Bogdanov was busy suturing the uterine incision. Pausing for a moment, he reached over and grasped Ben's gloved hand firmly. The look in his eyes conveyed a gratitude beyond words.

Ben pulled off his gloves and stepped back from the table. Walking over near the warmer where the pediatric team continued to work with the baby, he became conscious of his own heart rate. He felt both energized and exhausted.

I just delivered this baby.

A fresh wave of emotion rose in him as he watched the baby's chest moving steadily. Up . . . down . . . up . . . down.

She must weigh over ten pounds. I can't believe she looks so good. I can't believe she's alive!

He searched the little girl's face for damage, but instead saw her slowly beginning to turn pink. Though still swollen from her eventful journey into the world, she seemed fine. Ben continued to watch in silence as her condition improved by the minute. He didn't realize that fresh tears were staining his face until he impulsively reached up to wipe them with the back of his hand. Dr. Pereideri came over and wrapped a beefy arm around him. The Ukrainian doctor laughed, saying something with great conviction. Ben looked to Vladimir who chuckled and motioned toward Dr. Pereideri. "He said, 'This is why I didn't go into obstetrics.'"

This is why I did, thought Ben.

The mother still lay unconscious as the nurse prepared to move her to recovery. As Dr. Bogdanov pulled off his mask and gloves, he flashed Ben an enormous smile. He walked over to him and wrapped him in an embrace exclaiming, "Doctor, *spaciba!*" Ben returned the hug, saying, "You are most welcome!" in his best Russian.

Having assessed the two patients, Ben now turned his thoughts to his own state of health. He felt energized. *I've come through this surgery in pretty good shape, too. Thank you, Father. This came close to ending so differently for all of us.*

"Hungry?" Vladimir tapped Ben on the arm.

"Not any more!" the American doctor laughed.

"Me, either," agreed Vladimir. "Maybe next year."

At first Ben thought he might have misunderstood, but Vladimir's chuckle told him he'd intended the hyperbole.

The translator was quiet for a moment, then he asked Ben, "Tell me, Doctor. How do you spell 'symphysiotomy' and 'Zavanelli'?" He pronounced the words perfectly.

Ben sensed Vladimir's sense of failure and answered his heart, not his question. Looking him straight in the eyes, he said, "Vladimir, in a hundred years of English class, you would *never* have learned those words. Your English was flawless. I couldn't have done it without you."

Vladimir looked at his feet and breathed quietly, "Thank you. Thank you, Doctor."

Dr. Pereideri got the two men's attention and motioned them to the door. They left the operating room and walked to the health director's office, where someone had prepared for their arrival with an impressive spread of fruit and tea. Dr. Pereideri went to the cabinet behind his desk and pulled out a bottle. He filled several shot glasses, then handed one to Ben with great ceremony.

"What is this?" Ben asked Vladimir.

Dr. Pereideri smiled. In Russian-flavored English he answered, "Balzam. For 'medicinal purposes.'"

Ben nodded to his host and raised the glass to his lips. *Now I know what turpentine must taste like!* he thought as the fiery liquid burned its way down his throat. He discreetly caught his breath, then smiled and thanked his host. There was a quiet knock at the door and Dr. Bogdanov and Dr. Kutzenkova joined the celebration. The younger doctor gestured dramatically as he spoke to Dr. Pereideri. Ben, who was feeling the warming effects of the shot of balzam on an empty stomach, paid no attention until he heard Vladimir clear his throat.

"Excuse me, Doctor."

"Yes?"

"That would be almost twelve pounds. Yes. Twelve pounds baby." Ben's eyes widened and he shook his head. "Incredible!" he said in Russian, and they all laughed.

Vladimir clarified, "That would be weight, not cost, Doctor." The two men laughed again, not bothering to share their joke with the others.

As the celebration wound down and the Ukrainian doctors became engaged in clinic talk that excluded Ben, he turned to the translator and asked quietly, "Do you have a Bible, Vladimir?"

"No. I am atheist . . . until today, Doctor."

"That delivery *was* pretty amazing. God truly worked."

"Nyet. I mean your kindness, Doctor. You are Christian, yes?"

"Yes, I am." Ben, touched by this remark, smiled gently and reached into his coat pocket. He pulled out a tiny New Testament with a Russian tract tucked inside and handed them to Vladimir. The young man nodded deeply and reached to receive the gifts.

"I want you to have this, Vladimir. The best place to start is John's gospel, which I've marked with this tract." The doctor spent a few moments explaining to the translator how to get the most from his reading.

"Thank you, Doctor. You are so kind. I am honored. Of course I will read it." Vladimir handed Ben a pen and asked him to sign the Bible. He spelled out his own name, signaling that he wanted an inscription. He watched closely as Ben wrote.

"But, we must go!" Dr. Pereideri announced. Having forgotten for the last hour that any other world existed, Ben glanced at his watch and realized he'd barely make it back in time for his next lecture. Fortunately, this would be the fourth time he'd given this particular talk, so he had the outline practically memorized.

"Before we go, however, we have gift for you, Dr. Ben McKay." The three physicians ceremoniously presented him with a watercolor painting. "This is scene of St. Sophie's, Kiev's most famous monastery," Vladimir explained.

Ben received it gratefully. *"Spaciba.* It is beautiful." He spoke in Russian, and the doctors seemed delighted that he liked the painting. "I have had a most memorable day at your fine clinic. Thank you so much for inviting me here. And thank you for allowing me to share in your work. God bless you!"

After another round of generous thank yous, both for the medications and for his help in the delivery room, the doctors bid Ben good-bye. Ben hunkered down in the car to endure another white-knuckle ride, this time back to the Polytechnic Institute.

Back at the lecture hall, Ben and Vladimir hustled across the parking lot and headed for the Institute's grand hallway. Marnie and Emily were standing just inside the front doors with a group that had spent the morning together visiting an orphanage. Marnie had been comparing notes about their trip with other group members when she saw Ben coming up the steps.

She walked to the door and opened it, greeting him warmly. "How's it going? Where've ya been?"

Ben grabbed her shoulder and gave it a spontaneous squeeze. "Trying out a new procedure at the hospital," he grinned.

"What? Really?"

"One he wishes not to repeat soon, I think," Vladimir offered with a chuckle.

With no time to spare before Ben's scheduled talk, the two men excused themselves and headed for the lecture room. Marnie watched, smiling and shaking her head, as they went. Before he rounded the corner into the hallway, Ben turned back, pointed at her and said, "Dinner cruise on the Dnieper River tonight. Be there!" Then he winked, turned, and walked off to talk about reproductive technologies.

As the dinner boat cruised the river, Marnie was content to eat her meal quietly and watch Ben having a good time with the other doctors. She had encouraged him just to enjoy the company of his colleagues without feeling the need to translate for her. She and Emily sat at the table with him—and with Vladimir and several Ukrainian doctors, including Dr. Pereideri. There was a Canadian couple there as well who had a daughter Emily's age. They engaged her in conversation, wanting to know all about her Ukrainian experiences. Midway through dinner, Dr. Pereideri told a story bragging on Ben—that much Marnie could deduce—which drew admiring "ooohs" and "ahhs" from the other doctors, who raised their glasses and toasted "Zavanelli." Then Vladimir added a few comments, which made Ben throw back his head and laugh heartily. Marnie had never seen Ben so joyous and full of life.

After dinner, he looked over at her and asked, "Want to walk the deck?"

The Canadians motioned for her to go, saying they would keep an eye on Emily, so Ben and Marnie excused themselves and strolled to the back of the boat. Alone together for the first time since the trip began, they leaned on the rail and watched the moonlight dancing on the water.

"Where's the North Star?" Marnie asked, turning her attention to the sky. As she looked up, she unintentionally leaned back against Ben's chest.

Ben put his hand on her shoulder and pointed with his other hand. "There it is."

As Marnie peered into the evening sky, Ben became more conscious of his elevating heart rate than the stars. The motion of the gently rocking boat caused Marnie's shoulders to sink more completely against Ben's chest. He inhaled her fragrance and touched his lips to her hair.

When Marnie didn't move away, Ben moved his arm off her shoulder and ran it gently down her arm. He picked up her hand in his, touched his fingertips to hers and said quietly, "Did you know there are five million touch receptors in each fingertip?"

"Mmm, that's nice—and only a doctor would talk about nerve fibers in such a romantic setting!"

They both enjoyed the moment. "I love having you here, Marnichka," Ben murmured softly in her ear.

"I love being here." Marnie leaned her head back against him, intentionally now. She continued to look at the sky, and Ben tilted his head to gaze down at her profile. He noticed that her breathing increased slightly as she settled back fully against his chest.

What a gorgeous neck . . . beautiful ear . . . pretty earrings. Remarkable lips—I'd love to kiss them.

As his thoughts began to drift toward temptation, Ben caught himself and redirected his focus to enjoying her perfume, the sensation of her hair against his lips, and the press of her back against his chest.

"Actually, I mean, I love being with *you,* Benichek," Marnie's eyes had a dreamy look.

A loud crash behind them startled them apart, and they turned to see a young waiter scrambling to pick up the shattered remains of china from the tray he had just dropped. They turned back to look at the river as the boat approached a suspension bridge. "Nice bridge," Ben said as they floated beneath it. He was momentarily embarrassed by his own vulnerability.

Marnie drew a deep breath, and it seemed to Ben that she was trying to regain her composure. The breeze blew a strand of hair into her mouth as she opened it to speak. Pulling it back and looping it behind her ear, she said, "May I ask you a question?"

"Sure."

Marnie hesitated, then asked, "What's a Zavanelli?"

"Is that really what you wanted to ask me?"

"Honestly? No," Marnie smiled. "But why don't you go ahead and answer it."

Ben looked down at the water, taking his time in answering. "It's a medical maneuver named after a Dr. Zavanelli. I'd never done it, but I was forced to use it today when I visited the hospital."

His eyes met hers. "I delivered my first baby in six years today. A little girl."

Chapter Eighteen

As he bid Marnie and Emily good night at the door to their hotel room, Ben told Marnie, "In the morning, be sure to pack some snacks and get some bottled water. You can't buy any decent food or decaf drinks on the train to St. Petersburg." Their group was scheduled to leave the next afternoon on an eight-hour train ride to the capital city of the old Russian empire for three days of touring before heading back to the United States.

Marnie nodded. "Bottled water. Good to know, thanks. So we have a free day until we leave?"

"Uh-huh. But before we go, I'm dropping in at the hospital to check on the new mom and baby. I'm meeting Dr. Bogdanov at ten. Would you and Emily like to come with me?"

Marnie and Emily looked at each other. "Sure!" they answered in unison.

Once Emily was tucked in, Marnie did some light reading, then opened one of the windows several inches and turned out the light. She curled up and made herself comfortable, but she couldn't sleep. Instead, she lay hugging the feather pillow and staring at the curtain swaying in the breeze. Her mind kept drifting back to how it felt having Ben's lips so close to her ear. She could almost still feel the touch of his fingertips, his chest against her back, his voice saying he loved having her there. On a night like tonight, she could almost believe that he felt the same way about her that she felt about him. But then she couldn't shake her fear that his interest in her was purely spiritual and that she was letting herself care way too deeply.

Across the hall, Ben lay on his back on top of the covers, staring at the ceiling. He tried to remember the last time he'd been that close to a woman. Marnie had rekindled strong desires in him that he hadn't felt in a long time—desires and feelings he had wondered if he ever would feel again.

He pictured them together—with more time, more privacy—and wondered if she felt the same way. He wondered how she might like to be kissed . . . if such an opportunity would one day present itself. As his imagination began to run free, he caught himself. *I better quit this or I'll need a cold shower—which is the only kind of shower they have in this hotel anyway!*

On their last morning in Kiev, Ben, Marnie, and Emily flagged down a cab and sped off to the First Clinic. Dr. Bogdanov met them at the door and ushered them into the director's office, where white starched hats, cloth boots, and cotton gowns awaited them. "Usually, we do not allow children on the ward, but you are honored guests, and today we make exception," he managed in passable but heavily accented English.

The doctor handed Emily a child's gown and asked Ben to carry her. From there, he led the way up to the women and children's wing, stopping briefly to let everyone gaze through the window into the newborn nursery.

Emily stared at the ten tightly wrapped linen bundles—four blue and six pink—arrayed in functional glass bassinets. "Don't they wish they could move their arms and legs?" she asked Ben.

"I don't think so, Emilichka."

Emily flashed him a big smile, and he continued. "They seem to like being bound up snug." The four onlookers watched as a nurse picked up a crying pink package—unwrapping, changing, and rewrapping it in mere seconds.

"She's fast," Marnie observed.

"Probably does it a hundred times a day," Ben said. Then he looked over at Dr. Bogdanov. "Which one is 'our' baby?"

Dr. Bogdanov pointed to one of the bassinets where a rosy little face, with eyes squeezed shut against the light, protruded above the pink cloth wrappings. They all admired her tiny lips as she moved them slightly in her sleep. After a moment, the doctor motioned for his visitors to proceed. He led them to the room where the exhausted mother lay resting.

Awakening her abruptly, Dr. Bogdanov spoke, motioning to Ben with the word "Doktor" and to Marnie with "Journaliska." Marnie took Emily from Ben's arms, and the patient nodded her greeting to both, then rested her eyes back on Ben with a look of deep gratitude. She reached out her hand to him and spoke in a gentle tone. The only part Marnie understood was *"Spaciba, Doktor."* Ben held the patient's hand in both of his, nodded deeply, then gestured to Dr. Bogdanov.

"What did she say?" Emily wanted to know.

"She's thanking us for saving her baby's life," Ben said to Emily without taking his eyes off the woman.

"You saved her baby's life? Wow." Emily looked at Ben with fascination.

Just then, one of the physicians who had joined them on the cruise stuck his head in the door. "Doktor McKay!"

Ben looked up and waved.

The Ukrainian doctor held up his hand in an imaginary toast and said, "Zavanelli!"

Luc propped his feet up on his desk after returning from evening rounds. He sat sipping on a diet soft drink, looking at a patient's chart, and trying to determine the amount of medication to prescribe. Then he picked up the phone.

The force of a sudden blast threw him hard across the room. He hit the bookshelves with his knee and shoulder as his head slammed against the floor. A sharp pain stabbed through his side and he grimaced as he struggled to bring his breathing under control.

He wasn't sure if he had blacked out, but when he suddenly tasted smoke, he realized that the place was on fire. Blinking his eyes rapidly a few times, he wondered how long he'd been dazed. As he regained full use of his senses, he coughed hard and thought to himself, *I'd better get out of here—and fast.*

He felt excruciating pain in his leg. A file cabinet full of charts had fallen on him, pinning his knee and thigh. Yelling in agony, he pulled his leg free. He was pretty sure it was broken.

Flames covered the wall, and he knew that, even if he could climb to the windows in his office, they were sealed for security purposes. His only hope was to crawl into the hallway and try to find his way to the doctors' entrance—a small corridor beside his office that led to the front corner of the building. He had often used it for discreet entrances and exits.

The blast had knocked out the electricity, and flames lit the room. He dragged himself across the carpet to the open door, wishing he could plug his ears to screen out the drone of the smoke alarm. He looked down the hallway toward the lab. Red and orange light flickered along the walls, signaling an inferno in the making. He felt the heat of the growing blaze on his back as he crawled away, skirting pieces of debris from the blast, and keeping his mouth and nose to the ground to avoid the heavy smoke.

When he got within ten feet of the outside door, a second, smaller explosion dazed him again. When he was able to focus, he saw that a mangled metal stool had landed in the hallway in front of him. Lying on his side, he grasped it with both hands to shove it to the side. The hot metal seared his palms and fingertips, and he screamed in agony. He lay still momentarily, squeezing his eyes and holding his breath in pain. Then he struggled out of his lab coat and used it to cover his burned hands as he grasped the stool and hurled it out of the way. Struggling at last to the door, he grasped the handle and inched his way out on the ground.

Luc heard the sound of sirens and saw a crowd gathering. A man ran up and dragged him away from the building, which was now fully aflame. Luc blacked out from the pain.

When he awakened, two paramedics stood over him, trying to determine his condition. They asked if he knew of any others in the building. As the medics air-splinted his leg and started an IV, Luc heard one of them express concern about a significant concealed hemorrhage from a possible fracture of the femur. They braced his dislocated arm and loaded him into the ambulance. Luc looked back in a daze of pain and watched as the roof of the clinic slowly collapsed into the fiery blaze.

"Why don't you go home and get some good rest?" the nurse asked Leigh Rivera. Though she had been at the hospital since the twins had been admitted, the medical staff had limited her visiting hours in the pediatric ICU. She'd had comparatively little time with her girls and had hardly slept for days—yet she refused to leave. She couldn't remember the last time she'd eaten a meal from anywhere other than the hospital cafeteria or vending machines. And the complete lack of any encouraging news reflected itself in her washed-out countenance and red-rimmed eyes.

Leigh glanced up at the nurse and smiled wanly. "Thanks, but they need me," she said quietly, motioning toward the door to the ICU.

The nurse patted her shoulder and nodded, then disappeared-.

The mayor's schedule had prevented him from visiting for the past three days, so Leigh had kept vigil by herself. With a chemotherapy regimen fully underway, the babies now had zero resistance to any kind of infection. The mask, cap, gown, and glove routine had become critically important. For all her efforts, Leigh had no idea if her babies knew she was there. Her songs, caresses, and coos brought no response.

Amid the professional detachment of the medical staff, Leigh felt isolated. As the days stretched on with no discernible change in the twins' condition, the physicians had stopped talking to her. The nurses also said little. Though Leigh spoke fairly fluent Spanish, the staff seemed intimidated by her status and obvious Anglo appearance.

Nobody cares. I haven't slept—not really—in weeks. My babies are dying. I don't have one good reason to go on. I must be strong for the twins. They need me. But if they don't make it, what's the point?

Marnie, Emily, and Ben enjoyed their day at the Hermitage Museum. Marnie focused on the intricate mosaics and the Picassos, while Ben and Emily were more taken with the Rembrandts, especially *The Return of the Prodigal Son*. At seven o'clock, after quickly freshening up back in their rooms, they hurried off to the ballet, where Emily fell asleep during the second act.

By ten, when they arrived back at the hotel for dinner, they were famished. Though the meal was one of the better ones they'd had on the trip, everyone rushed to finish, because they wanted to get plenty of rest for another full day ahead, starting with the Peter and Paul Fortress at eight in the morning.

As the waiters were pouring coffee, Marnie stood and excused herself from the table. "I need to take Emily back to the room. She's exhausted."

The others at the table bid them good night, but Ben said, "Bummer. I was hoping we could at least enjoy dessert together—if not a chat in the lobby afterward."

"Sorry," Marnie said with genuine disappointment.

"That's okay," Ben replied. "Leave us if you must. Duty calls."

"Good night, everyone," Marnie smiled. She squeezed Ben's shoulder, then helped Emily out of her seat and guided her toward the door.

Once Emily was settled for the night, Marnie showered, and then pulled out her phone card to call her father. She had promised to touch base with him and confirm their return flight information. They would be home in three days, and he would meet them at the airport.

Forty minutes after Marnie and Emily had left the restaurant, Ben returned to his room and got ready for bed. He had just dozed off when he heard a knock on the door. Pulling his slacks back on as he walked across the room, he opened the door to find Marnie standing there, looking alarmed.

"What is it? What's wrong?" He squinted against the light in the hall and felt suddenly self-conscious that he wasn't wearing a shirt.

"I just talked to my dad. Luc's in the hospital."

"What?"

"Ben, somebody bombed the clinic. It's totally destroyed."

"What? When?" Ben, now fully awake, started firing questions at her, then stopped himself. "Wait, come on in and sit down. You don't have to stand out there." He reached over and turned on the room light and opened the door so it rested against the wall. "We can leave this open so you'll hear Emily if she wakes up."

Marnie followed Ben into the room, looking away while he threw on a tee shirt. Then she sat knee-to-knee with him on the narrow Russian twin beds and told him everything she knew, which was only the little bit that Will had read in the newspaper.

"I have to get back there," Ben said. "I wonder if there's a flight out tomorrow morning. I could probably get one through Frankfurt."

Marnie nodded. "I told Dad we'd probably come back early."

"You don't have to come with me, Marnie. There's

no reason for you to cut short your time here. There's nothing you can do for Luc. Emily will. . . ."

Ben stopped short when he saw tears fill Marnie's eyes. He'd said the wrong thing. Searching her face, he tried to figure out whether it was the bombing of the clinic that had upset her or his words.

"I don't want to stay here without you," Marnie told him.

Ben was touched, and he smiled tenderly. "Good. Because I'd rather have you with me." He stood and drew her into his arms. "Okay?"

Marnie nodded and seemed content to have him hold her for several minutes.

Finally, she looked up at him. "Ben, I'm scared. What are the odds that two doctors from the same clinic. . . ."

The sensation of having Marnie's face so close to his made him momentarily deaf to what she had said. But recognizing her fear, he responded. "I know. It *is* scary." Cradling the back of her neck, he leaned down and rested his cheek next to hers. The warmth and moisture of her face brought him a deep sense of contentment.

Marnie sniffled and held on tightly. Ben waited until he was sure she was okay before speaking. Then he wiped her tears with his hand. "Let's see what we can find out," he told her. "Is it all right with you if we leave in a few hours—assuming we can get a flight?"

Marnie nodded again. "Are *you* okay?" she asked, searching his eyes. "I mean, Luc's your best friend. You're a part owner in the clinic. You've already lost one partner. That's a lot to deal with."

"Yeah, I'm okay, Marnie. And I'm really, really glad you're here. It takes some of the sting out of the news.

Thanks for asking." Ben felt a warm sensation inside his chest. He was accustomed to taking care of others, but it had been a long time since anyone had been concerned about *his* feelings. He offered a tired smile, pulled Marnie close again, and guided her head to lean on his chest. "This is nice."

"Do I have to let you go?" Marnie asked.

By four in the morning, the three travelers were on their way to the airport.

"I want to sit next to the window," a yawning Emily said as they boarded the plane after an hour in customs. Marnie followed her daughter and slid into the middle seat, while Ben took the one on the aisle. They settled in quickly with pillows and blankets from the flight attendant, and Emily was back asleep before the plane even took off.

As the jet taxied out onto the runway, Marnie leaned her head back to rest. Before long, she drifted off to sleep, and her head strayed over onto Ben's shoulder. With appreciative eyes, he looked down at her face as she dozed. *Such long, dark eyelashes. She looks so sweet and peaceful.* Leaning forward, Ben kissed her tenderly on the forehead. Marnie's eyes remained closed, but she smiled and snuggled in closer.

When Dr. Allan Brown read the *Washington Post* website story about the explosion at the IVF clinic, he threw his empty coffee mug against the wall of his Dallas office. The article identified the injured Dr. Luc Morgan as a physician currently involved in a lawsuit involving an international dignitary. It also alluded to his partnership with President Sullivan's deceased nephew. An initial investigation revealed that the bomb, which had been placed in an air-conditioning unit outside the back wall of the lab, had been detonated using a complex timing device. Allan picked up the phone and called his contact at the FBI.

"We had absolutely no prior knowledge about the bombing," he was told. "Some pro-life group did it. Claimed they didn't like the clinic's embryo policy."

"That's so lame," Allan snorted. "If their beef is that life begins at the moment of fertilization, why would they blow up the lab and destroy all the frozen embryos?"

"That's the report I have," the FBI agent replied flatly.

Allan rolled his eyes and gritted his teeth. "I'll tell you this—and listen good. You'd better not mess with *her*."

"Then perhaps you can find a way to make sure she remains quiet. Your work has top security clearance. We can't let anything stand in the way of your research, and any kind of leak would jeopardize the project, you understand."

"I mean it. You'd better keep her out of this."

"Then see that she remains quiet."

When Will met the weary threesome at the airport late the following afternoon, he suppressed the urge to ask Emily all about her trip. He knew that his daughter, ever the journalist, would want to grill him about Luc. As they stood waiting for their bags, Will told them as much as he knew. "The clinic's destroyed. Luc's out of commission for at least several months, but apparently he'll be okay. I'm not exactly sure about his injuries, but the paper said he was in stable condition and expected to make a full recovery." He looked at Ben. "All the newshounds are claiming you guys were targeted because of your frozen-embryo policy."

"The media? Never trust 'em," Marnie quipped, trying to lighten the somber mood.

As they watched the bags circle the carousel, Ben and Marnie exchanged looks that said they were both sorry to see this trip end. A few minutes later, as Will and Emily led the way to the car with the baggage cart, the couple lagged a few paces behind. "It was a great trip until last night, Marnie. Marnichka. Or perhaps you prefer the French, Grand Marnier."

Marnie smiled.

"I'm so glad you came," Ben continued as they walked. "And you sure made the flight home a lot more bearable." He looked over at her and added, "This may be the end of the trip, but I hope it's the beginning of a journey."

Marnie raised her eyebrows and nodded with a smile. "I hope so too," she answered softly. "Marnier and McKay. Sounds like a good team."

"The best."

They continued silently across the parking lot to Will's

car before Ben spoke again. "I'm gonna go home and shower, then head out to the hospital to see Luc. I'll call you later if you think you'll still be up."

"If not, go ahead and wake me. I want to know how Luc is, and I'd sure like to have some clue about what's going on."

"I could e-mail you."

"I'd rather hear your voice."

Ben reached over and pulled her closer in a side-to-side hug. "Oooh, good answer," he said.

Chapter Nineteen

MARNIE HAD THROWN IN A LOAD of laundry and finished going through the bills and letters when she decided to check her e-mail. After logging on, she scrolled through about fifty messages. Suddenly a dialog box opened on her screen: "Will you accept a message from Humpty Dumpty, unknowndomain@unknown.com? Yes? No?"

What an odd joke. She clicked "yes" out of curiosity. Immediately, a message appeared.

HumptyDumpty: Hey Aurora! Been watching for you to come on-line.

Marnie's heart jumped, and her mind went aswirl with questions. She typed, "Who is this?"

HumptyDumpty: Humpty Dumpty swims!

Marina106: Who are you?

HumptyDumpty: Uncle Cal's nephew. Honest.

Marina106: You're scaring me.

HumptyDumpty: Aurora, you need to get to Dallas tomorrow for a few days. Don't bring Emily. Can't write details. American flight at 7:03 tomorrow morning out of Reagan National. Tickets waiting for you at the counter. I'll explain it all when you get here. Gotta go. Could be traced. Erase this! Tell no one.

Because Luc was an esteemed staff physician and the hospital wanted good publicity in this high-profile case, he lay in traction in a hospital suite instead of a regular room. He had been assigned to the orthopedics floor instead of the burn unit, because his burns were less severe than his leg fracture.

Ben took the elevator up and checked in at the desk. "Good evening, Virginia," he said to the nurse. She knew him from his chaplaincy work and often directed him to patients in special need of prayer.

"Good evening, Dr. McKay. So nice to see you again. I knew you'd be up to visit Dr. Morgan before long. I'm so very sorry to hear about your clinic."

"Thank you," Ben replied with a warm smile. "Where can I find the good Dr. Luc?"

"In 714." Virginia nodded toward the hallway on the right. "He's quite a sight," she said softly.

"How's he doing?" Ben asked, leaning over the counter and dropping his voice.

"Pretty well. I'm the charge nurse tonight, so he's actually not my patient. But he seems to be doing okay."

"Thanks, Virginia. See you in a bit." Ben stepped away from the nurses' station, then turned back. "Hey, what are visiting hours around here?"

"Oh, the usual. But we're running a 'chaplain special' tonight, so you can stay as long as you like," she said chuckling. "That is, unless you get too rowdy, or the patient complains."

"Got it!" said Ben as he moved down the hall.

When he reached Room 714, Ben rapped softly on the door, hoping his good friend wasn't already asleep. He was glad to hear Luc's familiar voice, sounding relatively strong. "Come on in."

As Ben pushed open the door, the hospital smells stirred his senses—the sweet smell of the silvadene gauze that wrapped Luc's hands, the odor of burnt hair, and the medicinal scent of Hibiclens soap. He suppressed a wince when he saw Luc, who lay imprisoned by the traction apparatus surrounding the bed like a cage. His leg was pinned and suspended above him. A sling immobilized his shoulder, his hands were wrapped like mittens, and his face—that fair, handsome face—was blotchy and red, with the eyebrows singed black and almost gone. Ben realized how fortunate his friend was to be alive.

"How you feeling, old buddy?"

"I would say 'death warmed over,' but I don't do heat or fire humor anymore," Luc said with a slight grin. The first degree burns across his cheeks and nose looked like a pretty fair sunburn, and Ben knew it felt uncomfortable.

"Well, you *look* terrific," Ben replied, almost convincingly. "How's Janelle?"

"She's fine, though she worries a bit. She spent most of the day up here but went home about an hour ago to corral the kids and get the house reorganized. She's quite a trouper in the midst of crisis. Really."

"Glad to hear it. And you know I'm here to help," said Ben. "Reinforcements from Russia have arrived."

"Thanks, buddy. So how was the trip?"

"No way," Ben replied. "You think you can get out of telling me what happened?"

Just then, the evening shift nurse knocked and came into the room. "Dr. Morgan," she said, "I need to take your vital signs."

Ben relaxed in the chair beside the bed while the nurse took Luc's temperature and blood pressure, then measured the urinary output from the Foley bag hanging beside the bed.

"Can't wait until they can take the catheter out," remarked Luc.

"I'll bet," replied Ben. "But considering how much IV fluid they're pouring through you, just think how many trips to the john you've saved."

"Right. Like I'll be making any trips soon. They're planning traction here for several more weeks and then a cast all the way to Cleveland."

"Ah. A lesser man would surely complain."

"So, dial the phone. Let's call that 'lesser man,'" Luc chuckled back.

Ben was pleased that Luc still had his sense of humor. The nurse completed her examination and left the room with a cheery, "Everything looks good. Thank you, Doctor."

Ben resumed his questions as soon as the door closed. "Okay, Doc, looks like we're out of business for a while. So what happened?"

Luc motioned for his friend to come closer. The smoke he'd inhaled made it uncomfortable for him to project his voice. But he also didn't want anyone else to hear what the investigation had showed clearly. Someone had detonated the bomb at the clinic by remote control. As he explained the early findings to Ben, his partner sat in astonishment.

"Who would want to destroy the clinic?" Ben asked.

Just as he finished the question, the full impact of what had happened struck him like a bolt of lightning. "Remote control? Someone detonated it when they *knew* you were in the clinic." This thought made him shiver. He sat forward and looked Luc in the eye. "Talk to me, buddy. What are we up against here?"

Luc began, "It may just be a coincidence, but I gotta tell you—I figured out what happened in the Rivera case. Then I called Chris—you know, Chris Winston, my attorney?" Ben nodded, but remained silent. "And Chris was going to make some calls to the feds to follow up on it. Next thing I know, less than forty-eight hours later, I'm at the clinic reviewing charts and doing dictation when, *bam*. I'm splattered against the wall, and the clinic's on fire."

"Hmmm. Yeah, I drove by. There's not much left."

"We lost it all. Records, equipment, everything. All the cryopreserved material was wiped out." A faint hint of a tear began to form in Luc's eye. He eased his head back into the pillow.

Ben gave him a moment and then asked, "So what *is* the Rivera story? Tim mixed up the sperm with somebody influential?"

Luc paused, unsure whether to keep silent or share the truth—and the danger—with his friend. But, if he was right, Ben was in trouble too. "Are you ready for this? Tim was cloning eggs. Not embryos—eggs! He cloned Leigh Rivera's eggs. We ran tissue samples through the lab, and they came back saying the Rivera twins have no paternal genes—only maternal ones."

Ben's face showed his disbelief. He sat in silence for a long time. "I didn't even think that was possible. Nobody's even trying that. Cloning embryos maybe, but not *eggs*. Tim must have been trying to get stem cells to work on his akenosis project. I guess it makes sense—that is, if you don't have an ethical problem with the whole notion." He thought for a moment longer. "Do you think Rivera figured it out? Did he knock off Tim, and you were next?"

"Actually," Luc replied, "I hadn't thought of that." He lay silent for a long time. Finally he offered somewhat less confidently, "I was thinking that when Chris called the feds, what if—maybe they knew I was getting too close to some 'secret experiment.' So they wanted to shut down the clinic and shut me up."

"The government?" Ben was frowning. "You think?"

"Sure. If Tim was working on something to help the president, I'm guessing there were others doing research, too. So when Tim died, they just moved on to the next scientist."

Ben thought through Luc's theory and had to ask, "Then you don't really think Rivera is behind all this? I mean, obviously he was unhappy with his blonde twins, and the lawsuit proves he has some strong feelings about you and the clinic."

Luc shrugged.

"You think the government would go this far to protect its 'discovery'?"

"I don't know," answered Luc. "All I know is, a phone call goes to the Feds one day, I get nuked the next. If it was supposed to serve as a message, they certainly got my attention."

"But what if they really want you out of the picture?" Ben asked quietly.

"I'm afraid I won't be able to run away," Luc quipped, waving his hand at the pulley that suspended his injured leg.

"Right," said Ben. "But you can always pull the sheets up over your head, and they won't be able to see you."

Once again, laughter broke the tension in the room. Both men seemed glad to have the opportunity finally to talk over what had taken place. After they'd tossed around the apparent options, including a timely and quiet settlement of the Rivera suit—and no more calls to anyone—Ben offered to pray for Luc before leaving. He grasped his friend's good hand, undeterred by the bulky dressing. "Heavenly Father, thank you for sparing Luc's life. I'm so thankful he's here. I ask that you would give him a speedy and uneventful recovery, and I ask for full restoration of his hands. And for peaceful rest during his recuperation. . . ."

A few moments later, as Ben rose to leave, Luc asked, "Aren't you going to tell me about your trip?"

"We'll talk later when you're rested," Ben answered, then stopped and smiled a sly grin. "I've got just one word for you: Zavanelli."

"You mean the maneuver? Or some Italian actress?" Luc laughed.

"You wouldn't believe it. . . ."

Ben left the room shaking his head. As he walked down the hall, his smile evaporated, and he focused his mind on the conversation he'd just had with Luc. *If he's in danger, maybe I am too. If the Riveras are tak-ing revenge . . . and if Tim is at the center of this, what about Marnie?*

≈≈≈

"Jet lag's a killer, huh?" Will intended his comment as an expression of empathy for his daughter as she emerged from the office. "You look like someone zapped you with a stun gun."

Normally, Marnie would have rolled her eyes, but she acted as though she hadn't even heard her father. She sat down on the couch in a daze, raked her fingernails through her hair, and leaned her head back on the cushion. Noticing her father's searching eyes, she feigned interest as Emily and Will sat on the floor sorting through her travel treasures.

"This is called a *matrioshka,*" Emily told Will as she began to open layer upon layer of the Russian nesting doll.

"Dad, do you think you could keep Emily for a couple days?" Marnie asked quietly, exhaustion in her voice.

Will looked at her with surprise.

"An emergency came up in Texas while I was gone," she said. "I need to go down and handle it right away."

"Good night, child. What could possibly be so important that you can't give yourself a day to recover from being a world traveler?"

"Please, Dad." It was more a request not to argue than a request that he keep Emily.

Just then the phone rang, and Marnie walked into the next room to grab it.

"Hi, Marnie." It was Ben.

"I didn't expect to hear from you for a few more hours," she said, struggling to figure out what to tell him about Dallas.

"I decided not to wear out the patient tonight, though he looks pretty good under the circumstances."

"Uh . . . okay. Well, I need to talk to you," she said.

"I need to talk to you, too."

"Yeah, well, this is sort of an emergency. I need to go to Dallas for a few days."

"Oh. Okay. When? What's up?"

"Seven A.M. flight, tomorrow."

"What? No way! Why?"

"Something happened while I was gone. I need to take care of it right away."

Ben was silent for a moment. Then he managed to muster up some enthusiasm. "Then why don't I go with you? It's not like I have to be at work in the morning, with the clinic out of commission. And I have a few more days off from the chaplaincy. I've got a sister who lives in Dallas, and I'd love for her to meet. . . ."

"No, I need to handle this on my own," Marnie interrupted.

"What is it? Some story you're working on?"

"I really . . . uh . . . it's sort of complicated."

"Hey, I'm a gynecologist. I understand women's hormones. Nothing comes close to being *that* complicated. Try me."

Marnie sighed. "Just the paperwork alone could be a nightmare. Really, there's too much involved. . . . I'd rather not discuss it." She fought hard to stay within the truth.

"You have an emergency, and you'd rather not discuss it?" Ben's voice told her she'd done a lousy job of keeping any red flags from waving. She was too tired to pull this off well. Ben sighed. "You're sure a mysterious one, Marnichka." He was quiet for a minute, then added, "I'd sure feel better if I were close by. Why don't you let me fly down with you?"

Marnie softened. "Ben, any other time, I'd love the idea. But I really have to do this alone."

"Well, if I can't go with you, will you at least let me take you to the airport?"

"I need to leave by five-thirty in the morning, and I know you're beat. I'll just drive my—"

Ben interrupted. "Not a problem. I'll be there."

"You sure?"

"Yep. You can't shake me that easily," he said with a note of affection in his voice. "Now, since you're so set on deserting me, how long are you planning to stay gone?"

If you only knew. "Just a few days. I think."

As Marnie and Ben drove in the morning darkness to Reagan National Airport, Marnie leaned her head against the door and closed her eyes. Ben wanted to ask more questions, but he did not probe.

Her mind felt like a gerbil in a treadmill, working endlessly, going nowhere. *What if Tim is alive? What if he's not? What if it's a hoax? But how could it be? Nobody but Tim and my junior high friends called me Aurora. And who but Tim would go by Humpty Dumpty? But then, anyone at the funeral would know that part. Why would he leave like that? It must have had to do with the project he was working on. If it's really him, how could he do that to me? To Emily? To his mom? I'll kill him. Still, if he's reappeared, maybe there's a reasonable explanation. And all those unsaid words I've longed to say, the flowers he was bringing me that night. . . . Maybe we'll have the second chance I wanted.*

Continuing to rest her head, she opened her eyes and looked over at Ben for a long time. The sunrise added a faint glow to his face. *But I love this guy. He led me to Christ. I've never had a relationship like this one. My mentor. My confidant. The shoulder I've cried on. My best friend. I'm pretty sure he's finally starting to love again. And I have to tell him our "journey" has to end? Father, it doesn't seem fair.* A silent tear rolled down her cheek, taking mascara with it. She closed her eyes again. In a moment, she felt Ben reach over and tenderly wipe her tear away with his thumb.

She opened her eyes and saw on Ben's face a look that told her how he felt about her. And in that moment, she felt bottomless pain.

"You're a mysterious one, Marnie," Ben said once again as he turned the car toward the entrance for departing flights.

"You don't need to park and come in with me," she said in an insistent tone. "You can just drop me off."

He knew from the way she said it that he'd better not press the issue. So he pulled up to the curb, got out, and retrieved her bag from the trunk. As she reached out to take it, he set it on the ground and grabbed her outstretched hand instead, pulling her into a strong hug. "I'm not letting you get away that easily," he said.

She didn't even try to resist. Instead she clung to him, suppressing a sob. Finally, she stretched up and quickly kissed his cheek. "Good-bye, Ben," she said, intending to pull away.

He held her tighter. "Oh-h-h, Marnie, please be careful," he spoke into her ear.

"I will. I promise," she answered. "Pray for me."

"You know I will."

Turning her face away so he couldn't see the tears, she grabbed her bag and walked into the terminal. Ben stood watching as she went through the glass door.

Once inside, she walked up to the American ticket counter and showed her ID, suddenly wondering if there would actually be a ticket waiting for her. *I should have called. I'm too tired to think straight.* But, indeed, a paperless ticket had been purchased. Her heart was pounding so rapidly in her chest that she glanced down at her blouse to see if it was as visible as it felt.

"Now, what was the return flight on that?" Marnie asked the ticketing agent, trying to keep her voice from quivering. *I must be an idiot to be doing this. What time zone am I in, anyway?*

The agent looked at the computer screen as the ticket was printing. "It says here the twenty-third, ma'am, which is the day after tomorrow. Is that correct?" The woman raised her eyebrows and awaited an answer.

"Yes. Thank you." Marnie waited another moment for the agent to hand her the boarding pass, then she stared at it for some clue as to who had purchased it. *Nothing, of course.* She walked down the concourse to the metal detectors, passed through, and then walked slowly to the gate, deep in thought.

After watching Marnie board the plane to Dallas, Victor emerged from the seating area of the adjacent gate, bought a pretzel and left the airport. Later he reported to Carlos. "That 'good-bye' hug was more than, 'Thanks for the ride.'" Then he raised the question that Carlos had asked of him earlier. "Do you suppose Dr. McKay had something to do with Dr. Sullivan's death?"

Several hours after leaving Marnie at the airport, Ben drove to the local nursery on what had emerged as a beautiful Northern Virginia morning. He was grateful for the lack of humidity and breathed the cool air in deeply. After thirty minutes spent choosing just the right flowering rosebud plant, he backtracked to Highway 50 and made his way to the cemetery in Arlington. Entering the front gate, he wound his way slowly and solemnly through the beautiful park. Stopping on the side road closest to the graves of his wife and daughter, he got out and walked over to the concrete bench he had often occupied. He sat for a long time in the stillness, meditating and praying.

As the sun began to chase dew from the green expanse, Ben walked back to the car, got out the trowel he had brought, and picked up the plant. Returning to Juli's grave, he knelt down and dug a small hole until it was large enough for his purchase. Then, reaching into his right pocket, he pulled out his wedding ring. He held it between his thumb and index finger for a long moment, staring at his reflection in the shiny surface of the gold. Finally, he kissed the ring, placed it in the ground and gently set the rosebush on top of it. He tamped the soil down around the tiny trunk, then stood, dusted off his knees, and walked back over to the bench.

Twenty minutes later, he was ready to go. "Good-bye, Juliet. Good-bye, Mandy," he whispered, not bothering to restrain the tears. He walked back to his car, which smelled faintly of roses, and slowly drove away.

Chapter Twenty

MARNIE WALKED DOWN THE jetway and out into one of the American Airlines terminals at Dallas/Fort Worth International Airport. She wiped sweaty palms on her pants as she anxiously looked around the room for Tim. Her heart sank when she saw a uniformed man holding a sign that read, "Marnie Sullivan." She walked over and identified herself, then asked who had sent him.

"Dr. Allan Brown has ordered limousine service for you," he said checking his paperwork.

"Forget it," she said. "I'll take a cab."

The limousine driver looked confused.

"Where were you supposed to take me?" she insisted.

"Highland Park," he said, then checked his records for a more specific location. "A residence on Turtle Creek Boulevard, ma'am. All the arrangements have been prepaid."

"Look, I've never heard of any Dr. Brown. I don't know why he would send you to pick me up. So call me paranoid. Whatever. But I'd rather take a cab. I'm sorry for your trouble." She handed him a fifty-dollar bill. "You said it's an address on Turtle Creek Boulevard?"

"Yes, ma'am." The driver wrote down the exact address and handed it to her.

Marnie looked at the paper with a weary sigh. "Where exactly is this?"

"Near downtown, ma'am. Any taxi driver in this city will know how to find it."

"Thanks. And tell me again the name of the guy who sent you. Andrew Brown?"

The driver checked his paperwork. "Dr. *Allan* Brown."

"Thanks." Marnie grabbed her wheeled carry-on and dragged herself outside to hail a cab.

The limousine driver went back to his vehicle and reported the strange incident to the dispatcher, who then placed a call to Dr. Brown's cell phone. When informed that his guest had chosen to take a taxi rather than the limousine, the doctor merely laughed and said, "Well, good for her!"

Thirty minutes later, Marnie and the cab driver had circled the block twice trying to find the correct address. They finally realized that the number they sought was for the carriage house behind an English Tudor mansion. As the cab pulled into the main drive, Marnie told the driver, "Wait here until I wave you on, please." Her voice shook as she handed him the fare.

Lugging her overnight case up the outside staircase to a door above the garage, Marnie rang the bell. Heart pounding, she reached into her pocket to make sure her mace was accessible. It seemed like forever before the door opened, and her eyes froze on the face of a man who was so familiar, and yet not.

"Hello, Marnie," he said. "Didn't think you'd see me again, did you?"

Her hand flew up to cover her mouth. "Tim?" she gasped as she grabbed the rail behind her to keep from falling to her knees. The voice was his, but the face was not. This man had more hair, a broader chin, and a smaller, straighter nose.

"Call me Allan," he said. "Amazing what they can do with plastics, isn't it?"

Marnie stared in disbelief, her brain swirling with confusion. She felt like she was going to throw up.

"You'd better come in," he said. Then looking down and seeing the taxi, he reached for his wallet. "Did you forget to pay him?" he asked, motioning down to the driver.

She forced out the words, "I paid him." Taking a deep breath, she released her grip on the rail and motioned to the driver to leave. As the cab backed down the drive, Marnie leaned down and grasped her knees with her hands, trying to overcome the effects of the shock.

"Did you come alone?" Tim asked sharply. "Do you think anyone followed you?" He pulled her into the one-bedroom apartment.

"Yes," she was working to breathe deeply, trying not to hyperventilate. "I came alone." She began to shake her head slowly, then violently.

Tim was oblivious to her distress and then her mounting rage. He guided her to a large chair next to his computer and headed over to a nearby wet bar. Marnie remained standing as he continued what he was saying. "Good, because we have to protect the research I'm doing. It's imperative. It's all very. . . ."

"Tim Sullivan! Have you been in Dallas all along?" Marnie was suddenly near hysterics. "Why didn't you contact me?"

Tim reached out to hand her the water, but she slapped him hard across the face, batting the glass out of his hand. Water splattered his nearby computer. The sight of his processor shorting out sent Tim running for towels and screaming profanities at Marnie.

After a paint-peeling ten-minute exchange, Marnie and Tim had calmed down enough to at least cover the basics.

"You wrecked my computer, Marnie," Tim complained. "Good thing I have a backup at work and the budget for speedy replacement." He watched her eyes as she glanced around.

"This place isn't much to look at," he conceded. "I don't spend a lot of time here, but it's home. I'm sure it needs a woman's touch." Stacks of shirts just back from the cleaners lay on the back of the couch next to a hamper of clothing ready to be sent out. Several candy wrappers, an empty bread bag, a calculator, and yesterday's paper lay on the coffee table. It was obvious that any time Tim spent here was in front of the now defunct computer screen. And though Tim was highly organized when it came to his work, no one had ever accused him of being a good housekeeper.

"Actually, I was looking for photos of your family," she said. "Your wife? Your daughter?" She scanned the stacks of medical books, genetics texts, piles of photocopied journal articles, and downloaded pages from the Internet, but there were no reminders of their life together.

"Sorry about the mess," Tim apologized as he watched her. "The maid comes twice a week and today wasn't her day. Please, please, sit down Marnie," he said pointing to the chair. "Can I get you something?" he asked. "That is, if you promise not to throw it."

"No thanks, Tim." She tossed a stack of magazines off the couch and sat there instead.

"Sorry, but you're going to have to call me *Allan*, even in private. Don't even think that other name any more. Think *Allan*. Say *Allan*. That's the way this new identity thing works."

"What are you talking about? What new identity thing?"

"I have a lot to tell you—can't wait to tell you. I'll explain all that."

"Not that you asked," Marnie said, reaching into her wallet for a photo of Emily. She handed it to him, and Allan stared at it. "She's beautiful—just like her mother."

"Thanks. I guess that's as close as you're going to get to 'I love you, I've missed you,' huh?"

Allan shrugged.

"You may keep the picture," she said.

"Can't." He handed it back to her.

"Fine. Whatever." Annoyed by Tim's perfunctory rudeness, Marnie said, "I'm listening, but this had better be good."

Allan was too excited to sit, so he half-reclined, half-stood to tell Marnie his story. She sat stiffly, trying to veil her total confusion. Under the circumstances, she was not at all thrilled by the reappearance of her dearly departed husband, and she was exhausted from her trip. She studied the subtle changes in his face and nose, and the hair implant. He definitely looked better. She folded her hands and leaned forward on the edge of the couch. As she stared at Dr. Allan Brown, she looked for Tim Sullivan behind the new and improved façade, trying to feel something for this man and wanting to understand what was happening.

"I think I've found it!" Allan exclaimed. "I believe I've found the cure for akenosis."

"Really? Is that what this is all about?"

Allan nodded enthusiastically.

"And for that you had to fake your own death? What's up with that? Where've you been? Here? And how did you escape in the water? How could you do this to me? To Emily? Why the rearranged face?"

Allan interrupted her with an impatient wave of his hand. "I'll get to all that, but first you must understand that there was no other way. I was getting so close to this major breakthrough when the lawsuit against the clinic threatened to expose all my work—*before* it was time."

"What! How in the world did the lawsuit threaten your research? Come on, Tim, or Al, or whatever you're calling yourself now. . . ." Her voice betrayed her seething rage.

"It's *Allan*. And you said you'd calm down. It really does make sense. Just give me a chance to explain."

"Explain? What possible explanation could justify . . . ?

We had a funeral and everything." Marnie's voice cracked as her volume escalated. "Why did you fly me down here like it was some big emergency? Why all the drama? Because you finally cured some mice, or what?" Catching her breath, she leaned back on the couch and crossed her arms. This reunion was not going well.

Allan ignored her blasting sarcasm. "Marnie, it *is* an emergency. The situation is *very* dangerous. Do you think the bombing of the clinic was a coincidence?"

"What?" She sat forward again. "What do you know about that? Are you responsible for *that?*"

"No, no, but I think I know who is. See, Luc had started to figure out the situation. He's close to exposing this research before I have it completed, and the publicity would be devastating."

"Publicity? Devastating? Have you seen the clinic? I thought Luc was your friend," she shot back vehemently.

"Will you just listen?"

Marnie resisted the urge to answer with a huffy "Fine, talk away." For the first time since she'd arrived, she remembered that she now had a relationship with God, and that gentleness and patience might be a more appropriate response. Struggling to bring her mounting fury under control she blinked, nodded, and said quietly, "Sorry." She sat back against the cushions and forced herself to relax.

Allan pulled up a chair across from her. "I know this is all a huge shock for you, Marnie, but I never intended for you to know I was alive." Seeing the cloud that passed over her eyes, he added hastily, "We were unhappy together—remember? Well, I'm legally dead, and you're free to get on with your life."

"Hold on, Tim. Can we start at the beginning?"
Allan nodded.

"The accident was staged?" Marnie asked.

"Uh-huh."

"By whom?"

"I'm not sure, exactly. Uncle Cal's paying for the research privately, with some help from friends. But he
has people in the government who handle some of the
"details." I'm just not sure which set of initials are behind it. The FBI for sure. Maybe the CIA. And maybe
some other people."

"So your uncle knows you're alive?"
Allan nodded.

"But he was at the funeral."

Allan shrugged. "Wouldn't that be expected?"

"What about the flowers on the front seat? And the
note?" Allan's blank stare told her that the FBI had fab-
ricated the one story that had given her hope. The disappointment hit her like a stone.

"He forced you to leave your family?"

"No." Tim's voice softened. "But I knew you'd never
come with me. You have your own work. It would have
meant never seeing your father again at a time when
you were still grieving the loss of your mom. It would
have meant asking Emily never to see her grandfather
again."

"So you opted never to let her see her dad? Your research is that important?"

Tim looked away. "I was doing some research involving material from a former patient, and a mix-up in the
lab caused a lawsuit. I didn't expect it to come to all
this."

"And you know the clinic was bombed?" she asked.

Allan nodded. "I suspect—don't know for sure—but I think some moonlighting FBI agents are trying to silence Luc. That's why I got you down here. I had to warn you—for your sake and Emily's. I disappeared because we had to keep the project ongoing and secret."

"What lab cover-up is worth giving up your family, blowing up a clinic, and almost killing a friend?" Marnie asked, honestly bewildered. Then she had an afterthought, "Not to mention that you sank my classic Mustang!"

Allan spoke softly, almost apologetically. "Luc picked up the wrong petri dish and transferred the wrong embryos into Mrs. Rivera. Those embryos didn't have any of Mr. Rivera's DNA. That brought the lawsuit, which would have started an investigation. It would have uncovered the highly classified work I was doing."

"So Luc made a mistake. I still don't get what that has to do with you, with us."

"Luc transferred some special embryos that I was cloning for research. I never intended for them to be used for transfer. I had no idea they could become viable fetuses. I was working on developing a pure line of stem cells to treat akenosis. You *know* I'm concerned not only about myself but also about all my brothers and Uncle Cal as well. He's beginning to show some of the early signs. The time is right for launching a cure based on biotherapy, using stem cells that can repair the damage. I believe I've done it!"

"Good for you." Marnie worked to suppress a biting tone. "But what's the big deal with your experiment that you have to 'die,' and the clinic gets destroyed? Why didn't you just come forward with your work and explain Luc's error?"

"Couldn't. The research is secret because some parts of it are currently illegal. And the urgency of Uncle Cal's condition required that I stay on it after the experimental trials. He could die a slow and miserable death even before his term is over if I don't find a cure. And beyond that, it could really damage him if anyone finds out that he's ill, or that he's behind 'questionable' research. So the security's very tight."

"Come on, now! What makes stem cell research so top secret? What exactly are you doing that's illegal?"

"You remember all the research that lead to the FUI discovery?"

Marnie nodded.

"And remember how so many couples benefited from that therapy?"

She nodded again.

"I think this has the potential to do even more good. Stem cells are a type of body cell—actually one of the smallest independent units of the human body. They can differentiate into any kind of body cell if you can isolate them early enough and 'flip the genetic switch' to make them mature into the cell type you want. Like a muscle cell, for example, or in the case of akenosis, a nerve cell."

"You mean the kind of research where you grow skin or a kidney in the laboratory?"

"I've developed a line of cells that can be injected into an area of damaged nerves and new, healthy nerves will be generated. The stem cells attach, activate, and grow as healthy nerve cells."

"But why all the secrecy?" Marnie wanted to know. "Seems pretty straightforward to me."

"Yeah, but in our country, and many others around the world, national ethics committees have banned research on human embryos. You know, those pro-life clowns that think a fertilized egg is a person."

Marnie winced, recognizing that she had become just such a "clown" since Tim's disappearance. "You're destroying human embryos?" she asked softly.

"Actually, no," smiled Tim. "But *creating* embryos with unfertilized human eggs is, shall we say, a 'gray area.'"

"A gray area," Marnie repeated. "So Tim Sullivan had to 'die' to avoid being exposed by the lawsuit?"

"Right. I had to disappear and take my research with me."

"And now you're alive again?"

"Not exactly. Tim is dead, and though I can't fully explain it now, Allan Brown will need to remain a stranger to you—or an acquaintance at best."

"What?" Marnie stood up and started to pace. "Then what am I doing here?" Her voice began to rise again.

"It's for your own safety, Marnie," Allan said gently. "Listen to me very, very carefully. You were never here. You don't know me. You know nothing about this research. Things are precisely as they were yesterday—except now you know that you need to stay away from the clinic and anyone associated in any way with the doctors at the clinic. You're not here because we're getting back together again. You're here because you're in danger, and this was the only way to convince you to lie low."

"You've gotta be kidding! You're dead, you're alive;

you're here, you're not really here. And now I need to stay away from people who have cared for me while I mourned *your* loss? Anything else I need to know? Like, am I married—or widowed?"

"We're both single. Marnie, for your safety and for Emily's. . . ."

"What? You've endangered our *daughter, too?*"

"This research is a top national priority, with security at the highest levels. I have one chance to gain your silence, Marnie, only one." Allan spoke with a sincerity that communicated the gravity of the situation. "I never meant to hurt you."

"Me? Forget about me! How could you do this to *Emily*? And your mother? What about *her?*"

Allan ignored her questions. "In fact, I did it partly for you," he said. "This way you didn't have to file for divorce. I knew you were unhappy. I thought it would be easier for you. Honest, I really didn't mean to hurt you."

This pseudo-nobility was more than Marnie could stomach. "You didn't want to hurt me?" She raised her voice again. "This is your idea of a divorce? You never said you wanted a divorce. *I* never said I wanted a divorce. I wanted a husband! You didn't want to hurt me? How do you think it felt to put a stone on your grave site? Huh? Try watching your mother suffer the loss of her son." Marnie was crying now. "Or watching your business partners messed around so their lives are ruined. I'm glad you weren't only thinking about yourself!"

"I regret all that, Marnie. Really, I'm sorry. But I had to do this. The investigation in the malpractice suit would've uncovered my crowning achievement. My life is literally on the line with the akenosis research. And it has the potential to help so many people. I couldn't think only of myself. Remember how your pregnancy almost ruined us? Well, maybe I can prevent that from happening to another couple."

"My pregnancy didn't almost ruin us. Your *response* to my pregnancy almost ruined us."

Chapter Twenty-One

"THAT'S A LOW BLOW, MARNIE. Look, I don't want a fight. You know everything I've ever done has related to akenosis research. It's my life," Allan said. "My lab research in med school. My residency at UT Southwestern. And there I was in D.C., closing in on a breakthrough when the malpractice suit got filed. I *had* to 'disappear.' And I think you'll believe it's worth it in the end. We're close to a cure."

Marnie heard the excitement in his voice more than she caught his words. She saw that she would get nowhere expecting him to value the relationships in his life. She figured the best she could do was to try to understand what he had done from *his* perspective. "I just don't get it," she sighed.

"What don't you get?"

"Exactly what you're doing. And why."

Tim sat back down in the chair across from her. "Remember those late nights back in D.C., when I was working on FUI? I told you then that there was more to my research than just improving our in vitro success rates. Well, what I didn't say was that I was taking some of the extra eggs—the ones that didn't grade out high enough for fertilization. And I subjected them to rigorous, experimental environments and stimuli. In fact, the enzyme that was so helpful in activating the implantation process from the sperm head, with slight modifications, could also trigger DNA replication in the haploid gamete!"

"The what?"

"The egg cell itself. I took the chromosomes from one egg and added them to the chromosomes of another egg. The nucleus of one egg actually acted like sperm would have when I combined it with the other—it contributed genetic material. So I was able to get the egg cell to replicate and divide. Do you get it? I used two X chromosomes—from one egg of the mother inserted into another egg from the same mother. And by doing that, I produced a cell line of pure chromosomes from a single X of the mother, along with all the maternal chromosomes in that egg!"

"You mean you *cloned* the mother?" Marnie asked in hushed tones.

"No, not exactly. See, each of us is made up of duplicated double strands of genetic material. DNA. So the egg cell contains half of the mother's chromosome sequence, and instead of joining it with the chromosomes of a father, I took the half set of chromosomes from one egg and inserted it into *another* egg. I added a little bit of electricity, and the DNA aligned! *Voilà!* I really did put Humpty together again!"

"Whoa. So there isn't any father, but it isn't a clone?"

"All of the genetic material is from the mother but, as this set of chromosomes duplicates, it won't be precisely like the mother. It'll be extremely close, though."

"So, genetically, Leigh Rivera is both the twins' mother and their father?"

Allen nodded.

"Good night, Tim! What are you *doing*?"

"Marnie, I'm serious—you've got to stop calling me *Tim*. I'm *Dr. Allan Brown* now. It's imperative for everyone's safety that you abide by that."

"Fine. Okay, *Allan*. But why? Why would you 'create' these people?"

"I never intended to develop *people*. I just wanted to create a pure, reliable cell line that I could use to produce totipotential stem cells for my research."

"Stem cells? I thought they came from embryos, from clinics or abortions," Marnie said.

"Yes, that's how they were obtained originally. And you remember the outcry from the pro-life folks . . . all the regulations? Plus, it wasn't easy to get the cells, and they all had different genetics. Not the kind of control I needed to proceed."

"Proceed with what?"

"The experiment, the treatment for MHS. You know, akenosis."

"You've lost me again," Marnie said, shaking her head.

"All right, I'll try to simplify it. Once I had a pure cell line of identical genetic makeup, I could test my theory. I figured that the stem cells—which are able to develop into any cell line in the human body—from a healthy donor, should be able to recognize disease or damage and mature into the proper cell line to effect a permanent healing. A full restoration of function. I believe that with this technique, I may have discovered the permanent cure for Parkinson's, Alzheimer's, Huntington's Chorea, MS, and, of course, akenosis. Basically any of the neurological diseases. Leigh Rivera's genetic history was free from any hint of neurological problems, making her an ideal candidate."

Marnie shook her head. "But are *you* having symptoms? Do you feel all right? Is that what's driving you?"

"I'm fine. But Uncle Prez has been showing some troubling signs, so we've accelerated the program."

"Uncle Prez?"

"You know, Uncle Dufus. I assume you've listened to the news. That dive on the dance floor wasn't accidental. He's developing memory problems, emotional swings—he's almost manic-depressive. Not what you want in the most powerful man in the world. And he's starting to show the more obvious physical symptoms—tremors and weakness, difficulty with balance."

"So, does it work? Have you treated him yet?"

"I said we were accelerating the research. I haven't quite got to the miracle-making stage yet."

Marnie leaned forward. "So where does it stand now?"

Allan paused and took a sip. "I'll get there. Hang on. First I have to tell you that the animal work was extraordinary. I started with mice." Allan cracked a smile and said, "Here's a new nursery rhyme to teach Emily: Hickory, dickory, dock; the mouse ran up the clock. The clock struck one, but that's okay because your dad already made ten clones just like him."

"Very funny."

"Then there was the neurosurgical placement with the chimps."

"Chimps?" Marnie shook her head, and gave him a puzzled look. "Where do you do all this?"

"I'll take you down and show you. With basically unlimited resources, it's amazing how fast things can happen. Come on. Let's go over to the lab now, and I'll show you how well it's going."

Marnie was too stunned to refuse. She walked down the steps and got into Allan's car for the short drive to the research hospital.

"I'll give you the grand tour," he said, excitement in his voice. Marnie rode in silence. After a few minutes, Allan spoke. "I really am sorry I had to do this to you. Even though I had to stay gone, I missed you. And Emily. And I hope you'll be happy in the long run."

Marnie said nothing, but her mind was in high gear. *I don't know which is more painful: the death of my husband or his rejection of me. One or the other is bad enough, but I've been abandoned twice. By his choice and by his actions. Divorcee and widow. So am I still married or not?*

Allan's magnetic card gave him access to a secure parking area. He turned off the ignition but, before he got out, he turned to Marnie and spoke firmly. "I am Dr. Allan Brown, Marnie. Do you understand? Don't call me by that other name, not even once."

She nodded, feeling like a preschooler receiving a scolding.

"Good."

"Are you sure it's safe for me to be seen here?" she asked.

"Yes, but we'll have to be careful."

They took a secure elevator up to a hospital-like floor. Allan used another card to open the elevator door. Seeing all the signs that said "Infectious Disease Precautions," Marnie hesitated. Then she noticed the security and "No Admittance" signs. When she read the "Radioactive Materials in Use" warnings, she said, "Whoa. What's going on up here?"

Allan smiled. "If you believe all the rumors, we're trying to find a cure for a very contagious, rapidly virulent mutation of the AIDS virus."

"Oh, my! Shouldn't we be gowned, gloved, and masked or something?"

"I said, *if* you believe the rumors. Which I don't, since I started them!"

Marnie glared at Allan. "Why in the world would you start a rumor like that?"

"I like my privacy, and nothing discourages visitors like a juicy fatal infectious disease lurking about."

"And the radioactivity?"

"I have a radio, and it's active."

"Not funny. So what is this place?"

"This is my lab. This is where the miracles happen— at least, that's what I'm counting on. See, I developed this cell line using Leigh Rivera's eggs—I call it LG for Leigh Genes—remember you always used to wear Lee Jeans? Like the word play?"

"Impressive," Marnie said, trying hard to keep from saying the angry words she was thinking.

"Using Leigh Rivera's eggs, I created a cell line that was able to survive in the laboratory situation, both in mice and in chimps. In fact, in the chimps, I got the cells to attach to the damaged areas and survive. You want to see the chimps?"

"You've got chimps up here?" Marnie looked around, bewildered. "This looks like a high-class hotel. And the nurses' station down there looks like a control room at the space center." Marnie pointed down the hall. "I've never seen so many monitors and machines."

"The chimps are down in the lab in the basement. This is the research hospital wing—my own human laboratory. And the experiments are well underway."

"*Human* experiments?" Marnie was appalled. "Didn't you say the LG cells or whatever they're called—didn't you said they didn't even cure the chimps? How could you give them to people?"

Allan nodded, understanding her point. "Yes, it was a dilemma. But I proceeded under the assumption that the subtle chromosome differences between primates and humans were sufficient to prevent the new, healthy cells from reading the problem and encoding the solution in the primates. In the chimps, they went to the site of injury, and they caused no harm, but they couldn't 'flip the switch' and begin the restorative process. I think in humans, they will."

"And *that's* your theory?"

"Yes," he said almost indignantly.

"So, what have you done?"

They walked over to the unmanned nurses' station and looked through the chart rack containing the ten names of ten patients, each color-coded differently. The four red tags were Parkinson's disease patients. The three blue tags were severe Alzheimer's patients. The three green-tagged charts had MHS stamped in the corner. Tim pulled one of each color from the rack and pointed to the date of surgery on the chart—roughly three weeks before. Marnie read the notes and asked, "What surgery?"

"Microscopically guided, computer-enhanced trans-phenoidal placement of the LG cell culture," he responded proudly.

"What?"

"You know how I loved to work with microscopes and manipulate cells, right? It turns out that, with minor modifications, I was able to use my technique to place the cells I've developed into the part of the brain where the disease occurs. It's remarkably simple with the computerized scans and magnet scans here."

"You? Doing brain surgery?"

"I wouldn't exactly call it that, but I did place these cells. I'm actually quite good at it. It involves meticulous placement of a needle through certain portions of the skull and brain. Then I inject the cells. All in a perfectly sterile environment, of course."

"Of course," she said, almost mocking his arrogance.

"In fact, I've developed my own technique. I can reach the target through the nasal cavity. It leaves no visible scar, and it's essentially painless. We don't even need general anesthesia—though because of their deteriorated mental status, we had to put most of my patients under so they'd hold still."

"How many have you operated on so far?"

"Ten in all."

"How many have gotten better?"

Allan walked over to the cardiac monitors and the video camera readouts displaying each of the patients' rooms. He glanced at each methodically, from the earliest surgical candidates to the most recent. "Don't they look good?" he said. Marnie looked at the monitors. Each patient seemed to be resting comfortably. She repeated her question. "How many are getting better?"

"Each has recovered from the procedure. The tests on the early operative patients show that the LG cells are alive and thriving in the areas where I placed them. It takes time for the cells to differentiate and begin the healing process, but we're looking good so far. Very good," he said, looking across the bank of monitors.

A nurse, back from making rounds, approached and asked whether the doctor needed anything. Allan shook his head, then escorted Marnie toward the elevator, without introduction and without comment. "Unless you want to see the chimps, let me take you home now. It won't be good if people see us together."

Marnie had seen enough. All the way back to his apartment and then, as they ate take-out baked potatoes from Jason's Deli, Allan talked about his research. More than once he mentioned that he'd taken the day off to be with Marnie. He was at a critical point in the work, but if he expected appreciation for his sacrifice, he did not receive it.

Marnie, who for years had done most of the talking in their relationship, remained silent while the animated Dr. Allan Brown rambled about his exciting work. She noticed that he had not asked about her life after his disappearance. She had no real opportunity to mention Ben, the mission trips, even Emily.

In the middle of a long explanation about his mastery of primate brain function, Allan's beeper went off.

He looked down at the LED display and said aloud, "Emergency?"

Stepping quickly to the phone, he placed a call. "Dr. Brown here. . . . What! One of the Alzheimer's . . . ? Expired . . . ? Cardiac arrest . . . ? But he was doing so well!" Marnie watched the color drain from his face. His voice revealed his immense disappointment. When he got off the phone, he told her, "Sorry to do this to you, but I have to go back to the hospital right away. I'll be back as soon as possible. One of my Alzheimer's patients just died. It's crushing news."

How many times had she heard, "I'll be back as soon as possible"? Marnie knew that even though it was only five in the afternoon, she'd be spending her first night in Dallas alone. She tried to find some sympathy in her heart for Allan, but it was hard.

After receiving the page, Allan rushed to the research building, bolted over to the elevator, and hurried out to the nurses' station. Because of the tight security in the research wing, the information about the sudden death had been restricted. So far, only the nurse and the on-call house physician, Dr. Kenneth Newton, knew. Dr. Newton stood waiting at the nurses' station. He was not allowed to review the chart—he was told only that the patient was a long-term Alzheimer's victim with assorted health risks who had had suddenly arrested.

By the time Dr. Newton made it onto the ward, he saw little point in a full-court resuscitation effort. So he did a perfunctory evaluation and shocked the patient a few times. But on noticing that the pupils were fixed and dilated, the doctor called the code, declaring there was no brain function left to recover.

When Allan Brown arrived, Dr. Newton asked him about the rumors of infectious disease research and radiation therapy. He was satisfied to learn that this particular patient was not involved in those studies, but was being tested for brain abnormalities found in Alzheimer's patients and structural changes demonstrable on a CT scan. Dr. Newton expressed his sympathy and suggested that an autopsy might prove valuable in clarifying the findings on the CT scan.

Allan thanked him for his time and effort and escorted him onto the elevator. Turning back to the nurse's station, Allan asked with great emotion, "What *happened*, Sheila? Everything was looking so good. I can't believe this. Tell me."

"Everything was quiet," the nurse replied. "Just like every other evening. Take a look at the chart. All of his vitals were absolutely normal. In fact, he seemed to be improving in the mental-status exam. His face was more expressive, he was smiling and responding. I introduced myself every time I entered the room, and he seemed to be recognizing me. Then all of a sudden this. . . ." While she spoke, she was rewinding the video surveillance tape from the room and preparing to replay it for Allan.

As the tape ran, Allan noted that the patient seemed peaceful. *She's right,* he thought as he fixed his eyes on the screen, searching for every detail. *His facial expression is improved, and so is the muscle tone. He does look better.* He could detect a slight smile on the man's face, even in his sleep. Suddenly, things changed dramatically. The patient took on an agitated posture and an expression of horror. Allan's mouth dropped open. "That's unbelievable!"

They watched as the patient tossed and turned, waving his hands over his face as though something were flying right at him. Then he sat up, let out an agonized wail, and opened his eyes briefly, sweat beading on his forehead. Right after that, he fell backward in full cardiac arrest. Tim reviewed the monitor strips and watched the heart rate move from a regular slow rhythm in the early sleep section to a dramatic acceleration. Right at the end, when he sat up and screamed, it slowed quickly then finally stopped.

Over and over, the doctor watched the tape, looked at the monitors, and reviewed the lab work. "Nothing," he muttered to himself. "Absolutely nothing to explain this."

He called his government connection and briefly recounted the events, asking for an immediate autopsy. *I've gotta find out what caused this.* Arrangements were made. A pathologist known for his discretion would come over from the med school first thing the next morning to do the postmortem.

For a while after the man she had known as Allan left her alone, Marnie channel surfed. She was exhausted, but her mind wouldn't slow down enough for her to sleep. Every time she tried to close her eyes, the pain inside grew worse. She missed Ben. And Emily. She even missed the other members of the Russia team. And she felt so abandoned by her husband's choices. Her most depressing thought was what Tim's reappearance meant to her relationship with Ben.

Wanting to relieve herself of some of the loneliness, she set up her laptop, connected it to the phone line, and cruised the Internet for a few hours. When she realized that she was doing more staring at the screen than reading, she logged off. In the fridge she found enough ingredients to make a ham sandwich but, after one bite, she decided she wasn't hungry. Logging back on, she visited a few chat rooms. She wished Ben had sent her some e-mail, but she had no messages other than a few unwanted solicitations.

Around eight o'clock, she picked up the phone to call Ben, knowing that with the time difference he was probably close to turning in. She punched in his number, then put down the phone again. She didn't know how secure the line was, and she didn't want to run the risk of jeopardizing his safety.

For the first time in her life, Marnie was aware that there was nobody she could talk to. She had never felt so alone—as if something might break inside. Ben had given her two mild sedatives on their flight from Russia to help regulate her "internal clock" after the jet lag. She was glad she hadn't taken them then. Now she opened her cosmetic case and swallowed one. Then she walked into the bedroom to scope out the sleeping arrangements. To her surprise and disgust, Allan had secured a cot for her. She hadn't seen it until now because it lay against the wall with the door. Even though the one bed in the apartment had a king-size mattress clearly, in his mind, they were no longer husband and wife. This visual reminder jolted her more than anything he'd said all day. She stared out the window, letting the reality sink in anew.

His work is his god. He doesn't love me or Emily or anyone else. He loves his research and himself. He never intended for us to work it out. The flowers weren't from him. It was so much better when I thought he was gone.

With the new perspective she had gained the past few months, the reality of her husband's coldness seemed even more crushing. She could hardly believe the contrast between all the joy she'd experienced in Russia and the misery now. She felt the exhaustion of too many time zones.

Who am I supposed to love. And how?

Oh, Father, give me wisdom. I'm so angry at Tim, but he'll never see your light in me if all I show him is my own rage. Today didn't go the way I wanted it to. I'm too tired to communicate well. Give me strength. Am I really in danger? Protect me! What do I do now? How do I explain? Tim needs you the way I did. I guess I should be thankful that he has a second chance. Open his heart to you, Lord. And what about Ben? Am I single or still married in your eyes? What do I do now?

Sometimes journaling helped, so Marnie went back to her computer and opened a Microsoft Word file. "I can't help but compare Tim's disregard for my feelings with Ben's kindness and concern for me," she wrote. "Here I thought my husband had died, but today I learned the honest truth: he has abandoned me for another lover—his work. Ben is attentive to me; Tim doesn't care about my needs. Ben loves me—and has perhaps even fallen *in* love with me; Tim is indifferent. The contrast overwhelms me, especially when I think of the vows I made to Tim."

She fell asleep crying and praying. At four in the morning she awoke, still alone in the apartment. For a few moments, in that hazy state between sleep and consciousness, she had a vague sense of dread. *Why do I feel so depressed?* she wondered. It took her a minute to remember where she was. Then it all came back to her, and she felt the terrible ache in her heart take hold again.

In the quiet hours before sunup, Allan reviewed the charts of the other patients. The deceased patient was the first to have received the operation. Allan had also done one Parkinson's patient and one MHS patient that day. His eyes were drawn to the monitor in the rooms of the MHS patients, each of whom appeared to be resting comfortably. There was no evidence of any problems. He breathed a short sigh, reminding himself that the man who had died had been old and chronically ill. *He did beautifully during the surgery but, after all, the LG cells aren't the fountain of youth. They're not supposed to cure everything.* Feeling slight relief, he returned to the charts, reviewing once again the nurse's notes, looking for any clues that might unravel this setback.

Only after a thorough perusal of the charts did he remember that he had left Marnie alone at the apartment. But just as quickly, he dismissed the thought. The clock told him it was time to head down to the morgue to observe the autopsy.

Chapter Twenty-Two

COLD. THIS KIND OF ROOM IS *always so cold,* thought Allan. *Though I can't even remember the last time I attended an autopsy. Probably back in residency.*

He surveyed the stark room, with its stainless-steel tables, tile floors, multiple drains, and "the wall." The wall held the refrigeration units, which contained the corpses awaiting autopsy. The scales, instruments, stainless pans—everything was clean and neat. No other autopsies had been done recently, and Allan felt grateful for the absence of any odor. Neither was there any sound until Dr. Johns came in and flipped on the tape deck. Apparently, he liked Strauss while he worked. "Good morning, Allan," he said. "How goes it?"

"I don't know, Johns. I'm hoping you can tell me."

"Well, what do we have?" Recognizing the urgency and secrecy of the request, Dr. Johns opened the refrigerated unit while Allan brought over the chart. The refrigerators looked like household units laid on their sides and stacked four high. Inside the huge doors were large metal trays on rollers. They held the human remains. As he slid out the tray with Allan's deceased patient, Dr. Johns asked, "Can we get some help, or is it just you and me?"

"He's not so big," answered Allan. "We can move him."

"Sure. He's just 'dead weight,'" the medical examiner said chuckling.

This was the sort of warped humor that Allan appreciated. "You're sick," he said with a grin.

"Gotta keep a sense of humor, though the crowd isn't very responsive," Dr. Johns smirked, eyeing the cadaver.

The two men moved the patient over to the dissection table, and Dr. Johns asked, "Anything in particular you're looking for?"

"Sudden death, in the middle of some cutting-edge research on brain function and neurotransmission," said Allan.

"Well, I'll show you some cutting edge," Dr. Johns said, smiling again, as he began with the traditional Y incision. "Shoulder to mid-chest, same on the left, then mid-chest to pubic bone, stem to stern," he muttered.

Allan interjected, "I'm thinking cardiac, or maybe cerebral hemorrhage. Plus he had some neurosurgery that involved transplanting some material into his midbrain. I really need to see that."

"Okay, let me take a quick look at the heart. Then I'll do the head and get the info you need."

"Thanks, man. Sorry for the inconvenience."

"No prob. I'm sure I'll be well compensated," Dr. Johns said with a smile. A moment later he clicked on the tape recorder and began his dictation: "Sixty-four-year-old white male, appears his stated age."

Allan interrupted, "There won't be any record of this post." Their eyes met. Dr. Johns nodded, clicked off the recorder, and proceeded with his examination.

"Heart looks pretty good. No evidence of anything acute by gross exam. I'll do the complete workup later, but let's take a look at the brain." He picked up the scalpel and cut the scalp flap, lifting the skin off the cranium. Then he reached for the bone saw.

Allan cringed at the sight and sound, but a "cap" was made at the top of the skull, allowing the brain to be exposed by simply lifting off the bony cranium.

"Oh," sighed Dr. Johns softly. "Here's your problem. Evidence of a massive bleed. Can't tell where it started, but I'm betting this was the 'eject button' for our friend here. No history of hypertension though?" he murmured, half asking, half stating.

"No. He didn't know who he was, but he had great blood pressure," Allan replied.

"Too bad. It'll take a while to do the sections and tell you the wheres and whens, but this gentleman died of a cerebrovascular accident. Acute bleeding into the brain."

"That's what I needed to know. Thanks again. I'll call you later for the rest of the report." Allan's face revealed his uneasy feeling.

"What goes on the chart 'officially'?" Dr. Johns asked.

"I've got it covered. Don't worry."

"Okay. You're the doc."

Allan pulled off his mask and shoe covers and left the morgue, uncertain what to make of this event. Coincidence? The tragic, untimely death of one of his subjects? Or something more? Only now did he realize how tired he was. He'd been up all night and was ready to crash—but he made himself go back up to the ward. He *had* to look at the patients one more time. They were all awake, receiving their morning care. Everything looked fine. *Now I can head home and get some sleep.*

After a long, hot shower, Marnie dressed, dried her hair, and made her way to the kitchen to brew coffee. She smiled when she found French Vanilla Café in the cupboard. It was her favorite, and Tim liked it too. It was one of the little things they had shared in common. She mixed herself a cup, plopped down in the easy chair with her feet up on the coffee table, and opened her Bible. Before she'd become a Christian, she had never read the New Testament. Now, with Ben's encouragement, in the past few months she had focused on reading it cover to cover. She'd finished Hebrews on the plane, and this morning it was time to begin the book of James.

She prayed for understanding and began to read. Within five verses, the words jumped out at her: "If any of you lacks wisdom, let him ask of God, who gives to all liberally and without reproach, and it will be given to him." She remembered pleading for wisdom the previous night. Reading this promise was as though God had spoken directly to her need. *Oh, Lord, please do give me wisdom. I need it so much right now!* She read on for two pages, devouring the words. When she came to the end of the third page, the words again caught her by surprise, only this time they brought guilt: "The wisdom that is from above is first pure, then peaceable, gentle, willing to yield, full of mercy and good fruits, without partiality, without hypocrisy." *Ouch. Not exactly the way I acted yesterday.*

She reread that part and tried to think of some justification that would keep her from having to apologize. *I was tired. He left me! He's made life miserable for a lot of people. He abandoned his kid. Why shouldn't I be angry? His job is his life.* It was all true. Still, she had no peace about brushing off her actions. *He's not a believer. How can I expect him to have God's value system? I didn't have it myself until after his funeral.*

She was beginning to realize how God had changed her heart through the very thing she abhorred—Tim's abandonment. It had begun with Ben's words at the funeral. She knew she would have to let go of the desire to be bitter, because God had used her greatest hour of pain to give to her a new life.

She decided she would have to apologize to Tim, though she wasn't looking forward to it. Nevertheless, she asked the Lord to give her the strength to humble herself. Her eyes returned to the text. What she read next spoke directly to her heart: "But he gives more grace. Therefore he says, 'God resists the proud but gives grace to the humble.'" *That's it, Lord. I need your grace. I can't change in my own strength. It's not all Tim's fault. My anger didn't help our marriage either. Forgive me, Lord. Give me the strength to swallow my pride.*

Her time in the Bible and in prayer helped her focus on what was bothering her most, and she made a list of items to discuss with "Allan" when he got home.

He arrived mid-morning, exhausted. "I'm so sorry,"

he said as soon as he walked in the door. "I didn't mean to desert you like that. Honest."

"Rough night?"

"Really a bummer."

"Sorry," Marnie said.

Allan raised his eyebrows. "Thanks. Gee, what a surprise. I figured you'd blast me the minute I got home."

Marnie ignored this remark. "Hungry?" she asked.

"Famished."

"I made your favorite breakfast—cheese soufflé."

"Marn, no kidding?" He looked at her with wonder. "Gee, thanks."

"And the French vanilla's ready as soon as I boil some water."

"Awesome."

She set the food before him, and they sat across from each other at the kitchen table. Allan said, "Mmmm!" with every bite of the soufflé. When he had finished, he looked at her kindly and said, "Thanks. Thanks a lot."

"I'm sorry for some of the things I said yesterday."

Allan swallowed hard, and his eyes got huge. "You? Apologizing? Wow." He sat speechless. Finally, he reached for his cup of coffee.

"I think some of my anger was justified, but my words didn't need to be so harsh. Will you forgive me?" she asked.

Allan struggled to keep from sputtering. He swallowed his coffee and shrugged. "Yeah, sure."

"Why don't you get some sleep. You must be exhausted. When you wake up, I have some questions to ask you, but we'll probably do better if you're not so tired."

"Thanks, I appreciate that. I *am* beat." His eyes narrowed slightly, and he added, "You're not trying to seduce me or something, are you? 'Cause, if that's what you're doing, I'm really not interested."

This comeback caught Marnie by surprise, and she fought to keep from answering him with the first insult that came to mind. "No. I'm not," she said evenly. *Does there have to be some ulterior motive behind kindness?*

"Okay. Good. G'night." As always, her husband remained oblivious to the pain he had inflicted. He dumped his dishes into the sink, walked into the bedroom, wrapped himself in a blanket, and quickly fell into a sound sleep.

After cleaning up the breakfast dishes, Marnie stood in the doorway looking at Allan. *Must be nice to sleep so soundly.* She hadn't fallen asleep that easily since the day before he'd "died."

Four hours later, Allan emerged sleepy-eyed from the bedroom. Marnie had watched some TV, had a good cry, drafted a long, unsent e-mail to Ben, and written more in her journal. "Better?" she asked.

"Not great, but definitely better. I'm going to clean up, and then you can interrogate me."

She wanted to tell him what a great way with words he had, but she held back the sarcasm. "I'm not planning to interrogate you. I just have a few things I'd like cleared up. Can I order us in some food?" She changed the subject.

"Good idea. Crone's Pizza delivers lunch. Pizza okay with you?"

"Sure."

"The number's posted on the fridge."

"The usual?" Marnie was momentarily reminded of how much detail couples share, even when they aren't getting along—how they take their coffee, what they want on their pizza, whether they like the car seat close to or far back from the steering wheel.

"Uh-huh. Back in a few." He shut the bedroom door, and a moment later she heard the shower.

She ordered the pizza, wrote a little bit more in her journal, then sat nervously praying through her questions. When the pizza car pulled into the driveway, she put her hand on the door intending to walk outside with the cash. "Marnie, don't," Allan stood in the bedroom doorway, running a comb through his hair.

She wrinkled her brow as if to ask why.

"He comes here all the time. It'd be better if he didn't see you."

"Okay." *Is it that dangerous?*

Allan laid his comb on the table, took the cash from her hand, and met the delivery guy halfway down the steps.

Once they each had a slice on their plates and had opened a soft drink, Allan said, "Fire away any time."

"Okay." Marnie picked up her steno pad and tried to steady her shaking hands.

"You interviewing me like a reporter?"

"Just like old times," Marnie responded, trying to lighten the mood. "So can you tell me, sir—who arranged the accident?"

"Classified."

"Some government agency?"

"Probably. It had the approval of a high-ranking source who's been known to reside at 1600 Pennsylvania Avenue. Beyond that I frankly don't know which set of initials put the package together, as I said yesterday. I was told not to ask too many questions."

"But you had a choice, right?"

"Yes, but it wasn't much of one. I could've stayed and endured the scandal when the world found out that Leigh Rivera's kids were from my unauthorized stem cell research. But that would have been bad for the clinic, bad for my job security, and bad for my uncle. And I could have destroyed everything I'd ever worked for. . . ."

"But you'd have kept your family." Marnie worked to keep the emotion out of her voice.

"Do you think you and I would have survived that? I don't think so. Besides, a public relations nightmare is not exactly what someone in the PR business needs."

"It would have been nice if I'd been consulted!" Marnie blinked quickly to get rid of the tears that had filled her eyes.

"I thought it would be cleaner this way. Obviously, it didn't turn out the way I'd planned, but then not much did," Allan said.

"The point is, it was your choice, right?"

"Bottom line? Yes."

"And, in your mind, is it over between us? Do I just get on with my life?" Marnie braced herself for his answer. It wasn't that she harbored a great deal of affection for him anymore, but she still felt his rejection deeply.

"That's pretty much how I see it."

"So you feel *nothing* for me?" she half-whispered.

"I wouldn't put it quite in those terms, no," Allan laughed. "Geez, Marn, this reminds me of high school when we'd say that couples had the 'DTR Talk.' You know, 'Define the Relationship.'"

"It's pretty pathetic to have to do that with your wife," Marnie responded.

"In my mind, you're not my wife. Legally, you're no longer married to Tim Sullivan. He's dead. I'm Allan Brown, single white male. I'm sorry if that sounds cold. I didn't mean for all this to happen. Look, you know I'm not one of those guys who 'gets in touch with his feelings.' Ever since Dad died—of a disease that could kill me and all my male relatives—I've tried not to stop long enough to feel. But if I didn't bear some sense of responsibility, some desire to protect you, I wouldn't have contacted you. I think they could hurt you, so I want you to be careful. I don't want you to get hurt."

"Too late for that." Marnie swallowed hard.

"I mean physically hurt."

"Who is this *they* who could hurt me?"

"I'm not sure exactly. But they're government people."

"So what do I need to know to keep from getting hurt?" Marnie set her notebook down and stared at him.

"Realize your phones are probably tapped. And probably your e-mail—maybe not your instant messages but certainly your memos. Someone in the government found out how much Luc knows. I imagine someone's monitoring his calls. That means you're probably being watched, too."

Marnie shook her head and shuddered at the thought. "What is it that Luc knows that got him into trouble?"

"He knows that Leigh Rivera's children are hers and

only hers, if you know what I mean. Frankly, I have to admit I'm rather pleased that the lives I created actually became human beings."

"Excuse me? The lives *you* created?"

"Uh-huh."

"I thought only God creates life," Marnie tried to speak her piece gently, but his arrogance was more than she could stomach.

"God? God! I don't think I've ever heard you refer to God since the day I met you, except when you swore," Allan snickered.

"A lot has changed, Allan." She forced herself to call him by his assumed name. "After your funeral, I talked for a long time with Ben, and I believe in Jesus Christ." Marnie could feel her heart rate picking up.

Allan looked half shocked, half amused. "No way! Not *you*, Marnie. I thought you'd be the last person Ben could convince to become a right-wing, pro-life zealot."

Marnie squinted. "Is that what you think a Christian is?"

Allan thought for a minute. "I guess it makes sense. You'd endured a huge shock. It's to be expected. I imagine it helped you to believe in some greater purpose when nothing else made sense."

Marnie felt insulted by his patronizing, but she determined to focus on him, not herself. "You were raised in church. We've never even talked about what you believe. What *do* you believe?" Marnie wondered.

"I believe in myself."

"I mean about God."

"So do I."

"What?" Marnie figured she must be misunderstanding him.

"I believe man is the center of the universe. We get one shot at it, and then we die. That's it. It's over. If there's any intelligence, it's ours."

"What do you think about Jesus?"

"A good man. Great moral teacher. I think he'd believe I did the right thing—to give up my family for the good of the country and the sick people who can be helped through the research. But I don't think Jesus was God, if that's what you're getting at."

They talked a while longer, and then Allan made it clear that they'd exhausted the subject of "religion."

"What else is on your list of questions there?"

Marnie looked down at her paper. "Who may I tell that you're alive?" She looked up at him and searched his face for a response.

"Um, no one." He pretended to think for a moment. "Yeah, that about covers it. And especially for people like Mom. It's better for them to move on with their lives. And for Emily—she'll be better off thinking I died than knowing I'm out there somewhere but never contacting her."

Marnie absorbed Tim's cold logic, then changed the subject. "What if I want to remarry some day?"

"Then I hope you're happy."

"But, I mean, don't you think he would have a right to know what happened?"

"As far as I'm concerned, no. No way."

Marnie looked at her list again. "Before you contacted me, I thought you *were* dead. So why did you bring me here only to tell me about keeping silent? What is it I'm not supposed to say?"

"You need to get Luc to settle out of court, and you

need to find a way to convince him without telling him what you know. No more test results that point to my research. No more detective work from you, Luc, or Ben. You know the truth now. No more digging. Nobody talks about it on the phone or to colleagues. It's over."

"And why did I have to come here to hear that?"

"If I'd written it, it would have been documented. Too risky. Besides, you needed to chew me out in person." Allan's eye twinkled.

Marnie pursed her lips. "Okay, then. Last question. Can you think of a good reason why I should stay another day? You need sleep, and there's nothing for me to do here."

"You bored? We could rent a movie if you like. Suit yourself. But the return ticket is for tomorrow. I didn't know how long it was going to take to work things out with you. If you can wait until tomorrow, it'll save you about nine hundred bucks. But suit yourself." Allan shrugged and reached for another slice of pizza. "Besides, what do you have that's burning in D.C.?"

Marnie looked at him with guarded eyes to see if he was making a perverse joke about the clinic, but he was oblivious to the irony of his question.

"Well, I got back from Russia the day I got your e-mail," she answered plainly, "and I have a lot of other things going on."

"Russia? What were you doing there?"

"It was a mission trip."

"Oh." Marnie could tell from his tone that Allan didn't want to pursue the subject.

"Will I ever see you again after this?" Even as Marnie asked the question, she told herself she was a glutton for punishment. Every way she'd asked it, he'd made it clear that it was over between them.

"I'd like to think so."

Marnie looked up at him hopefully.

He continued, "When I come up with the cure for the Prez and all these diseases, and I'm famous as all get out, I'd like to think you'd cover the story."

"Somehow it always comes back to work, doesn't it? All business, all the time. Typical!"

Chapter Twenty-Three

MARNIE GOT UP FROM THE TABLE and went to the stove to mix herself another cup of coffee. "Why haven't you asked me about Emily?" she demanded with her back to Allan.

"Too hard," he responded.

"What do you mean?"

"It's easier to get on with my current life if I don't dwell on the past." Allan paused for a moment, before adding, "You interpret my 'lack of interest' in her as not caring about her. But it's precisely because I do care that I have to distance myself from both of you. The less I know, the better." He stood up from the table and walked over to the couch. "Want to rent a movie? I haven't seen one in months." He'd had enough talk about relational issues.

Marnie had one more nagging question. She knew this was her last chance to lay her fears to rest. "Did you bring anyone else with you when you left D.C.?"

Allan's furrowed brow told her that he wasn't following her.

"Was there someone else? Anyone who came with you?" she rephrased.

"You mean like another researcher? No, I've always worked alone. You know that. The only people who knew were Uncle Cal and his people."

"No, that's not what I meant."

Understanding finally began to dawn on Allan's face. "Is that what you think this is about? Another woman? Is it so hard for you to understand that I would do this because it was *right?*"

"You didn't answer me."

"Look around you, Marnie. Do you think any woman would put up with *this?*"

"You still didn't answer me."

Allan cursed and raised his voice. "No. There's no one else. There wasn't then; there isn't now."

"You can't really blame me for wondering, though, can you?" Marnie remained calm.

"I know what you're thinking. Well, all men are *not* alike! Women don't enter the picture here. I've got enough on my mind without any new distractions. Besides, I couldn't share my work with anyone even if I wanted to. It's classified. So any sort of deep sharing is out." The way he said "sharing" made it sound like a disease. He sat looking at her for a long time then sighed. "You think I'm selfish, don't you? You know, I honestly thought that once you saw the importance of all this, you'd understand—and maybe even appreciate— the choices I've made. But apparently you have trouble seeing the way millions of families will have their lives changed when this works, thanks to my sacrifice."

"You're right. If you expect me to thank you for your

sacrifice, it'll be a long wait," Marnie shook her head in disbelief. "The sacrificial lamb never feels too excited about the slaughter. The blade lands a little too close to my neck, I suppose." She knew there was a spiritual analogy somewhere in what she'd just said, but she felt too frustrated to think in that direction right now.

"Just promise me one thing," Allan persisted. "Even if you never understand it all, at least tell me you'll stop my partners from nosing around in this case. Tell me you won't be stupid."

"You don't have to worry about that. I have this thing about not wanting to find myself or my kid attached to a concrete block at the bottom of the ocean." Seeing that the discussion had gone about as far as it could, she offered, "How about that movie?"

"Is that your way of getting the last word?" Allan asked.

Marnie resisted the urge to glare. "If you have something else you want to say, I'm all ears."

They stood with their eyes locked on each other for a few moments. Finally, he managed a thin smile and said, "Comedy or drama?"

"Don't you think we've had enough drama?"

"Good point."

On the way to the video store, Allan called the hospital to check on his patients. During the movie, he checked his beeper periodically to make sure it was working. At one point, he paused the film and asked Marnie if she wanted a drink. When she shook her head, he got up and called the hospital again. After the movie, they ordered in Chinese food, which they ate in virtual silence. Then Allan excused himself and left for the hospital.

Around seven, the cell phone in Marnie's travel bag rang. It was Ben.

"I thought you might call last night," he said by way of greeting. "Guess it was just wishful thinking."

"I wanted to," Marnie said softly.

"Great. Well, next time *follow* that good impulse," he admonished her teasingly. "So, when ya coming home? I'm dying to see you. It's bad enough that I have 'team withdrawal'—missing the whole Russia group after working together for so long. But then you take off on me like that right after we get back. Ow!" His tone was sweet, not at all accusatory.

"I miss you, too, Ben."

"Get all the mess cleared up with your client?"

"Not exactly. But I'll be heading home tomorrow morning."

"Best news I've had all day! Can I pick you up?"

"I can take a cab—or call my dad. You don't have to come."

"Wound me, why don't you?"

"I didn't mean it as a rejection. I just don't want you thinking you have to run an airport limo service. I read somewhere that the difference between friendship and love is that friends don't *expect* you to pick them up at the airport." As soon as the words were out of her mouth, Marnie regretted them.

"Ah, so you're telling me you want to be 'just friends'? Okay I can take a hint." Ben exaggerated an injured tone, but he didn't believe her for a second. If he had he wouldn't have said it.

"No, that's not what I—"

"What time shall I find the fair maiden at her gate?" Ben interrupted. "My trusty steed awaits to serve her every request." The contrast between Ben's attentiveness and Allan's lack of interest was almost overwhelming.

"Don't bother to meet me at the gate." Marnie didn't want to give any information over the phone that might identify where she'd been. She now worried that her world was less private than she'd assumed. "Just meet me at the door where you dropped me off."

"Suit yourself. What time?"

"Tomorrow at eleven."

"A.M.? P.M.?"

"Morning."

"Excellent. I'll be the guy standing there with roses. And in case you're wondering, they won't be yellow; they'll be red."

After Marnie hung up, she realized she hadn't even asked him about his day, his life, anything. *Maybe I'm more selfish than I thought.*

Marnie had never been so glad to see Ben as when he wrapped her in a long bear hug, then held her face in his hands. "Great eyes. I've missed those eyes," he said.

"Thanks, Ben. I could use a little boost about now."

"Do I have to take you straight home, or can we take a detour for lunch?" he asked.

"Lunch would be great. They tried to feed us on the plane, but I was holding out for a better offer."

"You got it! Hungry for anything in particular?"

"Something private."

"Mmmm. Good idea."

"We've got a lot to talk about," Marnie clarified.

"Oh. Yeah." He placed her carry-on in the back seat and opened her car door. A box of red roses lay across the seat. "I know I said I'd be holding them, but I thought they might get in the way of saying hello," Ben charmed her with his words.

Marnie leaned down to pick them up. "Oh, Ben, they're beautiful." Their eyes locked and she gave him a warm, appreciative smile.

Ben gave a slight nod and winked.

"Thank you!" She quickly reached up and pecked his cheek.

"Wow, if that's the kind of thanks I get, I'll bring more tomorrow!"

They both laughed. When Marnie was seated in the car, Ben jogged around to the driver's side. "How does seafood sound?" he asked as he slid in behind the wheel.

"Just perfect."

"I love the way you said that."

As they sped toward Ben's favorite seafood place over-looking the Potomac River, Marnie kept the conversation light. She hated to launch into all the negative news, and she hadn't yet decided how much she planned to say. But there was so much to discuss in such a short amount of time. She wanted to find out to what extent Luc had confided in Ben about the latest developments in the lawsuit, but she feared his car might be wired. Instead, she told him about the lame movie she'd seen in Dallas.

Once inside the restaurant, they placed their orders,

then focused their full attention on each other. The hostess had seated them at a two-person table in a corner, far removed from the other diners. Marnie eyed the white starched tablecloth and the vase with five or six exotic flowers. "Very nice. Though with today's company, even a greasy spoon would be okay."

"Thanks," Ben smiled and reached out. "Give me your hand."

"Why?" Marnie smiled at him curiously as she extended her palm.

"You see these fingertips?"

"Uh-huh."

He examined her fingers. "Did you know that our fingertips have five million nerve endings? Each?"

"Actually, yes. I believe you told me that once," Marnie smiled as he gently touched his fingertips to hers.

"Uh-huh. And every one of mine is glad you're back," he added.

The waiter interrupted by bringing a loaf of garlic bread and iced tea, and they pulled their hands apart.

As Ben cut the bread, Marnie launched the conversation. "You saw Luc before I left."

"Yeah."

"How is he?"

"He's gonna be okay, but it was a close call."

"Tell me about it," Marnie said.

"Not here."

"I think here's really the best place, don't you?"

Ben gave her a puzzled look, then shrugged. "Sure. Whatever."

Marnie feared that Ben would resent such a drastic change in the subject, but he seemed relieved to finally have a chance to tell her about the bombing. By the time they'd finished most of their lunch, he had filled her in on Luc's condition, the rumors, the big developments in the case, and Luc's call to Chris Winston. Then he answered most of Marnie's questions, holding back nothing of what Luc had told him.

"Do you have *any* idea who Chris called after Luc told him?" she asked.

"Just someone in the Justice Department. That's all I know."

"Sounds like it's time to stay away from the government."

"Yeah, unless the timing was a coincidence, and the Riveras had something to do with it. But that seems unlikely."

Marnie took a deep breath. "No, it was the government." She had lowered her voice, and her tone was insistent.

Ben stared at her. Finally he spoke quietly. "How do you know?"

"I know."

"*What* do you know? Did you already know what I just told you?"

"More on that later," she demurred. "But Luc needs to back off on the investigation. You guys need to settle—do whatever it takes. The nosing around and uncovering new evidence has to stop. Or we could all end up in the headlines."

"Did someone threaten you, Marnie? Is that why you flew to Dallas?"

"No one threatened me, exactly." She skirted his second question. "But I do think we need to assume our houses, cars, and phones are no longer 'private.'"

Ben stared at her. The waiter picked up his credit card and went to process it.

Sensing his frustration, Marnie assured him, "I want to tell you everything, Ben. I'm still trying to decide what's best."

"I hope you'll tell me what happened to you, and what you know. I have a vested interest in it all—on several levels." Ben's eyes revealed his anxiety.

Marnie weighed her options. Finally she spoke. "Tell you what. When I was a kid, my dad took me for canoe lessons down at Thompson's Boat Dock. Let's go down there. I don't want to talk in your car or at either one of our homes. Or on the phone."

Ben searched her face and saw that she meant business. "Okay, sure."

They waited impatiently for the waiter to bring the receipt for Ben to sign. Then they drove in near silence to the boat dock across from the Watergate Apartments. After parking the car, they found a place to sit on the grass nearby and looked out at the water. Marnie hugged her knees, fixed her eyes on a canoe going by and began. "What would you say if I told you I just found out Tim was still alive?"

The color drained from Ben's face. "No way." He was rarely shockable, but this one got him.

"Way." She didn't want to look at him.

"Marnie!"

"But it's not like we're still married, if that's what you're thinking. He's legally dead, and in his mind, we're divorced."

"Slow down! What!? When did you find this out? When did you talk to him?"

Marnie finally turned to meet his eyes and saw the pain in them. "The night we got back from Russia, I got an instant message on e-mail from him. He told me to fly to Dallas. Apparently, Luc got too close to something that was going on, and Tim was told to silence us, or 'they' would."

"Unbelievable."

"Quite."

Ben thought for a moment. "So, Tim was the 'emergency' in Dallas?" He didn't try to hide his wounded tone. "So was this a romantic reunion with hubby?"

"Not even close. I think he loathes me. Okay, maybe 'loathe' is a bit strong. But it wasn't anything I would describe as remotely romantic or conciliatory. The accident last December was staged to cover up some stem cell research he was doing that would benefit the president. They relocated Tim before it got exposed. Who knows? Maybe he'll save the free world." Ben had never heard Marnie use such a biting tone. "And remember the flowers they found in the submerged car? The ones that gave me so much hope? He knew nothing about them."

"I'm sorry."

"Yeah." Marnie didn't try to hide the hurt. "He had not one word of warmth for me. He left his wife and kid for *research*, and he thinks he's being noble. He forbade me to tell anyone, but I had to tell you. I need your wisdom, Ben. Besides, I'm having trouble figuring out how God views my marital status."

Ben thought for a long, long time then swallowed hard. "Marriage isn't just a commitment or a contract, Marnie. It's a covenant. And you don't need a 'relationship' with me clouding your judgment right now. I'm glad you told me."

"What do you mean?"

"I mean just that. If you're still married, well. . . ." Ben's voice cracked.

Marnie had not anticipated this response. She burst into tears. "I hate him! I hate him! He keeps ruining my life!" She stood and picked up the closest item—a life vest lying on the ground—and hurled it into the water. "I hate him!" she screamed.

Ben blinked hard. Then he stood and wrapped Marnie in a hug. "I can't believe what you've been through," he said into her ear. She sobbed on his chest, and he blinked rapidly to keep from joining her tears.

Why did he wait until I fell in love with you to tell me? she thought.

Ben closed his eyes tightly for a moment. Then he rested his cheek against Marnie's and held her tightly until her tears subsided. Finally, he reached for her right hand and placed his left hand on the small of her back, then gently rocked her, slowly shifting his weight from one leg to the other. Anyone looking on from a distance might have thought they were dancing.

Chapter Twenty-Four

CARLOS RIVERA PULLED INTO HIS GARAGE and headed straight for the bar in his office. Having just come from the hospital, he poured himself a double Scotch. All this waiting agitated him. The girls had been finished with chemotherapy for several weeks, and the doctors had closely monitored their blood work. So far it all looked good, but it was still too soon to tell. And there had been no new developments on the case for weeks.

He paged Victor, who called twenty minutes later.

"What are you working on, Victor? It's been too long." Carlos sounded impatient.

"There is not much to report, señor. I've continued monitoring phone calls, but they've said nothing relating to the case. After the clinic bombing, I wired Dr. Morgan's home as you requested. But his calls have added no information."

Carlos cursed. "They must know." He was silent for a moment. Then he insisted, "We need more. I want visual surveillance."

Victor reminded Carlos that he had already arranged for Marnie, Ben, and Luc to be followed. But having hospital chaplaincy work, church activities, and physical therapy appointments watched had done nothing other than make him question his earlier suspicions that Ben McKay and Marnie Sullivan had a romantic relationship.

Dr. Allan Brown sat resting his head on his hands, staring at the view boxes. He put up each of the patients' CT scans in turn, studying the subtle changes in the pre- and post-transplant films and comparing each set from first surgery to last.

"It's right there," he murmured, pleased with himself. "The cells are aggregating on each point of damage."

In the Parkinson's patients, he looked at the motor fibers. These patients had experienced some restoration of the missing neurotransmitter dopamine, and they showed early evidence of improvement in their symptoms.

The Alzheimer's patients showed signs of new cell growth where the myelin sheath function had been absent or diminished. *The LG cells are attaching and "patching" the problem,* he observed with a look of satisfaction on his face. Like the Parkinson's subjects, these patients also showed external signs of improvement, judging by their facial expressions and alertness. Allan felt a rush of hope that memory, emotional response—everything—would also return.

The final group, the MHS patients, clearly received most of his attention. They showed dramatic improvement in the overgrown areas of the nerve myelin. As with the others, the new cell line was attaching. Yet, uniquely in these patients, the cells were slowly breaking down the extra myelin, raising expectations that normal nerve function might be restored. *They're in the areas where permanent damage has occurred—surely the new cells will correct that damage,* Allan hypothesized, then hoped his personal involvement was not clouding his objectivity.

He made an overall assessment. *The transplants are working. They've attached themselves to the abnormal areas of myelin in each of the different patient groups; they're activating and starting to correct the problems.*

He sighed, a deep, prolonged sigh. It looked so good. *But then a patient goes and dies on me. The postmortem shows a massive intracranial hemorrhage. Every area of new cell growth also had new, fresh bleeding. Massive multi-site bleeding. So far, no problem with the Parkinson's patients or the MHS patients. But why? Why such an awful outcome? Maybe it has nothing to do with this. Maybe he was just too old.*

Allan's beeper interrupted his thoughts. Recognizing the number, a rush of dread washed over him. He went to the phone and dialed.

The phone was answered with a curt, "Yes."

"This is Dr. Brown," he offered.

"One moment please." His call was processed and transferred to Dr. Harrison's office.

"How are things going?" the doctor wanted to know.

"Fine. Just fine," Allan assured him in his most professional voice.

"Are we ready to proceed?"

"Almost," replied Allan. "We're seeing all the right changes. I expect some definitive results, within a week or two at the most. I'm pleased with the way things are going so far. The Parkinson's patients are—"

"We need to move ahead as quickly as we can," Dr. Harrison interrupted. "When will you be ready to treat the president?"

"Sir, there have been a few setbacks. Not with patients like the president, sir, but we have seen some worrisome side effects."

"Worrisome?"

"Yes. Unexpected complications. One of the patients—"

"Doctor!" Dr. Harrison interrupted again. "We're running out of time. Correct the problems, and let's proceed. We're counting on you. We've extended to you every advantage for your research, and we've kept your family out of it, in return for your diligence on the president's behalf."

"I understand fully," replied Allan. *In fact, all too well.* "I'll have it ready as soon as possible."

His promise was met with a long silence, followed by, "When was the last time you caught the news?"

"I read the *Dallas Morning News* this morning, sir."

"Then you haven't heard about this afternoon's embarrassing mishap."

"Sir?"

"He had lunch today at a big, informal Republican fund raiser. A barbecue. He was holding a full, thirty-two-ounce drink when he lost his grip on it. Drenched himself and everyone around him. It's all over the media. They're comparing him to Gerald Ford."

"Gerald Ford, sir?"

"You're probably too young to remember, but when Mr. Ford was president, he stumbled a time or two, and it greatly hurt his credibility. Your uncle appears to be getting worse, Doctor. And it's getting harder to cover for him."

"I understand, sir. Believe me, I'm doing everything I can."

"Good day." Dr. Harrison hung up without waiting for a reply.

Allan cursed into the dead phone.

When Ben called to offer Luc a ride and some company during his hydrotherapy session, the recovering patient enthusiastically agreed. Luc's wife, Janelle, wheeled her husband to the curb after Ben pulled up. She thanked him profusely for giving her the morning off, saying, "I appreciate your giving him a change of scenery. I think he's getting tired of seeing my face everywhere."

"Not a chance," Luc said, winking at his wife.

Once they were on the road, Luc told his partner, "We got the insurance check on the fire this morning. You and I can eat for a while longer."

"Great," Ben said without much enthusiasm.

"Just kidding on the amount," Luc clarified, curious about his friend's apparent lack of interest. "It was really quite generous. We'll all be fine."

"Good." Ben clearly wasn't in a talkative mood. Finally, Luc asked if he could turn on the radio, and they rode without speaking further.

Once inside the physical therapy facility, Ben wheeled

his friend past the curtained areas and the four-leaf-clover-shaped stainless Jacuzzi. He sat quietly as Luc endured hot soaks, dressing changes, and range-of-motion exercises. It was tedious and somewhat painful work. An occupational therapist with strong hands worked him hard, expressing her desire to help him optimize his surgical skills. Luc called her Bertha; it was his lighthearted way of complaining that she was such a taskmaster with his therapy. She ended the hour by handing him some red putty, announcing to no one in particular that he had graduated to the hardest level of hand exercises.

Afterward, Luc looked surprised when Ben asked if he could take him to lunch. Ben's company had been disappointing so far, but Luc hoped it would get better. Ben seemed to be moping, and Luc was curious to know why. Once they were ushered to a table at the country club and had ordered their BLTs, Luc asked, "Are you okay, buddy?"

Ben looked puzzled.

"Something on your mind?"

Ben nodded. "Lots of stuff. But most of it doesn't concern you. I do have something I want to talk to you about, though."

"Fire away."

"The case. Where are we on it?"

"In deep trouble," Luc chuckled.

"That's not what I meant."

"Hey, lighten up," Luc said. When Ben still didn't smile, Luc got serious and answered the question. "Chris thinks we should offer a settlement. I told them no, but that was before the DNA tests showed the fault was mine. It also was before I practically got my brains blown all over the office wall."

"Nice image," Ben said dryly. "You gonna go for it now?" It was the first time Luc had seen Ben smile all day.

"I'm thinking about it," Luc said. "We have some time. Besides, I wanted your input first. The lab error was—technically—mine, so it's not like I can prove my innocence. It's not a case we can win."

"You've got a point."

"The Riveras don't know about the twins' genetics and, while I'd like the truth to come out, it may be more than they can deal with. And it would certainly drive up the price of the settlement. If I press forward with the case, it'll hit the news. If we settle, it can stop here. My sense of justice has been violated—there's no question. And there's a lot I'd still like to know—like the whole truth. But the truth appears to be kind of threatening in this case."

"Sounds like you think a settlement would be the wisest move," Ben summarized.

"Probably. But don't you think the Riveras have a right to know about their kids?"

"Sure I do."

"But you still think we should settle?"

"Two separate issues," Ben said. "You can settle now and figure out later how to deal with what you know and how much to tell them."

Ben saw Marnie at church a few days later. It was the first time she'd insisted on driving herself, and her decision had been painful for both of them. She had lashed out in anger when Emily asked her why they were on their own this time. Even though she had apologized before taking her to Sunday school, Marnie still felt pangs of guilt for unleashing her feelings on her daughter.

Ben hoped that Marnie would join him in their usual place for worship, but she elected to sit elsewhere. Determined not to miss her altogether, he hurried to catch up with her after the service. He intercepted her downstairs just before she got to Emily's classroom. Grabbing her arm, he said, "I wish you'd return my calls. I have some good news."

She stopped and turned toward him. "Yeah? What?" The hopeful look in her eyes sliced through him.

"It was easier than I thought it would be," he said.

"What?"

She couldn't help but notice his gentle touch as he guided her by the elbow into the uninhabited corridor that led to the rest rooms. "Getting Luc to settle. I didn't have to tell him anything."

"Ah." Marnie nodded, looking at her shoes. This was not the sort of good news she'd had in mind.

"He's going to try to settle with the Riveras and avoid going to court."

Marnie continued to stare at the floor. "That *is* good news, Ben. Thanks for telling me."

"There's more. Apparently Chris's contact in the Justice Department seemed very pleased to learn that Luc wanted to mediate a quick and quiet settlement."

"Interesting."

"So I think, at least for now, you're safe."

She looked up at him, grateful that what had initially

appeared to be a "strictly business" conversation was actually an expression of his care for her.

"Thanks, Ben. Thanks for telling me."

His look pierced her. "And can I tell you one more thing?" he asked.

Marnie shrugged her consent.

"When I said you didn't need me complicating your life, I didn't intend for you to treat me like a stranger."

Swallowing hard, Marnie fought to remain emotionless.

Ben continued. "I miss you. You're the dearest friend I've got. So I'm asking you, please don't go writing me out of your life."

Marnie stared off at a door down the hall and finally answered softly, "I was an idiot for opening myself up to you."

"Marnie, if you weren't married, it would have been the greatest gift you could have given me."

"Honestly?" She looked up at him, surprised.

"Honestly." The gentleness with which he answered and looked at her caught her off guard.

"So what am I supposed to do, Ben?" she pleaded in a half whisper. "Spend time with you every day like we used to do, only convince myself I feel nothing?"

"That's not at all what I'm suggesting."

"Then what *are* you suggesting?"

"I don't know yet. But you've left a hole in my life. I mean, can't we at least talk? You rode home the other day in silence and haven't returned my calls since. That feels a little harsh. You tell me you're not coming to church with me by leaving a message on the *machine*? I wear a pager, Marnie. We can talk about that sort of thing in person."

Marnie had a puzzled look. "I thought that was what you wanted."

Ben shook his head. "Not even close."

She thought a minute. "Whether or not I am married—and I'm not sure I am—I need your advice about what to do. I don't know what God expects of me. But I heard you saying you had to get out of my life—to 'uncomplicate' it. I thought I was acting honorably."

"You don't have to be cold to be honorable." The wounded tone in his voice conveyed his true feelings.

The following Thursday, Dr. Allan Brown practically cheered when he learned that the MHS patients had started showing improvement in their motor nerves. Their strength was slightly better, and their tremors had decreased, although they'd experienced no improvement in mental or emotional function yet.

The Parkinson's patients had plateaued, showing no further improvement from the prior week—no discernible change at all. The therapists had remarked that this was fairly normal in the rehabilitation of other muscle injuries. There was no hint of worry on the chart.

Allan focused again on the MHS patients. Their CT scans were clearly better. And now, as he had expected, the nerve transmission was occurring and improving. *I did it! My cell line is growing and fitting in—as a nondifferentiated stem cell! It's becoming precisely what's needed—adapting and activating.*

Allan was so excited, but it frustrated him that he had nobody to tell. He looked down at his pager, daring it to go off so he could tell Dr. Harrison he had found a cure for akenosis. He could save the president—and ultimately himself.

He walked back to his office and pulled an X-ray folder out of his desk drawer. Placing the film up on the view box, he flipped on the light. This CT scan was his own.

He could see early indications of MHS. *Subtle, but obvious to the trained eye.* He stared at the film evidence, meticulously studying every panel, every angle, every level. Then he rubbed his tired eyes and snapped off the light. Though he hadn't yet developed any symptoms of MHS, he saw unmistakable evidence of early trouble on his scan. He noted several areas of myelin sheath overgrowth, and he knew it was just a matter of time before the symptoms manifested themselves. An odd smile came across his face. *Save the world, save yourself.*

If the special cell line could replace the neurotransmitters quickly, as the nerve sheath was repaired, function should return. Pleased with himself, he sat back in his chair to relax and savor the possibilities. *I'm sitting on the edge of a dramatic medical breakthrough. Fame, spelled N-o-b-e-l. Will they let me accept it as Dr. Allan Brown, or will the risk be too great? After all, my work will save the functional life of the president and extend his actual life.*

On the basis of his "gut feeling" and the preliminary results, he elected to press on. Drawing a deep breath, he resolved, *I'm going to have the LG transplant myself.*

Holding the scan up to the overhead light, he said, "Gotcha! You aren't going to get me." Returning the film to its protective sleeve, he placed it back in his drawer and picked up the phone.

"This is Dr. Brown. Schedule the OR for another transplant in the morning. Seven-thirty."

"Will you be needing the neuro room again?" asked the scheduling nurse.

"Yes, everything just like before. I know it's been a few weeks, but I need all my equipment—the micro needle, the CT scanner on standby. Dr. Dehmer will assist me again."

"OK," said the nurse. "Patient's name?"

"Brown," he said. "Lane Brown." He chose his former middle name.

"Got it. Seven-thirty. Neuro room. Who's doing anesthesia?"

"I've got that covered," said Allan. "No problem."

"General or local?"

"We'll do it under local. And I'd like the fiber optic video camera, also."

"We'll have it there for you."

"Thank you."

"No problem, Doctor. See you in the morning."

"No regrets," he breathed, barely audibly.

The next morning, Allan explained the procedure and the location for the transplant, step-by-step, to Dr. Dehmer. He held back, however, from divulging the source of the cells. Under his colleague's steady hand, everything went off without a hitch. Allan was even able to stay awake and position the monitor so he could observe the procedure.

Chapter Twenty-Five

TWO DAYS AFTER BEN'S ENCOUNTER WITH Marnie at church, he sat praying in the hospital chapel alone. The family of a car accident victim had just left, and he had felt their sorrow acutely. But when he looked up and saw Marnie slide into the pew in front of him, he struggled to suppress the huge smile that lit up his face. She turned to face him, resting her arms on the back of the pew.

"I thought I might find you here," she whispered.

"It's amazing you did. I actually don't come down here much," he said. "And you don't have to whisper."

"Confession," she said, holding up her right hand. "I've spent the last hour looking for you. It's not like I just stumbled in here."

"What's on your mind?" he asked, both pleased and puzzled.

"You got a few minutes?"

"For you? Are you kidding? I've got all the time you need. It's great to see you."

"Thanks," she smiled sadly. "Is it okay to talk here? Or will we keep people from praying?"

"This is fine, unless you *want* to go somewhere else. Sadly, this place doesn't get a lot of use."

"Here's fine." Marnie looked down at the pew for a few moments while she worked up the nerve to ask her questions. She picked at a thread on one of the cushions. Finally she spoke. "It's a good thing you're not afraid of silence," she said. "Not that it happens much when I'm around." She glanced at him and smiled self-consciously, then drew a deep breath. "Ben, I need to know if God considers me still married. And I know it puts you in a really awkward position, but you're the only one I can ask about this. And even *you* aren't supposed to know about Tim." Her voice revealed her stress. "So I sure can't ask anyone else."

Ben nodded. "Don't think that I haven't given it all plenty of thought."

Marnie looked at him contemplatively. "When I made my decision to follow Christ, and when I got baptized—I made a choice to follow him all the way, no matter how hard it would be." She stared up at one of the stained glass windows, and the light shone down on her face. "I understand the redemption deal—I know I'm not my own."

Ben thought she had never looked more beautiful.

"But I sure have some questions," she continued, gaining enough confidence to look Ben straight in the eye. She was gratified to see gentle concern for her there. "It's so hard to go from being a widow for six months to being married again—yet without a husband. What made you say I was still married, if I'm legally a widow?"

Ben gulped hard and prayed for wisdom. "Because three times in the Bible we read that marriage is a covenant. Hard as it is, you made vows before God. It's more than a legal contract. You're joined by more than a court of law; you're joined by God, even if you didn't believe in him at the time."

"Yeah, I get that," Marnie nodded. "I figured that's what you'd say. I went to the Christian bookstore, and I've been reading up on what the Bible says about divorce."

"Good for you," Ben said tentatively.

"Doesn't 1 Corinthians 7 say that if an unbeliever abandons his spouse, the believer is free?" she asked.

Ben nodded. "Indeed. And many scholars believe that means you may remarry."

"But *you* don't?" she asked, dreading his answer.

"I'm open to that possibility in the text. But it's not that simple, Marnie."

"What do you mean?"

"I know it's a hard line to draw, but I think the spirit of a covenant would suggest that you should at least try to make it work before seeking other options."

Tears welled up in Marnie's eyes. "But Ben, he was so *cold* to me when I was there. He rejected me in every possible way. And you're telling me I haven't tried?"

"No. I'm not saying any of it is your fault, Marnie," Ben assured her. "Honestly, I'm not." He didn't like how this was turning out. "Tim left two incredibly beautiful people—Emily and *you*. I think he's absolutely crazy. But I also know that you weren't a Christian when the two of you were together. Now you're a new creation. He doesn't know the Marnie I know."

"He'll never know me the way you do, because he's not you. You view me through loving eyes, and his are so critical."

Ben smiled gently at the compliment. "My point is that you're different now. And he needs Christ, too, Marnie. He's lost. And maybe God wants to use you to help him find life."

"What do you expect me to do, Ben? Move to Dallas? Leave my church and my friends and my business and drag my daughter away from her grandfather to chase after someone who's abandoned me, and who would be furious if I came after him? Someone"—her voice cracked—"Someone who wants to remain anonymous for the sake of 'saving the free world,' who would fear the exposure my mere presence could bring?"

"I honestly don't know what you should do, Marnie. We need to spend some time praying to discern God's leading. A lot of life is gray, and this is one of those times when I see no easy answers."

They sat in silence for a long time. Finally Ben spoke again. "I'll tell you the truth—I wish you were free as much as you do."

Marnie looked him squarely in the eye. "It's hard. I'm trying to figure out how you fit into my life now. How much of you is it right for me to have? What am I allowed to feel and do so that our relationship pleases God."

He nodded his understanding. He had asked himself the same questions and he hadn't liked the answers, but he knew they were right. "We've both made a choice to love God first, correct?"

She nodded.

"For me that means I have to deal honorably with

you as Tim's wife. And the fact is, Tim's still alive, and he hasn't divorced you. And you can't file for divorce."

Marnie nodded. "I thought that's what you'd say. I guess I just needed to hear the hard, cold words. But I'm still not sure how my married status should work itself out on a day-to-day basis." She stood to go, signaling the end of the conversation.

"Well, it doesn't mean you have to dump me as a friend."

Marnie didn't respond. They walked out silently and started down the hall. "Hungry?" he asked her as they neared the corridor leading to the doctors' dining room.

"No. Sorry. Lost my appetite," Marnie said sadly. "See ya around." She walked away, her eyes glued to the ground. He watched until she turned the corner and was gone.

Two weeks after his self-prescribed implant, Dr. Allan Brown sat staring at his postoperative CT scan with a grin on his face. The results showed a change in the brain cells affected by MHS. By all measures, this was wonderful news. While still conscious of the risk involved, he felt tentatively optimistic. However, he checked his own enthusiasm by reminding himself that since his procedure, a second Alzheimer's patient had died.

After a few moments, Allan took down his own film and pulled out a confidential file from a locked cabinet. It held the most recent CT scans of the president of the United States. Allan shook his head when he saw the multiple areas of MHS. The dropped drink was no random slipup. Uncle Cal was clearly showing the effects of progressive akenosis.

Allan stood up and paced, knowing he had little time. He still had some lurking doubts about injecting the president. Was LG the answer, or a horrible mistake? It was too soon to tell; he simply didn't know. *Still, within a month, I'll have the information I need. Why not go ahead and schedule him for four weeks from now? It would buy me some time and get Dr. Harrison off my back.* He picked up the phone and made the call.

Allan had no solid working theory as to why he'd lost the Alzheimer's patients. He did know he was going to stay at the hospital tonight and watch Mr. Gray, the last of his "blue-tag" patients, for abnormalities. He had done three LG cell transplants exactly a week apart in each of the three Alzheimer patients. It certainly seemed like more than a coincidence that the sudden deaths of the other two occurred the same number of days following their LG cell transplants.

If there was some connection, tonight was the night for Mr. Gray. His CT scans showed excellent evidence of viable cells and early repair. And he had displayed other favorable signs—facial expression and recognition of his nurse. So Allan felt guardedly optimistic.

Meanwhile, each of the Parkinson's patients showed significant progress. The first had even shown improved motor control and a decrease in the classical "pill rolling" tremor. As for the MHS patients, so far he had seen no clinical response, but lab and X-ray evidence had consistently encouraged him.

Nevertheless, the two sudden Alzheimer deaths were troubling. Same cause of death—sudden, multifocal hemorrhage, each surrounding an area where the LG transplant had healed damage. Allan had looked at both the pathology and the microscopic slides. And both showed that the tiny capillaries supplying the nerve had exploded. Yet the nerves had been healing, and the level of neurotransmitter had tested normal. *Why? Why would they have vascular problems?* he wondered repeatedly. He simply couldn't make any sense of it.

"Doctor?" the nurse asked. "Mr. Gray seems to be getting restless."

Allan felt his heart begin to race. "When did you give him the sedative? Did you give him the higher dose? Are you sure he took it?" He fired off questions in an excited tone as he watched the monitor.

The nurse opened her mouth to answer, but Allan had rushed out, headed for the patient's room. "Bring the crash cart," he yelled back to her.

As he entered the room, Allan pulled the emergency code switch. Mr. Gray lay sweating and flailing. The doctor was about to order an injection when his patient had a sudden grand mal seizure. Moments later, he lay motionless. His pulse, which had skyrocketed, now began slowing steadily. Before initiating the full-court resuscitation, Allan quickly opened Mr. Gray's eyes. They were dilating rapidly, already unresponsive to light.

"No!" he yelled. "We *can't* lose him," he barked at Sheila, the nurse. Cursing, Allan began administering chest compression while Sheila tried to oxygenate the patient with a mask and ambu bag. The nurse supervisor arrived quickly and manned the cart. Allan, sweat beading across his brow, called for the usual cardiac medications, trying to get a response.

⊰❧⊱

"Your policy covers two million," Chris told Luc after Janelle had wheeled him into his attorney's office.
"Rivera's attorney initially asked for four. That was the
offer we rejected."

Luc glared at his friend. "No way!" he exclaimed, incensed at the greed.

"So we have two choices."

"And they are . . . ?"

"You can make him a counteroffer and hope he comes
down in what he's asking. Or you can pay what he's
asking. Otherwise we go to court."

"You're sure you don't have another option?"

"Like what?"

"I don't know. You're the attorney!"

⊰❧⊱

By the time the elevator alarm signaled the arrival of
the Code Blue heart team, Allan had pronounced Mr.
Gray dead. *Probably a cerebral hemorrhage,* he concluded
with a sinking feeling.

"What do we have?" asked the arriving doctor, out
of breath from his rush to respond.

"Seventy-eight-year-old, white male. Alzheimer's. Ar-
rest. No response to CPR. Bradycardia, then asystole.
Unresponsive to meds. Pupils fixed and blown. . . ."
Allan's voice trailed off.

"Not much left for me to do here then. Need me for
anything?"

"No," replied Allan. "Thanks for coming up. Guess

it was just his time," he said softly. *Yeah. Time. Right on time. And I'm the one who set the alarm.* It was deeply disturbing that all three of the Alzheimer study patients had died suddenly this way and almost exactly the same number of days after their transplants. Judging from the sequence of death events, Allan was betting on the cerebral bleeding again in this case. *What have I done to them?*

Allan walked slowly back to the nurse's station. He paged through the chart, not really looking for anything, just occupying the moments. Then swallowing hard, he walked down the hall to the Coke machine and stood facing it for several minutes. *How did I get here? I don't even remember walking down the hall just now,* he told himself. *What have I done to them? And what is going to happen to me?*

Because Marnie suspected her phone line was tapped, she quickly got used to the fact that Ben no longer made a nightly call to her house. Once she suspected listeners on the line, she avoided talking on the phone—even though she had nothing to hide. She felt incensed at the violation of her privacy but knew there was nothing she could do about it.

It was harder for her that Ben filled his e-mail messages with the idiom of introduction—hi, bye, good morning, good night—and with business and impersonal news such as, "I spent the evening playing racquetball again." In his careful removal of any romantic undertones, he had also excised any hint that they had built a righteous friendship over the past months. Still, when he called one evening about a week after their chapel conversation, she was glad to hear from him.

Ben arranged to pick her up for a church singles' group function. They were going to a play at Ford's Theater, followed by dessert at a nearby coffee house.

When he met her at the door, he smiled. "You look like a million bucks," he said.

"Are you still allowed to compliment me?" she asked, almost mocking, as she stepped out and locked the door behind her.

Ben felt his blood pressure going up. "Why would you say something like that?" he asked in disbelief.

"Because I'm a married woman. You're not supposed to notice how I look." Ben started toward the car, but Marnie remained on the porch.

"Correction," Ben said, turning back to face her. "It's one thing to look; it's another thing to drive around the block for a better look."

"Very funny."

"I'm quite serious," Ben said. Then, seeing Emily waving in the bay window, he asked, "Would you like to continue this discussion in my car?"

Marnie shrugged, then followed him.

He opened the door to his Explorer and helped her in. Once he had seated himself on the driver's side and fastened his seat belt, Marnie spoke again. "Look, if you don't like being around me, don't feel you have to do this kind of thing."

"Who said anything about not wanting to be around you?" Ben gave her an exasperated look.

When she didn't answer him, he spoke again.

"Marnie, I've never heard you talk this way. Why are you saying these things?"

Marnie stared out the window on her side, not wanting to see his expression. Finally, she looked over at him. "I guess I'm just having trouble getting used to my new, ultra-confused status. I shouldn't be taking it out on you. You're just trying to be nice to me, and I'm pushing you away. Maybe it's because I'm afraid you're going to leave me anyway. I'm sorry, Ben."

"Forgiven," he said, working to make his feelings match his words.

"Actually, my status isn't so confused. It's pretty clear. That's what really stinks."

"You're not the only one who's having a hard time with it, Marnie." Ben's voice had an edge.

"I know."

"Then I'd appreciate it if you'd try to make this easier for both of us."

"Are you suggesting I should be handling this differently?" She didn't like the accusation.

Ben thought for a long time. Then he answered firmly, "Yes. I am. I know you're miserable. Well, so am I."

Marnie noticed he was holding the wheel in a vicelike grip. He hadn't turned the ignition key yet.

Ben continued. "I'm trying to do right by you, but I don't want to lose you as a dear friend in the process. It's tricky."

"Well, that's good to know," Marnie said sincerely. "I wasn't so sure you wanted any sort of relationship at all. You've seemed so cold. I've had warmer e-mails from angry clients." Marnie was relieved to know he still cared and was ready to lighten the mood.

"Sorry. I'm still trying to find my footing. But is it any consolation that I really respect you for doing what's right?" he looked over at her kindly.

"Actually?" Marnie cocked her head and smiled. "Yeah. It helps. It helps a lot."

After the play, they sat at separate tables. It felt awkward initially, but they both managed to overcome it and have a good time. On the way home, they had a great discussion about the deity of Christ. Ben loved her enthusiasm when he shared new truths with her.

But as they pulled up in front of her house, she hit him with another bombshell. "I enjoyed the evening immensely, but I have the gnawing feeling I may need to find a different Sunday school class."

"What? Why?" His voice registered his disappointment. "These are your closest Christian friends, Marnie. Considering all you're going through right now, do you really think you should pull out of the best support system you've got?"

"It's not what I *want* to do. But it doesn't feel honest."

"What do you mean?"'

"When you go to a singles function—or a singles class of any kind—without a ring on your finger, you're saying that you're free. It feels a bit like false advertising."

"Advertising to whom? It's not like anyone asked you out, right?"

"Correction."

Ben turned off the ignition and looked over at her. He felt a twinge of jealousy. "Honestly?"

She nodded. "Uh-huh."

"Who?"

"As we were leaving, one of the guys at my table asked me out for this weekend."

"Which guy?"

"That's not the point. I told him no. But Ben, this is getting more complex instead of less."

Ben heaved a reluctant sigh and opened the car door.

Never one to seek patient contact, Allan kept to his charts. He had concluded that the LG therapy provided an unacceptable answer for Alzheimer's, but he still held out hope that it would cure Parkinson's and, more importantly, MHS.

It had been three weeks since the death of the last Alzheimer's patient yet, despite the setbacks, Allan had to work to control his elation because the Parkinson's subjects were an entirely different story. They had shown significant improvement. Their tremors were disappearing; motor function had measurably improved; they could even walk, smile, and converse intelligently. Allan felt his confidence growing again. As he reviewed each chart and the physical therapists' daily notes, it pleased him to see clear results measured by "non-biased" professionals.

Finally, he turned his attention to the charts of the three MHS patients. Their symptoms still showed no improvement, but they had not deteriorated. The encouraging news was that the serial CT scans showed dramatic changes in the areas where the myelin problems had previously existed. Allan sat staring at the view box, studying each of the scans, patient by patient, scan by scan, watching the buildup areas slowly, almost imperceptibly, disappear.

It's only a matter of time, he told himself. *These nerves will begin to conduct normally. I just know it.* As he viewed the films, he guessed that within another week or two he would see some outward changes. Perhaps the large motor fibers would be the first to respond, and the tremors would dissipate. That was his calculated opinion, based on the response of the Parkinson's patients.

His pager vibrated, interrupting his musings. He looked down and recognized the classified code that meant he was getting paged by "the president's men." He returned to his office on the fifth floor of the research center, picked up a secured line, and dialed the number as instructed.

Steven Harrison got right to the point. "How are things going?"

Before Allan could say "Quite well," he heard, "Are we still on schedule?"

Chapter Twenty-Six

BEN CRUISED DOWN HIGHWAY 50 into Washington, D.C., heading for a luncheon. A U.S. Representative, a heart attack survivor whom Ben had befriended in his chaplaincy work, was returning to work today. The patient had honored Ben by asking him to join the celebration his colleagues were hosting for him on his first day back. *Heady stuff,* Ben thought, as he hummed along with the radio.

Suddenly, the lyrics of an old hit caught him by surprise: "I didn't think it could happen again, but I've fallen in love with you." He let out a tiny gasp. He remembered so well the years he'd spent convinced of this very thing—that he would never again care deeply about any woman after Juliet. But then, in the last few months, Marnie had rekindled the light he'd buried deep inside. Ben had even begun to dream that he might be able to share his life with her, and where had it gotten him? He reached over, snapped off the radio, and drove in silence the rest of the way.

He thought about the doctor from Romania who had called recently. He'd asked if Ben could come for six months and help set up a medical facility. At the time, Ben had had a job at the clinic and his developing relationship with Marnie had made the prospect of going overseas unappealing. But now he wondered whether he should reconsider. Maybe it would be best if he went away for a while. It would be several months before Luc reestablished the practice. And his relationship with Marnie had certainly turned out differently from the way he'd expected.

Marnie made herself a sandwich and picked up the *Washington Post*. Her eyes widened, and she bit her lip when she read the headline at the bottom of the front page. It was the first article she had seen suggesting that the president might have some kind of disease. The investigative reporter listed minor occurrences that the general media had not reported, events that seemed insignificant until added together. The president had fallen asleep at a meeting, he trembled when he held a pen. Then there were the public stumble and the spilled drink.

The article said that the president's personal physician had been unavailable for comment. As a publicist, Marnie was astonished at how badly the White House had handled the story. She thought they should have taken a more proactive stance, and she momentarily pondered the possibility of getting involved.

Later in the morning, Mavis Beth called to express

her concern. There was no doubt in her mind that her brother-in-law was showing signs of akenosis. The *Post* reporter had called her in the process of writing the story, and the information he had given her had shaken her. Marnie didn't have the heart to tell her the story had made page one in the capital.

Conscious that her every word was probably being recorded, Marnie swallowed hard and kept quiet. When Mavis Beth talked on for a few minutes only to find her words met with silence, she said, "Well, maybe not. You probably think I'm an old fool, honey. It's probably nothing. The media's always trying to sensationalize everything. It's just that after losing Horace, I see akenosis in every male family member."

"I'm sure it's scary for you, Mom."

Mavis Beth felt stupid. "Well, I don't mean to keep you. Glad I caught you at home. I always used to have to leave messages, but it seems like I'm having more luck lately."

"I *am* here more this year, thanks to satellite e-mail, FedEx, faxes, and cell phones. I don't have to go out as much. In fact, some of my clients are in other states."

"Then why live in D.C., honey? Why not live in Rhode Island or somewhere prettier? Somewhere slower? And cheaper—a nicer place to raise a child?"

Marnie laughed. "And take Emily away from my dad? Not a chance? He'd have me tarred and feathered."

"Well, take him *with* you, for Pete's sake! He's no landlubber. He adores the coast."

She had a point. Marnie didn't like the thought of dragging her dad away from his retired government buddies, but then, anywhere he'd gone he'd made a circle of friends immediately. He'd never met a stranger.

"Or are you wanting to stay near someone else special?" Mavis Beth asked.

Marnie was glad her mother-in-law could not see her turn red. "No. Uh-uh. That's not an issue. Not at all," Marnie stammered.

"Oh, dear! I didn't intend to pry. I'm sorry, honey. I just want you to know that I don't expect a pretty young thing like you to pine for my son forever. You'll always be a daughter to me. I just want you to be happy."

"It's okay, Mom. Really. You're sweet. And maybe you're right. I could use a change of scenery." Starting over in a new Sunday school class had left her feeling rootless.

After she hung up, she thought for a long time. Maybe she *should* consider a move. She really could serve most of her clients from anywhere in America. She propped her elbows on her desk, closed her eyes, and rubbed her temples. Then she reached over and turned off the lamp.

Allan sat in his office, sipping French Vanilla Café and feeling satisfied that his follow-up CT scan showed he'd made the right choice. The LG cells were alive and had attached in his brain.

The phone once again jarred his thoughts. It was his fifth call in as many minutes, and he hurried to take one more sip of coffee, burning his lips.

"Dr. Brown?" The physical therapist's voice immediately betrayed concern.

"What is it?"

"Sorry to bother you, sir. But I figured you'd want to know—I thought a verbal report would be appropriate." The PT had been involved with each of the post-transplant patients from the beginning. Allan liked him for his detailed notations, but lately his chart notes had been a bit vague, particularly for the Parkinson's patients.

"There's been a significant regression. I can't explain exactly why."

Allan's e-mail screen blipped the arrival of an incoming message, another in a stack of correspondence he had no interest in answering today.

"In the MHS patients?" Allan strengthened his grip on the phone.

"No, sir. Just the Parkinson's. Muscle strength and range of motion are deteriorating in each of the patients. And the faintest signs of tremors seem to be returning. I have no explanation for it. It may simply be a temporary setback. Only thing is, all three of them are showing this negative change."

Allan said nothing, so the therapist filled the silence. "But on the bright side, sir, I've seen incremental improvements in each of the MHS patients."

Allan leaned forward. "What kind of improvements?" His tone changed dramatically.

"Definite improvement in the tremors. And some of the emotional lability, which was causing the abrupt mood swings and uncontrolled laughing and crying. They appear to be stabilizing. The three patients are definitely improving."

"I appreciate your personal attention. Good work. You were right to call me." After Allan hung up, he sat back to assess the new data. The X-ray studies of the

Parkinson's patients showed no change. So as far as Allan could tell, the LG cells were still viable. Yet the patients were deteriorating. *There really is no explanation,* he thought. *But at least the MHS patients are improving. I knew they would. The CT scans show dramatic changes now. The built-up areas are almost gone, and the LG cells are apparently laying down new myelin, which is just now starting to show improved transmission.*

The CT scan data, combined with the physical therapist's assessment, was wonderful news for the MHS patients. And the timing could not have been better. Allan had an appointment in the morning with Dr. Harrison, who was flying in to arrange the particulars of the president's procedure. Everything would have to be done with the greatest discretion, in the middle of the night, with only Allan and the president's men around. Allan was ready, but part of him was vaguely uneasy.

The phone rang again. Allan handled the call quickly and hung up. He tried to recall where he'd been in his thinking process.

The others aren't looking so hot. But after all, the MHS patients are the people I'm really trying to cure. His lack of success with the other diseases disappointed him, to be sure. It would have been nicer, in terms of international fame, if his therapy had worked for the more common neurological conditions. But saving the president wasn't exactly a failure, he assured himself.

The e-mail screen beeped again. Another incoming message.

Allan hadn't slept well for days. He couldn't seem to clear his mind. And all the distractions were really starting to annoy him. He had this nagging suspicion that he was overlooking something. He needed to think. If he were back home in Westfield, he would have instinctively headed out to Mindowaskin Park to sit by the lake. Instead, he settled for the Dallas equivalent.

Twenty minutes later, Allan was guiding his car around White Rock Lake. The city had just finished a dredging operation that had turned the murky six-mile-long lake into a pristine stretch of blue water. He drove by the sailboat docks and made his way to the top of a hill on the east side, just up from the old bathhouse.

He parked the car, got out, and walked a few yards down to a bench that provided an inspirational view of the lake and downtown Dallas. Shoving his hands in his pockets, he stared past the bikers and occasional joggers on the road below.

Allan mentally replayed the events of his research, from eggs to mice to chimps to humans. He recalled his anticipation and confidence in those first days. He had made a pure cell line—a replicated gamete. No one in all the earth had anything precisely like these cells. The birth of the Mexican twins demonstrated how accurately his procedure had replicated the genome from the mother, duplicating the X chromosome.

Though the "mistake" of Luc's implantation had been unfortunate, Allan took a certain amount of pride in knowing that his LG line was so perfect—and not just as stem cells. Under the right conditions, they had gone on to develop into children.

To his mind, Allan had made no mistakes; his logic was flawless. A pure cell line, all stem cells, at the totipotential stage, should be able to adapt, adjust, activate, and fill in anywhere. And the neurological system was just the beginning of the useful applications. Once the proper gene "switches" could be located and "flipped on," this cell line could develop into anything—cells, tissues, organs, and, of course, human beings. The potential for curing diseases was staggering.

The implants had been perfect. The cells went where they were supposed to go, and began almost immediately to "switch on" and restore the abnormal cells to normal.

So what went wrong? Why would fresh, healthy, normal nerve growth trigger an electrical storm so strong that the localized blood vessels would "explode" and kill the Alzheimer's patients? It makes no sense. But they are dead—and all in a similar, horrible way.

He shifted on the bench. When an elderly couple walking hand in hand nodded their friendly greeting, Allan looked right past them.

He considered the Parkinson's patients. Getting better—and they knew it! Even the therapist was impressed. Yes, they'd plateaued, but they'd also stabilized. The studies had all been good. The neurotransmitter was producing at normal levels. But then there was today's news.

He compared the different diseases to the different responses: Neurotransmitter production involving motor nerves in the Parkinson patients; sensory nerve output in the Alzheimer's. Different type of fibers; different diameters. *I wonder if that's significant?*

And then there were the MHS patients—a definite mixed bag. These patients had both the smaller sensory fiber involvement of emotions and memory, in addition to the larger, thicker motor nerves. Yet so far, both seemed to be responding. The built-up "callus" of myelin seemed to have dissolved in each of the abnormal areas, and normal function appeared to be returning in both types of nerves. It appeared that the LG therapy was appropriate for both types of nerves. But why? Why did the Alzheimer patients have such dreadful outcomes? Why did the healing process evoke such a devastating electrical response from the nerves, overwhelming the patients' circulatory systems and leading to violent, sudden death?

Added to that, the Parkinson folks' improvement seemed to have hit a brick wall. *But there's no X-ray evidence of deterioration. I just don't get it! This should work. It has to work. Dr. Harrison arrives tomorrow. And something just doesn't fit yet. I have to be missing something here.* Suddenly, a voice behind him jolted him out of his contemplation.

Marnie was approving photos for a client's press packet when the phone rang again. She recognized her father's cell number. "Hey, Dad. You and Emily having fun?" she asked, before Will even had a chance to identify himself. But she immediately knew something was wrong. She could hear her daughter screaming in the background. Will's voice cracked as he said, "I'm on the way to the hospital with Em."

"What! What have they done to her?" she demanded, a hundred terrifying scenarios coursing through her brain in an instant.

"Excuse me, sir?"

Allan turned to see a young biker carrying an expensive racing bike over his shoulder. The doctor's initial response was annoyance that this stranger had invaded his world. But then he figured he'd done enough thinking for one afternoon. "What d'ya need?" Allan asked. "Got a flat?"

"Naw," said the youth, who looked to be no older than eighteen. "Broke the chain pounding up the hill. Mind giving me a lift? I left my car over at Winfrey Point."

"Sure," said Allan, impressed by the young man's boldness.

"I noticed your sport utility—figured you were a biker, too."

"Actually, no," said Allan. "I'm not. But I do love the lake." The young cyclist popped off the front wheel and loaded his bike into the back of Allan's car. As they drove along the road, Allan asked, "Can you repair the chain with an extra link?"

"No way. Got a bunch of miles on this chain. If I clip in a new one, it'll just break again where the old meets the new—you know, the 'weakest link' deal."

"Right," said Allan. They passed the park museum and came up the hill to Winfrey Point.

"Thanks a lot, man." The cyclist pulled his bike out of Allan's car and carried it over to an old Toyota. As the doctor drove around the lake on his way home, his thoughts kept settling on the fact that he had transplanted LG cells into his own brain and couldn't be sure what would happen. It was a fear he worked hard to suppress.

"Emily, um . . . she fell off the jungle gym in the condo courtyard," Will told his frantic daughter. "I think she may have broken her arm." Marnie could hear the guilt in her father's voice, but she knew it wasn't his fault. Her daughter made a habit of attempting balancing acts in high places. Marnie felt as much sympathy for her father as she did for her daughter.

Though upset for Emily's sake, Marnie felt relief. This was bad, but nothing like what she'd feared. "I'll meet you in emergency. But first, let me talk to her, okay?"

In a moment, the crying grew louder. Through her sobs, Emily managed to communicate, "Mommy, it hurts, and I'm scared."

"It'll be all right, baby. I'll meet you at the hospital, okay, honey?"

"Will you bring Molly?" Emily wanted her favorite worn-out rag doll, the one with a hole in her cheek and a face smeared with lipstick.

"Yes, sweetheart. I'll have Molly with me."

On her way to the hospital, Marnie instinctively paged Ben. When he greeted her in a matter-of-fact tone, Marnie wanted to say, "Never mind." Instead her voice cracked as she worked to get the words out.

Ben listened carefully and warmed to the distress in Marnie's voice. "Are you okay?" he asked.

"Yeah. I guess I'm all right."

"I'll meet you down in emergency."

"Okay." She was hoping he'd say that.

"I'll be there by the time you arrive," he assured her.

When Marnie rushed in the emergency entrance, clutching Molly in one hand and her purse in the other, Ben enveloped her in a hug. She felt grateful for the familiar face. "They're not here yet," he told her, guiding her to a place where she could sit and watch the street for Will's car.

"I don't know why I'm such a wreck. A broken arm isn't exactly life-threatening."

"You thought they'd hurt your kid, didn't you?" His eyes searched hers.

Marnie sat down, buried her head in her hands, and nodded. Ben sat down beside her and rubbed her back as she choked back sobs.

"Is it ever going to end?" she murmured. "Are the fear and pain ever going to stop?"

Ben handed her a tissue. She appreciated that he always seemed to carry a few. "Look! They're here!" he stood, handing Marnie her purse and Molly.

Marnie wiped her face and blew her nose as she rushed out the door to comfort her daughter.

When Allan's phone rang around four o'clock the next morning, for a minute he thought he was in his house back in Virginia with Marnie. He struggled to orient himself.

"Doctor, I thought you'd want to know. . . ." The nurse sounded agitated. "Mr. Abercrombie just had a seizure."

Allan cursed.

"It was only a short petit mal. I wasn't even sure it was a seizure, but I couldn't get his attention. He just lay staring for about two minutes. And when he came to, he couldn't remember any of the previous moments. I checked his chart, and he has no history of a seizure disorder or epilepsy. So I thought I'd better call."

"Thank you," replied Allan. "You were exactly right. Is Mr. Abercrombie okay now?"

"Yes, Doctor. He took a sleeper, and I think he's already fallen asleep."

"All right. Thanks again. I'll come on in and check on him."

Before Allan had hung up the phone, his mind raced ahead of him. Mr. Abercrombie was the first of the MHS patients. What was happening? Could he have been an epileptic? Maybe the nurse was wrong, and it wasn't a seizure at all. But what if it was? What did it mean?

He pulled on a scrub suit and headed for his car, ignoring the speed limit on the deserted streets as he hurried to the research center. He pulled into his parking stall and took the elevator up to the research floor, thinking through the workup for seizures.

Right away, he ordered an EEG and scheduled a CT scan for the morning. Mr. Abercrombie was resting comfortably, with no evidence of any serious complications. Vital signs were normal. Allan requested the usual laboratory blood levels. Then he dutifully pulled the chart and wrote a note.

With nothing more to do until he had more information, Allan decided to sleep in the hospital call room.

He left his room number with the nurse and told her to page him when they had the EEG strip. Then he shuffled off drowsily, hoping to take the edge off his weariness. But as he settled into the narrow bed, his mind was still racing. *What if it doesn't work? What's going to happen to* me?

Chapter Twenty-Seven

"GOOD MORNING, LITTLE SWEETIE." Marnie greeted her groggy child and stroked her dark hair. Emily rubbed her eyes, licked her parched lips, and looked around as though lost.

"You're in the hospital, honey," her mother said soothingly. "Remember? You broke your arm and had to have surgery, punkin."

Marnie and Will had waited in emergency, finished in X-ray, and sat through the hour or so it took to do the surgery. By then it had been midnight. Before Marnie had even arrived at the hospital, Ben had contacted a buddy in orthopedics, who helped expedite the process. When the attending physician had determined that Emily needed surgery, Ben had offered to stay by her side until she got into recovery—an offer that Marnie gratefully accepted. The surgical nurse joked that Emily was the youngest patient she'd ever known to have her own personal OB/Gyn.

Now Emily looked frightened. "You're okay now,"

Marnie continued. "You had a nasty break, and the doctors had to make your arm better, but it's going to be good as new very soon." Holding up Molly in front of her daughter's face, Marnie wagged the doll back and forth as she spoke in a high-pitched tone. "Wow, we get to be in the hospital, Emily. We can watch videos *all* day."

Fear melted into delight as Emily grabbed Molly and hugged her. Marnie was glad her daughter didn't seem to be in any pain. The cast on her slender arm was awkward enough.

Around nine, Ben poked his head in the door. "Such lovely scenery we have in the hospital this morning! How are you, princess?" he asked Emily.

"I didn't like the oatmeal."

"Yucky hospital food, huh?"

The patient wrinkled her nose and nodded vigorously.

"Sorry. You'll have to get your mom to smuggle in some toaster pastries for you." He handed Marnie her briefcase.

Will had brought a change of clothes, then had gone home. Marnie's father loathed hospitals, and he could always call. Ben also had his own delivery, a small box for the patient. Emily carefully opened it with her free hand. Inside, Ben had tucked a pair of heart-shaped, red sunglasses. Emily adored sunglasses; she had at least eight pairs. The gift delighted her, and the grown-ups chuckled at the sight of her lying in bed wearing them. "Thank you, Benichek," she said reaching up with her good arm to pull him near.

"You were a brave girl last night," he said, nudging her cheek with his nose. Then he leaned back. "And now you look like a movie star."

Emily beamed as Ben turned back to Marnie. "I called the church prayer chain this morning. Lots of people are praying for you both. But I should warn you—after twenty people have embellished the story and passed it on, you probably won't even recognize it."

It felt good to laugh together. "I'll check back in on both of you a little later, okay?" he said.

Marnie walked him to the door. As he left, he leaned back and said under his breath, "By the way—next time you're in emergency, I suggest that you hide that pitiful-looking doll. It's *so* pathetic."

Marnie put her nose in the air and feigned great dignity. "But she's real. And Emily loves her dearly."

"Yeah, well, as your friend, I believe it's my duty to tell you that you looked pretty silly holding on to a dolly in front of God and everybody."

Marnie worked to suppress a grin. When she couldn't hold it back, she giggled, punched his arm, and said, "I hate you, Ben McKay."

Later that afternoon, Ben returned to check on Emily. Finding Marnie dozing in the chair and Emily asleep, he tiptoed in, picked up Marnie's magazine where it had fallen at her feet, and sat down to read. When Marnie opened her eyes a few minutes later, she was startled to find him sitting there. "How long have you been in here?"

Ben raised his eyebrows and assured her, "About a minute and a half. I told you I'd be back."

"Thanks," she said barely audibly. "I can't tell you how much . . ."

Ben raised his palm to silence her. "I know," he whispered, nodding. "Really I do." He edged his chair closer to hers and said, "There's something I want to talk with you about."

"What is it?"

Ben mulled his words carefully before he spoke. "I'm thinking of going to Romania for six months."

Marnie looked stunned. "Romania?"

Ben nodded. "I'm just at the early stages of thinking about it. But I've been asked to help set up a Western clinic to serve American missionaries over there—as well as a lot of other people."

"Wow." Marnie didn't know what else to say. After seeing him at work in Russia, she knew he'd be great, but the thought of his disappearing completely from her life was hard to bear. She leaned forward and searched his face. "You really feel like that's what God's telling you to do?"

"I'm not sure."

Victor answered his page and immediately punched in the numbers for Culiacán.

"We're on the right track," Carlos Rivera told him. "They know it's their fault."

"What do you mean, señor?" Victor wasn't following, but he could hear the seething anger that punctuated the mayor's words.

"They did something wrong or they would not be pursuing a settlement. So stay at it until you find something." Carlos was indignant. "They *must* be protecting someone. And I want to know who." He raised his voice as he spoke. For Carlos Rivera, knowledge was power. He hated the thought of someone trying to hide something from him.

"But señor, all the records burned with the clinic," Victor tried to reason with him.

"Yes, how convenient! But that doesn't matter; we can work around it. Even if Dr. Morgan is not the father, he must know who is. I tell you—they know something! Someone connected to the clinic did this evil thing. Otherwise, they would not want to pay for it to go away."

"What do you wish for me to do, señor?"

"Stay on them."

"If they know, they are not talking about it on the phone." Victor was tired of wasting endless hours listening to boring calls.

"Bug their cars. And Dr. Morgan's attorney's office. Do whatever you must. But stay on it."

Sitting in front of his computer screen, Allan continued to puzzle over the recent events. When Sheila called to tell him that Mr. Abercrombie had died, despite full anticonvulsant therapy, it shook him to the core. He had managed to control the patient's symptoms for a few days. But then, *status epilepticus*—a neurological emergency consisting of grand mal seizures without interruption—put the patient at risk of death by insufficient oxygen. Allan had tried all the usual—and even some unusual—drug therapies. Nevertheless, Mr. Abercrombie, his first MHS patient, had succumbed.

Allan had scanned the Internet for every available

piece of medical information on seizure disorders, but he'd found nothing to explain why these seizures had become totally resistant to treatment.

The postmortem exam, on the other hand, had been very revealing. All the areas of akenosis had been restored! The body's natural "cleanup" cells had broken down the disease's abnormal thickening, removing the excessive myelin, and relieving the buildup. Healthy, new cells had replaced the damaged nerve sheath. The healing looked perfect. So what had triggered the seizures? And if the nerves were just "adjusting" to the new tissue, why hadn't the seizures responded to any medications?

Allan leaned back in his chair, propped his feet on the corner of the desk, and stared at his screen saver. He hadn't even noticed the storm that was approaching Dallas until a loud crack brought him back to reality. His computer screen went blank. *That was some major thunder.*

"Stupid surge protector," he murmured to himself, moving to reboot his PC. He was glad he'd had nothing critical open when the system had crashed. The screen flashed a message that the computer had been "improperly shut down." Allan paused. Leaning back in his chair again, he stared at the power unit on the floor, where the glowing red light confirmed that it was still working. Yet the electrical storm had hit something close enough to blast his computer, despite the surge protector.

That's it! The truth suddenly seemed so obvious. *A 'power surge' in the brain! These new cells are too good. They connect too perfectly, and the older, surrounding nerve cells—being fifty-plus years old—can't handle the surge.* Allan was certain he was right. The new cells laid down by the LG cell line were perfect—too perfect for the surrounding nerves to sustain.

His mind shifted back to the words of the young cyclist he had helped at the lake.

"If I clip in a new link on the chain, it'll just break again where the old meets the new—you know, the 'weakest link' deal."

"Of course!" Allan exclaimed out loud. "Why didn't I see it?" The Alzheimer's patients had deteriorating sensory nerves. By patching in new, healthy nerve cells, he had subjected their brains to terrible "electrical surges" whenever the nerves fired. Eventually, the localized seizures led to massive hemorrhage and sudden death. He shook his head in amazement.

No wonder the autopsies showed such good nerve healing and such disastrous damage in the surrounding tissue. But, what about the Parkinson's patients? Allan considered how regression to baseline symptoms had followed their early improvement. The patients had gotten better, then plateaued, and then got worse again. He had no autopsy specimens, because all of the Parkinson's patients were, fortunately, still alive, but he knew that the problem was with the neurotransmitter, dopamine. Obviously, the LG cells had recognized the deficit and differentiated into a cell type that could replace the missing chemical, but it had stopped working. No seizures, no problems, just the disappearance of the early signs of improvement.

Why would the cells begin so well and then stop producing the needed chemical so quickly? As Allan reflected, he recalled his early cloning days in the animal lab in Kentucky, when he had created artificial twins. The identical offspring thrived and lived normal lives. Yet when researchers had used the nuclear transfer technique, as with Dolly the famous sheep, they'd found that the genetic codes were disrupted such that the animals had greatly shortened life spans. When they'd taken a cell from an older animal and cloned it, though they could get the DNA to "restart" and "flip the switch" to begin a new animal, some of the effects of aging had shown up in the genome.

"I took the genome from the mother, with the existing effects of aging, and merely duplicated them," he muttered to himself. "It wasn't the normal chromosome aligning between father and mother, which seems to 'reset' the genetic age clock."

Allan paused and rubbed his forehead. "There was no way to know. No way to know! And if that's true," he mumbled at the computer screen, "the LG cells ran through their life span quickly and then failed."

He sat for a moment with furrowed brow. *That returned the patient to the pretreatment state in the Parkinson's folks, but in the Alzheimer's patients, the new cells' nerve conduction was simply too strong for the nervous system to bear. Result—overload.*

A wave of satisfaction washed over him as he settled back into his chair and folded his arms across his chest. He understood. His mind had solved yet another medical mystery. But as Allan began to relax, the nagging sense of dread that had been lurking in the back of his mind jumped to the forefront. He cursed. *What if I'm right?*

Luc played telephone tag with his attorney all morning before they finally connected. When Chris came on the line, he told his friend, "You're not gonna like it."

"What did they say?" Luc asked.

"Basically, they rejected our offer."

"No counter?"

"Well, yeah. But hardly. They originally said four million. We came back and offered two. They countered with three-point-eight million or nothing."

"Three-point-eight! What kind of negotiation is *that*?" Luc demanded.

"Pretty hard nosed, but understandable. The Riveras do have two children who are going to require a lifetime of care."

"Yeah, but Mexico has government health care. It's not like it's going to bankrupt them. I mean, I feel bad about it, but I don't have four million bucks."

"Do you have any resources outside of your insurance, Luc? Got anything that might allow us to restructure a deal? Any resources you haven't told me about?"

Luc groaned. "Not two million bucks' worth!"

That afternoon, Luc relayed the information to Ben, who gaped in astonishment at the news. He had expected an easy settlement. Later, Ben dropped back by the hospital to tell Marnie. Emily had started running a fever, and her surgeon had decided to keep her in for another day. Ben was glad he knew where to find Marnie, but he wondered how she would respond.

Allan Brown tried to sleep but, instead, he kept breaking into a cold sweat. Dr. Harrison's response to the delay of the president's procedure had frightened him. Equally troubling was the realization that the symptoms of MHS were much more like those of Alzheimer's than those of Parkinson's. Both diseases affected the delicate sensory nerve fibers that carry emotion and memory, in addition to the larger, sturdier motor cells. But the Alzheimer's patients were the ones who had died.

If Allan was right, the other two akenosis patients he had transplanted with the LG cells were destined for an acute onset seizure disorder that would ultimately lead to death. He had no effective medications to offer. If the usual time sequence held true, the next patient would be entering the "danger zone" within two or three days, followed shortly by the final MHS patient.

Allan tossed and turned, considering different anti-convulsant regimens, different combinations of Dilantin, Tegretol, and Benzodiazepines and its derivatives. He tried to avoid thinking about the LG cells in his own brain, which likely were placing his life on a short timeline. Never a particularly emotional man, Allan blinked back tears. The work of his lifetime, his great quest for deliverance for himself and the men of his family, seemed to be proving futile. In fact, his magnificent advance, "the cure," was looking more like a "curse."

He was beginning to fully recognize that his death was imminent. He had no idea how he might escape. His hopes were pinned to the possibility that his relative youthfulness, compared with the other patients, might work in his favor. Perhaps the LG cells would "grow old" quickly, thanks to genetic aging, and die before they killed him. He managed to sink into a fretful sleep.

He woke at three in the morning with a sense of resignation. After getting up, he called the research center and instructed the nurses to start the two surviving MHS patients on a therapeutic dose of Dilantin. He also instituted seizure precautions. It helped him to order a preemptive strike—at least he was doing something—though it felt a bit like fighting a blaze with a water pistol. Still, he was a doctor and a scientist, and he was going to stay at the helm, captain of the ship, even though the outlook was bleak.

Later that morning, no longer caring about high-level security, he picked up the phone and punched in Marnie's number.

Chapter Twenty-Eight

"DO YOU BELIEVE IN MIRACLES?" Marnie asked Ben, after he'd answered her page.

"Sure! What's up?"

"I just heard from Allan."

Ben's lips parted. "Really? He called you at *home*? What's going on? Or would you rather tell me over lunch?"

"That's okay. Anything he said to me is already a matter of public record, if you know what I mean," Marnie told him.

"Good point. So what happened? Were you surprised?"

"Cold stunned. My stomach's still quivering."

"What did he say?"

"He wants me to come to Dallas again. And he wants me to bring Emily. When I was there, he had no intention of ever seeing us again. Now he wants us. He's always so zipped up, so closed. But now I get, 'Marnie, I have to see you. There's so much I need to tell you.'"

"Hmmm. I guess it sounds promising."

"Only one thing that's kind of weird."

Ben leaned forward and tightened his grip on the phone. "What's that?"

"He doesn't want Emily to see him or know about him."

"Huh?"

"He wants to set it up for her to see the research monkeys or something so he can view her from the next room."

"How do you feel about that?"

"Good, actually. Imagine the turmoil otherwise. Until I know what he's thinking, and what he wants in terms of a relationship, I'd rather not upset her."

"It still seems pretty odd."

"So, naturally, he needs us to stay in a hotel instead of at his bachelor pad."

"Why do you think he's had a change of heart?" Ben felt suddenly less than enthusiastic.

"Answered prayer!" As Marnie said this, Ben felt a pang of guilt. For her, this *was* an answer to prayer.

When Ben remained silent, Marnie filled the void. "Okay, it's not like he was making romantic overtures, Ben. That's what I find so puzzling. I can't imagine what he's thinking. Anyway, before I forget to tell you—I told him about the Riveras rejecting Luc's settlement offer."

"And?"

"It was interesting," she said.

"Why's that?"

"Well, he said he would handle it."

"What does *that* mean?"

"I'm afraid to ask. What do you make of it all?"

Ben thought for a long time. "I really don't know. But I have a favor to ask."

"What's that?"

"My sister Carolyn lives in Dallas," he said. "And she's got plenty of room. Let me go down with you two."

"Sorry, Ben. Allan would kill me if I took you to see him."

"That's not what I meant. I don't intend to see him."

"Then why go?"

"I haven't seen Carolyn for a while; we're overdue for a visit. And, honestly, I'm a little nervous about your safety. Call me overprotective, but I'd just feel better about it if I went."

"You don't have to do that. We'll be fine."

"I want to."

"Well, suit yourself. I wouldn't mind the company."

"Then it's settled?" Ben found Marnie's enthusiasm underwhelming. "I'll call Carolyn and tell her to expect us."

"Wait. I don't want to inconvenience your sister. I don't even know her. Why don't you stay with her, and Emily and I will get a hotel."

"But Marnie, really. Trust me. The two of you will really hit it off. Carolyn wouldn't mind at all." When Marnie didn't respond, Ben added, "But if you'd be more comfortable—whatever."

"Yeah, thanks, but I'd really prefer our own place."

"Okay."

"I've been *praying* for an opportunity like this!"

"Yeah? Well, good for you," Ben said, hoping the jealousy he felt didn't show in his voice.

"You paged me?" Carlos Rivera's question was sharp, impatient.

"Señor, we have a development."

"What is it?" Carlos demanded.

Victor relayed the details of Marnie's conversations.

"Who is Allan?" Carlos wanted to know.

"I'm not sure, señor, but he told her he would handle the settlement, so he must be linked to the clinic."

"Si."

"I think I should go to Dallas, señor."

"Certainly."

On his way home that evening, Allan had a hard time shaking the feeling that someone was following him.

The next morning, he received a call from his government contact who reamed him out for the security breach. Allan held the phone loosely and stared at his office ceiling as he listened. He just didn't care any more. Not even when the caller threatened that the government might not fork over the 1.8 million dollars needed to help Luc settle the suit immediately.

That's your *problem*, he thought. "Listen to me," he said through gritted teeth. "If anything happens to my family, I've seen to it that this whole thing will hit the news. And your name will be all over it," he lied.

"That would be a very unwise move, Doctor. Your wife and the clinic are also being tracked and tapped by one of Carlos Rivera's men. How would you know who was really responsible?"

"I guess you'd better make sure that *no one* is, then!"

Allan arrived at the crowded airport in the early evening, forty minutes before his family's scheduled arrival time. He had no intention of making his presence known. He merely wanted to catch a glimpse of his wife and child as they exited the airport. He sat in the waiting area of the adjacent gate, patiently reading the *Dallas Morning News.* When he saw Emily emerge holding Ben's hand, his mouth dropped.

Victor sat drinking a sloe gin fizz in the airport bar on the American Airlines concourse at the Dallas airport. When the flight from Washington D.C., arrived, he stood up to watch the exiting passengers. Out of the corner of his eye, a man sitting at the next gate caught his attention. It seemed to Victor that the man was paying particular attention to the same threesome that he himself was watching, and the stranger's reaction to seeing them suggested something was amiss.

Ben pulled the rental car up to the curb where Marnie and Emily, who had gone to the rest room while he was at the Avis counter, were waiting with the luggage. After piling their bags into the trunk, they exited the north airport entrance and headed east on LBJ Freeway. In thirty minutes, they pulled into the parking lot of the Westin Hotel. While Marnie checked in at the front counter, Ben walked over to a pay phone to call his sister.

"Use my cell phone," Marnie called after him. "It's cheaper."

Shortly after the three of them had ridden the elevator up to the room, Marnie's cell phone rang.

"It might be Carolyn," Ben said. "I just gave her your number."

"Marnie Sullivan," she answered.

"This is Allan."

"Oh! Hello." Marnie gave Ben a funny look, then walked into the bathroom and shut the door. "I didn't expect to hear from you so soon."

"I'd like to talk to you tonight, if I may."

"Okay, fire away." She shut the lid on the toilet and sat down, expecting a long conversation.

"No, I mean I want to see you."

"Oh, well childcare is a bit of a challenge."

"Can't Ben stay with Emily for awhile?"

Marnie stared at the towel rack, eyes wide. "How did you know Ben was here?"

"I have my ways. Just ask him to keep her."

"Uh, okay, I guess I could."

"Why's he here, Marn?"

"His sister lives here. He came to visit her; he's not planning to see you."

"So he knows about me."

"Yes."

"I see." He did not sound happy, but his reaction was milder than she expected.

"Then as long as he knows, I'd like to see him while you're here."

"Yeah?" Her voice registered pleasant surprise. "So where do you want to meet tonight?"

"Star Canyon."

"You want to meet in a canyon?"

"No. It's a restaurant. Near downtown." When Marnie exhaled her relief, she realized she'd been holding her breath.

"You hungry?" he continued.

She had eaten the airline food, but she didn't want to discourage him. "What time?"

"Seven."

After Marnie took down the directions, she freshened her makeup and redid her hair the way Tim had always liked it best. When she emerged from the bathroom to Ben's searching gaze, she was glad to see that Emily had engrossed herself in *The Swan Princess*.

"You're white as a sheet," Ben said under his breath.

"That was *him*. He wants to meet tonight for dinner."

"That must be why you look so sharp."

"Ben. He knows you're here."

"How?"

"I'm not sure. Strange, huh?"

"Very." Ben looked concerned.

"And, obviously, I need to ask a favor."

"You need me to stay here with Emily."

"Do you mind?"

"Of course not. Just let me call Carolyn and tell her not to pick me up for a few hours."

"Sure you don't mind?"

Ben winked at her as he reached for her cell phone. "Still sorry I tagged along?"

Twenty minutes later, Marnie grabbed her keys, kissed

her daughter and gave Ben a knowing look. He hugged her and said in her ear, "I'm praying for you. Hope it's all you're hoping it will be." She knew from his tone that he feared she had set herself up for disappointment. She prayed he was wrong.

Ben sat on the bed and stared at Emily's movie, but his mind was a million miles away. He'd sounded so confident when speaking to Marnie, but now his words to God were far more honest than his words to her had been. He asked forgiveness for wishing Tim had really died.

Marnie searched the restaurant for her husband's face. She didn't see Allan anywhere. As she stood wondering whether she should go ahead and get a table, he emerged from the rest room. His altered appearance caught her off guard all over again, even though it hadn't been that long since her last trip to Dallas.

"Great to see you. Thanks for coming, Marnie." Allan loathed showing affection in public, but he leaned over and pecked her cheek.

"You, too," she replied, reminding herself not to put too much stock in his greeting. At least he seemed to mean it.

He had made reservations, and the maitre d' led them to a table in a secluded corner.

"Nice place."

"You'll love the food," he assured her.

"Come here often?"

"Actually, no. But when I entertain government big shots, this is where we go. One of the nurses tipped me off to it."

As they studied their menus in silence, Marnie noticed that Allan was nervously tapping his foot. Once they'd made their selections, he took the menus and carefully placed them on the corner of the table. Then he sat staring at them. The silence felt awkward. He shifted in his seat without looking at her and finally spoke. "I guess you wonder what this is all about."

"That thought had crossed my mind, yes," Marnie smiled.

"No point in pretending."

Marnie raised her eyebrows while she waited for him to elaborate.

"It looks like Humpty Dumpty's shattered, and no one can put the pieces back together, after all."

"Someone blew your cover?"

"Worse."

Chapter Twenty-Nine

MARNIE'S BRAIN SWITCHED to fast forward, trying to figure out what might be worse to Allan than someone uncovering his identity. She hoped it was safe to be sitting here. She fixed her eyes on him as he stared off into nowhere. Finally, she asked, "So the 'cure' isn't working?"

"You could say that," he said, still not making eye contact. After another long silence, Allan looked up. "It's like this. I had four akenosis patients. Three of them died. I injected the stem cells in them a week apart, and each one expired exactly one week after one another."

"Oh, my! I'm sorry."

Allan looked away again. "The cells mature to a certain point, and then they explode inside the patients' brains."

Marnie grimaced. "So your solution didn't work." It sounded so matter-of-fact. She immediately regretted her words—but her husband had gambled with the patients' lives. He'd even gambled with their marriage. She struggled to suppress her anger.

As he stared off in silence again, she tried to imagine how difficult this must be for him, and she softened. "I'm sorry. How disappointing for you."

Allan half smiled but still averted his gaze.

Then it occurred to Marnie that this might be the answer to her prayers. She felt a ray of hope that he'd give up the life of researching a cure for his uncle. Maybe now he'd return home. Still, she caught the seriousness of it all. "Not great news for the president, though. Huh?" she said soberly.

Allan shrugged. "Yeah, I guess not." His response surprised her. It seemed so callous, considering how important it had all been to him the last time they'd talked. The waiter brought their salads, and Marnie breathed a silent prayer for wisdom before taking her first bite. *So far, so good; at least he's talking to me.* "You said three died. What about the fourth? Any hope there?" she asked.

"We'll find out soon enough. Due in two days." Allan picked at his salad.

"Oh. Male or female?" she asked.

"Male."

"Is he lucid? If so, he must be terrified."

"Yes, on both counts." Allan paused before adding, "He is." Something about the way he answered made her glance up. They sat with their eyes locked for a moment. Finally he spoke. "Marnie, I'm the fourth."

Outside in the parking lot, Victor snuffed out his Marlboro and walked over to Allan's car. He had tried to get a hair sample earlier, but the signs at the hospital

had scared him away. And Allan kept his car in a secured garage at home. After the doctor left for dinner,
Victor had tried to break into his apartment, but the
most sophisticated security system he had ever seen kept
him out. Victor would have to come up with another
plan. As he crouched down trying to gain entry to the
vehicle, he again discovered to his dismay that Allan had
a complex security system. *Just like at his home. What's
with this guy?*

Across the garage, a woman in a dark, calf-length coat
stood in the shadows watching Victor. After several minutes, she got into her car and made a call. "He was unable to access either the house or the car," she said
crisply. "Good work."

Marnie went to the ladies' room and sobbed. Finally,
she rinsed the red out of her eyes and reapplied her
makeup. She reminded herself to address Allan's spiritual need, to keep her brain in charge.

Allan looked like a lost child. This was not the confident young man she'd known. She slid back into her
chair and touched his hand. "So you're telling me that
you may live only two more days?" Her voice cracked
as she asked it. It seemed impossible; he looked fine.

He nodded. "I'd say I have a 95 percent chance of
that. There's an outside possibility that the new cells
will degenerate. If so, I could live. Otherwise . . ."

Marnie grasped at the thin sliver of hope and started
praying for a miracle. Unconsciously, she shook her head
in disbelief. How strange to bury the same husband twice.

"So I guess I'll find out soon enough if I'm right—or if you and Ben are," he said.

Marnie's quizzical look told him she wasn't following his train of thought.

"Whether I'll meet my maker or just that expanse of nothingness that awaits our evolutionary bodies. I'll try to come back as a ghost and let you know either way," Allan told her.

Marnie sat unamused and tried to stay focused. "Somebody already has come back from the grave to let us know. His name is Jesus Christ."

"Yeah. Right. All I have to do is believe in Jesus," Allan said in a mocking tone that brought another tear welling up in the corner of Marnie's eye. She turned her head away at his sarcasm.

"Look, I don't want to argue religion with you, okay?" Allan said softly.

"You brought it up," she reminded him.

"Yeah. And I appreciate your concern for my soul. But remember, I was raised on Easter and Christmas. I know this is your first experience with religion, but I've heard it all my life."

"From what you've told me," Marnie countered gently, "you didn't grow up hearing the truth. What you learned was that, if you were good enough, you'd get into heaven."

"That seems more logical than thinking I'm in as long as I'm willing to receive grace—even if I murder someone—but a great philanthropist with no belief in Jesus won't make it. Is that fair?" He asked the question, but had no interest in the answer.

"If God were fair, none of us would make it," Marnie

spoke with urgency. "Don't ask for fair; ask for mercy. But you have to humble yourself enough to ask."

"I take pride in the fact that humility has never been my strong suit, Marnie. You know that," he smirked.

"How could you do all that work with human embryos and not marvel at God's creation of human life?"

"They were *pre*-embryos, Marnie."

"Semantics, Tim. Call them what you want, but the sperm and egg had met and the DNA had lined up, creating a unique being, right?"

"Sure, but they hadn't yet developed the primitive streak."

"You mean they were younger than fourteen days old."

"Basically." Allan was surprised. "You've been talking to Ben, haven't you?"

"Uh-huh."

"So now you're some pro-life radical, eh?"

"If that's what you call someone who respects the dignity of human life, even at the one-celled stage. I think you've overstepped the bounds of 'dominion' that God established for humans. I have no problem with the cloning you did in Kentucky, because it involved animal life. But human life is different. We can mess with plants and animals, but humans are made in God's image."

"Save your little speech, Marnie."

This was not the direction Marnie had planned to go, and now she regretted going there. She had little experience sharing her faith, and it felt awkward.

The waitress came with the entrees. Marnie and Allan waited patiently until she had finished grinding fresh pepper over their dinners before they resumed the conversation. When they did, Allan spoke first. "Look,

Marnie, I'm happy for you. I'm glad you found what
you were seeking. Honest, I am. In one sense, it looks
good on you. From the little I've seen of you, your rest-
lessness has disappeared. You're more serene. No more
hopping from seminar to workshop looking for something, but not knowing what. It's great for you. But I
just don't believe it. So don't annoy me, okay? We don't
have time for this. We have a lot of ground to cover."

Marnie felt a kind of grief different from any she'd
ever known. The gospel had been such good news to
her. It startled her to see him hear it and reject it, especially when death stood waiting for him, right around
the corner. She blamed herself. Perhaps it was her inability to explain it well.

"I want you to bring Emily to the clinic tomorrow,"
Allan told her. "There's a two-way mirror in the chimp
lab. I just want to see my little girl one last time."

Marnie swallowed hard.

"I'll have it all set up with the nurse, Sheila." Never
had Marnie heard such sadness in Allan's voice. "You
can tell Emily that her dad used to do this kind of research. It'll be true." Allan paused, reflecting. "I used
to. Too bad she'll never know just how brilliant her old
man was." Allan's voice trailed off at the end. He stared
away momentarily. "I'll bet she's a smart kid, huh?"

Marnie nodded.

"How'd she break her arm?"

"How did you know?"

"I was at the airport last night."

Marnie's lips parted. Knowing he had watched them
gave her a creepy feeling, as though he had violated her
privacy. "So that's how you knew Ben was in Dallas?"

"Uh-huh. And he seemed pretty attentive to you two, I might add."

This surprised Marnie. "How so?"

"Oh, I don't know. Just a sense I got. But then, it's not like you're my wife."

"Sure, I am."

Allan glared at her. "No, you are not. Are we clear on that? You're *not.*"

Marnie shrugged and said, "Whatever."

Allan changed the subject. "I'd like to talk to Ben while he's here. I owe him an apology for all I've put him through. I need to do that before I . . . check out."

The words made Marnie gasp. She looked at his face for some sign of pain but saw none. "Have you noticed something?" Allan asked.

"What?" Marnie had noticed a lot of things.

"Neither of us is eating."

"I'm not really hungry."

"Me neither." Allan said. "Whose dumb idea was it to have this talk over dinner, anyway?" It was the first time all night he had smiled.

Marnie wept all the way back to the hotel. She sat in the parking lot for a long time, trying to pull herself together. Instead of going straight back to the room, she walked around the Galleria Mall, which was connected to the Westin. She moved from window display to window display, not really seeing any of them. Eventually, she leaned over the rail and stared down at the ice skaters. It reminded her of the ones she and Ben had seen back in Westfield, and she wished her husband had died then. Once was enough. But then she felt pangs of guilt for having such a thought, and she asked the Lord for a miracle.

Suddenly, she recognized Ben and Emily below her on the ice. *How sweet of him to take her skating.* Marnie watched for a while, until Ben skated over and spoke to a spectator. *That must be Carolyn.*

Meeting Ben's sister seemed like an awful idea at the moment. Marnie was dying to tell him everything that had happened, but the presence of a third party would make that impossible. After watching the skaters for a few more minutes, she took a deep breath and made her way down the elevator to say hello.

Carlos had been sitting in his home study staring at the computer. For the better part of an hour, he had studied the downloaded pictures Victor had sent. He got up and paced rapidly. Then stalking back to his desk, he paged Victor. When the return call came, he snatched the receiver up from the phone cradle.

"You paged me, señor?" Victor asked.

"Yes, I have seen the pictures. He looks very familiar. Tell me what you have found out about this man."

"He's a physician. Dr. Allan Brown. Works in contagious diseases at Doctor's Surgical and Research Center." Victor paused, giving his words even greater impact. "Señor, I am certain that he is the egg man—the one who disappeared mysteriously after the lawsuit."

Carlos slammed his fist on the desk. "I knew it!" His

thoughts came rapidly. "It all makes sense now. The president's nephew! He gets involved with my wife and they can't have him embarrassing the president of the United States. So he disappears."

"Yes, señor. So it would appear."

"Well, he will pay!"

"What do you want me to do, señor?"

"Get evidence so we can prove paternity."

"Yes, señor. I have been trying to get a hair sample."

"Yes, get one. And get phone records confirming that he has been calling Culiacán. But don't bother to wait for any test results. He's the man. Why else would he be hiding? Get the hair sample and then take care of him."

"Take care of him?"

"Yes. You know what I mean. The man . . . he was with my wife. Get rid of him."

The next afternoon, Marnie and Emily went to see the chimps. Emily especially liked Moe, who mimicked everything she did. When she touched her ear, he touched his. When she stuck out her tongue at him, he did the same back. Meanwhile, her mother stared steadily at the reflective glass of the observation window, imagining the man who sat watching some of the most precious moments of his life.

Shortly after they left, Allan had his first petit mal seizure.

As soon as he regained his composure, Allan admitted himself into a research ward hospital room. He asked to be placed on monitors with self-administered anticonvulsants, then he called Marnie. "I'd like to see Ben tonight," he told her. They arranged for a seven o'clock meeting.

As Allan awaited the hour, he thought about his former business partner. Ben's care for Marnie in her grief had come as a surprise. He hadn't known Ben had it in him, and something about it felt strange to Allan. Perhaps it was a twinge of jealousy. His own inability to feel an attraction for Marnie made him sensitive to other people's appreciation of her.

More than anything, though, Allan was glad that Ben had kept Marnie from bearing the entire burden alone. And he figured Ben would understand. He was a smart doc—a good diagnostician with a good mind. Ben was the only one he wanted to speak to now. Allan had something he needed to say. Nobody else knew he was alive, and the medical jargon would only confuse Marnie. There were a few important loose ends to tie up, and Ben was the one guy who could help make it all right. As Allan lay on his hospital bed, mentally rehearsing what he wanted to say, a nagging thought kept occurring. No one besides Ben, Marnie, and a few of the local staff would note his passing. Everyone who cared anything about him had already grieved. Even his only child.

A knock at the door brought Allan back from his contemplation. "Come in," he called out.

Ben poked his head inside. "Hello," he said quietly. "We meet again." He stepped into the room and shut the door, then stared at the patient, trying to see the man he had once known behind the plastic surgery and hair implants. "Well, Allan, or whatever you call yourself," Ben began. He felt acutely aware of the pain this man's choices had caused his friends. "You look pretty good for a dead man. Nice funeral. You should'a been there."

"Sorry," Allan replied. "I know that doesn't help, but I didn't mean to cause so much trouble. I guess it proves I never should have gone to Hawaii on vacation."

Ben was not about to let him off the hook so easily. "Trouble? *Trouble*? Aside from the multimillion-dollar lawsuit, almost closing the clinic thanks to bad publicity, the loss of the world's best embryologist, Luc's burns and broken bones, the torching of our facilities, hey, no trouble at all." Ben looked Allan squarely in the eyes. "Not to mention the pain you've caused your daughter and Mar . . . , your wife!"

Allan had never seen his former partner so animated. He returned the glare but averted his eyes after a brief moment. "I had to pursue this experiment. I *had* to," he said. "It's of utmost national significance—security and all that."

"Right," Ben replied, without sympathy. "So what's this all about?" He leaned against the wall. "I've figured it's got akenosis at the heart of it. True? And what are you doing in this hospital bed?"

"Yes. I've got akenosis, and so does my Uncle Cal. Sit down, and I'll bring you up to speed."

Ben pulled up a chair, and they sat together—colleagues, past friends, at a crossroads. Allan explained the months of seclusion and secrecy that he had spent working on a cure for akenosis. "I gather you've learned a bit about the disease. Kenosis means 'emptying,' so akenosis is the opposite, an adding on," he said.

Ben nodded. He'd first learned the word in Greek class at seminary.

"It's a buildup of the myelin sheath, which leads to compression, nerve damage, and ultimately cessation of nerve function. It results from an enzyme defect and manifests itself around the fourth decade," Allan continued. "Somatos, the guy who discovered it, suggested that the normal nerve life cycle—with growth, aging, removal, and replacement—becomes impaired. Consequently, the old, aging sheath remains while more and more new myelin piles up, until the excess sheath compresses the nerve."

Ben nodded, so Allan went on. "Though Dr. Somatos offered no treatment options, he accurately pinpointed the problem to a genetic enzyme defect on the Υ chromosome. Thus it passes from father to son, usually showing up after reproductive age."

"I'm with you so far," said Ben. "I researched your work on the Net and figured you were particularly interested in MHS, or akenosis as you call it."

Allan nodded. "When Uncle Cal started exhibiting signs, even before he was president, I agreed to do the research."

"And your theory of treatment involved stem cells?"

"Yes. If I could develop a pure cell line of totipotential cells without the damaged gene, I figured the cells might 'recognize' the abnormal areas, then attach and activate. So I pursued genetic therapy, trying to insert the corrected gene using a viral probe. But I was too far away from isolating the segment to develop it in time.

So, I focused on putting it into the brain cells that could identify and correct any abnormality."

"And your animal studies?" Ben asked.

"Very encouraging," Allan replied, choosing to withhold the details that would have suggested that his results were insufficient to justify research on humans. "Then I did human trials with eleven subjects. Four with Parkinson's, three with Alzheimer's, and three MHS patients."

Ben thought for a moment. "That's ten."

"There was a fourth MHS patient. I'll tell you about that later."

"And the response?" Ben asked, listening intently, the scientist in him riveted by the incredible story.

Chapter Thirty

"THE CELLS GREW AND ATTACHED to the damaged areas. They seemed activated," Allan eyes danced as he described to Ben the research that had consumed him for years.

"Amazing." Ben shook his head in wonder.

"The early Parkinson's patients showed a decrease in tremor, and better muscle tone, though nothing too dramatic. The Alzheimer's patients grew more alert. Some memory returned for a while. On the MHS folks, the CT scans showed the hypertrophic areas slowly disappearing. I really hoped that the new cells would eventually replace the damaged nerves." Allan's voice changed to near despair.

"This all sounds terrific. So what's the problem?"

"The first Alzheimer's patient I transplanted died in his sleep."

"Oh." Ben felt his friend's disappointment.

"Then eventually, the rest of them died in a similar way. It seemed like everything was going great, but then, . . ." Allan snapped his fingers. "Gone. Massive cerebral hemorrhage, big-time bleed."

"All of them?" Ben asked.

"Yep. Each one in turn. Same way. Sudden massive bleed in the brain. And the bleeding sites were right where the transplanted cells had repaired the nerves."

"Really?"

"Uh-huh. For a while, the Parkinson's patients improved nicely, but now they've all reverted to their former status."

"And the akenosis patients?" Ben leaned back in his chair, taking in all the data.

"No actual symptomatic changes, but as I said, the CT scans showed gradual removal of the built-up nerve areas. Then they died, too."

"All but one, right?" Ben asked.

Allan nodded.

"What about that patient?"

Allan tucked his chin down and stared into Ben's eyes. "You're looking at him."

Ben's eyes widened.

"Based on the time lags with the others, I give myself about forty-eight hours." Allan expected his next question.

"Does Marnie know?"

"Yes, I told her the night she got here."

Ben suddenly felt sorry that Carolyn had been at the skating rink when Marnie had returned from dinner. He remembered her anticipation, her face full of hope, as she left to meet her husband. The news must have devastated her.

"I'd rather not talk about me," Allan told him. "Can

we go back to the research? We have a lot of ground to cover tonight."

Ben nodded. "Sure."

Allan picked up where they'd left off, and Ben struggled hard to concentrate on his friend's words. He felt too concerned about Marnie to focus properly on medical facts. "The Parkinson's patients show most of new growth in the midbrain and hypothalamic area, the crossover of the motor nerves. The Alzheimer's and MHS patients had more diffuse disease, so the clusters of LG cells scattered more widely out into the temporal lobe."

"Different nerve cell types?" offered Ben. He tried to reenter "doctor mode."

Allan thought for a moment. "Yes, though in the brain itself, the difference between motor nerve origins and various pain and sensory types is fairly insignificant. Good thought, though."

"Different kinds of pathways," muttered Ben, not particularly looking for an answer, just recalling that different nerve fibers carry different types of messages.

A nurse, entering to take Allan's blood pressure, interrupted his concentration. After she left, Ben asked Allan, "What are LG cells?"

"They're the totipotential cells that I used for the transplant," Allan said abruptly.

"What's LG, and where did they come from?" Ben pressed on.

Allan hesitated, then spoke barely above a whisper. "This is classified information. I developed a pure cell line that I used in every experiment, so quality control was absolute."

Ben looked Allan squarely in the eye. Suddenly he

knew. He knew this was where the story involved the clinic, and probably where it involved the lawsuit as well. He also knew it wasn't the time to discuss it. His face softened, kindness returned to his eyes, and he relaxed back into the chair. He turned away with a gentle "Hmmm."

Allan grew uncomfortable with Ben's silence. He began again, this time telling him about his bike-chain theory. "I thought I had it," Allan said, somewhat dejectedly.

Ben nodded and leaned forward, signaling to Allan that he could continue if he wished.

"I really thought my cell line was the answer."

"How *did* you do it?" Ben asked.

Allan smiled. "I'd been working with eggs for years; I figured I knew how they 'thought.' I took the excess eggs, the slightly imperfect ones from IVF cycles, and I carefully incubated them in solution. It was a mix I developed that allowed healing from the trauma of the egg aspiration process and maturation for the ones we picked before they were ripe. I extracted the DNA from one egg, quite easily actually, and inserted it microscopically into another egg. The trick was to get the nucleus to activate, pair up the chromosomes and divide. That took time."

"So, the Rivera twins were actually the result of combining the chromosomes from two eggs and getting them to divide?" Ben asked. *That's why all the twins' genes came from their mother.* This was astonishing. He had known it *had* to be this way, but still, hearing it from Allan came as a shock.

"Right. I was trying to develop a pure cell line using just the *X* chromosomes from a donor."

"An unwitting donor," Ben interjected.

"Yes, but the potential good. . . . I believed that if I could develop this cell line and grow it sufficiently, I'd have the key to unlock the mysteries of Alzheimer's, Parkinson's, MS, and, of course, akenosis. The possibilities were limitless."

"Tell me how you put together what's happening. What do the cells actually do?" Ben asked.

"They do precisely what I'd hoped they'd do. Only they do it a bit too well. They survive and attach to the damaged areas. Then they activate and grow. These cells splice into the diseased portions and generate perfectly normal tissue—in these cases perfect, pristine nerve cells."

"Yet everyone either relapses or dies," Ben said sadly. "What have you discovered, mechanism-wise?"

"Good question. That had me puzzled for the longest time." Allan detailed the theory he'd discovered the day of the power surge. "The autopsies demonstrate that the new cells are *too* good. They conduct the nerve impulses well—so well, in fact, that the older cells on the other side of the splice can't handle it. So it triggers seizures, awful seizures, eventually leading to hemorrhage and death. I've already started the process. It shouldn't be long for me now." As Allan picked up a cup of water to take a sip, Ben noticed for the first time that his hand was shaking. "I've already had a few petit mal seizures," Allan told him.

"I'm so sorry," Ben said gently. "Sorry for you . . . and for Marnie and Emily."

"I was so close, so close. My one hope is that the implant cells will grow old and degenerate before the seizures get too severe."

"I hope so, too," said Ben, aware that this possibility was highly unlikely. "I don't know how much time you've got. I've been praying for you. In any case, are you ready to step into eternity?"

Allan turned and stared impassively at Ben.

"I know you know *about* Jesus, but do you *know* him?" Ben looked into Allan's eyes, imploring him to listen.

Allan pitied Ben, knowing what his friend was trying to do. "Forget it. I've made my choices; and if you can help me, I'll make my peace with the world. Science is all there is to me. I'm not interested in all that 'if you come to our church you can go to heaven' stuff."

"It's not about church, Allan. It's about being forgiven by God, having peace with him in Jesus Christ. It's about believing that Jesus took your punishment. It's not about doing some great thing to be worthwhile to God. It's about finding that there is nothing you can do, except give yourself to Christ."

Allan interrupted. "If you don't mind my changing the subject, I need to ask you a few favors."

"Sure. If there's anything I can do, consider it done." Ben leaned forward.

"First, when I'm gone, I need to you to notify a Dr. Steven Harrison. He's my government contact. I've withheld the fact that I'm ill from him, so it will come as a surprise. You must call him and explain." Allan handed Ben a business card with the number.

"Okay," Ben said, reading the card.

"Next—here's my access card and combination." Allan handed Ben a plastic card and a piece of paper from the table next to his bed. "Over at the lab, in the refrigeration unit, I have all the Rivera embryos—all seven in good shape. Plus the cell line."

Ben's mouth dropped.

"The culture dishes labeled LG are the purified cloned cells from the Rivera egg harvest. In the shelf above the desk are all my notes. I've printed out all the results and steps. There's a researcher over at UT Southwestern who's doing work on adult stem cells. His number is on the paper next to the combination." Allan looked at the paper that Ben held and gestured toward it with his head. "It's possible that the mature cell line I have can help the twins. I understand they have an atypical leukemia, and they have no good bone marrow matches."

Ben's lips parted. "Sure! Wow! I don't know what to say."

"You're okay with adult stem cell research, right?"

Ben nodded. "I think it holds a lot of promise."

"I figured you'd say that, considering how you feel about embryos."

"I'm all for research, if we can still protect the sanctity of human life. And I think *adult* stem cell research does that," Ben answered. "But the Riveras. . . . I don't know how they'll react to the reappearance of their embryos. You really know how to shock an old friend."

"Maybe something good can come out of that egg harvest. So far, it's been lethal to everybody, including me. But perhaps there is some hope for the Rivera twins in those cell lines. Or maybe there's new hope in the extra embryos."

"So they weren't destroyed in the fire?"

"No, they were in good shape at the freeze, and I've

kept them in perfect condition ever since. I had to bring them to Dallas with me to cover the evidence trail."

"Amazing." *So, once again, God has made something awful work for good.*

"I *am* sorry for all that mess, but the research was too important to risk interruption." As he said these words, the irony finally struck him. At the time, he couldn't risk interruption, but he had risked his life.

"I know you'll do the right thing, Ben." Allan's voice trailed off, his eyes fixed at a point far away. A few seconds later, he emerged from another of his brief petit mal seizures and picked up the conversation as though nothing had happened. "I appreciate all you've done for Marnie and Emily. I know they're in good hands. Will you please make sure they're okay?"

"Certainly. Of course," Ben said quietly. "But I haven't given up on *you* yet!"

"Pray all you want, buddy. As for me, I need some rest," Allan said, pulling the covers up and closing his eyes.

Leigh Rivera brushed her teeth in the sink of the twins' special-care isolation room. She washed and dried her face, then rubbed her sore hip, counting the days since she'd last spent the night in a real bed.

Carlos poked his head in the door and asked, "How are the niñas this morning?"

Leigh smiled slightly and motioned for him to enter. At the same time, she shook her head. "About the same. Critical condition."

"I see." Carlos entered and patted his wife on the back. After looking tenderly at each of the twins, he sat in a large chair in the corner and looked at Leigh. She raised her eyebrows as if to ask what he wanted to know.

"Allan Brown," he said, searching his wife's face for a response.

"Yes?" Leigh asked.

Her husband stared at her.

"Who is he?" Leigh wanted to know.

"Tim Sullivan," Carlos continued.

"What about him?"

"These names mean *nothing* to you?"

"I don't know anyone named Brown. Tim Sullivan was the embryologist at the IVF clinic. He's the one who died."

"Did he?"

"Didn't he?"

"How well do you know him?"

"You mean how well *did* I know him? Hardly at all."

"I find that hard to believe. Very hard."

Leigh stared blankly in return, wondering if the stress was getting to him.

"When you went to Dallas, I sent a traveling companion with you. But she did not accompany you to the clinic. You were apparently very busy while you were there. You and Dr. Sullivan both thought I would not find out?"

Chapter Thirty-One

A GENTLE KNOCK ON THE HOTEL room door signaled Ben's arrival. He had come to stay with Emily while Marnie went to visit at the hospital.

Emily jumped up to answer the door. "Did you bring me anything?" she asked, spying the sack that Ben carried.

"Emily!" Marnie warned.

"That's okay," Ben said. "Actually, I did bring a present."

Emily shot her mother a superior look, then pulled on Ben's arm. "What is it? What is it? What did you bring me?"

"I brought a game for us to play while your mom goes out for awhile," he told her.

"Let me see!" She grabbed for the sack, but Ben held it higher than she could reach.

Ignoring her daughter, Marnie asked, "How did it go last night?" She searched Ben's face for any sign that he knew of her husband's true condition.

"Maybe we can talk for a minute before you go?" he asked, and Marnie nodded.

Ben settled Emily by pulling a board game out of the bag and promising to play with her in a few minutes. While Emily opened the box and took out the pieces, the adults stepped into the hall.

Ben looked down at Marnie with a look of deep compassion. "You okay?" he asked softly.

"He told you?"

Ben nodded.

Tears welled up in Marnie's eyes. "I'm glad you know. It makes it easier."

Ben wrapped her in a hug. "I'm so sorry, Marnie," he spoke tenderly into her ear. "I'm sure it was a shock. You were so optimistic."

"I was so *stupid*," Marnie said, burying her head.

Ben pulled back, and Marnie looked up at him. "It's not over yet. And you weren't foolish, Marnie. Yours was a holy response. You've lined up your feelings with what God wants, instead of rushing off to have your own way. I've got so much respect for you."

"But he's still lost, Ben. I tried to talk to him about Christ, and he had zero interest. I feel like I've failed."

"It's not you, Marnie. Don't beat yourself up. I tried to talk with him last night, too. I'll try again tonight."

"You're going back?"

"Yes, he asked me to come back."

"Good. What happened when you tried to talk with him last night?" Marnie looked up at him with hope in her eyes.

Ben shook his head. "He changed the subject."

Marnie hung her head again.

"It's not your fault. He made up his mind about Christ a long time ago."

Marnie let out a deep sigh and stood staring at the carpet for a long time. Finally, she looked up at Ben and said, "I'm so glad you're here. What would I do if you weren't?"

Ben smiled down at her, a gentle look in his eyes. "I'm glad I'm here, too. I really felt like I was supposed to come."

"It was God's kindness to me that you did."

Ben gave her another hug. He prayed with her before she headed off to the hospital again.

When Marnie returned after ten that evening, Ben lay on one of the queen-size beds watching ESPN, while Emily slept on the other.

"Guess I wore her out," he said pointing to the sleeping child. He turned off the TV, and Marnie sat down at the end of the mattress.

"How'd it go?" Ben wanted to know.

Marnie shrugged and sat quietly for a long time, tracing the curtain pattern absently with her eyes. Finally she asked, "Do you think he'll live, Ben? What are the chances?"

Ben shook his head. "Not good, Marnie. God can do miracles, but humanly speaking, I think it's pretty bad news."

A tear ran down Marnie's cheek. "That's what I thought. He said good-bye to me tonight, Ben. I don't think he expects to make it through the night. And he may be right; I think he had a couple of little seizures while I was there."

"What did he say to you?"

"He was pretty much all business, other than that brief good-bye."

Ben shook his head in amazement.

Marnie looked at Emily to make sure she was sound asleep, then looked back at Ben. "I still don't get why this incredibly complex research was worth his wife, his child, his life. Not to mention blowing up a clinic and ruining his partners' lives."

"You really don't know?"

"Well, maybe I do intellectually," Marnie nodded slowly. "He wanted to save his uncle and himself and all the people suffering from diseases like Parkinson's."

Ben nodded. "Right."

"Very noble. So why should I object to that?"

"Because he gambled too much away."

"But wouldn't you feel differently if he had actually found a cure for these diseases?"

Ben shook his head. "I'd be glad for the relief of suffering. But I'd still feel he chose badly."

"You would?" Marnie was surprised.

"Of course. You don't sacrifice embryos and your family on a slim chance like that. There were other ways he could have gone about trying to achieve his worthy goal."

"Thanks, Ben. He thinks I'm selfish to see it that way. It helps that you see it the same way I do." She rubbed her eyes.

"Why don't you get some rest? You must be worn out."

"I don't want you to leave, but I know you need to talk to him. I keep hoping he'll see the truth."

"If you want, I can call you when I get back from the hospital," Ben told her. "But it may be the middle of the night."

Marnie nodded. "I'd appreciate it."

When Ben arrived at the hospital around eleven-thirty, Allan showed him the results of his latest CT scan. The LG cell line was "setting up shop," and it would shortly conduct nerve signals at such a proficient rate that his brain would hemorrhage. Then he would die. The two sat in solemn silence. Finally, Allan flipped on CNN, and they stared at the tube for more than an hour. Ben was content simply to sit in the corner, offering his silent presence.

Finally, Allan reached for the control and turned off the TV. "You've done this before, haven't you?" Allan broke the silence.

"What do you mean?"

"Sat with the dying. I suppose, as a chaplain, you've spent a lot of time with dying patients."

Ben nodded. "I've kept company with lots of patients but not just the dying. Being alone can be pretty unsettling sometimes."

"Yeah, alone. The irony is, I'm already dead! You've already preached my funeral. I just haven't gotten around to keeling over yet," Allan chuckled softly.

"I'm glad your life was extended. I believe God has given you time to reconsider who he is."

"Forget it, Ben. God didn't give me anything. If he's even there," he looked up at the ceiling, "then thanks a bunch for this akenosis treat." He looked back at Ben. "Besides, the death was a fake. God didn't spare me or anything."

"Perhaps," said Ben, "but still, you're alive now, and you have a chance to consider your destiny."

"Look, Ben, I'm a scientist, and you know it. Save all that pie-in-the-sky stuff for somebody who'll buy it. Remember, I've held life in my hands. I've created it. Those Rivera twins are alive because I created them. That's about as much 'God' as you're ever likely to see."

"You really think so?" Ben asked. "You took one set of genes and started them dividing. That triggered the mechanism already present within those genes. You didn't create anything. For the record, God creates out of nothing. Allan, Tim, you are a fine scientist, but a lousy God."

"Yeah, yeah," said Allan, dismissing Ben's words out of hand. "Let me tell you what I was able to do. I was the first to take the genome from a viable ovum, extract it, implant it into a sister ovum and stimulate it to grow—and not just a few divisions. Not just a stem cell line, but into human embryos. And *voilà*—the Rivera twins. *My* work. I made embryos out of eggs alone. No one else has done that. And you should be pleased. After all I didn't destroy any 'embryos.'"

"What you did was remarkable, scientifically. But, ethically, it's troubling. The Rivera twins are proof that you *were* working with embryos, and your transplant research does, in fact, destroy them. God is the author of all life, and humans are uniquely created in the image of God. The Bible tells us that he gave dominion—or authority—over creation to humankind."

Allan loved intellectual sparring matches. Having waited patiently for his shot, he seized the moment. "If God gave us dominion, why do you object when I 'exercise dominion' and manipulate the genome for the good of humankind? Isn't God good? And loving? How could he possibly object to work that's for the benefit of afflicted 'humans in his image'?" Satisfied with his own reasoning, Allan settled back into the bed.

Ben gave thoughtful attention to what his friend had said. "You're right. God is good, and he *is* a God of love," he nodded. "But you've misunderstood dominion."

Allan leaned forward, listening carefully so he could formulate his counterargument.

"God has given humans dominion, authority over creation," Ben said. "But God has also established limits. For example, my 'dominion' doesn't extend to committing murder or stealing another person's property."

"I'll buy that," said Allan, "but those are bad acts, and curing the sick is good. I mean, you use medications, surgery, and all kinds of therapy to fight disease, even when you have no chance of succeeding. And you support scientific research to relieve suffering and pain, right?"

"Correct," Ben replied softly. "You know that I believe the Bible is God's communication to us—that in its original form it was perfect, without error—and that it can teach us who God is, and what God wants."

"Yeah, I know you believe that, though I can't say I understand why. I mean, walking on water and raising the dead? Ever seen that?"

"No, but that's another discussion. Let's stick to dominion," Ben said, wanting to keep the focus. "Right after God created humans in his image, the Bible says he gave us dominion over all the plants and the animals. God never gave the kind of dominion over humankind that would entitle one human to destroy another for the purpose of research."

Before Ben could even finish his thought, Allan broke in, "Yet you did surgery for tubal pregnancies, effectively killing one 'person' for the sake of another."

"Yes, the removal of a tubal pregnancy interrupts one life to save another. But the lives of embryos destroyed for research are certainly not threatening anyone else's life. My point is, humans are fully commissioned to explore and research within the animal and plant kingdoms. Cloning in these realms, I believe, is within our dominion. But when you try to coerce a new person from a laboratory experiment, you've exceeded dominion. God never gave us that authority. We are to reverence individual life. I can't say with certainty the exact moment it possesses an immortal soul. Yet what we know scientifically suggests that a human has its full complement of its unique genetic sequence immediately after the egg is fertilized. The chromosomes align and begin to divide."

Allan pondered Ben's words. "So you're not sure the pre-embryo is a person? I mean, when I'm looking at eight cells, any of which could become the fetus, the rest *do* just become the supporting tissues."

"Right, I'm saying I don't know. But God knows, and I believe he has already determined which cell or cells will develop into a person. And I will respect that mass as life from the moment the DNA lines up."

"What about the Rivera twins?"

"They are alive in accordance with God's plan. You wouldn't have succeeded without his permission. How God plans to use the outcome, I don't know. But I believe he is in control over every moment of every life."

"Seems a little too neat," said Allan.

Ben smiled and said, "Yeah, that 'all-knowing' thing— there are certain advantages to really being God."

Allan chuckled. "I'm getting tired, my friend. I do appreciate what you have to say. I don't agree, but I know you believe it, and I respect that."

Chapter Thirty-Two

CARLOS WAS ATTENDING a state dinner. He was annoyed with his wife for remaining at the hospital instead of joining him for the important event. He had tried to convince her that she needed to get out, that she could do nothing to help the children, anyway. But she had become irrational, and he had stormed out of the hospital.

As the waiter served the *flan*, Carlos glanced down at his vibrating beeper and recognized Victor's number. He excused himself from dessert and went to make a call.

"The doctor never came home last night, and there's been no sign of him tonight, either," Victor told him.

"Where is he?"

"He's been inside the research hospital for a few days."

"So maybe he spent the night. Go inside and find him."

"He works in a wing with dangerous and contagious diseases, señor."

Carlos smiled cruelly. "Well now, that's *your* problem, isn't it, Victor?"

After another hour of CNN and ESPN, Allan turned to Ben with fear in his eyes. "I told Marnie good-bye a few hours ago, Ben. I'm pretty sure I won't make it through the night. And I'm feeling really weird right now."

Ben felt his palms getting sweaty. "Anything I can do?"

Allan shook his head. "Nothing to do, really."

Ben asked Allan if he could pray with him, and the patient reluctantly agreed. Ben placed his hand on Allan's arm and thanked God for their years of friendship, asking for insight in the last hours. He asked for a good life for Marnie and Emily. Both he and Allan breathed hard.

Before Ben reached the "amen," Allan pulled his arm away and punched the button on his patient-controlled pain machine. He had rigged the PCA with high-dose anticonvulsant medications, which he could administer whenever he felt pre-seizure symptoms—flashing lights and an awful smell. So far, it had kept his convulsions from progressing to grand mal seizures. And none of the seizures had lasted very long. Allan had classified himself as a DNR, a "do not resuscitate" patient. And he repeated his wishes to Ben.

Despite the huge dose of anticonvulsant medicine, Allan's eyes rolled upward, leaving only the whites in view. Then his whole body stiffened. Ben hastily finished the prayer and checked to assure that Allan's airway remained unblocked by his tongue. He didn't bother to raise the rails, sure that he could keep Allan in the bed.

The seizure progressed from total body stiffness to violent jerking motions. Ben breathed a prayer of thanks that Marnie had made it back to the hotel before this happened. Grand mal seizures were terrifying for first-time witnesses.

Ben remained alert and attentive to Allan's needs. In about a minute, which seemed like an hour, the convulsive motions began to subside. Ben felt his own body starting to relax as well. But then Allan's body stiffened again.

Not again! thought Ben, his heart racing. Though he was no expert in neurology, Ben recognized the emergency. He put an oxygen mask over Allan's face hoping the seizure would break quickly so his friend could inhale. He injected another dose of the medication into Allan's vein, then punched the nurse's "call" button. Ben hadn't expected this seizure to last so long. The floor was almost deserted now, and the nurse joined Ben quickly.

Allan's stiffness subsided. He began to shake, indicating that his body's large muscle groups were contracting and relaxing. Slowly, full relaxation came. Ben waited eagerly for him to take his first deep breath. He had begun to turn cyanotic, the bluish-gray skin tone that occurs when the tissue lacks oxygen. Just then, Allan stiffened again. *Status epilepticus*—an unbroken string of seizures.

"Come on!" Ben said under his breath. He knew that Allan's need for oxygen was reaching a critical stage. He watched as the cardiac monitor registered abnormal beats, interrupting his rapid heart rate. "Crash Cart?" he asked the nurse.

"It's here," she replied, "but he gave himself a DNR. No code."

"I know," Ben said, his medical reflex taking over. "But if the seizure breaks, I'd like a shot at bringing him back."

"Doctor, he didn't want to be brought back," replied the nurse. "He'd just go through this again. He sat with his last two patients as they died. I mean, he tried everything, and nothing helped the seizures. There wasn't even the slightest improvement."

Ben stared wide-eyed. *He was fine a minute ago. Surely this isn't it.*

Allan lay stiff and extended as all of his muscles tried to fully contract at one time. Then the alarm on the cardiac monitor went off.

"V-Tach," said Ben. His teeth clenched involuntarily. Ventricular tachycardia meant Allan had an elevated heart rate beyond the safety setting of the machine. His cyanosis deepened. He was still unable to take a breath because of the sustained seizure.

Then—inevitably—Ben muttered "V-Fib," for ventricular fibrillation, a cardiac rhythm in which the heart muscle flutters more than it contracts, producing no actual blood flow to the body. *No oxygen, no blood flow, no chance,* thought Ben. He realized in that moment that there would be no return.

Ben closed his eyes, grabbed Allan's stiffened arm, and offered a silent prayer as tears streamed down his face. He felt his friend's arm relax and heard the steady noise of the cardiac alarm. Allan's heart had stopped, and his body at last, lay at rest. The nurse turned off the monitor, looked Ben in the eye, acknowledging his tears with a look of compassion. Then she silently left the room. Ben stood quietly beside the bed. He and Allan had been talking just minutes before, and now they were separated for all eternity.

Finally, Ben pulled over a chair and sat beside the bed. He closed Allan's eyelids for the last time and stared at his friend's lifeless face. Then he buried his head in his hands. He knew he needed to deliver the news in person to Marnie, but he dreaded the task. Regretting his promise to call, he wished instead that he could wait until the morning. He sat for a long time, thinking about the conversation he'd just had with Allan. And he thought through how he would tell Marnie. He prayed and grieved for a few moments before tenderly covering his friend's head with the sheet and walking to his car.

Victor slipped into the janitorial changing area and searched the overalls hanging along the wall until he found a pair with a magnetic card key left in the pocket. Grabbing a plastic garbage sack, he made his way up to the third floor of the hospital. He used the card key to gain entrance, sighing with relief when he saw that the nurses' station was vacant.

Victor wandered from bed to bed. The hall signs warned of highly contagious diseases, but all he saw were four rather harmless-looking patients. And still no sign of Dr. Allan Brown.

The fifth bed held a corpse, its face concealed by a white sheet. He hesitated to enter the room, fearing that whatever had killed the patient might kill him, too. But, finally, he worked up the nerve. When he pulled the sheet back and saw Allan's face, he stared in disbelief. *How could someone else have beat me to it?*

After his heart rate slowed down, he began to think methodically. He lifted a hair sample and placed it inside the garbage bag he had brought. Then he covered Allan's face again with the sheet.

"You're here early tonight. Sorry. They'll be here in a minute to take him to the morgue," a voice said behind him. He spun around to see the nurse. "Not much to clean up here," she added. "You new?"

"Yeah," Victor mumbled something about mopping a floor and got away as fast as he could, checking to see if anyone had followed him. He never stopped until he got back to his hotel twenty minutes later. Once inside his room, he washed his hands for five minutes, then chain-smoked three cigarettes.

The insistent rap on the hotel door jarred Marnie out of her fitful sleep. Instantly, her heart was racing. She glanced at the clock. *At this hour! Someone must have the wrong room. Either that, or I'm dreaming.* But the knocking continued.

Marnie rose, turned on the bathroom light, and donned her bathrobe. She raked her fingers through her hair, pulling it back from her eyes. As she looked through the peephole, she swallowed hard when she saw Ben. She unhooked the chain and opened the door.

"What are you doing here?" she whispered, searching his sober face. But she knew.

Ben said nothing as she gestured for him to come into the room where Emily lay sleeping. He stepped inside.

Once she had shut the door, he spoke softly, "Marnie, I'm so very sorry. I just couldn't tell you over the phone."

"He's gone?" she asked, looking into his eyes for the answer.

Ben nodded.

As her hand shot up to cover her mouth, he wrapped strong arms around her. She suppressed her sobs as well as she could to keep from waking Emily. After a few minutes, she motioned toward the hall. She managed to say, "Can we talk outside? I don't want to wake her up. It upsets her to see me cry."

Ben nodded. Marnie grabbed the tissue box off the vanity and slipped the room key into her bathrobe pocket. Then two sad souls went into the hall and sat on the floor outside Marnie's door, leaning against the wall and staring straight ahead. Marnie dabbed her eyes and asked, "When did it happen?"

"About an hour ago."

"How?"

Ben briefly rehearsed the conversations and events of the evening as Marnie sat taking in every word he said. She probed for more details, and Ben told her everything.

"I knew when he said good-bye tonight that he truly believed he would never see me again," she said.

Marnie spoke slowly with a faraway look on her face. "It reminded me of the day he told me good-bye before his car went into the Potomac. Tonight, he spent most of the time talking about his research. He said how much he wished I'd understood and supported it. Seemed like he wanted me to feel guilty. But when it was time for me to go, his tone changed. He told me he was sorry for what he had done to me." Her head gestured back toward the hotel room. "And to Emily. He reached out for me to hug him, and when I got my face down next to his. . . ." Marnie's voice cracked and she fought to regain composure. "When I got my face down next to his, he said, 'Good-bye, Aurora Borealis' in my ear. Then he kissed me." She had never intended to share this intimate detail with anyone, but Ben had a way of making her say what was on her heart.

As she leaned forward and cradled her chin in her hands, Ben rubbed her back and let her ramble on. She went over and over the evening, repeating what had happened many times and in many different ways. Ben leaned his head back against the wall. He had seen her do this before. This was how she processed her grief. While Ben worked through his pain internally and alone, Marnie needed to talk, to recount every detail. So he sat and listened, content to be the one with whom she shared her sorrow.

Before long, Marnie began to focus on the tasks ahead. "He said he wanted to be buried at his plot in Westfield."

"I'll handle the arrangements, if you'd like," Ben offered.

Marnie looked at him gratefully. "You wouldn't mind?"

"Of course not."

"Thanks, Ben. Could we have some sort of memorial service, even if it's just you and me? I need closure on this."

"If you'd like."

Marnie sat silently for several minutes before speaking. "He wanted nothing to do with the Lord right to the end?"

Ben shut his eyes hard and nodded. "Right."

"That's the hardest part," she said, and they both choked back tears. Finally, Marnie spoke again. "When do you want to head back to D.C.?"

"There's no reason to stay here."

"What about your sister?"

"We've had a few good days together. That's all we needed. I should get back to work, anyway. It's time to go home now, Marnie, don't you think?"

She nodded and squeezed his arm.

Once they had decided on the details, they slowly rose to their feet. "I wish you didn't have to go, Ben. It's so late. You must be wrung out. How long is the drive to your sister's from here?"

"About forty minutes. But I'm not going back there tonight. I'll get a room here. It's late, and I want to be nearby."

"Won't Carolyn worry?"

"No. I told her I planned to spend the night at the hospital, anyway, so she's not expecting me."

"It's such a comfort to have you here," Marnie told him. "It's going to be hard to keep Emily from sensing something's wrong. I'll have to work to keep from crying when she's around."

Ben looked at her with compassion in his eyes. "You're incredibly selfless, Marnie," he said. "I want you to feel free to cry when *I'm* around."

She looked up at him and tears filled her eyes again.

"You've seen me crying more than you've seen me happy, haven't you Ben?"

He smiled gently. "I suppose so. But then you've experienced the death of two husbands and the abandonment of one of them in less than a year's time." He reached out and drew her into a hug again, holding her in the hallway as they wept together.

The next morning, a florist delivered a beautiful arrangement of cut flowers to Marnie's room. She assumed they were from Ben, but when she opened the card, she stared in disbelief. The note said, "You are not alone." It was signed by the president of the United States.

Chapter Thirty-Three

THE FOLLOWING MORNING, the hotel service where Victor was staying delivered the *Dallas Morning News* to his room. He immediately turned to the obituaries, looking for news of the physician's death, but found nothing. *Probably too early for a death notice,* he told himself. After refolding the paper, he tossed it onto the coffee table, but a headline at the bottom of page one caught his eye: *Body of President's Nephew Finally Found in Potomac.* He grabbed the paper and quickly scanned the article for details. It said that Timothy Sullivan's body, badly decomposed after months in the water, had been recovered and now lay in a Washington, D.C., morgue. Dental records had confirmed his identity. Victor shook his head, his mouth agape. For a moment, he felt tempted to let Carlos think he had murdered an innocent doctor in Dallas due to the mayor's haste. But he was too afraid of Carlos to risk such a lie. Instead, he would let Carlos think he had done as he had been instructed.

He paged the mayor and when Carlos returned the call, Victor told him, "Allan Brown is dead. I sent you his hair sample by Federal Express this morning, so you can confirm paternity. In the meantime, look for news that Dr. Sullivan's body has been found."

"Good work!"

"Come on in. Pull up a seat and sit down!" said Luc with a spark in his voice. His wife Janelle escorted Ben into the spacious living room that she had remodeled to accommodate her husband's motorized wheelchair. He sat with his leg still in a cast, a sling around his shoulder, and gloved hands.

"I like what you've done with the place," Ben said as he glanced around.

"Having Hot Wheels makes getting around a challenge. So my better half had things remodeled to make it easier." Luc muted the TV, which was showing a Redskins preseason game.

Ben went to extend his hand but, thinking better of it, leaned over and hugged Luc gently around the shoulders. "You look great for a man of your age and mileage," he said with a grin.

"You laugh," replied Luc. "But you wouldn't believe the mileage I get on this baby." He patted the arm of his wheelchair. "At top speeds, it makes my Jag jealous." Luc's tone quickly became more serious. "I haven't heard from you in a few days, buddy. How've you been?"

Ben opened his mouth, but the words weren't coming. So Janelle asked, "Can I get you something to drink?"

"No thanks. I just guzzled a fruit ice on the way over here."

Harmless noises of sibling rivalry emerged from a back bedroom, and Janelle excused herself to look into it. "Please stay," Ben offered, but she smiled back and said, "I think he needs your kind of conversation. A little high-tech medical lingo might be a welcome change. To the kids, *A* is for apple; to Luc, *A* is for anticardiolipin antibodies."

The men chuckled as she disappeared. Ben settled in comfortably across from his friend and asked, "How's it going, Luc?"

"I was asking about *you*. But I'm pretty well, honestly. The occupational therapy on the hands is progressing well. They expect full return of function. And my shoulder has pretty much settled down. I may even propel my own wheelchair here soon. The X-rays show good alignment of the leg. So in the immortal words of Arnold Schwarzenegger, 'I'll be baaaaaaaaaack!'"

Ben's face showed his pleasure. "Great. That's just great, Luc. We've got the clinic site cleared, and I'm getting our old architect back to start drawing up some plans. The same, but better!"

"Nice," said Luc. "Sounds like things are lookin' good. I think the Rivera situation is finally behind us, as well. Chris is still working on the settlement, but it should be a done deal. I still can't believe that guy really thought I had a tryst with his wife. Anyway, I'm still pretty concerned about the babies. I've been praying that those kids would really turn around and respond to therapy."

"Me, too," said Ben. "In fact, there's a bit more to the story."

"Yeah?" Luc was all ears. "How do you know?"

Ben smiled broadly.

"So lay it on me," Luc pressed. "Were you off playing some sort of private eye or something? Tell me. I can take it. I'm sitting down! But then again, I'm always sitting down these days," he said with a gleam.

"You know, for a guy who got blown up recently, you sure are amusing yourself!"

"Right again. Nothing like an out-of-chair, almost out-of-body experience to put life in perspective," Luc laughed.

Ben shook his head and smiled. Then he grew serious. "Okay, here's the story. Remember when Tim's car went into the Potomac?"

Luc nodded. "Of course. And they've finally found the body."

"Wrong."

"What do you mean?"

"Tim wasn't dead. Enter friends from the federal witness protection program." While Luc listened in shocked silence, Ben filled in the details of Tim's disappearance and his subsequent research in Dallas.

"Unbelievable," Luc said, trying to take it all in.

"Oh, but there's more. As you know, he developed a cell line from Leigh Rivera's eggs. But what you don't know is that he took the Rivera's remaining cryopreserved embryos with him to Texas. I'm having them transferred to storage at our temporary clinic setup, along with the cell line."

Luc's mind raced to comprehend. "So Tim's alive?"

"Actually, . . . no. He did die this past week. He had injected himself with the cell line that he designed to cure akenosis. But it backfired, and he died of a massive cerebral hemorrhage, just like most of his patients. I reviewed the autopsy data."

Luc winced. "Oh, man."

"I sat with him the night he died, and he expressed to me a few final wishes. He asked me to tell you that he's sorry. And he also asked me to return the Rivera embryos to them."

Ben had never seen his friend so stunned. "Hmm. I wonder how they'll take *this* news. I doubt they'll even believe it. I'm not even sure that *I* trust the origin of those specimens."

"I think we can trust Tim here," said Ben solemnly. "It was really his deathbed wish to try to make things right with the Riveras and with you. Sadly, he didn't ever feel the need to make things right with the Lord. He had his chances, and now he's gone. . . ."

Silence filled the room for several minutes.

"Did you try to talk to him about it?" Luc asked quietly.

Ben nodded and stared into space, thinking aloud. "You know, back in Greek class at the seminary, I learned a word—*kenosis*. It means emptying. In Philippians 2, Paul writes that Jesus emptied himself, laying aside his attributes of deity to take on human form as a servant. It's so sad to me that Tim spent his entire life pursuing a misguided goal, however noble. He focused so much on *a-kenosis* that he missed the more important *kenosis*."

Janelle walked through on her way to the kitchen, and Luc said, "Honey, you gotta come hear this. You're not going to believe it." She started to take a seat on the couch, but the phone rang, and she rushed off to answer it.

When they were alone again, Luc spoke. "Are you telling me we have seven cryopreserved embryos from the Riveras?"

Ben nodded. "Indeed."

"Plus all Tim's research and the cell lines?"

"Right. And he has a contact from UT Southwestern who's working with adult stem-cell research. Tim thought perhaps he would be able to work with the genes from the LG cells to treat the twins. He told me this doctor might be able to build some bone marrow that the twins wouldn't reject, because the genetics would be the same."

"Amazing," Luc said softly. "Perhaps that 'all things work together' verse applies here."

"Sometimes, out of the worst disasters God brings something beautiful," Ben said. "Tim meant well, but he went out of bounds. Yet two beautiful babies resulted. Babies who need help."

"It would be nice if the research that proved so lethal to Tim . . . If only we could somehow see that it's used for some benefit."

"That raises many questions, my friend," said Ben.

"I know, I know. But the cells are there. They clearly have critical errors in the genetic clock, but they may hold the key for the twins at least," Luc said passionately.

"Perhaps. That's why I preserved them. I didn't want to put an end to the experiment and destroy the cell line. I don't even know what we have, or what I'd be destroying."

"If you don't know, with all your theological training, I'm sure I don't know!" Luc shook his head. "So how much does Marnie know about this?"

"We were in Dallas together with Emily last week."
Luc raised his eyebrows and started to make a comment, but then thought better of it.

"Señor Rivera?" the mayor's aide asked.

"Si," Carlos responded, looking up from a document.

"*El teléfono*. Señor Lucas Morgan."

Carlos bit his lip. He had been advised by counsel to have no direct contact with the defendant. He thought of the bombing and shuddered. But he was so puzzled by the call that he couldn't ignore it. Feeling confident that he could handle himself well, regardless of any problems, he picked up the phone and shooed out his aide.

"Yes, Señor Rivera here."

"Mr. Rivera, this is Dr. Luc Morgan."

"Yes, I know who you are." Carlos fell silent, waiting to see what was on the doctor's mind.

"Let me just say this straight out," Luc said. "Our attorneys are meeting to try to work out a settlement suitable to you, but I wanted to speak with you personally."

"Yes, go on," said Carlos, savoring the moment.

"We know that the twins are genetically unrelated to you, but I now know the details of the very unfortunate mistake, and I will take responsibility for everything."

It's about time. Running scared are you? thought the mayor. "How could this happen?" Carlos spoke firmly. "My wife had complete trust in you."

"Actually, Mr. Rivera, that is why I called. The babies do not have a father."

"Liar!"

"Please listen."

"Who are you trying to protect?"

"Dr. Sullivan, our embryologist, was working on a highly classified project to find a cure for some devastating diseases. He took extra eggs from several patients, including your wife—eggs that weren't quite suitable for fertilizing. He used some special techniques that he developed and was able to clone the eggs."

"Clone the eggs? What do you mean, Doctor?" Carlos asked with venom in his voice.

"He was able to take the chromosomes from the nucleus of one egg, inject them into another egg, and cause them to grow. He was just trying to grow a cell culture that could be used to treat disease. I mistakenly reimplanted some of these cells, not knowing their origin, when your wife came to the clinic. It was a holiday. Dr. Sullivan was out of town, and I thought I knew his storage system. The specimen had your wife's name on it and, as you know, the twins are definitely hers. In fact, they're completely hers. She provided all the genetic material."

Silence filled the room at both ends of the phone line as Carlos took in this information. It began to make sense. "There is no father?" he asked again.

"Correct," Luc stated clearly. "Mrs. Rivera would, in truth, be both the mother and the father. I can send you the test results to confirm that, if you'd like. The laboratory error was mine. The twins are fully hers; and there was no one else involved."

Carlos remained silent.

"And there's more," Luc continued. "The seven

embryos you had frozen before your wife's last IVF transfer. We have located them. My clinic is not doing business at the moment, but when we resume practice, if you wish, we will do another transfer for you at no charge."

Carlos Rivera was both thrilled and horrified. He had treated his wife cruelly. And unjustly so. The babies were the offspring of the woman he loved. He had ordered the death of an innocent man. Yet now all his anxieties— fear that perhaps his wife didn't want biracial children and suspicions of her infidelity—disappeared. And they still might be able to have biological children. It was the most wonderful, terrible news he had ever received.

"Mr. Rivera, I cannot undo what has happened," Luc told him. "But I want to do everything in my power to help make it right. Not only a monetary settlement, but also a research trust to seek a solution to the unique problems the twins may have. I'm so very sorry that they are ill."

After a long silence, Carlos spoke. "I must go to the hospital now and see my family. We will find a way to work through our differences. I will contact my attorney; there has been enough anger and pain. Good-bye," Carlos said, hanging up the phone before Luc could speak.

Luc sat in his wheelchair and sighed relief. He had taken the high road, confessed his error, and committed himself to making things right— at least as far as it was humanly possible. Suddenly, he felt five hundred pounds lighter.

Meanwhile, Carlos informed his aide that he was going to the hospital for the rest of the afternoon. He sped off, stopping first to go to confession and then to pick up some flowers for the three beautiful women in his life.

～ஜ௸～

"Aren't you looking spiffy?" Luc told Ben three days later, as he entered Luc's living room wearing a dark coat and tie.

"I'm headed for Westfield, New Jersey, this afternoon with Marnie."

"Memorial service, right?" Luc noticed Ben was wearing cologne.

Ben nodded.

"Please express my condolences to the family. I wish I were more mobile."

"Will do," Ben assured him.

"What's on your mind? You sounded kinda funny on the phone."

"I'm okay," Ben said. "It's just a big step for me, that's all."

"What's a big step?"

Ben struggled for a long time to spit out the words. Finally he managed, "I want to help you open a new clinic."

Luc stared blankly. This was no news. Ben had already been working with the architect.

"I mean . . . I want to practice medicine again."

Chapter Thirty-Four

"So, WHAT ARE YOUR PLANS?" Luc asked Ben, trying to pretend he wasn't out of his mind with joy.

"More than we have time to cover this morning, that's for sure!"

"Janelle says she's seen a change in you. A bit of sparkle. Wouldn't have anything to do with Marnie, would it?" Only Luc knew Ben well enough to speak so directly.

Ben paused and smiled just a bit before answering. "Luc, I don't know. So much has happened so quickly. But she *is* a wonderful, beautiful woman. And I do feel very alive when I'm around her. The Russia trip, . . . it seems like a million years ago . . . we were truly two hearts in sync. But this whole thing with Tim, the Riveras, the clinic. . . . I'm on overload big-time. Don't know if I'm coming or going. . . ." Ben's voice trailed off.

"Sounds like love to me," Janelle said playfully, passing through the room at just that moment.

"Yep," said Luc. "Sounds like he's got it bad . . . or good."

"You two are shameless!" Ben shook his head and chuckled almost shyly.

"And, now that I think of it, you pulled a Zavanelli. In Russia! It sounds like you *are* baaaaaaaaaack."

Ben grew serious. "Luc, I really do want to come back into more active medical practice. I still want to keep working part-time as a chaplain, but perhaps I could work with our clinic's patients as I treat their medical needs. I've given it a lot of thought. I believe I'm ready, if you can use me again."

"*If* I can use you? You gotta be kidding! Janelle!" Luc yelled. "Ouch!" He twisted in the wheelchair to call her again. "Janelle. C'mere, you gotta hear this!"

Luc's wife walked back in holding some flowers she was arranging, "What is it, dear?"

"Ben's coming back! Partners again!"

"Really? Oh, that's just great," she said rolling her eyeballs. "Two doctors—one in a wheelchair, one in love. . . . Keep me out of that clinic. Hey, you don't even *have* a clinic!"

"Yeah, yeah, but we *will,*" Luc insisted, his mind flying ahead to the possibilities. "You want to get things rolling until I get my leg back under me?" he said looking at Ben.

"I take it you like the idea?" Ben said with a grin.

"Like it? Man, I've been praying for this moment for six years. I thought God wasn't paying attention. Now I can see why. It took a bomb to get you to reconsider!"

"No, Luc, I just needed some time and perspective— and the chance to feel God work through these hands again to help a patient in a crisis." He held up his fingers and looked at them as he said this. "I'd forgotten how good it felt."

Luc's eyes welled with tears. "Fantastic!"

"I do have some new options I'd like you to consider, though," Ben continued. "Like how would you feel about establishing a system for accepting unwanted cryopreserved embryos for transfer or adoption by needy couples? I've been thinking we could set up a Christian adoption registry for unwanted frozen embryos. No more 'thawing to death' or anything like that."

The two doctors spent the next three-quarters of an hour discussing how they would operate their IVF clinic with the highest ethics in the country. No third-party reproduction; no cryopreservation unless thaw survival rates improved; no embryo "living out its natural life span in a petri dish." And they would encourage clinics planning to destroy embryos to give them instead to their clinic for donation to infertile couples.

"Wow," said Luc finally. "You really have given this some thought. I'm totally with you. I've had a lot of time here in the Morgan Rehab Living Room to rethink some of my own positions."

"Yes. I've noticed you've become a lot more comfortable talking about faith issues since the bombing," Ben said. "On you, it looks good."

"Once you appreciate the sacredness, the preciousness of human life, even at its very earliest stages, I think the right decisions become much clearer. In fact, I might even like to provide some 'chaplaincy' kind of encouragement myself while I'm recuperating. If you know any people in rehab from a fire, I'd be glad to go and spend some time with them."

Ben came over to Luc, wrapped his arm around his shoulder as he sat in his chair, and asked, "Could we pray together and dedicate the entire work to the Lord?" Janelle quietly walked over, knelt on the other side of Luc's wheelchair and joined them as they bowed their heads.

The publicity surrounding the "discovery" of Tim's body made Marnie's hope for a small, private, two-person service impossible. Yet, despite her annoyance over how the government had handled the situation, she felt relieved that Mavis Beth and Emily would have a sense of completion at the burial.

Marnie's Sunday school class had rallied. They prepared food and some even made the four-hour drive to support her and Emily. "But you didn't even know Tim," Marnie had told the leader.

"Yes, but we know *you*, and we love you. Isn't that enough?"

Marnie marveled at the difference between Tim's two "deaths." Her life had been so devoid of meaningful relationships the first time. Now, the support of loving Christian brothers and sisters overwhelmed her. She could hardly believe that one relatively new friend even closed her dance studio for the day to be there. And finally, Marnie could grieve in public and everyone understood. She was also glad that the president had an outlet for his overwhelming sorrow. In fact, he had originally planned to come, but a shake-up at the State Department had detained and then prevented him.

When Mavis Beth saw Ben before the service, she made a beeline for him. Wrapping him in a big hug, she got choked up. "Thank you for agreeing to identify the body, Ben," she told him. "It's a comfort to know for sure it was him. Otherwise, I might have always doubted."

Mavis Beth had opened her home to anyone who wanted a meal before heading back to Washington, D.C. So after Ben had said the final public prayer under the canopy, everyone filled their cars and headed to the old Sullivan place.

Ben, Marnie, Emily, and Will lingered. Finally, Will offered to take Emily along with him, discerning that Ben and Marnie might appreciate a few moments alone together. Grandfather and granddaughter walked hand-in-hand back to his Jeep. Will smelled the air and enjoyed the quiet walk with his favorite little girl. As he left, he noticed that the only other people remaining in the cemetery were the old caretaker—and a man at the other end of the yard, who stood watching, smoking a cigarette.

"How are you?" Ben asked Marnie a few moments later.

"Better now."

"Yeah?"

"Uh-huh."

"Why so?"

"I do better without the crowd. And with a good friend." She glanced over at him.

He smiled his appreciation.

"It was another beautiful service, Ben. Thank you. You've definitely done double duty on this one."

"It was an honor."

Marnie stared off into the distance. "Do you remember the very last thing that happened when we were standing here together last time?"

"We prayed?" Ben guessed.

She nodded. "And we asked the Lord to bring Tim's body back to this place."

"Hmm. I guess he answered our prayers, then."

"Talk about God's mysterious ways," she smiled sadly.

"Then, thank you, Lord," Ben said, looking at the hole in the ground below the casket.

"Yes, thank you, Father." Marnie slipped her palm against Ben's and they stood silently for a few moments. Finally she exhaled deeply and looked up at him. "I'm ready now," she said with calm determination and a slight smile.

Ben moved his hand to entwine his fingers with hers and together they walked away.